"I know I'm gruff with them most of the time…"

Gabe cleared his throat. "And they are all kinds of noisy, but…I have to say… Well, the little pink things have grown on me."

Once he had spoken the first words, it seemed as if Gabe must spit them all out before he came to his senses. "They steal my time, they invade my study, they run down my hallways, and yet I went crazy thinking about Debbie being hurt. And still, I know the minute she can, Debbie will be right back out on that swing fixing to break the other arm." He looked up at Avery as though she were a puzzle to solve. "How do you do it?"

Explain parenthood to a bachelor cowboy? She could gather every word in Texas and still not have enough. "You just…do."

Gabe was trying so hard not to care.

He was failing at it, and in a way that stole her heart no matter what she deemed best for her or the girls.

Allie Pleiter, an award-winning author and RITA®
Award finalist, writes both fiction and nonfiction.
Her passion for knitting shows up in many of
her books and all over her life. Entirely too fond
of French macarons and lemon meringue pie,
Allie spends her days writing books and avoiding
housework. Allie grew up in Connecticut, holds a
BS in speech from Northwestern University and
lives near Chicago, Illinois.

Tina Radcliffe has been dreaming and scribbling
for years. Originally from Western New York,
she left home for a tour of duty with the US
Army Security Agency stationed in Augsburg,
Germany, and ended up in Tulsa, Oklahoma. Her
past careers include certified oncology RN and
library cataloger. She recently moved from Denver,
Colorado, to the Phoenix, Arizona, area, where
she writes heartwarming and fun inspirational
romance.

The Rancher's
Texas Twins

Allie Pleiter

&

Claiming
Her Cowboy

Tina Radcliffe

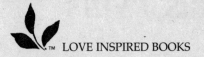 LOVE INSPIRED BOOKS

Recycling programs
for this product may
not exist in your area.

ISBN-13: 978-1-335-14610-6

The Rancher's Texas Twins & Claiming Her Cowboy

Copyright © 2019 by Harlequin Books S.A.

The Rancher's Texas Twins
First published in 2017. This edition published in 2019.
Copyright © 2017 by Harlequin Books S.A.

Claiming Her Cowboy
First published in 2017. This edition published in 2019.
Copyright © 2017 by Tina M. Radcliffe

www.Harlequin.com

Printed in U.S.A.

CONTENTS

THE RANCHER'S
TEXAS TWINS

Allie Pleiter

For Kelly
A mom with grace and humor

Rejoice before Him—His name is the Lord.
A father to the fatherless...is God in His holy dwelling.
God sets the lonely in families,
He leads out the prisoners with singing.
—*Psalm* 68: 4–6

Chapter One

Gabriel Everett had one job.

Well, two actually. One was standing in front of him, and the other was nowhere to be found. Spring in Haven, Texas, was shaping up to be one giant mess after another.

"So you'll consider it?" he said to the young woman sitting on the Haven Boardinghouse front porch. More like standing, for the pair of little girls at her feet hadn't let poor Avery Culpepper sit still for very long as he tried to hold a serious conversation. "You'll stay on just a couple more weeks until the celebration?" Gabe wasn't much for pleading, but she'd talked of heading back home and there was a lot at stake here. He had no intention of being the failing link in the long chain of events that led to the future success of the Lone Star Cowboy League Boys Ranch.

"Well," said Avery, handing a marker to one of her girls, "there's a reason I didn't respond to Darcy Hill's attempts to reach me. I didn't really want any part of this to begin with. And now, I have to say this isn't turning out well." One of the little girls began bickering with the other over the red marker. "I can't exactly put my life in Tennessee on hold while you all…look out!"

The box of markers tumbled off the table, covering

Gabe's left boot in a cascade of colors. One of the girls lunged after the spill and careened into Gabe's shin. Was it Debbie at the table, so Dinah was clinging to his leg? Or the other way around? He couldn't keep the four-year-old twins straight—did Debbie have the darker hair or did Dinah? Then again, did it really matter which pair of hands was now smearing marker on his jeans?

"Oh, Dinah, look what you've done." Avery fished in her pocket and pulled out a lint-covered tissue as Debbie began to chatter an explanation—or an excuse. Gabe waved off the suspicious tissue and instead began wiping at the purple streak with his own handkerchief. His housekeeper, Marlene Frank, would have fun trying to get that stain out.

Avery already sported three similar stains of her own. He'd met this young mother only a handful of times since Darcy had convinced her to come to Haven, but already it stumped him how the poor woman made it through the day with her sanity intact. Kids mostly annoyed him— how did she stand that whining hour after hour? A single mom with twin four-year-olds—that was the very definition of *outnumbered* in his book.

Appeal to her practical side, maybe, he thought. "I find it hard to believe you don't want to know what your grandfather's will has in store for you. Could be an explanation. Or an apology for the way he wasn't there for you. Or maybe he's left you something significant, something you could really use."

She blew her chin-length brown hair out of her face with a frustrated huff. "What I could have *really used* was to have a grandfather in my life. I doubt there are any pleasant surprises in that will, Mr. Everett. And in all honesty, I'm starting not to care."

She seemed so weary and bitter, Gabe found himself amazed Darcy had gotten her here at all. "What if it's enough money to get you well settled with the girls?"

"Who says I'm not well settled in Tennessee? I have a job, Mr. Everett. I have clients and decorating jobs waiting on my return. We have a house in Dickson. It may not seem like much to a big rancher like you, but it's the place the girls have known all their lives. I can't imagine needing whatever is in that will."

He noticed she had not mentioned friends or family. And she'd said *house* not *home*. Avery Culpepper might not have much, but she surely had her pride. "Please stay," he said as congenially as he knew how. "I know it's asking a lot, but lots of boys' welfare depends on us meeting the requirements of your grandfather's will. And you're one of those requirements, even though I know that doesn't sit well with you."

"You're right. It doesn't."

"Haven's full of good people. Kind folks I know would help with the girls while you're here and all." He was desperate for any argument that would convince the woman not to head back to Tennessee.

Exhaustion pulled at her pretty features. His mother had worn herself thin trying to raise him all on her own, and there had been only *one* of him. Almost every memory he held of his mother contained the same bone-tired countenance Avery Culpepper now wore. The pain that singed her brown eyes told him she was feeling alone, used and overwhelmed.

Could he really blame her for being ready to put the drama of Haven behind her? Her estranged grandfather, Cyrus Culpepper—who was evidently just as ornery on both sides of the grave—had ignored her all her life only to demand her appearance now. Half the town had been on a wild-goose chase to find her and bring her here. And to receive what? So far Cyrus had bequeathed her just a run-down cabin. True to Cyrus, he'd hinted that there might be more. Only how *much* more—and what—was anybody's guess until they opened a designated envelope at the seventieth anniversary celebration of the boys ranch a few weeks from now.

An unusable half an inheritance with a commanded appearance for a mystery other half—that was pure Cyrus. It was just like him to pull some ridiculous stunt as a final goodbye to the town that had put up with his bullheadedness all his life.

Gabe hated having to plead with this poor young woman. Was Cyrus fool enough to think an inheritance could make up for years of being ignored? At least Gabe had a mom— even if it was a tired one; Avery had been shuttled from foster home to foster home from what he'd heard.

No, Avery had dozens of reasons not to go along with that old curmudgeon's ridiculous set of final demands. Only Gabe didn't have the luxury of her refusal.

The eyes of the ranch's residents—problem kids through little fault of their own, just like he'd been— seemed to stare down the back of his neck as if the boys stood behind him. *Tomorrow is March 1.* The clock was ticking on the March 20th deadline for the anniversary celebration. *Keep her here. Do whatever it takes.* Grinding his teeth, angry that a coot like Culpepper could still stir up such trouble from the grave, Gabe tried again. "Please say you'll stay. Just until we get this all straightened out. We'll all pitch in to make it as easy on you as possible." He hated that it sounded like he was begging. He hated even more that he *was* begging.

"I don't know." She didn't look at all convinced. She was barely paying him any attention with the wiggly girls skipping all around the porch as they played some noisy singsong of a game. Mercy, but there was a good reason he'd never married or started a family. Gabe's fingers twitched as if he could reach out and grab Cyrus's spindly neck and shake the endless meanness from the man. "Honestly," she continued as she grabbed Debbie just before the girls started skipping in circles around each other. "I just can't see how…"

The porch door swung open and a very irritated Roz Sackett emerged holding a frilly doll. *Oh, no.* Roz owned the boardinghouse, and her doll collection was her pride and joy. Everyone in town knew it. Everyone also knew Roz was not a woman known for grace or patience. One look at the colored smears on the doll's china face told Gabe that Roz had reached the end of her already-short fuse.

"Miss Avery," the innkeeper began in a clipped tone, "I've told you more than once to keep those girls away from my collection."

At the sight of what was evidently her handiwork, Dinah left her skipping to head over toward the delicate doll. "She's pretty. Can I hold her?" Gabe grabbed the girl before she could reach her target. Nobody dared mess with Roz's precious doll collection—but Debbie and Dinah didn't know that.

Debbie, not to be bested by her sister, squealed, "Me first!" and darted around the table, rocking it and sending more markers rolling out over the porch floor.

Roz cried out in alarm, holding the doll above her head as if the thing was in mortal danger. While still holding Dinah by one elbow, Gabe managed to wedge a leg in front of Debbie. He'd hoped to simply impede her progress, but ended up tripping her instead, which sent her to the porch floor in tears. Naturally, Dinah began to cry, as well.

"I'm so sorry, Mrs. Sackett," Avery called over the increasing wails as she ducked around Gabe to reach Dinah and pick up Debbie. "It won't happen again."

"Oh, yes, it will," countered Roz as she continued to hold

up the doll, out of little hands' reach. "Bless your heart, child, I know you've got your hands full, but this simply won't work. They're too rambunctious." Given everything that had just happened, Gabe found himself surprised Roz hadn't called the girls flat-out wild. "I'm at my wit's end!" the innkeeper declared, throwing up her free hand.

She wasn't wrong. The girls *were* wild. That wasn't necessarily Avery's fault. From what Gabe knew about four-year-olds—which was next to nothing since the youngest guests of the boys ranch were in first grade—preschoolers didn't come any other way but rambunctious.

Avery's eyes went narrow with hurt. "Well, I suppose we'll just have to head back to Dickson."

Gabe threw Roz a look he hoped said "we can't let her leave." The Blue Bonnet Inn—the only other place in Haven to stay—was full up and, as fancy as it was, would be no place for these youngsters.

Roz threw back an exasperated glare. "Well, I'm sorry to say it, but you can't stay here." She didn't look one bit sorry to have said it. Avery Culpepper didn't need anyone handing her reasons to leave. Didn't Roz realize half the town had been working toward meeting Culpepper's absurd ultimatums—which meant finding Avery and keeping her here—since October?

Do something. Anything. It jumped out of his mouth before he had even a moment to think better of it, the foolish notion of a desperate man. "You don't need to head back. You can come stay at Five Rocks."

Roz Sackett's eyebrows nearly popped through her hairline at the offer. If a face could shout impropriety for no good reason, it was hers.

"With me *and Jethro and Marlene*," he clarified immediately, adjusting his hat, which had gone askew in the mayhem. "My housekeeper and her husband live on my ranch with me, remember?"

"Stay with you?" Avery looked shocked. She ought to. He was still shocked he'd made the offer at all.

"No," Gabe clarified a second time, "with me, my housekeeper and her husband." When both Avery and Mrs. Sackett still stared at him, he reached down and began gathering the markers off the floor. "If nothing else, four adults might give you a fighting chance against these two."

Debbie reached over and began picking up markers herself, but ended up knocking Gabe's hat off his head.

They all fell into stunned silence. No one, especially not a preschooler, knocked a cowboy's hat off his head. Gabe felt his face tighten into a frustrated scowl before he could stop it. Debbie, cued by his frown, caught on to the grievous nature of what she'd just done. Her bitty blue eyes went wide, the tiny pink lip below them jutted and quivered, and she dissolved once again into tears.

Gabriel Everett now added host to his list of demanding jobs—and it was the one that just might be the death of him.

Avery was sure she looked exasperated. Mostly because she was. Some days it felt like she hadn't known a moment's peace since Danny left.

No one should have to raise two precious little girls on her own. Debbie and Dinah should know their father, should see every day how much daddies loved mommies. How could any man she had been so sure she loved be capable of what Danny had done? Just up and decide that two children at once were too much? Had all his "faith" been false? He'd never been overly free with affection, but lately she wondered if he'd ever really loved her at all. Did the man ever give a thought to his dear daughters and how they fared?

Only her pride made her go on about *needing* to get

back to Tennessee. Dickson was where she lived, where she was trying to make a life without Danny, but the truth was, precious little was back there. A house, a smattering of clients, some acquaintances, but no true friends.

Not that she'd admit any of that to anyone here. Successful businesswomen didn't up and leave their enterprises for weeks at a time to help with some charity case. She'd end up a charity case herself if she kept that up. Every eye in Haven seemed to stare at her in either expectation or suspicion. And as for the whole town being ready to help, she didn't much believe that. Not after Mrs. Sackett's persnickety scrutiny.

"Avery?" Gabe was clearly expecting an answer to his startlingly generous offer. It was clear he would do anything to get her to stay, and the pressure of that choked any reply.

Life had dropped too many emotional bombs since her arrival here to let her think clearly. Coming to Haven had felt like stepping into a crammed-full kind of chaos. Really, who ever discovers they've been impersonated? Some gold-digging woman had actually come here earlier claiming to be her. Clearly, she was supposed to be someone important. The whole town was in an uproar over the fate of her grandfather Cyrus's estate. It had been set—along with a mountain of stipulations, one of which included her presence—to become the new home of a ranch for troubled boys. The huge house went to a worthy cause, while she, evidently his only surviving relative, got a run-down cabin. Everyone wanted something from her despite the fact that she was just trying to hold her life together. Someone important? Ha! The number of nights she fell into bed exhausted and near tears ought to be illegal.

Should she stay? *Could* she stay?

"You're serious?" she finally asked Gabe as she tried un-

successfully to fetch the poor man's toppled hat. "I mean…
look at them." She loved Dinah and Debbie to pieces, but
even she knew they could be a handful. Gabriel Everett
did not seem at all like the kind of man who would suffer
any children—much less four-year-olds—with any grace.

Time came to a prickly halt while the man bent over,
grasped his hat and settled it back on his head. He seemed
as shocked at the proposition he'd just made as she was.

"Marlene will love them," he said almost begrudg-
ingly. "She and Jethro have their grandkids in college
now, and Marlene needs someone to coddle. I caught
her staring at an ad for puppies the other day." Avery got
the distinct impression he was trying to convince himself as much as her.

"No, I'd expect it would be best if we just went back."

"You can't." He wiped his hands down his face. "I
mean, the whole town would be obliged if you'd stay.
I've got the space, and things aren't so—" he gestured
around the boardinghouse "—fussy out there. Not much
they could break or stain."

Dinah and Debbie had indeed excelled at breaking
and staining recently. Mrs. Sackett hadn't asked her to
pay for or replace anything the girls had damaged, but
she could tell the woman was getting close to drawing
up a bill. The dolls—which they had been warned about
several times—were clearly the last straw.

Would it be so awful to stay a bit longer? At a place
with extra helping hands? Experienced grandparent
hands? "Well," Avery said, pulling in a deep breath, "I
suppose we could give it a try."

Avery's eye caught Mrs. Sackett's hard stare, one that
practically shouted "you sure as shooting better give it a try."

Stay with Gabriel Everett?

Help with the girls was a hard prospect to refuse right

about now, even though Haven wasn't turning out anything like she'd hoped.

"How soon can you take them, Gabe?" Mrs. Sackett asked with a hurtful sense of urgency. Clearly, she meant every word of her threat to toss them out.

"Well, it's Monday. I think I can have them off your hands by tomorrow noon, Roz. Just a matter of a phone call and a bit of rearranging." He turned to look at Avery. "If that's agreeable to you."

"Well, then, I guess I should thank you kindly for the hospitality," she said, handing markers to Dinah to put back in the box. Just like that, the girls went back to their coloring. Her sweet little girls had returned—at least until the next calamity.

But something needed to be said. "Just for a week or so. Maybe less. I haven't made up my mind about anything after that." She'd gotten the distinct impression that being a Culpepper wasn't a positive in this town—nothing she wanted a big dose of, for her or the girls.

"Let's tackle that subject in a day or two." Gabriel turned his gaze to the innkeeper again. "After all, we can't have you run out of town now, can we?"

Mrs. Sackett just huffed, held the doll close to her chest as if the thing was alive and turned back toward the door.

"I don't know." Resentment at Cyrus for putting her in this position boiled in her blood—right now she could barely bring herself to care about whatever else the old man was leaving her, if anything.

Avery reached down to touch Dinah's soft brown curls. "They're not difficult all the time, you know. They really can be sweet as pie some days."

Gabe returned an orange marker to the table. "I'm sure that's true." He didn't look like he meant it.

"I'm sure the boys ranch is a fine cause, but I need to

think about what's best for the girls, and for me." Avery hated how tight and forced her voice sounded.

"No one can fault you for that. Just take some time before you decide." He stuffed his hands in his pockets, looking down at the little girls with a mixture of bafflement and irritation. "Give us a chance to work all this out."

She didn't have it in her to fight. At least not today. "We'll see."

It wasn't a yes, but he looked relieved anyway. "I'll come by tomorrow around eleven and we can load my truck with whatever doesn't fit in your car. I'll call Marlene right now. I'm sure it'll set her into a storm of happy preparations. Is it okay if I give her your phone number if she has any questions?"

"Sure." The prospect of getting out of the boarding-house lifted a weight off Avery's shoulders she hadn't even realized was pressing down so hard. "Thank you," she said, fighting the awkward and indebted feeling that settled cold and hard against her rigid spine. "Really. It's a very kind offer."

Gabriel shrugged. "I've got the space, and nothing gets solved if you leave. It works for everybody." He seemed more at peace with the idea than he had been even two minutes ago.

That peace wasn't likely to last. "We'll see if you say that after twenty-four hours of these two, cowboy," Avery teased. He couldn't really know what he was getting himself into, could he?

"I've handled far rougher bulls at the ranch. How hard can a pair of little girls be?"

Bless his heart, Avery thought, *he's about to find out.*

Chapter Two

Following a mountain of exasperating Lone Star Cowboy League business, Gabe came home that Monday afternoon to find Marlene and Jethro Frank cleaning a batch of old toys. Even the squeal of joy Marlene had given over the phone hadn't prepared him for just how much the older couple was going to enjoy this spontaneous setup. As he cut the ignition on his truck, Gabe couldn't help but wonder if he was looking at his last quiet evening on the ranch for a while.

"Evening, Gabriel," Jethro called from over a bucket of sudsy water. "Just getting things ready."

Gabe looked to his left to see child-sized pastel sheets hanging on the line. "You had all this?"

"A few calls around church was all it took," Marlene said with a smile. She chuckled as she handed a bright green doll carriage to Jethro. "Little girls! And twins at that!"

Jethro shot Gabe just a hint of a "you sure you know what you're doing?" glance, one gray eyebrow raised as he plunged a sponge into the soapy water.

Gabe had no idea what he was doing. He'd been asking himself all afternoon what on earth had made him offer to house Avery and the twins. He didn't especially like children—but he liked failing a whole town even less.

It wasn't as if life hadn't complicated itself tenfold in the past few months. Cyrus's will was forcing him to hunt down Theodore Linley, his maternal grandfather—someone Gabe never wanted to see again. Worse yet, Linley clearly didn't want to be found. No one else in Haven had been able to locate him, and even the private investigators hired to find the man had failed.

Cyrus Culpepper's set of demands was beginning to look more impossible with each passing day.

Desperation, he decided. That's what made him do it. The desperation he felt to save the boys ranch from losing the larger facilities it so dearly needed.

If necessity was the mother of invention, it seemed desperation was the father of foolishness.

"Supper's in the slow cooker," Marlene called as Gabe pulled his briefcase from the truck. His stomach growled at the mention of supper—Gabe hadn't had time to eat lunch today. He'd spent the time after seeing Avery in an endless stream of appointments for his role as president of the Lone Star Cowboy League's Waco chapter. The civic organization did important work supporting area ranchers, but lately it seemed the league devoured all his time. Gabe was a highly organized and precise man, and the length of his list of undone tasks was making him nuts. "We'll eat in thirty minutes," Marlene advised. "We've got enough for Harley, if you want to fetch him over."

Harley Jones was an old ranch hand who had been here since Gabe's stepfather owned the ranch. Gabe could never bear to put him off the property, even though the man had long outlived his usefulness.

Much as he liked Harley, Gabe was too tired and hungry for extra faces around the table tonight. In fact, if he thought Marlene would let him get away with it, he'd prefer to spend the evening eating at his desk, working through the pile of emails and other documents that still needed tending today. "Put some in the freezer and I'll drop a pot of leftovers over on Friday." Gabe grinned at his cleverness—it might serve him good to pile up a bunch of reasons to visit Harley and escape the house once those girls descended.

Marlene cooed at a doll she had plucked from a box. "Your mail's on your desk."

"Thanks. Did you manage to make it out for extra groceries?" he asked as he walked up his ranch house's wide front porch. The house was expansive—"too large for one man alone" Marlene never stopped saying. He would always point out that he wasn't alone—he had her and Jethro—but she would just scowl and give him a "you know what I mean" motherly glare.

On his worse days, Gabe called her Meddling Marlene. On his better days, he tolerated her attempts to fix up his life as well as his house with a begrudging affection. Much as he preferred solitude, the Franks were good company. Big-hearted people, faithful, loyal and kind. What would the state of that beloved solitude be after the three weeks he needed Avery to stay? Shredded, no doubt, but the boys ranch was worth the price.

"We stocked up at the store," Jethro informed him. "Marlene's baked cookies already."

Gabe's stomach paid attention to those words. "Cookies?"

"Gingerbread," Marlene said. "You don't want something too sugary with little ones in the house."

Marlene had better be more worried about her cookie jar being raided by the *big* guy in the house. "Better hide those cookies," Gabe teased as he pulled open the door. "I've always liked gingerbread."

"I knew that," Marlene declared. "Why do you think I made a double batch? No sneaking till after supper, Gabriel."

Gabe laughed, but detoured through the kitchen to what he knew to be Marlene's hiding spot. He grabbed half a dozen of the delicious-smelling goodies before dragging himself to his desk. Only a fool would attack the mail on an empty stomach, he justified.

On top of his far-too-tall stack of mail was a hand-addressed envelope from Mike Tower. Gabe smiled as he broke the seal to open an invitation to Mike's thirty-fifth birthday party in Houston.

That's why I'm doing this. Mike had been a best friend during Gabe's years at the boys ranch. They'd both had tough starts in life, but turned out fine. Gabe ran a prosperous ranch and was president of the Lone Star Cowboy League. Mike ran one of Houston's top law firms. The boys ranch turned lives around and deserved to expand. If he had to suffer a pair of little girls for three weeks— *three weeks*! He surely hadn't thought this through carefully—to ensure that the ranch could continue its good work, he could ride it out.

He started to fill out the reply card, then changed his mind and picked up the phone. The mountain of mail could wait another five minutes.

"Howdy there, Gabe!" The sound of a squalling baby filled the air behind Mike's distinctive drawl.

"Caught you at a bad time, did I?"

"It's Terri's night out with the girls. Me and Mikey are just a couple of happy bachelors tonight."

Gabe winced at the weariness that tugged at the corners of Mike's joke. "One of you fellas doesn't sound too happy."

"Teething," moaned the new father. "I'll never take a set of pearly whites for granted ever again. My little buckaroo's been miserable for days, and he's taken Terri right down with him. She needed to get out of Dodge tonight, that's for sure, and I'm coming to realize why." As if to underscore Mike's point, Mikey let out an enthusiastic howl.

Gabe tried to imagine the halls of Five Rocks Ranch reverberating with a pair of such howls. Just the five minutes of crying on Roz's porch had set his nerves on edge. Four-year-olds didn't cry as much as babies, did they? "I guess I should let you go, then."

"No, please," Mike begged above the wailing, "I need the human contact."

"Aren't lawyers humans?" Gabe replied with a laugh.

"Only barely. One of my cases has the staff in fits, so work isn't as much fun as usual. Speaking of fun, how are those investigators working out? My or Phillips's guys turned up anything on your grandfather yet?" Mike had added the best private investigators he knew to a set hired by local attorney Fletcher Snowden Phillips. All in an effort to find Theodore. All without success. After today's complication, Gabe had a few choice words for the late Cyrus and his preposterous demands.

Gabe tossed his hat onto the bentwood coatrack that stood in the corner of his office. "Nothing past the jail term we knew about before. Honestly, Mike, it's like the guy disappeared into thin air. I hate having to hunt him down. The only good side to finding him is that I can finally give him a piece of my mind. What man gives his daughter the slip like that? Leaving Mom and me to scrape by in the world?"

Gabe tamped down the burn of resentment that rose too easily these days and eased himself into the big leather chair behind his desk. Right now he could see exactly why Avery might want to put Cyrus and all of Haven behind her. Not much in life stung worse than being abandoned by the family that was supposed to love and care for you.

He heard Mike's sigh above the baby's noisy cries. "Think of it this way. That's what makes the boys ranch so important. A boy can go so wrong so fast when he's ignored or abandoned."

"True, counselor." Gabe pinched the bridge of his nose and reached for a cookie.

"And that's why you've got to find him," Mike said. "It's up to you to ensure the boys ranch won't lose the chance to expand. That place can't be sold to a strip mall and half those kids sent elsewhere. You and I both know that."

"I know, I know. And I've gone to extremes, Mike, believe me."

"How so?"

"I invited the real Avery and her girls to stay here since Roz Sackett was fixing to kick them out of the boardinghouse on account of their 'rambunctiousness.'"

"You what?" Mike was understandably shocked at a move so far out of character for Gabe.

"You remember Roz Sackett."

"I remember she can be mean."

"Mean enough to hand Avery a reason to head back to Tennessee and keep us from our goal. Who boots out a single mom with a pair of four-year-olds?"

"Wait a minute," Mike said, nearly laughing. "You mean to tell me you invited *children* to stay at *your* house? Just how pretty is this single mama?"

Avery Culpepper was pretty, but that didn't have any-thing to do with it. Even the prettiest mom, if she came with kids in tow, wasn't for him. Gabe was many things, but a family man hadn't ever been one of them. He'd stayed a bachelor all his years by choice, thank you. "I had to keep her from heading out of town, Mike. She's got to stay for the seventieth anniversary party—you know it's one of Cyrus's cockamamy demands. I was fresh out of options."

"I'll say. Boy howdy, I'd like to see you with a pair of little girls pulling on your pant legs. Sounds enter-taining."

"About as entertaining as that opera singer you got there," Gabe joked back. Every minute Mikey kept up the crying dug a deeper hole of doubt regarding what he'd just done in offering his own home. Little girls. What had come over him?

"You coming to my party?" Mike asked. "I mean, if you live that long?"

"Wouldn't miss it for the world," Gabe growled, think-ing it would have been far smarter to just fill out the reply card.

"Good," Mike replied. "Say, when do the kiddos move in?"

"Tomorrow afternoon."

Mike laughed. "I'll call you Thursday and see if you're still standing. Let me know if my guys find your grand-pappy. Sure would be nice if this whole circus actually worked out, but then again, this is Cyrus we're talking about. Anything could happen."

"Don't I know it. Cowboy up and get through the night watch, okay? I'm worried about you."

"Don't you worry about me," Mike responded with

a weary laugh. "I'm not the one about to be surrounded by females."

Gabe ended the call with the sinking feeling that Mike was all too right.

"This place is huge." Avery stared down the long hallway that led to the pair of rooms she and the girls would occupy. They had their own wing, which was practically the size of their house in Tennessee. Back at the boardinghouse, they'd been all stuffed into one room with a bathroom down the hall. Avery felt like she hadn't had the space to take a deep breath since she came to town.

Marlene, Gabe's wonderfully friendly housekeeper, put an encouraging hand on Avery's shoulder. "We've definitely got room to spare, honey. I'm so glad you took Gabriel up on his offer." The woman was a natural-born grandmother if ever there was one. The girls had taken to her and her husband, Jethro, instantly. Of course, the freshly baked gingerbread cookies may have had a great deal to do with that, but right now she didn't care. This place felt miles better than where they had been, and Marlene felt like desperately needed support.

Debbie raced past them, nearly knocking the housekeeper over as she catapulted into the room and flung herself onto one of the two small beds. In seconds Dinah was right behind her, flopping with a squeal onto the bright pink gingham sheets that topped each bed.

"Everything's so pink, Mama!" Dinah called, arms and legs flailing in little girl delight.

Marlene chuckled. "What little girl doesn't love pink?" She gave Avery a knowing look. "You've got your hands full, bless your heart."

If I had a dime for every time I heard that, Avery thought. She did hear it all the time. Everyone always said it back in Tennessee, but folks rarely lent a hand to help with the twins. Avery sighed. "I do indeed. I'm sorry for the racket."

"Don't you be one bit sorry. Five Rocks is a big and beautiful place, but I've always found it far too quiet. Oh, I know Gabriel says he likes his peace and order, but I think it'll be nice to have some happy noise around for a change," Marlene said as she walked into the room. "Now," she said, pointing to one girl, "are you Dinah or are you Debbie? I'm gonna have trouble keeping you two straight."

Any version of the "who's who?" game sent Debbie into peals of laughter. "I'm Debbie," she said, rolling over to grin at Marlene and point at her dark hair.

"Well, I'm glad for that hair," Marlene said as she eased herself onto Debbie's bed. "I need all the hints I can get. Tell me, Debbie, are you ready for lunch? I have bologna sandwiches cut out into heart shapes with carrots and sweet, juicy peaches."

"Dinah's a notoriously picky eater," Avery offered from the doorway, hoping to spare dear Mrs. Frank one of Dinah's all-too-frequent mealtime tantrums.

"Oh, that don't scare me none. I raised three sons and five grandchildren. I've seen it all." She winked at Avery. "This grandma's got a few tricks up her sleeve."

Avery couldn't help herself. "Use any on Gabe?"

Marlene gave a hearty laugh. "Don't tell. It works best if we let him think he's in charge."

"That's because I am." Gabe's voice came from the hallway behind Avery. His dark eyebrows furrowed down over the man's astonishingly blue eyes as he peered into the room. "Where'd all this come from?"

"Rhetta's twins outgrew their beds last year. Jethro went over and borrowed them early this morning."

"It's a whole lot of princess pink!" Dinah called with glee.

"I'll say," Gabe said, wincing. "My teeth hurt just looking at it."

"Girls, you should say thank you to…" Avery stopped, realizing she wasn't quite sure how to finish that sentence. "What do you want them to call you?"

It seemed like a land mine of a question. Gabriel Everett was an imposing figure of a man. Tall and dark-haired with strong, solid features, he certainly wasn't the "Uncle Gabe" type. Not even "Mr. Gabe." Still, Mr. Everett sounded like a mouthful for a four-year-old.

"Do they have to call me anything?" Gabe seemed to find the question just as daunting.

"Well, of course they do," Marlene said.

Gabe gave a bit of a twitch, as if he'd just realized housing the girls was going to mean he'd have to *actually talk* to them on occasion. Avery would have classified his behavior yesterday as an awkward tolerance—or perhaps it was more of a cornered surrender, now that she thought about it. The discomfort seemed to grow larger as Gabe scratched his chin and considered how the girls should address him. "Mr. Everett?" he offered halfheartedly, as if he couldn't come up with anything better.

Avery was afraid he'd say that. She really didn't think she could refuse, so she was especially glad when Marlene countered, "Don't you think that's a bit formal for someone their age?" The housekeeper shot a disapproving look Gabe's way.

Avery was wracking her brains for a suitable moniker when Debbie bounced off the bed and walked right up to Gabe with the air of a woman in possession of the solution. "Boots," she declared, pointing to Gabe's large brown cowboy boots.

Gabe looked around, waiting for someone to pronounce what a bad idea that was.

"You can be Mr. Boots!" Debbie said again, this time squatting down to pat her hand up against the dusty leather.

Dinah, not to be outdone, slid off her bed and began to chant "Mr. Boots" while pointing at Gabe's other leg. Poor Gabe, he'd been christened against his will now; once the girls latched on to something like this, they rarely let go.

"Could have been worse," Marlene offered with a grin that broadcast just how much she was enjoying this. "They might have picked 'Mr. Scowl.'"

Avery felt like she had to at least try. "Don't you think you girls could learn to say 'Mr. Everett'?"

In reply, the girls only chanted "Mr. Boots!" louder.

"Um, I'll try to keep that down to a minimum," she said above the noise as the girls began to circle around Gabe's legs like little pink cats, patting Gabe's boots while he stood there in mild shock and not-so-mild annoyance.

Avery was composing a suitable apology when Gabe just seemed to shrug and resign himself to the new nickname. "I've been called worse."

The man was huge and intimidating—she didn't doubt he'd been called a great deal of things. Only right now, she called him her host, and that deserved whatever kindness she could provide. "If it helps, I promise *I'll* never use it." It seemed slim consolation to a man whose spare bedroom had just been transformed into a tidal wave of pink gingham.

Gabe stuffed his hands in his pockets. "Well, I'd be much obliged for that."

"Well, *I'm* making no such promises," Marlene offered with a wink and a grin. "I rather like 'Mr. Boots.'"

Gabe gave her a dark look and carefully extracted his long legs from the girls' endless circles. "I've got to return a couple of calls, ladies. Marlene, how long before lunch?"

"We were just discussing lunch now. It'll be ready in twenty minutes. So no cookies." Marlene slanted a sideways glance at Avery. "That man always sneaks food into his office."

"Too late!" Gabe called, and Avery caught sight of the man producing a stack of cookies from his shirt pocket and waving them in the air like a schoolboy who'd just gotten away with a prank. Clearly, Marlene and Gabe one-upped each other on a continual basis.

Such behavior didn't fit the domineering, driven Gabriel Everett she'd met on her first day in Haven. That man was bent on getting what he needed, pressing for her compliance, pushing hard for whatever it took to secure the boys ranch. His own ranch was huge and clearly prosperous—those sorts of businessmen didn't sneak cookies or open their homes to little girls.

Of course, Gabe Everett had opened his home because he needed something from her—she knew that. He hosted to keep her from leaving because he needed her here for the celebration. Cyrus's will stipulated that she, as well as the three other original residents of the Lone Star Cowboy League Boys Ranch, had to be present on March 20. If not, the property left to the ranch would be sold to a strip mall, which would send half the ranch's current residents elsewhere. *Well*, she told herself as she led Dinah and Debbie to the bathroom to wash up for lunch, *if I'm going to be stuck between a rock and a hard place, at least the hard place is looking nicer every minute.*

Chapter Three

"I hate him, you know."

Gabe looked at Avery later that evening as she stood on the porch watching the stars come out. Jethro had taken the girls inside to read them one of his cowboy stories—Jethro had written down stories for as long as Gabe could remember, and was taking full advantage of his tiny new audience. The quiet of the falling dusk was as thick as a blanket after the commotion of moving-in day. Gabe felt like he could exhale for the first time since that wild meeting on Roz's porch.

"Who?" Gabe replied. He had a notion who she meant, since she'd just refused a tour of the ranch—her grandfather's home—but felt he ought to ask anyway.

"Grandpa Cyrus. Well, Cyrus Culpepper to all of you. Even before I knew who he was, I hated him."

Between the imposter Avery and the real Avery, Gabe was having trouble keeping his Cyrus stories straight. "I thought you never knew Cyrus." Of course, Gabe knew *knowing* didn't really come into a situation like this—he, of all people, knew how easy it was to hate someone you'd barely known. In fact, it was almost easier to hate the *idea* of someone than to hate an actual person. He resented his own grandfather deeply for abandoning him at a young age; it wasn't hard to believe Avery felt the same.

"Daddy would always say that if things went bad, Grandpa would come and save us. 'Grandpa will do this' and 'Grandpa will do that.'" She turned to look at Gabe, pain filling her eyes. "I know I was only six, but I remember the promises. And I waited. After Daddy died, I waited in one foster home after another. Only Grandpa never came. Never. That man never did a single thing to help me." Her words were sharp and bitter.

"You're sure? I mean, he could have been trying." Gabe remembered harboring the silly hope that somehow his own grandfather had tried valiantly to get in touch with Mom. He made up all kinds of reasons how their many moves had stumped Grandpa Theo's efforts. After a while, the hard truth of his abandonment won out over the optimism of such stories. Gabe knew what a hollow space that left.

Avery turned to look at him. "That'd make a nice story, wouldn't it? Only no. The foster service tried multiple times to find him and reach him. They had contact information for him. No one ever answered." She hugged herself, shoulders bunching up. A sore point to be sure, and who could blame her?

"That must have been hard," Gabe offered.

She didn't answer, simply nodded.

"I'm sorry," he tried again, even though it felt intrusive and inadequate. Gabe was all too familiar with how rejection brewed a slow, sour kind of pain, one that was deep and hard to shake. "I think maybe Cyrus regretted it in the end, if that helps."

She gave a lifeless laugh. "It doesn't."

Gabe walked over beside her, putting one boot up on the lower rung of the porch rail. It made him think of the chorus of "Mr. Boots!" he'd heard all afternoon, and he felt the surprise of a smile curl up the corners of his mouth. "It's why the boys ranch is so important, you know."

"The bumper crop of lousy parents in the world?"

It was becoming clear that Avery Culpepper rarely minced words. In that way, she was a lot like her grandfather—not that he'd be foolish enough to point that out at the moment. "Sure, some parents are lousy," Gabe replied. "Some are just gone. And some just plain don't have it in them. More helpless than mean."

"No one has the right to abandon a child. I'd bleed to the last drop before I'd walk away from my girls." She didn't say "like their father did," but Gabe felt it hang in the air just the same.

"That's the way it should be. Only it doesn't always happen that way, does it? The kids at the ranch did nothing wrong—well, some of them have acted out in bad ways, but you know what I mean. They didn't set their lives up badly, but things haven't worked out for them just the same. And that's not fair."

"I suppose not. I never felt much of life was fair, to tell you the truth."

"It isn't. That's what keeps me working for the boys ranch. Every boy we house and counsel is one less man who grows up hauling a ball of hate around." Even as he spoke the words, Gabe wondered if he really believed them. After all, he'd been a resident at the ranch some twenty-odd years ago, and the ball of hate was still following him around like a lead shadow.

Avery leaned up against the thick porch column, her arms still wrapped around her chest. "I didn't ask to be the only thing saving the Culpepper land from becoming a strip mall. I can't say for certain that I can stay all the way until the twentieth."

"I understand you need to do what's best for you and

your girls. But that doesn't change how much we need your cooperation. Think about it this way—if you'd had a girls ranch to go to instead of that long string of foster homes, would things have turned out differently for you?"

She didn't reply, which told Gabe he'd perhaps made his point, so he went on. "The boys ranch is a good thing. It's worth expanding." Gabe planted his hands on top of the porch rail and looked out in the direction where the ranch lay beyond a line of trees. If he could just get her there, even once, it would help to convince her.

"And while I wish old Cyrus would have been nice enough to help that without all these hijinks, I've got to take his help the way it came."

Avery's dark laugh returned. "'Hijinks.' That's one way to put it." She ran one hand through the neat fringe of brown hair that framed her round face. "You know, those messages and emails from Darcy Hill just about knocked me over. I didn't know what to think. It's a crazy scheme, even you have to admit that. I only decided to come on the hopes I'd get some answers. Or maybe I came half out of curiosity. Or amusement." She paused for a long moment, then added, "I didn't count on it hurting so much, you know?"

Gabe shifted his gaze to her, startled by the admission. "How so?"

"To walk around here and see this picture postcard of a little town. To know I could have been here rather than those dumps of foster homes if only he'd…" Her words fell off and she turned away. "Like I said, I know it's not very Christian of me, but I hate him."

Up until this moment, Gabe hadn't been able to fathom what would allow Avery to walk away from a possible inheritance. Here he'd thought it was just the frustration of living under Roz Sackett's glare, that getting her here would solve everything and be worth the chaos he'd just launched upon his household.

That wasn't the half of it. What was eating Avery Culpepper was so much more than just squirrelly twins. Cyrus Culpepper cast a long, cold shadow here in Haven, and he couldn't blame her for not wanting to spend any time in it. Neither her nor her girls. It was, as Pastor Walsh would put it, "a God-sized problem" of history and pain.

History and pain. The world was flooded with it. He'd lived it, she'd lived it. The boys ranch fought against it, one young life at a time. *How do I solve this, Lord? How can I override twenty years of a dead man's neglect? I've got to find a way.* Gabe pleaded to the heaven he'd once imagined hid behind the veil of stars. Somehow he'd have to convince this woman to set aside the mountain of pride and pain she clearly carried while trying to make his own grandfather appear out of thin air.

A God-sized problem indeed.

Avery groped her way toward the kitchen coffeemaker Wednesday morning, every bone aching from lack of sleep. How had the girls managed to be so sleepless and fidgety well into the wee hours after such an eventful day?

"Oh, dear," said Marlene as she stood slicing bread at the counter. "You don't look like you've slept a wink."

"I think it was three…four, maybe, by the time the both of them finally nodded off for good." Avery didn't even have the energy to stifle her yawn. "I thought they'd be exhausted. I sure am."

Marlene looked crestfallen. "They didn't like their beds?"

"Oh, they love them. I think the changes of location keep knocking them for a bit of a loop. By one a.m. I had both of them crawling in bed with me, all kicking and sprawling and fidgety." She spooned sugar into the strong-smelling brew. "It was like sleeping with a pair of mules on espresso."

That made Marlene laugh. "I was sure Jethro and I had worn them out. We tried."

The older couple really had gone out of their way to play with Dinah and Debbie, especially after supper, when Avery felt drained from the stresses of the day. "At least they're still out cold, the little darlings. My bed is up against the wall, so when I smelled coffee, I propped up a few pillows on the open edge and slipped out. I'm hoping that will buy me at least five minutes to grab a cup."

"Oh, honey, the way you look I ought to send you out to the porch swing with a thermos and a blanket. Young ones take so much out of you, don't they?"

Avery sipped the coffee, letting the bracing hot brew pull her toward clarity. The coffee at the boardinghouse was passable, but this coffee was marvelous. And not all the way down a flight of stairs, where she didn't feel right leaving the girls. She wrapped her hands around the stoneware mug and breathed a sigh of gratitude. A cup of morning coffee in quiet felt like the grandest of luxuries. "I wouldn't trade them for the world," Avery answered the housekeeper, "even when they stomp on my last nerve."

"And we all know little ones can surely do that." Marlene put a compassionate hand on Avery's shoulder. "I'm glad you're here. Truly."

"I hope Gabe can say the same." Avery ran her hands through what must be a bird's nest of bed hair. "Where is he?"

"Off into Waco on business bright and early this morning. That man has risen before the sun every day I've known him. If you like the coffee, you can thank him— he makes it before the rest of us even open our eyes."

Her mind concocted a vision of Gabe vaulting into his truck and peeling down the gravel road, eager to escape the girlish invasion. It would have been smarter to refuse his offer. He must be regretting it after yesterday's chaos, but he'd been a gentleman and hidden any sign of it. Either that or the boys ranch must be truly desperate to win her compliance.

The discomfort must have shown on her face, for Marlene squeezed her shoulder. "Oh, I know Gabriel can look like a stiff old bull sometimes, but he's got a heart of gold down under it all. It'll work out just fine, I promise you. Just takes a little adjusting."

Avery leaned up against the counter. "What I don't get is, why did he make the offer in the first place?"

"Well, you know the obvious reason."

Avery put her hand to her forehead. "My grandfather and his kooky demands."

Marlene sighed. "That old coot was a puzzle if ever there was one. Kept to himself mostly, and grumbled when he did speak up. You could have knocked me over with a feather when Gabriel told me about his bequest." She straightened up suddenly. "Listen to me talking ill of the deceased. Forgive me."

Avery glanced up from her coffee. "That's just it, Marlene. He *wasn't* my grandfather. I mean he was, but I never really knew him. I was surprised when Darcy found me and sent those messages. I ignored them at first, thinking they were some kind of internet hoax. Then I got to thinking…" She let her words trail off. "I don't know what I got to thinking." Avery knew she was too tired to get into this now, but the words seemed to tumble out of her without permission.

Marlene's hand covered Avery's own. "This has to be hard, all the demands and the messy history. And that other Avery! You two are night and day—and I can't tell you how glad I am it's *you* who's the real granddaughter."

Avery had heard a few harrowing tales of the woman who preceded her into Haven claiming to be Cyrus Culpepper's flesh and blood. The kind folks called her things like "a piece of work" and "up to no good." Others had far harsher terms for the woman. High heels, long nails, fancy cars? Avery thought she surely must look dumpy and unsuccessful when compared to that imposter! It just made everything in this crazy mess that much more complicated.

"I know Gabriel was downright relieved to know that other woman wasn't going to stay in Haven."

Avery didn't know how to answer. She wasn't going to stay in Haven, either.

Marlene clucked her tongue. "I wouldn't want that woman in this house, and Gabriel would have never made the offer, that's for sure."

Which brought the conversation around to Avery's original question. "Why did he offer to put us up? I don't get the sense he's fond of children."

Marlene let out a soft laugh. "Oh, he's not. Your girls stump him but good. Kind of entertaining, actually. His face when he saw those pink sheets? Priceless."

It would be amusing—if it wasn't so disconcerting—to see commanding Gabe Everett overrun by little people in pigtails. "All the more reason not to offer. I'm sure we could have found someplace else to go—if we chose to stay," Avery felt compelled to add. "Waited it out until there were rooms at the Blue Bonnet. Or convinced Mrs. Sackett to keep us on."

"If you couldn't contain the girls at the Haven Boardinghouse, they'd have been impossible at Carol's fancy Blue Bonnet place. And as for Roz Sackett? No one convinces that woman of anything but her own importance. Frankly, I'm amazed she put up with your sweet girls as long as she did." Marlene sipped her own coffee. "No, what got you here was Gabriel's determination to do whatever it took to save the boys ranch. Oh, I know he talks a good game, all serious and determined and the like, but if there's one thing that man can't resist, it's a good cause that needs saving."

Avery had no intention to be thought of as a cause that needed saving. She'd make it with the girls on her own without Danny. She'd head back to Tennessee when—or before—this was all over and give the girls a good life and fine futures.

"Comes from the way he was brought up, I expect," Marlene continued. "He and his mom went through some hard times. Makes him eager to give back now that he has so much." Marlene swung her hands around the large kitchen. "And so much space! This big old house practically echoes emptiness some nights. I'm glad for you and the girls. He will be, too, although don't hold your breath to hear him admit it. The girls will settle in, though, honey, you just watch. Why, in no time I expect—"

Her words were cut off by a loud crash, a tiny wail and the unmistakable sound of little feet running down the hallway floor. Avery practically tossed her coffee on the counter and ducked down the hallway to see Dinah tumbling at her with wide, frightened eyes. "Mama!"

"What's wrong, sweetheart?"

Dinah just buried her face in Avery's shoulder, clinging tight. "Mama. Mama. My pink's all gone. All the pink is gone."

It took a minute for Avery's undercaffeinated brain to process what Dinah was saying. "Your pink's not gone, sweetheart."

Dinah pulled away and rubbed her eyes while she looked at Avery. "I woke up and it was all gone." Her pout was as sweet as it was serious. Avery stood up, took Dinah's hand and began walking back toward their bedrooms. "It's still there. You and Debbie just crawled

in bed with me last night. Look." She reached the girls'
adjoining room and pushed the door open.

"My pink!" squealed Dinah, instantly joyful. She
grabbed at the candy-colored sheets and turned to look
at her mama. "I thought I dreamed it."

"Well, isn't she the sweetest thing ever," Marlene said
from behind her. "Do you like cinnamon toast, Miss
Dinah?"

"Cinnamon toast?" Dinah's eyes grew wide.

"I make the best cinnamon toast in the county. Want
to try some for breakfast?"

Dinah nodded. "Ebbie, too?" When Dinah was sad
or tired, she often dropped the *D* in her sister's name.
Avery, who'd never had brothers or sisters, adored how
her daughters always thought kindly of each other. Except when one had a toy the other one wanted, in which
case kindness went out the window in a heartbeat.

Marlene smiled. "Why, of course Debbie gets some,
too." She hunched down to Dinah's level. "Let's go roust
her up, shall we?" She slanted her glance up toward Avery
with a knowing grin. "That way your mama can have a
long, hot shower while we eat our breakfast."

That, and the hot coffee, had Avery ready to nominate
Marlene Frank for Woman of the Year. She'd have to find
some friends like Marlene back in Tennessee. There had
to be someone in Danny's hometown who didn't think
she'd driven him off, who would believe that it was *he* who
abandoned *them*. The only home the girls had ever known
was back there; she owed it to them to build her business
up enough to make it work with Danny's alimony.

She was a fighter, always had been. Maybe she'd consider staying just long enough to see if Gabe was right
and Cyrus really did leave her something worthwhile.

Chapter Four

Gabe knocked on the weather-beaten door of Harley Jones's small cottage on the west side of his ranch Friday morning. It was early, but Harley was an early riser like himself. The old man would be glad for the pot of hearty food, and Gabe liked to check in frequently on the widower's deteriorating health. "Harley?"

The sound of shuffling came from the other side of the door. "Hold your horses, I'm a'comin'."

The door creaked open, and Gabe made a mental note to bring oil on his next visit. Harley was trying to hold the place together on his own, but he needed help.

"Gabe." Harley pulled open the door, then hobbled on his cane back inside to the cabin's meager kitchen. "The league meeting's not today, is it?"

"Not today, Harley. I just thought you might help me finish off some of Marlene's good stew. She always makes enough to feed an army, and now with our—" Gabe groped for some way to describe Avery and her daughters' descent upon his quiet household "—houseguests, she's making even more."

He opened Harley's fridge, scanning the near-empty appliance as he settled the casserole dish Marlene had sent. Harley wasn't eating nearly as well as he should. Gabe made a note to visit again soon with some groceries. The pretense of escaping the noisy state of the ranch house would work well for everyone.

Not that he needed any incentive to visit Harley. Even as a young man on his stepfather's ranch—back when things were still tight, before Gabe stepped in as owner and made Five Rocks the prosperous ranch it was today— Gabe loved to spend time with Harley at this cabin. Leon, the last of Gabe's two stepfathers, had been a hard man who'd grown harder when Gabe's mother died.

Gabe warmed at the welcome sound of Harley putting on coffee—the old-fashioned way, in a blue enamel pot on a stove burner, never one of those "newfangled electric gizmos." Most of the happy memories Gabe had of his time on this ranch were his afternoons with Harley. Five Rocks wouldn't be Five Rocks without Harley Jones puttering around, even if he'd stopped doing any real work on the ranch years ago.

"Houseguests?" Harley had reason to look surprised. There hadn't been a houseguest at Five Rocks for years. "Who you got staying at the ranch?"

Gabe mused at his own reluctance to own up to what he'd done. "Tiny pink things." He'd found markers on his study desk this morning. Actually, he'd found marker *drawings* on his study desk blotter, too. A great big pink blob he suspected was supposed to be a heart. Or an elephant. Or a flower—it was tough to tell.

Harley turned toward him, cupping a hand to one ear. "Come again? You got piglets up at the house?"

Now Gabe laughed outright. "Not piglets. Little girls. Two little four-year-old girls and their mother. They're staying with us since Roz Sackett wasn't much for the noise and they need to stay in Haven."

"You took in little girls?" Harley shook his head. "That's a first. No wonder you're knocking on my door so early." Harley got two cups down from his cupboard. "Ain't nowhere for them to stay in town? Really?"

"The Blue Bonnet's full up with some women's thing and we need Avery Culpepper and her girls to be present at the anniversary celebration."

"Culpepper? More kin of Cyrus's, you mean?"

Gabe remembered that Harley's health had forced him to miss the last several Lone Star Cowboy League meetings—the old man knew nothing of the soap opera that had played out in the last few months. "His *real* long lost granddaughter, to be exact."

"I thought you said she showed up last month."

"Yes and no." Gabe reached for a simple way to recount the crazy turn of events. "Turns out that Avery Culpepper wasn't the real Avery Culpepper, but a gold digger out to grab Cyrus's estate."

"No kidding? Sounds just like ol' Cyrus to be stirring up trouble even from his grave." He pointed a bony finger at Gabe. "So you got the real Avery—and her daughters, no less—living with you down at the big house?" Harley began to laugh but it dissolved into a hacking cough that had the old man reaching for his handkerchief and sitting for a spell. "How's that working out?" he snickered in between wheezes.

Gabe felt himself smile. "I'm here before you put the coffee on. What do you think?"

Harley shook his head and dabbed his eyes. "You're a good man, Gabe. A bit crazy from the sound of it, but a good man." He made to rise as the coffeepot boiled, but Gabe stopped and got up himself so that Harley could sit and recover his breath. "The funeral was months ago. Why's she here now and not then?" Harley asked.

"Cyrus made his granddaughter's presence one of the crazy requirements in his will. You remember—we've got to have her here to deed his land and house to the boys ranch. We just found her. The real her, I mean."

"Requirements? There's more than that one?"

Harley must be the only person in Haven unaware of Cyrus Culpepper's wild scheme. Gabe must have told him about the Avery bit, but forgot to mention the other requirement of finding the ranch's original residents. Probably because the hunt for those three old men was making him crazy lately. "Nothing you need to worry about, Harley. We got it covered."

"Good place, the boys ranch." The words sputtered out between raspy hacks that left Harley reaching for his coffee. "You know that. Cyrus knew it, too. What a fool notion to play games with a good cause like that."

"I know. But the boys ranch will lose the best thing to happen to it in years if we don't play along. So we're playing along." Gabe put his hand on Harley's arm, disturbed to feel it tremble under his palm. "Don't you worry about it. I'll take care of it. You know me, I don't ever give up."

Harley looked up. "Never did."

"And I won't now." Gabe checked his watch, not wanting to bother the old man any further with the weight of his problems. "I've got to run by the sheriff's office and pick up some supplies at the store before I get back for lunch. I'll get some oil for that door while I'm out. You take care of yourself and I'll come out in a day or so to fix those hinges."

"Sure." Harley looked lost in thought. The old man really was declining, and way too fast for Gabe's liking.

"Thanks for the coffee. See you later, Harley. I'll see myself out."

"Sure."

Gabe pulled the squeaking door shut behind him. Harley wasn't doing well. Another problem to add to the growing mountain of challenges around him these days.

Avery was sitting on the porch emailing furniture websites to a client—she'd found quite a few ways to keep business going remotely once she put her mind to it—when Gabe pulled up. He hauled a pair of large boxes out of the back of his truck. "What's that?"

"Those," Gabe said with a sheepish smile on his face, "are two boxes of sanity."

Avery laughed as she closed her laptop. She couldn't remember the last time she'd gotten thirty uninterrupted minutes online in the daylight hours—extra adults were indeed a blessing and the sense of accomplishment had lifted her spirits considerably. "Sanity?" She put her hands up to her cheeks in mock surprise. "If only I'd known it came in boxes." Truly, not much in Haven had met the criteria for sanity since her arrival.

Gabe, who laughed, must have felt the same way, for he replied, "Well, if it came in spray bottles, I can think of a few people I'd douse in a heartbeat these days."

Avery walked up to the boxes to see a combination of wood planks, plastic pieces and lengths of rope. Sanity, evidently, came with the label Some Assembly Required. It struck her as a fitting metaphor. "Seriously, what are these?"

Gabe sat back on one hip. "Well, if all goes as planned, these will be swings tomorrow. Some boys from the ranch are coming over to help me put them together so Dinah and Debbie have some swings to play on while they're here."

Gabe was building swings? Was this some sort of incentive to keep them beyond a short stay? Gratitude and suspicion tumbled together in Avery's stomach—she didn't like being indebted to anyone, much less someone like Gabe Everett. And now she'd meet the boys from the ranch. She'd met supporters and volunteers from the ranch—Haven was full of them, as if the whole town had taken up the boys ranch cause. But until now, she'd deftly avoided spending any time with the actual residents. Or on the grounds. She didn't want to know the people whose lives would be directly affected if she didn't stay.

"You don't need to put up swings for us," she blurted out a bit more sharply than she ought to have.

"As a matter of fact, I do. I found markers in my study, and a pink blob colored on my desk blotter. Marlene suggested that if I wanted to avoid my house being overrun with tiny pinkness, we needed some outside playthings." He pushed the boxes up against the trunk of an expansive tree and started walking toward the house. "I've discovered I have a low tolerance for tiny pinkness."

His voice held the not-quite-disguised hint of irritation, making Avery think the "box of sanity" metaphor wasn't all fiction. Which, of course, only made everything worse.

As if to prove Gabe's point, Debbie and Dinah came barreling through the doors with Marlene behind them. "Mr. Boots!" they shouted, entirely too excited to see their host.

"We're getting octopus for lunch," Debbie proclaimed with a ridiculous air of authority.

Both Gabe and Avery looked up at Marlene for an explanation. Preschoolers didn't eat octopus. She certainly didn't, either.

Evidently Gabe did. "You're feeding the girls calamari?" Avery was glad to hear the same shock in his voice that currently iced her stomach.

That made Marlene laugh. "Of course not. I'd never think of such a thing."

"Hot dogs," Dinah said, looking as if she couldn't fathom why the grown-ups weren't catching on. A "box of sanity" was starting to look like a very good thing indeed.

Marlene planted her hands on her hips. "Land sakes, child, didn't your mama ever make you hot-dog octopuses growing up?"

The prickly ball of "I didn't have that kind of childhood" that usually stayed sleeping deep under Avery's ribs woke itself up. Foster homes weren't full of warm fuzzy childhood memories. The urge to mutter "I didn't have a mama like that—I didn't have a mama *at all*" crawled to the surface with startling strength. Avery took a breath, swallowed hard and answered with a simple "No."

"Me, neither." Gabe didn't sound eager for the new experience, either, despite the girls' delighted faces.

"Well, then, lunch ought to be a barrel of fun." Marlene clapped her hands together and headed back into the house for whatever preparations hot-dog octopuses required. Avery couldn't imagine what those might be.

"Watcha got?" Dinah said to Gabe, her eyes on the big boxes under the tree.

"A surprise for you and your sister," Gabe said. He started up the ranch porch stairs, clearly thinking that would settle the matter until after lunch, but he had no idea how wrong he was. At the mention of the word *surprise*, both girls launched on him with pokes and grabs and questions. Debbie grabbed his hand and practically dragged him over to the boxes.

At the mention of the word *swings*, the girls were all over him with squeals and hugs and even one squishy kiss on his elbow. It would have been totally charming if Gabe hadn't been turning shades of red and looking as if he'd contracted the adult version of "cooties."

Trying not to laugh at Gabriel Everett draped in tiny pinkness, Avery said, "What do you say, girls?"

A chorus of thank-yous erupted, complete with one girl clutching each of Gabe's pant legs so tightly he couldn't even walk. He stood there, enduring the outburst, with a face that was mostly long-suffering but not without a tiny sliver of amusement. "I hope it's nice to be appreciated," she offered.

He opened his mouth to say something, then simply shut it again, adjusting his hat, which had come askew in the assault of happiness.

"How about we go help Mrs. Frank with lunch and let Mr. Everett get some peace and quiet to settle in before we eat? I want to see these octopuses before I let you eat them."

Dinah giggled. "They're really hot dogs," she whispered.

"I sure hope so," Gabe said as he tenderly, but firmly, peeled each girl from his legs.

"Swings, Mama," Debbie said with wide eyes as she gleefully peered into the box.

"I like swings," Dinah agreed.

The happiness on the two girls' faces caused a giant lump to form in Avery's throat. Danny had always said he would put up swings but never did. Now, someone she barely knew was erecting swings just for Debbie and Dinah. Yes, it might be to gain her cooperation, but the weight of the gesture still touched her. *I'll buy the swings from him when we leave*, she promised herself. *I'll pay someone to put them up in our backyard. Little girls ought to have swings.*

Chapter Five

Saturday morning, Avery stared at the group of boys who had gathered on Gabe's front lawn to help put up the swings.

It was hard enough to see all those people gathered to do something just for her girls, but the boys themselves tugged at her heart in exactly the way she feared. It bothered her how she could see right into their hearts. That "I'm unwanted" look that lurked behind the eyes of every child in foster care, even on their happiest of days. Could other people see it? Or just those who, like her, had lived it?

"Morning, ma'am," they said in coached tones, as if boys ranch foreman Flint Rawlings had rehearsed them to greet her with good manners.

"Good morning, boys. These are my daughters, Debbie and Dinah." The girls waved, and the boys waved back, sort of. With a collection of boys between twelve and seventeen—near as she could guess—just a shuffle and a grunt was almost too much to hope for.

"Are you building our swings?" Dinah said, squinting up at one tall, lanky teen.

"They are," Flint said, placing a large tool kit down

with a thud beside the boxes Gabe had purchased yesterday. "We figured it was the least we could do seeing as to how you've agreed to stay until the celebration."

She hadn't actually agreed. She'd only agreed not to leave *yet*. No one seemed to recognize the distinction. The assumption—and now the swings—made her feel cornered, but she could never quite voice her growing concern. *Maybe you could try just being grateful*, she told herself as she forced a smile in the direction of the makeshift construction crew. *Maybe it won't be so bad to stay and find out what Grandpa Cyrus is up to.*

"I'll be back in two hours to pick 'em up," Flint said as he peered at his watch. "That'll be enough time?"

"I expect so," Gabe replied as he pulled the assembly instructions from the larger of the two boxes. "Five sets of hands ought to be able to get it done in half the time."

Avery settled down on the porch with the girls to watch the spectacle of the slowly rising swing set. She had two sets of paint colors and four other website addresses to send to another client to view products, as well as two estimates to send to potential customers, but it felt wrong not to at least watch since she couldn't hope to help.

Not that the girls didn't want to try. Avery was grateful for the porch rail to keep them corralled away from the sawing of beams and hammering of nails.

One of the older boys stopped and stared at her as he came back from using the ranch house washroom. "So you're her? The *r-real* her?"

Avery felt—again—the absurd sensation of having been impersonated. No one in Tennessee would ever believe a woman had come to Haven claiming her identity. Quite frankly, no one in Tennessee would think her important enough to warrant an imposter. And they'd be right; if there was any Culpepper fortune in the offing, she had yet to see any sign of it. "The genuine article," she answered the shy teen, who had a bit of a stutter. She tried to laugh off his question, but didn't quite succeed.

"Jake said the fake one was a money hunter, but there wasn't any for her to get, seeing as she wasn't the r-real Avery."

"I suppose so." Avery was of the opinion there wasn't any money for her to get, either, regardless of her genuine pedigree.

"But all you g-got is the house way over on the west side of the new ranch."

"Yes, that old cabin is mine now," she answered.

Even *old cabin* was a bit of an overstatement. In its current state, *shack* was a little bit closer to the truth, but the house had good bones, from what she could see from the outside. Some updating, a lot of large-scale repairs, a vigorous cleaning and a fresh coat of paint could make the place livable, but not for her and the girls. The best she could hope for would be sellable.

"The whole thing's crazy," the boy said, scratching his chin. "It's like one of them m-mystery movies on TV."

"I agree with you there." Wanting to shift the conversation, she looked at the tall, lanky boy with a head of curly brown hair, trying to remember which boy it was Gabe said had the speech impediment. "You're Johnny?"

He nodded. "Yes, ma'am."

"Are you happy living on the ranch?"

"I'll be sorry to leave when I turn eighteen soon." The boy shifted his weight on his long legs. "Dr. Wyatt's been r-real good to me. I ain't always d-deserved it. The ranch is the only place where I ever felt like I had a chance, you know?"

He was trying not to show the depth of emotion he felt

for the place, and it pulled at Avery's heart. She knew this would happen if she met the boys—it's why she had resisted it. That hollow place in a heart where it feels like no one cares? She recognized that hole, knew that particular strain of hopelessness.

I don't have to stay to help them out, she reminded herself. *I don't owe these people anything. I get to decide where life goes from here, not Cyrus. Not Danny. Not some scheme.*

None of that was the fault of the boy in front of her. "I'm glad things have worked out for you, Johnny."

"Dr. Wyatt says he'll h-help me go to vet school. I'll live with him and Miss Carolina."

Sometimes, all you need is someone believing in you, Avery thought as she saw optimism fill Johnny's features. She couldn't argue that the ranch did that. *It would have been nice if I'd had the chance for Grandpa Cyrus to believe in me.* She knew that wasn't exactly fair—Cyrus had evidently looked for her, although it didn't feel like he had tried very hard since the anniversary committee found her in a handful of months—but hearts didn't always play fair. These days, still smarting from all the wounds of Danny's abandonment, Avery had begun to wonder if she'd married Danny just because he was the first person to show her even glimpses of affection, rather than having been the best man to share her life. *Some day my girls will grow up with a daddy who treasures them.* If her prayers were answered, it wouldn't matter that the man wasn't their father.

"Sounds like you're moving toward a fine future, Johnny."

Debbie looked up from the plastic craft beads Avery had laid out on the porch table for the girls to make bracelets as they watched. "Are the swings done? It's taking *forever.*"

Avery was glad Johnny laughed. "I figure we're about halfway d-done." He hunched down to Debbie's height. "Fine swings, though. I think they'll be worth the long wait."

"Okay, I'll wait." Debbie said it as if the wait would stretch a thousand years.

"You do that." With a smile that lit up his features, the boy adjusted his hat and returned to the work crew just as Gabe was coming up the porch steps.

"You met Johnny Drake," he said, looking toward the young man as he settled into work again.

"Sounds like he has quite a story," she offered.

"He's one of our better successes over at the ranch. Not that it's been a smooth ride for him. A while back lots of people were ready to think the worst of him. Wyatt's pretty much turned him around—and turned him into a vet, I think." Gabe took off his work gloves and whacked them against his jeans, sending sawdust floating into the air. "We don't always get happy endings like that."

Avery thought of the dozens of unhappy endings she'd seen in the foster homes where she'd stayed. "I expect you get more of them than some other places."

"Flint Rawlings? The man who dropped them off? He's a big part of the reason why. And Bea Brewster—she's been running the place for over twenty years. And a whole mess of house parents. And volunteers."

"And half of Haven, it sounds like."

He smiled. "I suppose that's true. Might even be closer to all of Haven."

And there it was: the constant, subtle reminder that all this good work was riding on her shoulders. Well, hers and a bunch of old men who now had to be collected for reasons no one had quite figured out. Cyrus had boxed her in but good, and she didn't much care for the feeling.

"Is that why you brought these boys out here to build the swings?" That came out a little sharper than she would have liked, but she had good reasons to question his motives, didn't she?

"The swings are mostly for my sanity, like I said."

"You didn't bring them out here so I could meet them?"

"Well, now, I won't say I didn't consider it might be good for you to meet them," Gabe admitted. "Mutually beneficial, so to speak. I needed it done and they needed something to do. But mostly, I'm just quickly ensuring your girls have something better to do than finding my study or my library or any of the other places they'd be better off not finding."

He didn't mention the lamp Dinah had knocked over and broken yesterday, but he didn't have to.

"Well, it seems an awfully long way to go for sanity. Especially on a temporary basis." Again, she probably should have left off that last remark, but it bothered her how easily everyone seemed to think she'd become enamored of Haven and never leave.

"That depends. I value my sanity very highly."

"I think you valued your peace and quiet very highly, too." She placed an emphasis on the past tense. "Don't think I don't know how badly we've put you out."

"Maybe, but then there are hot-dog octopuses. Kind of balances out."

It does not, Avery thought, raising one suspicious eyebrow rather than voicing the words.

"I love hot-dog octopuses," Dinah chimed in. "We should make some for those boys."

"I don't think Mr. Everett would ever live it down if

we did that," Avery said, watching the horror on Gabe's face at the suggestion. "Let's just keep that our special meal. But I think we could muster up some cookies and lemonade if we asked Mrs. Marlene nicely and helped, don't you think?"

The girls squealed their approval—unfortunately scattering beads all over the porch in the process. Peace and quiet indeed.

"I like that idea much better," Gabe agreed.

As the swings were nearing completion, Gabe walked up to where Avery was sitting going through big books of fabric swatches on the porch steps. The girls were playing some beanbag game Jethro had set up for them in one corner of the porch. "So now you met the boys. Some of 'em, at least. You should go see the ranch."

She looked up at him as she aside set the book. "You really are the persistent sort."

Gabe settled himself on the top stair across from her. "Good work gets done over there. It deserves to be expanded."

"So maybe Grandpa Cyrus got his motives right. As for his methods…"

Gabe shook his head. "Yeah, well, I can't say much for those." He looked at Avery. "Your grandpa was a grouch in life. I suppose it shouldn't surprise me he found a grouchy way to pass." He cringed as he heard his own words. He hadn't slept well the last few days—the new noise all over the house was shaving the edges off his patience. Gabe valued his silence, and that was in desperately short supply right now. "That was a lousy thing to say. I'm sorry."

She gave him a thin smile. "Oh, no, you're absolutely right." Shrugging, she added, "I had this picture of Grandpa—a daydream, I suppose—of the friendly, happy old man who would come and save me. Take me on trips, read me stories, take me out for ice cream—" she motioned out to the construction taking place in the yard "—push me on the swings…the whole perfect grandpa package. Because of my dad and then my own lack of family, I built him up into this perfect antidote to everything wrong in my life. And then I watched as nothing happened. And no one came. And I got sadder and angrier." She hugged her knees. "You can say anything you want about Grandpa Cyrus and it won't bother me. I expect I'll agree with most of it."

She paused for a dark moment and then added, "He's my least favorite person right now."

Gabe felt a pinch in his chest at all that pain. He hadn't any notion of how difficult it would be for Avery to come here. He'd have thought she'd be curious, even eager, to see her grandfather's ranch. It was clear Avery had lots of baggage where her grandfather was concerned—and rightfully so. He knew a thing or two about baggage like that, so he couldn't judge. As a matter of fact, Gabe couldn't say he wouldn't have been far darker and angrier had he been in her shoes. But if he could just get her on the grounds, show her all the fine work and amazing outcomes the place made possible…

"Least favorite person, huh?" He laughed at her carefully softened choice of words. "Is that a step up from the 'I hate him' of the other night?"

He was glad that made her laugh even a little bit. "Not really. Maybe just a more polite choice of words." Her gaze slanted toward Debbie and Dinah, who were a few yards away. "I'm trying to watch how I phrase things, you know? About Cyrus. About my ex-husband."

Again, Gabe sensed a lot of pain lurking behind

that very short list of "things which must be carefully worded." He decided not to respond, but joined her in watching the girls as they played.

He heard Avery suck in a "that's enough of that" breath, and shift her weight. "Girls, come over here please."

The way Gabe was raised, a request like that—and now that he thought about it, it would never have been a request but always a command—would have been met with an immediate and often nervous "yes, sir." Gabe's stepfathers hadn't been affectionate men. It bothered him that he couldn't remember how his mother would have worded it. It bothered him that he couldn't call up the sound of her voice anymore, only the weary set of her eyes.

He found himself drawn by the way the girls reacted. Their eyes lit up, they dropped what they were doing and skipped—*skipped*, really, when was the last time he saw anyone skip?—over to stand next to their mother. There was something effortlessly joyous about it that fascinated him in a way he couldn't explain.

"Girls," Avery said as she smoothed out each girl's set of braids, "let's say thank you to Mr. Boots and the boys for building your swings, okay?"

Dinah looked out at the nearly finished construction. "Are they done *yet*?"

The girls were very much alike in many ways, but even he could already see their distinct personalities. Dinah was the thinker, the analyzer, while Debbie was the feeler, the instigator. That insight alone stumped him, because he didn't think of himself as a particularly perceptive man. Cattle, balance sheets, logistics, yes. People and personalities? Not so much. Children? Not at all.

And yet these girls intrigued him on some level—not that he'd ever admit that.

"We can still thank them," Avery explained. "So let's start right now. What do you want to say to our host?"

Almost in unison, the girls straightened themselves up and recited a very perfunctory "Thank you, Mr. Boots."

As heartfelt praises went, it wasn't much, but he couldn't deny it had an adorable charm. Gabe surprised himself by extending a hand. "You're welcome."

Dinah put her tiny hand in his—the sight almost comical with those small pink fingers wrapped in his large tanned hand—and shook it with pint-size importance. Debbie did the same, but added a vigorous shake and wildly happy grin to her gesture. Gabe ended up laughing despite himself.

There was an oddly warm moment where all the irritation dropped and everyone smiled at each other. He hadn't expected that, and it unsettled him enough to push himself up off the steps and back to the construction.

Debbie and Dinah followed him like a pair of puppies, skipping up to the pack of working boys with Avery trailing behind them. The girls went through the same routine with each of the boys, offering thank-yous and tiny handshakes to all of them.

He expected the usual grunts and nods, but the boys seemed as charmed as he had been. They laughed and smiled in response to the gratitude. Two of them tipped their hats, earning a fresh ripple of giggles from Debbie. Two of them invited the girls out to the ranch to see the baby goats—something that made them squeal with delight and turn back to their mother with a chorus of "Please, Mama, can we?"

Gabe began to think the impulse buy of the swings— actually more of a desperate act than an indulgent impulse, if he was honest—wasn't such a mistake after all. He hoped Avery wouldn't be able to refuse the boys' offer given the girls' enthusiasm.

"Did you plan that?" Avery said as she came up beside him.

Gabe was glad he could honestly say "No."

"Well," she reflected after a long pause and a large sigh, "I suppose we could manage a short tour as a way to say thanks for the swings."

Gabe smiled and offered his hand to her as he had to the girls. "It'd be my pleasure." He tried to convince himself it was an ordinary handshake.

It wasn't. Her hands were soft and a memorable tawny color, so different from his own skin. The backs of her palms held the hint of olive coloring that tinted the twins' cheeks. His calloused fingers took in the smooth texture of her skin, and he noticed the bare place on her other hand when she wrapped his hand in both of hers. The spot where her wedding ring should have been. All those details in the split second the gesture took.

Gabe was in many ways a detail-oriented man, but this was an entirely different "frozen in time" kind of detail that made his stomach twist and his breath catch.

Debbie broke the moment by tugging on Gabe's hand. "Can we have a sandbox next?"

"Deborah!" Avery chided.

Gabe managed a shocked laugh. "The girl's got spunk, I'll give her that."

"Apologize for that this instant," Avery said in "you're in trouble" tones, accompanied by a very demanding hand on Debbie's shoulder.

Debbie stuffed her hands in her jumper pockets and looked down. "I'm sorry I asked for a sandbox." Debbie did not sound very sorry. Instead of annoying Gabe, this made him like the spunky little girl all the more.

"No sandbox," he said, keeping the humor out of his voice in order to match Avery's disdain. "But I think the baby goats will make up for it."

"We get to see the baby goats!" Debbie squealed. He'd owned pigs and not heard so much squealing as he had today. "Can we ride any ponies?"

"Enough!" Avery replied, her color high with embarrassment and her eyes pleading for forgiveness. "Go on back to the porch now with your sister."

"I don't know where she gets it," Avery said, raising her hand to her forehead with an exasperated sigh.

He'd seen Avery stand up to Roz Sackett. Gabe had a crystal clear idea of where Debbie got her spunk.

Not that he was going to say. Every cowboy in Texas knew not to call the bull out for the size of his horns.

Or, in this case, a mama on the size of her spunk.

Chapter Six

Sunday morning, Avery sighed in relief. Between the four adults, they'd actually managed to get both girls ready on time to attend services at Haven Community Church. Back in Tennessee, she hadn't seen the first ten minutes of a church service in months—they were always horribly late. But at least they were there.

Not that today had been smooth sailing. Dinah had spilled orange juice on her dress, necessitating a last-minute change, which sent Debbie into fits because Debbie always wanted to match her sister. One double dress change and a quick swap of hair bows later, Marlene slid into the front seat of Avery's car while Jethro drove in the truck with Gabe.

"I imagine those men will have a thing or two to say about frilly dresses," Marlene laughed.

"How do you do that?" Avery asked as she checked the girls' seat belts and booster seats in the rearview mirror and turned the ignition.

"Do what?" Marlene asked, her words slightly garbled by the process of applying lipstick in the visor mirror. Avery wondered if she'd remembered to put on any makeup at all in the flurry of preparations.

"Laugh about it all." Did her words sound as weary as they felt?

"Well, I'm not much for the other choice. Better to laugh at it all than wear a sour face all the time." She turned to look at Avery. "A face as pretty as yours needs more smiles. I feel for how you've been slammed down in the middle of this with no warning. I sure can't figure out what the good Lord is up to in all this."

Avery shrugged. "Neither can I."

"Mama, my bow came out," called Dinah.

"Hang on to it and we'll fix it when we get there," Avery advised, giving her own hair a quick check in the mirror.

"You look just fine," Marlene said with a wink, then cast her glance back over to the backseat. "Little girls in Sunday dresses. Is there any sweeter thing?"

"*Quiet* little girls in Sunday dresses?" Avery often felt as if the entire congregation of her church back home barely tolerated her noisy girls. No one ever came out and said anything, but that might be due to the fact that people rarely talked to her at all since Danny left. It had been his church, and had never quite become hers. When she returned, Avery promised herself to find the energy needed to look for another one.

Marlene waved off the comment. "Don't you give a mind to that. We're a family church, and families are noisy. I expect those two will trot off to children's church and make loads of friends. My great-grandkids love to come to Haven because of how much fun the children's activities and Sunday school are. Next year your girls will be old enough to go to Sunday school, and they'll love that, I promise you."

There it was again. Why was everyone in Haven so quick to assume Avery was here to stay? No matter how many times she pointed out the temporary nature of her visit, folks talked as if her permanent residency was a done deal. Avery knew they meant it in a welcoming way, but given her circumstances she couldn't help but feel just the tiniest bit trapped.

"Have you met Pastor Andrew Walsh yet?"

"Only briefly," Avery replied as she followed Gabe's truck around a turn.

"He's a good man. Good-looking and single, too, but not for much longer. Everyone knows Katie Ellis—she's the boys ranch secretary, if you didn't know—won his heart. Bless that man, poor Katie had to wait forever for him to catch on and finally ask her out. That preacher may be wise in the Lord, but he sure was slow on the uptake in the romance department."

Marlene's chuckle made Avery smile. Small towns were pretty much the same everywhere. It was a sure thing Haven hosted a crowd of old-hen matchmakers the same as where she'd come from in Tennessee. She hoped those old wagging tongues wouldn't get any ideas about her—romance was definitely not on the table for her here. And not in Tennessee, either, until she and the girls were on more solid footing. The next man in Debbie's and Dinah's lives was going to stay and dote on them forever.

"Of course, love has had a good run in Haven lately. First there was Tanner and Macy—she has a nephew she's raising who's not much older than your girls." Marlene began ticking couples off on her fingers. "Then Heath and Josie—oh, she just had her darling baby, Joy. Cutest little thing, that girl. After that it was—"

"There's more?"

"Like I said, love has had a good run in Haven these days. Then came Heath's buddy Flint and sweet Lana. Has Lana showed you that photo she found of your grandpa yet? If not, you ask her—you ought to have it. Let's see, Nick and Darcy were next, and then I think it was Dr. Wyatt and Carolina. Carolina's got a little boy a bit younger than your girls."

Avery began to wonder if Pastor Andrew knew he ought to be ring shopping, given the town's romantic track record. She tried not to look stunned when it appeared Marlene wasn't yet done. "And…nope, that's all of them. So far, that is. Five couples since October."

"Maybe you ought to advertise," Avery quipped. "Clearly, there's something in the town water supply."

Marlene laughed. "Well, maybe, but I credit our mystery matchmakers for some of it."

"Mystery matchmakers?"

"Someone's been nudging those couples together. Or trying to—there have been as many hits as there have been misses. Notes, dance invitations, why, even pies have shown up in the name of romance around here. Someone—or a group of someones—seems bent on making sure there are no lonely hearts in Haven, Texas. Jethro says this town's a haven for the soul. I say it's just stepping up as a haven for the heart, too."

And a headquarters for crazy bequest schemes, Avery silently added. If she did give in to the town's insistence that she stay, would she end up in the sights of those overactive matchmakers before all was said and done? Avery didn't much care for that prospect, and chalked it up as another mark in the column of reasons she might be better off leaving.

She pulled her sedan into the parking space to the left of Gabe's truck. Gabe hopped out and opened the door for Marlene, gentleman that he was. Had Danny ever done that for her? To avoid letting that thought sour in her brain, Avery popped out and opened the back door to begin unbuckling the girls.

"Girls, what happened?" Not only was Dinah's bow missing, but both of Debbie's shoes were also nowhere to be found.

"They itched," Debbie offered, wiggling her toes under white tights.

"Shoes cannot itch," Avery explained as she unbuckled the seat belt and began thrusting her hands under the passenger seat until her fingers landed on the shoes. "It was a five-minute ride, Dinah. How did you manage to get both off?"

"It wasn't hard," Dinah replied, sliding off the booster as if walking into church in stocking feet would be fun.

"Sit," Avery commanded, working the patent leather straps through the buckles as quickly as she could. "I was really looking forward to walking into church on time, girls."

"The bell hasn't rung yet," Marlene advised. "In my book, if the bell isn't done ringing, you're on time."

"Is your church fun?" Debbie asked Marlene with as skeptical a look as Avery had ever seen on a four-year-old. Out of the corner of her eye, Avery saw an amused smile erupt on Gabe's face before he could smother it.

"I like to think so," Jethro said as if the question was perfectly natural. Avery loved that about Jethro—no matter what off-the-wall comment or question Dinah or Debbie dreamed up, Jethro spoke to them as if they were real, serious, worthwhile people. *Give me some of that kind of patience*, she prayed as she finished Dinah's buckle. *Slow me down enough to pay that kind of attention.*

"Take a deep breath, we're here," Marlene whispered in Avery's ear as if she'd heard the prayer. "God doesn't much care *how* you show up, just *that* you show up." With that, Marlene extended a hand to Dinah and walked toward the church as calm as could be.

Avery huffed a lock of hair off her forehead as she grabbed her handbag. "She's right," Gabe said. "Nothing too fancy for little ones inside. And when they scurry off to children's church, you get some peace and quiet of your own."

"I could use that," she replied.

"Couldn't we all?" he said with a grin as they started toward the door.

Gabe had never worked so hard to pay attention in church since he was five.

Normally, he liked church, welcomed the grounding it gave him for the often hectic week ahead. Pastor Andrew taught well, giving thoughtful and even challenging sermons, and what the choir often lacked in talent they made up for in enthusiasm.

This morning, it felt like God had hidden Himself behind a mountain of distractions Gabe was helpless to overcome. The girls were all squirms and whispers, dropping things and making noises. Marlene and Jethro flanked them on one side, with Avery and himself on the other, but even one body away the girls invaded his worship and concentration. It embarrassed him how he resented the intrusion—he shouldn't fault the girls for being four any more than he could fault a cow for chewing cud. Still, it seemed as if every corner of his life had been invaded—at his invitation, no less—by "tiny pinkness."

What are You up to, Lord? He prayed as the girls slid themselves off the pew and trotted forward for their children's moment with Pastor Andrew. *You know I'm out of my depth here. I need more calm and order in my life, not less. You've heaped enough on my plate without all this.*

Gabe had never much paid attention to the children's moment in services before, but today he found himself impressed with how Pastor Andrew boiled a gospel truth down into simple nuggets a little brain could grasp. He went out of his way to include Dinah and Debbie in the little knot of church regulars, talking to them and nodding at their answers to his questions. The girls smiled and nodded right back, even giving excited little waves and not-so-silently mouthed, "Bye, Mom" to Avery as they walked past her with the volunteer on their way to children's church.

The church always felt a little more settled when the young ones left, but today Gabe felt as if his entire pew exhaled in relief as the girls departed. He felt Avery practically slump back in her seat, newly aware of the tension she must have felt. Had he truly realized the scrutiny she must feel? If he felt as if the whole town was watching him fail to turn up Theodore Linley, how must she feel with all of Haven's boys ranch supporters hanging on for word of her decision to stay? *I've thought of her in all the wrong ways, Lord,* he confessed. *I've treated her like an asset to be managed, someone with something I need. Now I see what she needs: compassion. Only I'm not so sure I'm the one who can provide it.*

"Now you settle back and let the Spirit do It's thing," Marlene whispered to Avery as the organ started up for a hymn. "If anyone needs a few moments' peace, hon, it's you."

Thank You for Marlene and Jethro, Gabe continued as he opened his hymnal. *I don't know what I'd ever do without them.*

When Avery looked a little lost, Gabe handed her his hymnal already opened to the correct page and pulled another from the little slot in the pew. She looked up at him with kind eyes for the tiny gesture, a version of the look she'd given him over the swings. *She hasn't known much kindness*, he thought. *And don't I know how that wears on a soul.*

Her voice startled him. Avery had a sweet, clear singing voice. He wasn't sure why that was such a surprise—lots of people had pleasant singing voices—except that he'd never heard her use it, even with the girls. He'd have thought someone with that lovely a voice would be singing all the time, especially to her children. Life had certainly stomped too much joy from that woman's spirit. The dark circles that had lurked under her eyes that day back on the boardinghouse porch were only just beginning to leave her features.

As Gabe, Avery and the rest of the congregation finished the second verse, it struck him. Maybe this wasn't all about preventing her from leaving town and forfeiting the bequest. Maybe it was also about taking that abandoned look from her eyes, about wiping that air of desperation away. He only knew *what* she was—Cyrus Culpepper's granddaughter and one of the stipulations in his will. Maybe he ought to take the time to find out *who* she was—what she wanted in life, what obstacles she faced, how all that weight he saw pressing down her shoulders had come to be there.

And if that wasn't a revelation worthy of serious pondering, he didn't know what was.

Chapter Seven

The Lone Star Cowboy League Boys Ranch wasn't everything Avery expected. It was what she expected in terms of appearance—wide fields surrounding a large single-story building with a wide porch, brand-new barn, several outbuildings and the other elements anyone would expect of a ranch property. It was the atmosphere of the place, the warm bustle and happy noise of so many people, that caught her up short.

Without realizing it, she'd pictured it as an institutionalized home for troubled kids. A stern, productive place. The assumption made no sense, given that the estate had until recently been the private home of her grandfather and given how warmly the townspeople talked of the organization. As she walked around the buildings and saw the faces of the boys and the staff, Avery realized it was her grandfather she saw in those stern and unforgiving terms, not the boys ranch. This visit was jumbling up her emotions in ways she wasn't fully prepared to handle.

"This is the learning center we've finally had room to create," Gabe said as the girls ran toward a smaller building off the main house. "The littler ones get stories read to them here, and the bigger ones can check out books and get help with homework. It's a favorite place of lots of the boys—after the kitchen and the barn."

"Books can never compete with cookies," offered a slightly paunchy middle-aged man as he exited the building with a stack of books and some papers.

"They have cookies here?" Debbie asked with obvious hope.

The man leaned down to meet her wide eyes. "The cook, Miss Marnie, makes some of the best around. And she doesn't get too many chances to hand them out to sweet little girls." He extended a hand to Avery. "Fletcher Snowden Phillips. You must be Avery. The real one, that is."

Avery accepted the handshake. She wasn't sure she'd ever get used to being referred to as "the real Avery."

"Pleased to meet you, Mr. Phillips."

"Mama," pleaded Dinah, tugging on Avery's sleeve, "can we go see the kitchen right after we go see the goats?"

"I'd recommend we go visit Miss Marnie first, actually," Gabe advised, meeting with shouts of approval from the girls. "The barn can be a messy place and Miss Marnie may have a few scraps or treats you can bring to feed the goats."

Phillips fell into step with them as they turned toward the house. "You know, Miss Culpepper, I wasn't always a big fan of the boys ranch. I'm ashamed to say I misunderstood the place and even fought against it. I do hope the same won't be said of you, even if your grandpa didn't quite handle things the way we'd all have liked." He shifted his load to the other hand, stopping for a moment to gesture around the property. "This place deserves the chance to succeed. If there's anything I can do to

help you help us make that happen, I hope you'll let me."
With a nod of farewell, he turned toward the parking lot.

Gabe stared after the older man. "The boys ranch has a lot of turnaround stories to tell, but that one may just about top them all. Was a time we all thought Fletcher would fight the ranch to his dying breath."

That nice old man? "What happened?"

"It's a long story you'd best get from Darcy, but I'll just say he changed a lot once he discovered she was his daughter. Sometimes people just need to know there's someone they belong to, you know? Belonging here is mostly what turns these boys around. That, and a little care and a lot of hard work."

A sensible-looking woman with brown bobbed hair came out of the house's front door to meet them. "I'm delighted to see you here," she said, waving them up onto the porch. "I can't wait to show you what your grandfather's house is doing for these boys already." She looked down at Debbie and Dinah. "And I bet you little ladies don't want to wait to see what Miss Marnie might have for you in the kitchen."

"Avery Culpepper, meet our director, Bea Brewster. She knows everything there is to know about this place."

Bea smiled. "And then some." She pointed down a hallway. "Kitchen's just in there, girls. Follow the yummy smells." The house did smell delicious, with the scent of baking cookies. A lump rose in Avery's throat to be standing in her grandfather's house, where she should have been but never was. She took a moment to stare around the foyer, lost for words.

Bea's voice was tender as she lay a hand on Avery's elbow. "It's a beautiful place. So big for one old man to be rumbling around alone for all those years." Avery found it funny how Bea's words echoed what Marlene had said about Five Rocks. The two women seemed a lot alike to her—friendly and oh-so capable. "We're ever so grateful to be able to put the place to such good use."

One house tour, four cookies, one absurdly crazy and adorable goat-feeding session, and a top-it-all-off pair of pony rides later, Avery stood at a fence with Gabe, the girls between them, watching the horses wander about their pasture. Today she'd felt her heart lose some of the steely bitterness she'd held for this place. No, it hadn't been her home, but it was home to a lot of other people and a lot of good work.

"I'll stay," she said quietly.

Gabe turned to look at her, astonished gratitude lighting his eyes. "You will?"

"Just until the party. Then I have to get back to my life."

"Of course you do."

"I do have a life and job back in Tennessee, you know." She had an urge to keep saying that. "I can only do so much of my work from here and it isn't fair to uproot the girls." Even as she spoke them, the words rang hollow. No one had missed her in Dickson. She'd gotten only three calls from people who weren't decorating clients, and one of them was the preschool wanting to know if the girls should be registered for the coming year. Too much of that was her own doing—isolating herself in the eighteen months since Danny had decided life in Memphis suited him better than his family in Dickson. She should go back with her head held high and try to make Dickson the home it ought to be. At least she had a house and a business back there—one worth fighting to grow. Why on earth would she dabble in the idea that she could start over here, where she had only a run-down shack and where *Culpepper* was a dirty name?

* * *

Gabe was finishing up an agenda for the next Lone Star Cowboy League meeting Tuesday morning when Avery pushed open the door to his study and stared at him, wide-eyed.

"Gabe, I'm so sorry." She had on some kooky old hat that must have been Marlene's from years ago, with what seemed to be paper flowers poking out of it in all directions. Her parade-float accessory was alarming enough, but it was her genuinely mortified expression that turned his gut to ice. "I tried to stop them but…"

"Mr. Boots!" a pair of high, giggly voices called from the hallway, giving Gabe an irrational urge to duck under his desk and hide. Whatever was about to burst through his study door, Avery clearly predicted he wouldn't like it. "We have a surprise for you!"

Avery's face took on a helpless apologetic cringe. Gabe held his breath and made plans for a dead bolt on his study door.

Within seconds, two small girls in ridiculous dress-up clothes burst into the room. Debbie and Dinah sported frilly frocks twice their size cinched in at the waist. They also wore enormous wobbly hats with just as shocking a collection of paper flowers piled on top, gloves, pearly beads and bracelets. Debbie carried a handbag twice as big as her head.

Gabe could not form an appropriate greeting to his two guests as they clomped toward him in far-too-big high heels that held their little white sneakers with inches to spare. He could think of no safe or pleasant outcome of this invasion—not with Avery looking like that.

"Hello," they greeted him in unison, giggling the word in singsong, fancy-pants voices.

It was then he noticed Dinah held something behind

her back. Debbie fumbled with the clasp on the big hand-bag and produced a large colored piece of paper. "We've been baking like Miss Marnie at the ranch. And now we're having a tea party," she declared as if it explained everything.

"Good for you," he spit out, his own mortification growing. This was not heading anyplace he wanted to go.

"It's a *thank-you* tea party," Dinah said with great importance. "And you get to come."

Gabe shot his glance up to Avery, who was shrugging and cringing and giving him a "it couldn't be helped" look that was as infuriating as it was charming. *Are you sure about that?* he hoped his gaze conveyed.

"And," Dinah went on, "you're the guesty honor."

"The guest *of* honor," Avery amended, as if that made it any more palatable. "To say thank you for the swings and the pony rides. It was the girls' idea."

That wasn't hard to guess. "And clearly Marlene helped." Oh, he could just imagine how Marlene took that particular ball and ran with it. A woman who'd launched this granny-housekeeping stint with hot-dog octopuses couldn't be counted on for moderation in anything, much less dress-up tea parties.

"We helped her make gingerbread cookies and she helped us put flowers on our hats," Debbie said as she laid what Gabe assumed was an invitation—folded paper covered in crayon pink hearts and yellow flowers and something he could only assume were tea cups—on his study desk. Someone had doused the girls with a hefty dose of the perfume Avery usually wore. His stomach produced a wiggling sensation at his recognition of the scent, overpowering as it was at the moment.

Gabe was cornered as neatly as if the girls had roped and tied him at the rodeo. They were thanking him—

granted, in the worst possible way a busy cowboy could think of—and it would be mean to refuse their gratitude. After all, Avery had consented to stay as long as the anniversary celebration.

As if to test his resolve, Dinah produced what she'd been hiding. It was a dusty old gray top hat—from where, he couldn't hope to guess—with one enormous red flower tentatively stuck lopsidedly to the brim. Gabe fought the urge to gulp.

"This is yours," Dinah explained. "Everybody gets 'em. We're being fancy." She set it on the desk and wiggled her gloved fingers. The unfilled fingertips where her small fingers couldn't yet reach flopped absurdly as she did.

"A well-mannered cowboy knows he takes his hat *off* in the presence of ladies," he said, hoping to avoid the inevitable.

"That's not a cowboy hat," Dinah retorted. "You get to wear it specially."

Gabe raised an eyebrow directly at Avery, who was looking far too much like she was about to burst out in laughter. *Oh, no*, he thought as he pushed his keyboard drawer back under the desk. *You do not get to enjoy this. You could have—you should have—prevented this.*

"Those had better be the best gingerbread cookies in the world," he said with the nicest tone his rising reluctance would allow.

"Oh, they are," Debbie assured him. "They're *splendid*." She worked hard to get the fancy adjective out. Avery lost her fight to the giggles and he barely avoided chuckling himself.

Gabe scratched his chin as he eyed his new accessory. "So I'm to wear this hat, am I?"

Dinah nodded so vigorously her giant hat tipped down to hide her face until she pushed it back up again.

"Does Mr. Frank have one just as…fancy?"

"Oh, no, he had to go into town for something," Debbie said. *I'm sure he did*, Gabe thought darkly. *Let's hope it wasn't a camera.*

"The party's right now," Dinah said, pointing to some scribbles on the card. "So you hafta come right away."

Gabe stood slowly. Very slowly. "Condemned man going to his death" slowly.

"But with your hat on," Debbie insisted. "You need to put your hat on like all of us."

Avery made a big show of adjusting her hat. She most definitely was enjoying this far too much.

Gabe cleared his throat and reached for the thing. It smelled of the perfume, as well—one of them had sprayed the paper flower. *These had better be the best gingerbread cookies in the whole universe*, he thought to himself as he settled the silly thing on his head.

Debbie and Dinah greeted his new look with enthusiastic, if glove-muffled, applause.

There was nothing for it. The sooner he went, the sooner he got it over with. Gabe walked around his desk and held out an elbow to each of his flouncy escorts. "Well, ladies, I guess it's time for tea."

"You're a good sport," Avery whispered as he and the girls clomped past.

"I'm a dead man. Not one single photo or you're out on the curb by sundown," he whispered back, fully aware he didn't mean it.

"I'd never dream of such a thing," Avery said as she pulled the study door shut. "And I did try to stop them."

"Not very hard," he called over his shoulder. "Not nearly hard enough."

* * *

"Gabe Everett? The Gabriel Everett I know?" Rhetta Douglass threw her head back and laughed with one hand on her chest. "What I wouldn't give to see that man at a little girls' tea party." The children had made friends at church activity time and Rhetta had invited them for a playdate at the town library with Carolina and her two-year-old son, Matty. After checking out a stack of books, all three moms were sitting outside the library while the children played together blowing bubbles on the front lawn.

"I kept my word." Avery laughed alongside the woman, remembering the sight of Gabe's tall limbs folded around the small fussy table Marlene had set in the front room. "There are no pictures." She leaned in and lowered her voice. "But he never said I couldn't tell someone. I expect I'll have to swear you both to secrecy now that you know."

"We moms need to stick together. Some days I need someone who understands what it's like to raise double trouble. Someone other than their father, that is. Honestly, I think Deron eggs them on some days." Rhetta sighed.

"I can't fathom how you both manage twins," Carolina said. "Most times Matty's a sweet boy. Then other times…" She shook her head and made a weary sound Avery knew all too well. "How are you finding things over at the Five Rocks?"

"I don't know that I can rightly say. Some days are wonderful, and others make me want to pack up and head for the hills, where no one has ever heard of Cyrus Culpepper."

Rhetta looked at Avery. "You still have no idea what that old fool is up to? Making you wait on some celebration after waiting all those years?"

"Grandpa Cyrus has—*had*—a taste for the dramatic,

don't you think?" Avery shrugged. "When I'm feeling generous, I think Gabe is right—Cyrus is just trying to make up for all the years he didn't know me."

"And when you're not feeling so generous?" Carolina asked.

Avery scowled. "I think he's a mean old man who died alone because he manipulated everyone around him and I'm just the last one in line."

"Now you know why everyone believed the other Avery. She acted like a Culpepper." Rhetta shook her head again. "That woman. She ought to be ashamed of herself for how she acted, coming here trying to take what's rightfully yours. She thought she was waltzing into the high life, that's for sure." Smiling, Rhetta handed Avery an envelope. "I'm glad no one gave her this."

"What is it?"

"Lana gave it to me to give to you. It's a photograph of your father and your grandparents."

Avery pulled open the envelope to see an old color snapshot. *Dad.* He looked so young and hopeful—barely a teenager, from the looks of it. Too many of her last memories of Dad in his decline had drowned out the possibility of him youthful and happy. She touched the image.

"Lana found it one afternoon tutoring at the ranch. It's how we started to realize that the first Avery wasn't the real one."

"Well, that and her charming disposition and money-grabbing tactics," Carolina added. "She never looked anything like the family she claimed."

"I guess not." Avery found herself lost in the atmosphere of the photo. The trio looked like a family. Cyrus's hand was on her father's shoulder. Her father—not yet her father but just young and dashing John Culpepper—

looked up at his mother. June Culpepper. The grand-mother she'd never known—Dad had left home after his mother died, so this photo had to be before that falling-out. Her soured image of these people, the one she carried in her head for years, didn't match the people in the photo. It made her heart ache all the more for everything she'd never had.

"Lana felt you should have it," Rhetta said softly.

"Thank you." Avery touched the photo gingerly, wanting to feel them as real people instead of players in this game she'd been dragged into. "I'd like to keep it, I think."

"Grandparents can be good people—and not just for babysitting. Do the girls know their grandparents from your husband's side?"

"Ex-husband," Avery amended, trying unsuccessfully to keep the bitter edge from her tone. "And no, not very well." She sighed and tucked the photo into her handbag. "Danny was never much of a family man. We lived two hours from his folks and hardly ever saw them. That was fine when it was just us, but when we went from a duo to a quartet overnight…"

"That's a shame," Rhetta said, commiserating. "Those girls are adorable. And they must be loaded with charm if they managed to get Gabe under their thumb." Rhetta jumped up for a minute, waving her hand. "Get down off there, son, you stay away from that fence." She sat down again. "That boy. I ought to buy stock in a first-aid company the way he scrapes himself up."

"The girls adore Gabe. Although, if I'm honest, I have to say I'm not really sure why. He doesn't seem to especially like them."

Rhetta gave Avery a sideways glance. "No offense, but the man might be a bit short on the warm personality from where I sit. All alone up there on that huge ranch—seems to me a man with those looks and all that land is alone because he wants to be, not from a lack of female prospects."

"Certainly not with the way this town seems to match up folks," Carolina remarked.

"Marlene told me about the mystery matchmakers. Did they...?" Avery looked at Carolina.

"They did. Some rather obviously false dance invitations for Wyatt to be my pick at a ladies' choice charity dance," Carolina admitted with a smile.

"Not very original, but effective anyway," Rhetta laughed. "I wouldn't be surprised if our secret cupids matched you off—most likely with Gabe."

"He's been very generous to us, but it's because he needs to be."

"Needs? Darlin', that man didn't need to put you up in his own home," Rhetta replied. "He could have paid to put you up in the next town if he needed to keep you here. You've seen the size of Five Rocks—that man is well off."

Carolina leaned in. "Are you sure something else wasn't going on when he offered to take you in?"

"Nothing is going on." Even as she said the words, Avery knew they weren't entirely true. There was something going on between Gabe and the girls, between Gabe and her. She just didn't trust it or know what it truly was.

"That man put a froufrou top hat on. Trust me, *something* is going on." Rhetta sat back against the bench. "And that doesn't have to be a bad thing, you know. Have you decided you're going to stay in Haven?"

"I've told Gabe I would stay until the anniversary celebration."

Rhetta frowned. "But then you'll go back to Tennessee."

Avery felt her hackles rise. Why did everyone assume

she had so little life in Tennessee that it would be effortless to leave everything behind and come here? Leaving was what Danny had done—she wasn't about to do that to the girls. And not only that. "I'm not eager for my girls to grow up in Cyrus's long, cold shadow."

Rhetta crossed her arms. "You've given that man an awful lot of power from the grave. Not that I agree with what Cyrus did—I don't, although I sure am happy to see the boys ranch get a larger spread. It's a whole lot of manipulating nonsense, and you've a right to be annoyed. Only I don't wonder if you're letting the bad outweigh the possibility of a whole lot of good."

"You're forgetting that a lot of people here really like you," Carolina offered. "A whole lot more than that other Avery, that's for sure. They want you to be happy, to feel welcome. Surely, that's worth something. I know you didn't come by it in the nicest of ways, but you've got a place here. The girls, too. If there's nothing keeping you back in Tennessee, don't let everything Cyrus wasn't keep you from everything you could be here."

Avery offered no reply, mostly because she didn't know what to say. She didn't really agree with Carolina, but then again, she couldn't deny she was warming up to Haven—and to Gabe.

Chapter Eight

Avery spied the number on her cell-phone screen two days later and a lump formed in her throat. Danny hardly ever called, and when he did it was never for anything good. He couldn't have possibly heard her thoughts about what it would take for her to move to Haven—but she felt caught in the act just the same. She was glad Debbie and Dinah were helping Marlene make cookies in the kitchen so she could take the call in the privacy of Gabe's library.

"Hello?"

"Where are you?" It would have been nice if Danny's question held a tone of concern, but it rang far too much like an accusation in her ears.

"I'm in Texas, like I told you. The thing with my grandfather's estate."

"You said you'd only be a few days."

Why did he care? She needed his consent to take them out of state, but it wasn't as if he actually missed visits with his girls—she'd stopped trying to convince him to be part of their lives months ago. Danny's concept of fatherhood no longer extended beyond his child support payments, and Avery tried to feel grateful that he was at least dependable with those. "It's become more complicated. I'm going to need to stay here through the twentieth."

"What did the old man leave you anyway?" Avery resented the newly interested tone of his question. Did he hope Cyrus left her enough to live on so she could decline further child support? Knowing Danny, he'd looked up the size of the Culpepper ranch and was salivating over what she might now own. This man bore so little resemblance to the man who'd stolen her heart six years ago.

"So far, one run-down cabin. He left the ranch to a charity in town—well, sort of. There are a lot of strings attached, and that's part of the reason I need to stay here until the twentieth."

"So who's minding *our* house back in Tennessee while you're on your *extended* trip to Texas?" He emphasized the *our* and made it sound like she'd doubled her vacation.

"I paid the son of a client to stop by twice a week and check on things." He paid her alimony and child support, but little expenses like this and others necessitated that she keep up a steady stream of interior decorating jobs to ensure they weren't living paycheck to paycheck. She was responsible with the house. She wrote the check for the mortgage payment every month. She did everything, and did it alone.

"Would you rather I shuttle the girls back and forth while I get things settled here? We've got a place to stay. This isn't costing you extra, if that's what you're worried about." She hated the sharp tone of her words, but some days Danny could raise her hackles so fast.

"In that cabin he left you? Have you got my girls living in some ramshackle old cabin?"

My girls. The words burned in her ears. "No, that place isn't livable. I couldn't even sell it in the state it is now." Avery looked out the library window to see Gabe hauling something out of his truck. "One of the ranchers has let us use a wing of his place."

"His?"

"He and his housekeeper and her husband have been very good to the girls. They're helping us stay because I need to be here on March twentieth to find out what else Cyrus has left me. Like I said, Danny, it's complicated. The girls are fine. I'm fine." She tried not to sound exasperated as she added, "Is there a reason you called?"

"Do I need a reason?"

You never call without a reason. "I need to go soon. The girls are with Marlene baking cookies. Maybe you'd like to say hello?"

It saddened her how she knew that question would cut the call short. "No, don't bother them. I just wanted to know why you hadn't come back yet. Don't you have to be back to register for school?"

Avery was surprised he'd paid that much attention. "Registration starts April first—I've already talked to them about it. We'll be back in more than enough time to get all the paperwork done." Her mind thought ahead to parents' night, teacher conferences, school plays and everything else she would probably not be able to convince Danny to show up to. *But I'll be there. I'll make sure I'm there.*

"Don't you need my permission to keep them out of state like this?"

It bothered her that he was quoting regulations like someone who cared whether his children were nearby. For as often as he saw them—which was next to never—they could live halfway around the world. "I'm not moving here," she said, unsettled by everyone's assumption that she was, and her own tiny curl of curiosity that was starting to expand. How sad was it that she felt more welcome in a place she'd never known than the Tennessee town she'd lived in for six years? "Please don't make this more difficult than it already is. The girls and I are fine, we're sorting things out, and I'll be sure to let you know as soon as we're on our way back."

"You do that." Again, his tone was more of a power display than any show of concern. As she looked out the window, Dinah came running up to Gabe holding a heart-shaped gingersnap in her flour-dusted fingers. He stopped what he was doing and hunched down to Dinah's level to hear whatever she said as she presented him with the cookie. Debbie came right up behind Dinah with a cookie of her own, and Avery watched Gabe take the cookies with great ceremony, as if they were treasures. He smiled and talked with the girls as he bit into one cookie and tucked the other into his shirt pocket the same way he had done the day they moved in.

"Avery?"

She'd forgotten the phone still in her hand. "Sorry, I'm trying to keep an eye on the girls while they're outside."

"You're not with them? They're out there alone?" That was Danny—quick to criticize, but slow to offer help to fix whatever he deemed wrong.

"We're not alone here," Avery replied, the power of those words striking her even as she spoke them a bit harshly. "They went outside to bring cookies to our host, Gabriel Everett. I can see them from the window where I'm standing." Watching Gabe's reluctantly charming way with the girls, she assured him, "We're *fine*, Danny." Some small and bitter corner of her heart wanted to add "not that you care," but she bit back the remark. Danny was still their father, even though things had gone so horribly sour between them. A dead marriage was such a sad and ugly thing. She was grateful the girls were young enough that she had managed to hide most of the ugliness from them. She was also deeply aware of how the girls had taken to Gabe like thirsty deer to water. *They've taken to Jethro and Marlene, too*, she reminded herself. *And to lots of people here. Please, Lord, can't You help me find people like this in Tennessee?*

Danny was talking into her ear, going on about some business victory and his precious new truck. She used to love how he boasted, as if he could rule the world. As if they would have the grandest of lives together.

It all sounded like so much noise now. "I really do need to go, Danny. Is there anything else?"

"No. Just keep me posted."

She wanted to ask why, but chided herself. As she clicked off the call, a startling truth struck her like a physical blow to the chest. Danny and Cyrus were alike. She felt abandoned by both. She'd felt abandoned by nearly everyone. *How on earth do I fix that? How do You fix that, Lord?*

As she stared at Gabe, now sitting on the ground conversing with the girls and eating the cookie from his pocket, Avery couldn't help but wonder if God might have already begun that healing. Right under her nose in Haven, Texas.

Gabe walked outside Friday morning where the girls were "helping" Jethro fix some of Marlene's flower boxes. They had on small denim overalls, and even he had to admit they were adorable. Avery had done up each girl's hair in a set of bobbing pigtails topped with pink-and-blue bows—frilly compared to the overalls, but somehow cute as buttons nonetheless. *Cute as buttons?* When had he adopted phrases like that?

The day you invited all that tiny pinkness onto your

ranch, he answered himself as he walked up to where the girls were tapping nails with little flowered hammers.

"Where'd those come from?"

"Marlene found 'em at the Haven Tractor and Supply. Sweet, ain't they?"

Gabe wasn't sure hammers ever needed to be sweet, but the girls held the pair of them up like trophies. "Mind your fingers, girls. It won't feel so sweet if you miss that nail."

"I know," said Dinah with a pout, holding up one finger with a bright purple bandage. Now even his medicine cabinet had been invaded in girly colors? "Mom had to kiss it three times."

Gabe made a mental note to never do any activity with the girls that might end up with the need to "kiss boo-boos" or any such thing.

Dinah must have caught his sour expression, for she wiggled the finger in question. "It's better now."

"But you should still be careful like Mr. Jethro said," Avery said from behind him. She had on a pair of bib overalls, as well, but they didn't look anything like the girls'. She looked like a slice of down-home sweetness, a bit rustic, a bit tough on the outside, but still 100 percent curvy female. The sight grabbed a hold of him in a way he wasn't quite sure how to swallow. She smiled and shrugged, probably thinking he found the overalls amusing or silly, and the warmth of her grin slid under his skin in a very precarious way.

He coughed, scratched his chin and moved to the business at hand. "Avery, the Lone Star Cowboy League is meeting here this afternoon. I was thinking you might want to attend, if Jethro and Marlene can see to the girls for an hour or two."

"The league meeting?" Avery asked. "Me?"

"I figure you're mixed up in all of this, you might as well attend."

"Am I allowed?"

"Seeing as I am the president, I can invite any guest I see fit. I see no reason why you can't come and offer your views. Or at least get a better sense of what all this is about."

"Mom's meeting cowboys?" Dinah asked, clearly impressed.

"You've met a cowboy. You've met me." He tipped his hat, the gesture casting his memory back to the silly top hat he'd endured at that insufferable tea party.

Dinah laughed, something Gabe rather took issue with—was it so hard to think of him, a rancher and the president of the Lone Star Cowboy League, as a cowboy? "You're different," she said through her giggles. "You're Mr. Boots."

He widened his stance, only half joking. "And Mr. Boots is not a cowboy? These are *cowboy* boots, mind you." Gabe was glad to see the question stump the girls.

"Of course Mr. Boots is a cowboy," Avery added. "And a very fine one at that. Isn't he, girls?"

"S'pose," Dinah added with a suspicious eye.

"S'pose nothin'," Jethro said. "Why, Gabe here is one of the finest ranchers and cowboys I've ever known."

"I'll be glad to attend," Avery agreed. She tucked a thumb under one of the overall straps. "But I think I'll change into something a bit more meeting-like."

"It's casual," Gabe offered. Something about the way Avery dressed had caught his eye from the first. Sure, the activities of motherhood often meant she had smears and stains, but her clothes had an intriguing sense of style. She always looked just a bit different than the other women of Haven, but he couldn't put his finger on why. Was that a Tennessee thing? Or an Avery thing?

It shouldn't be a Gabe thing. The warning felt futile. Already he'd caught himself staring at Avery too many times. And now he was munching cookies with little girls when he ought to be checking on livestock. Or tending to this afternoon's league agenda. Or any number of tasks that had gone undone since Avery and the girls had begun to invade his days. *Things are slipping out of your grasp, and that's not good. Folks are depending on you, and Theodore Linley is still nowhere to be found. Mind you, don't get distracted by what shouldn't ever be yours.*

"I've got some errands to attend to, but I'll be back in time to welcome everyone for the three-o'clock meeting. That gives you four more than enough time to finish—" he waved his hands at the collection of dainty hammers, nails, benches and distracting females in overalls "—whatever it is y'all were doing."

"Fixing," Dinah proclaimed.

"Maybe we'll just have to use the league meeting as an excuse for me and the missus to take you girls into town for pie at Lila's Café."

"Pie!" shouted the girls.

"Can we, Mama?" Debbie asked.

Avery sighed. "It'll spoil your supper for sure, but I don't see how I can say no to an offer like that." She leaned down and tugged on Debbie's pigtail, affection washing over her features in a way that made Gabe's stomach do a flip. "I sure hope somebody remembers to bring me back a slice."

"I will, Mama," Dinah said. "You like cherry."

"That I do," Avery said, straightening up.

"Lila makes good cherry pie," Gabe offered, feeling

foolish for the heat he felt rising up his spine. He stopped just short of saying "I'll take you there some time."

Once the meeting started, Gabe questioned the wisdom of having Avery there. It wasn't her behavior—she was friendly and offered up so many good ideas for the anniversary party decorations that she ended up not only on the party committee, but she also got an invitation from Bea to come out to the ranch again and give decor advice. No, his doubts stemmed from how he couldn't stop looking at her. His brain kept overlaying the down-home girl in the overalls with the stylishly dressed woman spouting bright ideas across the table from him.

She fit in. Not just surprisingly, but effortlessly. As if she belonged here. Which made sense—she did belong here. She was a Culpepper and would own the cabin at the far end of the Triple C Ranch when this whole nonsense was finished.

No, it was the sense that she belonged right here. Debbie and Dinah belonged swinging under his tree out front, Avery belonged sitting on his porch watching the sun go down—a whole host of unreasonable images kept crowding his brain. Gabe had never seen himself as a family man. He was a leader, but he was also a loner. Relationships—the up-close and familial kind—never came easily to him. The few women he'd dated more than once or twice always ended up accusing him of emotional distance, and he couldn't say they were wrong. Children needed to be held close, and life had taught Gabe to keep folks at a comfortable distance.

Now, a trio of females was getting in too close, invading his thoughts. Avery was a woman who'd been abandoned not once, but twice by the men in her life—three times if you counted John's death. The men who ought to hold her close had mostly dismissed if not outright ignored her. She deserved a man who would dote on her, who would lavish her with attention—and that wasn't him, not by a long stretch. That sort of romantic bent had never been his thing.

He could never spout off about how the tawny-colored sweater Avery wore set off a dozen colors in her eyes. Or tell her how the sunlight made her hair gleam. A woman like that ought to hear elegant pronouncements of affection, and all Gabe could tell her was how he constantly thought about how her lips pursed when she was thinking. She'd probably find that odd instead of romantic, and he couldn't blame her one bit.

"So the new barn passed inspection with flying colors," Flint Rawlings reported. "Everything's up and running from after the fire." The burning of the boys ranch's old barn had been quite an ordeal, but some fund-raising by the loyal community and the sharp detective work of Texas Ranger Heath Grayson, who'd apprehended the arsonist, had put the matter behind them.

"I know that was a tough time for Johnny Drake, as well," Tanner offered. "He deserves some affirmation, which is why I'd like us to vote to offer him the scholarship we've been talking about."

"That's the boy who had the apprenticeship with Wyatt, isn't it?" Lena Orwell, the treasurer, asked as she looked up from her notes. "Can Wyatt vouch for the young man after all that running-away business?" The boy had run off in the middle of some earlier acts of sabotage aimed at the ranch. It had been a tense time for everyone.

"Here, Lena, read this. I think it speaks for itself." Gabe passed a letter Wyatt had written to him as president of the league. It was a heartfelt plea for scholarship funds so that the boy could continue his veterinary training. The letter was so compelling Gabe had already decided he'd write a check for the boy himself if the league somehow found a reason to decline him the scholarship. Someone with such obvious skills as Johnny shouldn't be denied the chance to put them to good use.

"The sign for the new ranch will be ready to unveil at the anniversary celebration," league fund-raising chairperson Katie Ellis said with obvious pleasure. "The sign maker donated half the cost, and I raised the rest in three phone calls." She held up a drawing of a horseshoe-shaped sign that read The Lone Star Cowboy League Boys Ranch, founded 1947.

"That's lovely. We should put it up the minute it's ready," Lena said.

"We should wait until the ranch is officially and irrevocably transferred," Gabe cautioned, keenly feeling the weight of the property's uncertainty. "None of this is set until we locate Theodore."

"But we will, of course," reassured Tanner. Gabe thought that was brave coming from Tanner, seeing as how the man hadn't come up with any hint of Linley's location and the whole matter had landed squarely back in Gabe's lap. Everyone was trying—even the private investigators were trying—but the pressure of finding his own estranged grandfather was starting to mount. Folks said they wanted to help, but it was equally clear they looked to him, as both the living relative and the president of the league, to solve this problem.

Avery caught his eye, and while her gaze wasn't the only one with compassion for his plight, somehow that's how Gabe felt. If it was up to him, Gabe wouldn't mind if he never spoke to Theodore Linley again—and Avery understood that. Yet, for the sake of the boys ranch, he had to leave no stone unturned and find Linley. The thought of that fine ranch being sold to become a strip mall burned in his gut. *Cyrus, you old buzzard*, he thought bitterly. *Why did you have to do this?*

"Is there any other business?" he asked, and the startled looks of the other league members told him his words had been sharper than was necessary.

"I think we're done," Lana said, one eyebrow raised.

"The only other business left is to find Linley," Tanner added. The guy didn't know the weight of his words. *Don't you think I know that?* Gabe wanted to shout. *Don't you think that's keeping me up nights?*

Chapter Nine

The house was so quiet after all the league members left, it was as if the world had temporarily shut down. Avery poured two cups from the coffee Marlene had set out for the meeting and went to find Gabe on the porch. He'd ended the meeting abruptly and sharply—well, more sharply than the usual Gabriel Everett efficiency, that is—and she could see how the whole boys ranch situation weighed on him.

Up until now, she'd only really thought about how the situation weighed on *her.* How so much was riding on her commitment to stay. Today showed her how much Gabe felt Cyrus's absurd demands rested on his shoulders.

He stood at the corner of the house's wide front porch, with shoulders tightly set and spine angrily erect. Like a man holding up the whole world and tiring of the strain.

She cleared her throat and offered the coffee when he turned. Dinah and Debbie were still out on their excursion to Lila's with the Franks, and with a start she realized this was the first time she had ever been alone with Gabe. The realization took her pulse up an irrational notch. "You okay?" she said quietly, even though she already knew the answer.

"I'll get by." His exhale said everything his answer did not.

"The boys ranch is really important to you."

"Yeah…" The single word was soft, as if it pained him to admit his loyalty. "More…well, more than most people know."

Was he hesitating because he didn't want to pressure her into complying, or was there something else behind the answer? Avery came around to rest against the porch rail and face him, so she could see his eyes. If you could see a memory in a gaze, it was clear Gabe had some kind of history with the boys ranch that stretched beyond Haven's collective civic pride.

"It seems like a good cause," she offered. "You know, kids straightened out, lives changed…"

"Mine," he said, shifting his gaze to look right at her. The intensity of his regard almost made her swallow hard—the man had such a powerful presence.

"Yours?"

"I was at the ranch when I was eight. I wasn't exactly a model kid, if you know what I mean. I was angry at my dad for dying, my mom was at her wit's end trying to make ends meet, and my grandfather—that'd be our long lost Theodore—just up and disappeared when Mom was hanging on by a thread. I took it out on the world in every way I could think of. And believe me, I thought of a lot of ways."

She knew what that anger felt like. They had that in common. "Why didn't you tell me that before? When we were visiting the ranch?"

"And make you feel further indebted to the man putting you up in his home? A 'force you to save the ranch that saved me' campaign? I'd like to think I can be persuasive, maybe even persistent, but I don't aim to be manipulative." He took a sip of the coffee. "I think Cyrus has given us enough of a dose of that medicine, don't you?"

Did he realize that the fact he *hadn't* used that information wielded twice as much power to convince her than if he had? For all of Cyrus's backing her into a corner, Gabe had held back to give her as much choice as possible. "I meant what I said. I will stay and meet the requirement." She'd told him that on their first visit to the ranch, but it surprised her how much she truly meant it right now. "And I will help Bea decorate the house—as much as I can while I'm here. You don't have to convince me to help anymore."

But it wasn't just about her help, was it? The final obstacle of Theodore Linley hung so heavily around his shoulders that Gabe looked beaten—something she'd deemed impossible in a man of his size and command. "You'll find your grandfather." It felt like hollow reassurance, but she wanted to say *something*.

"I'll have to. We're running out of time. Only I don't know what else I can do."

The end of one's rope was familiar territory to Avery. "There's always prayer. When I can't think of what else to do, it's the only thing left. I know it's supposed to be our first step instead of a last resort, but I guess I'm still working on that."

Gabe set down the coffee cup on the porch rail and leaned heavily against it with both hands. Again, the vision of him being pressed down by demands struck her with such force. Oh, sure, he seemed to hold himself at a distance from people, but it was clear to her that this man cared a great deal. Maybe even too much. *It'd kill him to fail the ranch*, she thought to herself. And that's just how he'd see it—that *he* failed the ranch. Not the dead man who set impossible demands or the lost grandfather who refused to be found, but him. And she knew, just as clearly, that no one would ever be able to convince him otherwise.

Find Theodore. She felt the prayer seep up with a fervor she'd never have expected. *You know where he is, Lord. Show him to these good people. I've decided to stay and do my part, but what good will that do if they fail on account of Theodore?*

And again, for what felt like the hundredth time, a stab of bitterness rose up in her chest against Cyrus. *Why'd you do this, you mean old man? Why put these people— and me—through this?*

Gabe's voice broke into her thoughts. "If this fails, it won't be your fault, you know." Avery couldn't believe he was attempting to console her when he was in so much clear pain. "No one will blame you if we have to send boys elsewhere and live with a stupid strip mall instead of what we ought to have."

He didn't say it, but it radiated out of him just the same: *They'll blame me.*

"It won't be your fault, either."

Gabe didn't respond, just shifted his weight against the porch rail. She put a hand on his shoulder, wanting somehow to make him see that this wasn't all on him.

The touch was a mistake. It startled both of them. They'd lived in the same house for almost two weeks, and the girls had flung themselves on him countless times, but *they* had never touched. In all honesty, she'd avoided coming close to him, subtly aware of the pull she'd started to feel, the humming connection that now seemed to fill the air between them.

She heard him pull in a breath, felt the muscles work under her hand. She told herself to pull the hand away, but didn't.

"It won't be your fault," she repeated. "It's both of our grandfathers' faults." Her use of the word *our* made the connection go from a hum to a roar. They understood each other. Each of them had a specific family connection to this whole nonsense that no one else in Haven shared.

And that was a dangerous thing to admit at the moment. It was as if that glimmer of attraction that she'd been denying since she had met Gabe suddenly stood up and demanded to be recognized.

Recognized, well, that couldn't be helped at the moment. Acted on? *That* she could control. Avery tried to remove her hand casually, inconspicuously, but it failed to feel anything like that. She couldn't look at Gabe, nor could he look at her, which meant that they both had felt that unwelcome zing that still coursed through her fingertips.

Looking down at her hands—because that was certainly a better place to look than at Gabe—she discovered she was running her thumb across the pads of her still-tingling fingers. She swallowed a large gulp of coffee and stuffed the offending hand in her skirt pocket.

I'm raw, that's all. Not in a good place to interact with the male species. Too many fresh scars. My heart is still screaming, "Man equals damage," and until that's no longer true, I'm a walking target.

This was a fine insight, to be sure, but not terribly useful to get her out of the wildly uncomfortable silence that hung gaping between them. "Family," she said in an awkward half laugh that fooled neither of them. "What are you gonna do, huh?"

While Gabe seemed to be able to keep up a calm exterior much better than she could, she did notice one hand's white-knuckle grip on the porch rail while he gulped the coffee with the same sense of "I'm hiding in this mug" she felt. At least the coffee gave them both something to do while she groped for a good exit line. The girls had always provided an easy out when things pulled a little too close between them, but they were in town.

"I think I'll take advantage of the quiet to start on some of those decorating ideas for the celebration and maybe a sketch or two for that parlor wall." She'd surprised herself by saying yes not only to party decorations, but also to coming up with some decor themes for the new ranch house. It was her family's property, after all. That first visit had dissolved such a startling load of bitterness that she actually found herself looking forward to going back. Who would have thought?

"Need any help? I've probably got some of the ranch floor plans around here somewhere."

Help? Gabe Everett did not look like the kind of guy to lend a hand with decorations. His eyes flashed a desperate sort of regret—the same flash she'd seen right after he'd offered to put them up here at Five Rocks. It made sense; Gabe was usually so deliberate and careful with his words that she guessed his blurting out something he regretted rarely happened.

Of course he didn't *really* want to help. Which gave rise to the second, far more unsettling thought: he just didn't want to be alone. This, from a man who struck her as solitary? He truly was rattled by all this. Couldn't everyone in Haven see that? Or had the similarity of their situations just offered her a clearer view?

He'd opened his home to her. Laid aside the peace and quiet of his home to help her. She couldn't decline, even though every time she looked at him she felt some little piece of her unravel, some little strip of hard scar peel away to expose the raw nerve underneath.

* * *

Like an idiot, he'd asked if she needed any help.

What on earth was wrong with him? Decorations were so far out of his wheelhouse he had no business asking that question. "Sorry," he said, backpedaling as he saw the shock in her eyes. "That was stupid. I didn't sleep well last night, and I clearly haven't had enough coffee yet today." Another dumb remark, considering it was four thirty in the afternoon.

"Awake all night worried about today's meeting?"

He wished. "Nightmare, actually. I dreamed Cyrus's strip mall was eating me alive."

"That threat does put a lot of pressure on you."

"No, literally, I dreamed the strip mall was eating me alive. Doors chomping at my boots, parking lot strip lines tangling around my heels, that sort of thing."

"Gruesome," she replied. "The demands are bad enough, and no one wants to send any boys elsewhere, but to hang the threat of a strip mall instead of the boys ranch over everybody's heads like that? Honestly, it's just plain mean." They both clung to the new subject like a lifeline pulling them out of the mire of her touching him.

She'd touched him. The girls had climbed all over him until he felt like a piece of playground equipment some days, but the tenderness of Avery's touch nearly knocked him over. He'd been strung so tight since last night's nightmare. Debbie and Dinah's sweet gesture of cookies had finally put a chink in that dark gray wall he felt around him today, and Avery had managed to waltz right through that crack and touch him just now. He wasn't ready for it, he hadn't put the wall back up far enough and she'd gotten inside.

Who has he kidding? She'd been getting inside since

that day on the porch. Her with those sweet, weary eyes and that all-too-rare smile and that stubborn independence.

"Sure, you can help." Her words had what he guessed was a professional confidence to them, but her eyes looked as if she was scrambling to come up with some way he could do the least damage.

Save yourself. "You probably should get a committee of ladies to do that sort of thing, not me."

Oops. One dark eyebrow rose, as if he'd challenged her without meaning to. "No, I think we can make it work. I have male clients back in Tennessee. And this is a boys ranch after all, so its decorative scheme should be masculine. A man opposed to *tiny pinkness* is a good place to start."

"I can't do anything like that. I don't even like parties, and you can see my home is no showplace, despite Marlene's endless efforts."

"All homes—and all events—can start on a basic decorative concept. A *feel*, if you will."

"Parties have *feels*? I know that I *feel* forced into a silly party Cyrus is shoving down my throat."

Avery laughed a little bit and then turned to start walking into the house. Her whole body had changed—spine straight, shoulders back, focused. Not as soft as she had been a moment before, but with a new, intriguing energy. "Well, that's no concept to launch a party on," she called over her shoulder. "Even one that's been shoved down your throat. We'd do better starting with your house. Come on."

He ran his hands through his hair. "Shouldn't you be doing this with Marlene?"

"It's your house—it should reflect you. I'm sure Marlene would agree. All you have to do is show me two things. Get some more coffee and meet me in the kitchen."

Now I've gone and done it. I'm going to be some weird decorating experiment. As if he hadn't already endured far too many new experiences since Avery's arrival. Gabe emptied his mug and headed into the kitchen.

She turned back up just as he was adding cream to his coffee, toting a notebook and the rectangular deck of colored cards bolted together at one end he'd seen her sorting through earlier. "Is this gonna hurt?" he asked.

"You may have to think. Will that hurt?" There was just enough teasing in her voice to let Gabe consider this might be more interesting than awful. He wasn't totally convinced which. He watched her refill her coffee mug, adding a generous amount of cream and sugar.

"Is there a piece of furniture or lamp or something in this house that you hate?"

He hadn't expected that as the first question. "How about we just focus on the party for now?"

"Oh, no, you don't. Come on, humor me."

I sat through a tea party—isn't that enough humoring for one guy? Still, he was a bit curious why she'd asked that question. It didn't take long to come up with a selection.

"That chair in the back of the library. The one with all the fussy flowers on it."

Avery picked up her coffee. "I hadn't noticed. Let's go see."

Noticed? The thing stuck out like a neon sign to him, all prim and proper in the warm woodwork of his library.

Avery studied it with her head cocked to one side. She took a long drink of coffee, then looked back at him and asked, "May I?"

"It's a chair. You're supposed to sit in it."

She settled into the old chair, wincing at the squeaks

and groans the piece gave under even her small weight. "You haven't sat in this, I take it?"

Gabe leaned up against the library shelves, watching her "work."

"Pretty sure I'd break it if I did. Not that I'd care."

Avery ran one hand down the worn upholstered arm. The realization that it was the same hand that had touched his shoulder kindled a small glow below his breastbone. "But you haven't thrown it out."

Now she was poking where he wasn't sure he wanted her to go. "It belonged to my mother."

Her eyes lost their analytical glare, softening as she looked at him. "But you hate it."

Gabe reached for the right words to explain it. "She used to say it was the one nice thing she owned. That wasn't a happy thought for her—I think it became a symbol for everything in her life that didn't work out the way she planned. She did a lot of crying in that chair. I suppose I should love it or something, but I don't."

"So you don't exactly hate the chair, you just hate what it stands for."

He wasn't in the mood to be analyzed like that. "I was thinking this was going to be more like 'what's your favorite color?' than dissecting my sorry past. I don't like it as a chair or a symbol, if that's what you're getting at."

"Fair enough. No fuss, useful is better than decorative. I can work with that." She stared at the chair one more time before squaring her shoulders and looking at him. "Okay, now show me something you love."

For some reason, this felt even more invasive than showing her something he didn't like. He made a show of thinking about it, but the truth was he knew almost instantly what he would show her. Only he was pretty sure it wasn't what she'd expect—and perhaps that was part of the allure of showing her.

Nodding toward the back of the house, he led Avery to the mudroom off the back hallway, the entrance where he came in from the fields or the barns. Once there, he pointed to a small shelf with three wooden tool carriers—long, deep rectangular trays with handles that ran from one end to the other. If anything in the house qualified as prized possessions, it was these, despite their "lowly" place in the back mudroom.

He was pleased to see his choice surprised her. She stared at the trio of toolboxes for a moment. "Makes sense," she said, looking up at him after a moment. "Definitely functional. Nothing fussy about these. Tell me why you like them so much."

He'd guessed she would ask for an explanation, but still felt unnerved at telling her. It felt absurdly revealing. He picked up the largest one, the handle warm and weathered in his hand. Could he explain how using these every day grounded him, reminded him of everything he'd overcome to get where he was today? It startled him how much he needed to touch these right now, feeling pressured and unsettled as he had since this whole business with Cyrus had hijacked his life.

Gabe started with the most important fact. "I made these. During my time at the ranch, there was a foreman there, Willy, who made the most amazing things in his wood shop. I wasn't an ideal resident at first, angry as I was for Mom leaving me on the ranch." He stole a glance at Avery before continuing. "I get why she did it now, but I sure didn't then. I felt thrown out, and I made sure the whole world knew it."

"That must have been so hard at your age. How could any eight-year-old understand something so complicated?" She ran a hand over the handle of the smallest box, and again the sight of her touching his things sent Gabe's innards tumbling.

"One day Willy took a bunch of leftover wood—discards from larger projects—and began putting them together to make a box like this. I watched him, fascinated that he could turn scraps into something useful." Gabe set down the box and picked up the smallest one, the one Avery had just touched. It was rougher than the other two, with mismatched joints and gaps in the bottom. "So Willy taught me to make one. I made a hundred mistakes and had to do things over two and three times, but he stayed at it with me." He put down the small one and picked up the middle one. "And then I made a second one, better and larger than the first. And then a third. All from pieces of wood other projects couldn't use."

Avery's eyes glowed with understanding. There were probably only half a dozen people in the world who knew the story of these boxes, and Gabe discovered he liked Avery being one of them. "What a wise man," she said quietly.

"Willy taught me a powerful lesson without ever saying a word. I was so busy being angry at everything I didn't have. Willy taught me to take what I did have and build it into what I needed." Gabe sighed. "Sure, lots of parts of the boys ranch turned me around, but none of them more than Willy and these boxes."

"Where is Willy now?"

"Oh, he passed on some years back. And I confess I didn't see much of him once I came back here after my stay on the ranch. Harley stepped in where Willy left off. My stepfather wasn't much of an influence, but Harley took a shine to me right away. He was a hand here on the ranch, and if there ever was a man who was a father to me, it's Harley."

"He's sweet. Don't you worry about him out there on that far corner of the ranch all by himself?"

"I do, but he won't come in. I mean, I bring him in for meals now and then and to league meetings when he feels up to them, but Harley keeps to himself. I go to him, but he doesn't come to me. Been that way his whole life, so I doubt it'll ever change. It worked for me, too—escaping to Harley's cabin is probably the reason I survived all the years on this ranch." He settled the trio of boxes back in order on the shelf. "Those weren't happy times. But I took what I had and made it into what I needed, thanks to Willy and Harley."

He reached to snap off the mudroom light, but Avery's hand met his as it found the switch. Again, the contact seemed to course through him like a current. "Thank you," she said. "It means a lot to me that you showed me these."

Gabe swallowed hard, knowing the spot where her palm lay on the back of his hand would still be tingling hours from now. "You asked," he mumbled as he walked out of the darkened room and into the bright hallway. It wasn't wise to linger for a single moment with her in the rose-gold sunset now filling the back of the house.

The whole house, big as it was, couldn't seem to put enough space between him and Avery. The woman had a talent for asking the most unnerving questions. He'd never been so happy to hear Jethro beep the horn and catch the sound of the twins clattering through the front door.

Chapter Ten

Avery stood with Bea and Macy Swanson in the living room of the boys ranch the next day, taking in the mix of decors. Bea had invited her at yesterday's league meeting, and Macy had come along because she was looking for help with her own house. Bea was right—the short notice and mishmash of existing and donated furniture gave the place a jumbled, disjointed look Avery knew she could improve with a few key touches.

When she told them so, Macy's eyes grew wide. "That's just it—my house doesn't feel like it fits together, either."

"Well, there's so much emotion in it, in your case," Bea said tenderly, touching Macy's arm.

"I'm transforming this house from my late brother and his wife—Colby's parents—but I want it to reflect our new life, too. And then I want to do the same thing with our life with Tanner, when we get married and move to his ranch. How can I mix all those different lives and spaces?" Macy had guardianship of her orphaned nephew, Colby, and was engaged to Tanner Barstow.

Avery smiled. This was her favorite kind of decorating challenge. "Well, I won't say it's not a complex task, in both your cases. And I'll come over to your place later, Macy, if you like, but I expect you can adopt what I'm going to suggest here without much trouble." She looked around the big room, her heart again twisting for a moment at what her childhood might have been like running these halls and being settled in large, sun-filled rooms like these instead of the cramped and make-do rooms where she had grown up.

Bea picked up on her hesitation. "I'm so delighted to have your help, Avery. I like the idea that the place will have a touch of you in it."

Avery swallowed hard. "The wall's a nice neutral, so colors and art are the perfect place to start." As Avery walked through the room, she pulled out the deck of paint color samples nearly every decorator used as a way to form palettes.

Fanning through it, she quickly located shades that matched one of the large landscape paintings over the fireplace and the couch upholstery. With a moment's thought, Avery added a third color that blended the first two into a pleasing trio of hues. She held the samples up to Macy and Bea. "If you added pillows in this accent color, the couch would blend in more easily. And you could find fabric for curtains that would have all three colors. That would alter the feel of the room with only two additions."

"Wow. You *are* good at this," Macy admired. She turned to Bea. "Isn't that armchair someone just donated the same color? We could put that in here, too."

"The one sitting in the back hallway? You're right— that would work to do the same thing. You're a natural, Macy."

"This place is so much bigger, but we can't afford to

buy a whole lot of things," Bea said as she scanned the room with a critical eye.

"But you can make the place feel visually pulled together, and that can do a lot for the boys' sense of calm, even if they don't realize it." She turned to Macy. "If Colby sees visual cues that his parents are still part of his life in your house, it'll help to ground him. Even when you move to Tanner's." After a pause, she added, "He'll feel like all the parts of him belong, and it will mean a lot to him later, if it doesn't already now."

Macy offered Avery a gentle look. "You lost both your parents, didn't you?"

"I lost my mom when I was about Colby's age. It sent my life into knots, and I think I gave my dad even more trouble than Colby gave you." Macy had told Avery that Colby had stayed on the boys ranch for a few months as he worked through his grief over losing his parents in an automobile accident.

Bea picked up one of the photographs of "graduates" they had hoped to hang on one wall—a family tree of past ranch residents, as it were. "It's so hard and sad. What turned you around?"

Avery sat down on the couch. "I didn't turn around, to tell the truth. I stumbled my way through a series of foster homes, making trouble in every one. I figured it was better to reject them first, before they could reject me. Only trouble was, that never gave them an opportunity to love me, either." She looked at Macy and the obvious care in her eyes. Colby's story was sad, but it had a happy ending.

Avery had photos on her wall at home—heartwarming pictures of Danny and her and the girls—that now were only images. And memories, she hoped. "I can't decide if it's a blessing or a curse if the girls might not remember much of Danny. But Colby? He should keep every memory of his parents that he can. And the boys here should see the long line of history and success that went before them. Here's what I had in mind." She gestured to the long wall opposite the fireplace. "If you gathered a collection of picture frames—lots of different kinds and sizes—and paint them all this shade of maroon." She held up one of the paint shades she'd suggested a few minutes ago. "Then, fill them with photos—black-and-white ones would be really stunning—of boys who've lived here. You could even have past residents send photos to you as part of the anniversary celebration."

Bea clasped her hands together at the idea. "That way folks who can't come in for the event can still be part of the celebration."

"You'd need a lot of frames, but if you got the boys to help you paint them it wouldn't be much work at all."

Bea narrowed one eye. "I could make that happen. The boys have a school holiday on Monday. Can you come by and show them what to do?"

Work with the boys? Was she ready to do that?

"Colby and I could come help if you'd like," Macy offered.

Now how could she say no? "You know," she said to Macy, "the same idea would work for photos of you and Tanner, of the three of you, of Colby, of his parents and any other family photos you have."

"It would show Colby all the different ways he has had and will have a family."

"And show our boys the bright futures they could have ahead of them despite how rough they may feel things are now. Oh, Avery, it's a brilliant idea—you'll do it?"

"You can always add more pictures or rotate pictures in and out. Include old photos and new ones—if they're all black-and-white, they'll look timeless. So yes, I'll do it." This was Avery's favorite part of the job. Her gift was to bring not just beauty and functionality to homes, but meaning. Anyone could make something pretty. Avery had always had a knack for making things that touched the deepest part of her clients. It felt so satisfying—reconciling, even—to do that here. Smoothing over, in one small way, the bittersweet journey of her path to this place.

Avery pointed to the fern-colored couch. "We can mix in a few botanical prints in this shade and some of those tin stars I saw in the hallway, too."

"Lana found those at a flea market," Bea said, standing beside Avery. "I'm sure we could get more." She gave Avery a warm hug. "You're a real star yourself, you know that?"

The praise glowed in Avery's heart. "If you ever give tours to donors, the wall could make a powerful statement."

Macy leaned against the blank wall. "I'm sorry you had it so rough growing up. Without folks and all. And then to learn Cyrus had been here all along? I can't imagine."

"It's no fairy tale, I'll grant you that." She sighed. "I won't say I wouldn't bend my grandfather's ear with a few choice words if I had the chance."

"Oh, I almost forgot!" Macy dashed for a bag that sat at the foot of a coffee table. "I was going through a box of books donated to the ranch learning center, and somebody seems to have forgotten that only boys live here." She produced a small stack of picture books. "Princesses, fairies, flowers, crafts and a few horse books that the boys would find too frilly. I thought they'd be perfect for the girls to have." She grinned. "Gabriel's library is beautiful, but I doubt there's much to entice Debbie and Dinah in there."

Avery took the gift with gratitude. "And a good thing they're not enticed to go in there. They've invaded enough of Gabe's house as it is."

Bea leaned in. "Marlene spilled to Marnie about the tea party." A soft laugh lit up the woman's eyes. "I'd have given just about anything to see that."

"Gabe? Our Gabe? At a tea party?" Macy laughed as well when Avery told her about what the girls had done. "I cannot imagine!"

"He was a good sport—well, sort of. I don't think the girls really gave him much choice."

"Those must be some girls you've got there," Bea said. "Not many people can claim they made Gabriel Everett do something he didn't want to do. Maybe the mystery matchmakers can build on that."

Avery scowled. "Marlene, Rhetta and Carolina have all told me about those stunts someone's been pulling to nudge couples together." She held up her hands in warning. "I'm in no market to be nudged. Not to Gabe or anyone else."

"Not even a little bit?" Macy teased. "After all this craziness has died down?"

When he told the story of those toolboxes, Avery was sure she'd seen a side of Gabe that he rarely showed anyone. Like the pictures she'd just described, it was part of his home that touched his heart. A treasure that she lacked. She wasn't succeeding at shielding her heart from such a powerful thing. Avery shook her head, hoping that would dissuade the women from their current train of thought.

"He's a good man," Macy persisted. "A fine leader,

from what I've seen. Seems a shame a man like that should stay alone."

Macy was in love and engaged to be married. Her starry eyes saw the whole world through romance-colored glasses. It wasn't Macy's fault that Danny had knocked that hope right out of Avery, and it wasn't coming back any time soon. Gabe was a fine man. But he wasn't big on emotion and kept most people at a carefully controlled distance. He'd even described himself—deliberately, if she had to guess—as "not a family kind of man." If there was one thing she needed from the next man in her life, it was a family kind of man. "I admit, he'll make a fine catch," Avery said, "but some other day and for some other woman."

Gabe was glad to see Nick McGarrett's truck come up his path. Avery had come back from her "decorating session" at the boys ranch with a stack of new books, and her girls were working their way through the pile in a warm patch of sunshine on the porch. Nick had come to borrow some tools—the perfect excuse for Gabe to hide out in the barn with someone his own size and gender.

Nick got out of the truck, eyeing the festivities on the porch with a welcome disdain. "You weren't kidding, Gabe. You're surrounded."

"They're not so bad," Gabe said, feeling compelled to defend them, even though he couldn't put much enthusiasm into his voice. "Well, most days."

Nick shook his head. "You with little girls. I'd have never seen that one coming."

Gabe adjusted his hat and nodded toward the barn. "I didn't see it coming, believe me. I just figured something had to be done to keep Avery in town and Roz sure wasn't helping. I thought I had enough space here that they wouldn't get in my way."

Nick laughed. "And you thought wrong?"

Gabe remembered the stuffed animal parade that clamored down his hallway yesterday. "Boy, did I think wrong. How big a hole in your fence do you have to fix?" He elected to change the subject as he gathered the tools Nick had requested. That was one of the best things about Haven—folks helped each other out. Gabe liked that Nick never hesitated to ask for a tool or a hand when he needed one. As such, Gabe knew he could always count on a fellow rancher like Nick whenever he himself got in a pinch.

"Far bigger than I'd like. I feel like I just got done fixing the last hole." Sure, Nick was struggling to put his family ranch back on its feet and Gabe's ranch was prospering with funds to spare, but that never came into it. A man could keep his pride and still ask for help in Haven because nobody looked at each other in terms of bank balances.

Nobody, that is, except the imposter Avery. Even Fletcher Snowden Phillips, who once could have rivaled the fake Avery for seeing the world with status-colored glasses, had stopped looking down his nose at everyone. Fletcher had softened since meeting his birth daughter, Darcy—the woman Nick would soon call his wife. It made Gabe wonder how Cyrus might have changed if he had had the chance to meet Avery.

Avery. He was going to have to fix this annoying tendency to keep seeing things in terms of Avery Culpepper.

"I got some extra wire from a job earlier this year. Could you use it?" Gabe asked as he kept filling the crate Nick had pulled from the back of his truck.

"Sure. And if you've got any smaller shovels, I'll borrow them if you don't mind. Corey wants to help me with the fences, and I don't think he can handle any of my bigger ones." Nick and Darcy and Corey had the makings of a nice little family going.

Again the thought sent his mind to the little family currently reading on his front porch. *That's not the same*, he reminded himself. *You've never wanted that sort of thing.*

"Darcy taking to ranch life?" Darcy had come from money and was used to life's finer things. She was pretty much everything the first Avery wasn't: big hearted, brave and not afraid to get her hands dirty.

"Makes me proud. I'm a blessed man." Nick beamed. "I gotta say, this fiancé gig has a lot going for it. Hey, the way folks are hitching up in Haven lately, even you could be next."

"Not likely." Gabe kept his eyes on the tools.

"Mr. Boots!" Dinah's voice came from the barn door. "Do you have any flower seeds?"

"Mr. Boots?" Nick asked, barely containing a laugh.

"Not one word," Gabe growled, trying not to be annoyed that even the sanctity of his barn had now been invaded by tiny pinkness. Couldn't Avery keep them confined to the porch and the yard? He turned toward the little girl dwarfed by the huge barn door. "It's not safe for you to be wandering around in here without your mama."

"But we were reading about flowers and now I want to plant some."

"Did you ask Ms. Marlene? She's the one with the flower boxes."

"She told me to go find you hiding in the barn and ask you myself."

"*Hiding in the barn.* She's got you pegged," Nick

teased, walking up to Dinah. "My name's Nick," he said, holding out a hand. "What's yours?"

"Dinah."

"Why do you call Gabe here 'Mr. Boots?'"

"Leave it, McGarrett," Gabe warned in the most pleasant tone he could manage.

Dinah simply smiled. "'Cuz he wears 'em. All the time."

Nick turned to peer back at Gabe with a mock investigative squint. "That he does. How do you like living with *Mr. Boots*?"

Gabe cringed at the emphasis Nick gave the title. Maybe it was time to take a few of those tools back out of the crate.

"I like him a whole lot," Dinah said, nodding. "He's really nice. One day he even came to our tea…"

"There you are, Dinah girl!" Avery came rushing though the door, clamping a hand over tiny Dinah's startled mouth. "Next time Marlene tells you to go to the barn, come get me first, okay?"

Debbie appeared right behind Avery. "Hi, Mr. Boots. Whatcha doing in the barn?"

"Hiding," Nick suggested in a whisper as he came over to hoist the box Gabe had filled. He stopped in front of the girls as he returned to head toward the barn door. "You must be Debbie."

"Yep."

"How is it living here with Mr. Boots?"

"It's very nice," Avery answered for her. "We're very grateful for his hospitality, aren't we, girls?"

The twins nodded.

"And we're going to leave Mr. Boots to his work in the barn and promise not to bother him anymore today, aren't we?"

"But my seeds…" whined Dinah.

"I'll take a look and bring you some later if I find them," Gabe offered as they left. He wasn't ready to admit to Nick or Avery how much he hid in the barn lately. He used to hide in his study, but the girls somehow always managed to nose their way in there—much like they did to his barn just now. It was starting to feel like there wasn't a private place left on the entire ranch.

"Flower seeds?" Nick snickered, grinning entirely too much as he came back from loading his truck. "Does Mr. Boots grow flowers now?"

Gabe considered asking for all his tools back. "Mr. Boots grows impatient and frustrated, that's what Mr. Boots grows."

"Hey, aren't impatients a kind of flower? That'd be kind of ironic if you had those, wouldn't it? Maybe I'll go ask Marlene."

Gabe stopped and glowered at Nick. "You don't need to enjoy this quite so much."

"Oh, I disagree." Nick leaned back against the wall, laughing. "I'm enjoying this very much. Corey's put me in my place a time or two, but he's got nothing on those two little girls."

"It's for the boys ranch," Gabe reminded Nick. "Avery has to stay, and she had nowhere else to go. Surely, you can see it's worth the minor inconvenience." Gabe nearly laughed at his own understatement. Avery's and the girls' stay on his ranch was fast becoming a major issue on several levels, not a minor inconvenience. For crying out loud, he had swings in his yard. And drawings of bunnies stuck up on his fridge door with cutesy little magnets. Was it any wonder he preferred the barn these days?

"How's all that estate stuff going?" Nick asked, thankfully taking the cue to change the subject. "You found everybody yet?"

Nick had managed to pick the only subject more painful than tiny pinkness. "Still no Theodore. I had Haverman look over the will again to see if there's a loophole like we had for Carolina Mason standing in for her great uncle Mort."

"Nothing, huh?"

"Either we prove Linley's dead, or we produce him. No other options."

Nick put a hand on Gabe's shoulder. "You'll find him. Or you'll figure something out. You always do."

He did. Gabe was the kind of man everyone counted on to set things right. He prided himself at being thought of that way. *This is gonna knock the pride right out of me, Lord*, Gabe groaned to Heaven as he walked away from the barn. *If that's what You had in mind all along, couldn't You find a way to do it that doesn't hurt all those boys?*

"Hey." Nick stopped walking. "Weren't you going to look for flower seeds?"

"No need to look. I don't have any. I'll swing by the supply store and grab something this afternoon."

"Gabe Everett buying flower seeds." Nick shook his head. "Next thing I know I'll hear about you buying flowers."

Gabe had actually seen some of the first bluebonnets of the season yesterday up on the eastern pastures and thought about—not actually done, mind you, but thought about—bringing some to Avery.

Not that anyone would ever be told a secret like that. Besides, that wouldn't have counted as *buying flowers* so when he gave Nick a decisive "Nope!" it was the truth.

Chapter Eleven

When Heath Grayson opened his door Monday afternoon, Avery recognized the universal countenance of a new father: equal parts wonder and exhaustion. Remembering the haze of days and nights in those first weeks with Debbie and Dinah, Avery had let Marlene talk her in to adding her name to a church sign-up for bringing the new parents supper. Everyone in Haven seemed to be taking a turn, and Marlene had said she already had a huge pot of chili planned, so all Avery had to do was deliver.

"Hey, proud poppa," Avery greeted. "How are you holding up?"

As if to answer the question, baby Joy's cries echoed from behind Heath. "Ranger duty has nothing on diaper duty. I feel like I'm in parenting boot camp."

Avery laughed. "I suppose you are." She pointed to the burp cloth still perched on the Texas Ranger's shoulder.

He pointed to the paint smears not quite gone from Avery's hands and arms. "And you're still purple from this morning's painting session. I heard you and the boys had quite the time of it." Heath ushered her in with a chuckle.

"It's maroon, actually. And it was fun. I'm pretty sure

most of the paint ended up on the picture frames, but I can't be certain."

"I'm still trying to make sure most of the diaper ends up on the baby," Heath admitted. "How'd you ever manage this with two of them?"

"I remember thinking I would never sleep again. I'll bring the girls for a shorter visit next time, but I left them with Marlene so I can give you both a shot at peace and quiet."

Josie came out of the kitchen holding a wailing little Joy tucked in a pale yellow blanket. If it was possible, Josie looked even more tired than Heath. "Peace and quiet?" Josie asked. "I forgot what those are."

Avery walked up close to see the tiny weeks-old newborn in Josie's arms. "Little Joy hit her first growth spurt, did she?"

"If you mean did she reach the point where she does nothing but cry and eat for hours on end, then yes, Joy is in a growth spurt." Heath moaned. "Or a whatever spurt. All I know is that I've done more laundry this week than in a month of my bachelor days."

Heath's words could be classified as complaints, but the affection on the man's face was nothing but pure love for his new family. If he wasn't Joy's biological father—Josie had been a pregnant young widow when she and Heath met—he was surely that little girl's daddy in his heart. Avery felt a stab of regret remembering that Danny had looked at her daughters that way once.

"Would you like to hold her?" Josie asked.

"I'd love to. Let me set my things down and wash my hands." She tucked the pot of chili and the pan of corn bread into the Graysons' kitchen and washed up. Coming back out into the living room, Avery took the beautiful little girl in her arms and sat on the couch while Heath and Josie settled across from her.

"Look at those eyes," Avery cooed. "And all that hair!" The baby had the gray eyes of so many newborns, but the full head of red-brown hair seemed to be the gift of her mother.

"She has her mama's hair, that's for sure," Heath said.

"And her mama's lungs, I'm afraid," Josie said with a weary smile. "A champion crier. I thought being a nanny before would make this easy, but…"

"It's a whole new world when it's your own baby, isn't it? Twice as wonderful but three times as much work."

"On half as much sleep." Josie yawned. "You were so kind to offer to come and bring supper."

"Marlene did the cooking, but I was happy to help. No one should have to do this alone." It struck Avery how poignant she found the words. She probably had looked as harried to Gabe when he'd offered his help back on Roz's porch. If Gabe had offered his help that afternoon, surely she could do as much right now. "When's the last time you two sat on your porch alone together and watched the sun go down?"

One look at their faces told Avery it had been quite a while.

Avery stood. "Tell you what—put the baby swing in the kitchen and I'll get supper on while you two get reacquainted on the porch. If I did it with two babies, heating up supper with one ought to be a cinch."

"But you don't have to—" Josie began.

"Sure, I don't have to, but I want to." She had no way of repaying Gabe, but she could "pay it forward" and help out Josie and Heath. It made her feel more human, less like a pawn in Grandpa Cyrus's from-the-grave chess game.

Joy fussed a bit, but settled drowsily beside an adorable small stuffed goat—surely a ranch gift—in the swing. After a few minutes of cooing until the child's eyes closed, Avery made her way around the Graysons' kitchen to prepare the meal. There had been one or two—not many, but a few—women who did this for her and Danny when the twins were first born, and she remembered being so thankful. Opening the fridge for some butter for Marlene's cornbread, she saw a list held to the fridge door with a magnet.

It was the same schedule for the next two weeks she'd seen at church. Supper was arriving via a different member of Haven Community Church each night. She saw Rhetta was on tomorrow night, and several other names she recognized. Of course, Marlene was on tonight's list, but Avery found herself glad to be taking the housekeeper's place. "Go get to know Josie," Marlene had encouraged her. "A new mom always needs another mom to help hold her up."

She'd never known a community as tightly knit as Haven. Sure, Haven had its share of small-town faults—judgmental old hens like Roz Sackett and grumpy, meddling old men like Cyrus—but it had a lot more of what small towns ought to have. Kindness and generosity and connection. It was getting hard to deny the fact that she felt more connected in Haven than she had back in Tennessee. Still, the obstacles to staying—no place to live, uprooting her business, getting Danny's consent to move the children out of state—weren't going away. It still made more sense to head back to Tennessee and redouble her efforts to build a better life there than it did to daydream about a life here.

The oven timer beeped, and Avery walked to the front door to call in the couple for their supper. At first she thought they'd been cuddling on the porch swing, but a closer inspection showed the pair to be fast asleep.

Oh, those sleep-deprived first weeks, she thought to herself. *Let them be, poor things.*

She walked back into the kitchen, covered the cornbread and turned off the oven. Avery turned to grin at Joy's bright gray eyes—the baby was now wide-awake. "Don't you know you're supposed to sleep when they do?" she cooed as she picked up the infant. "Why don't you and I explore the backyard while Mom and Dad nap?"

She scribbled a quick note to put where Josie or Heath would easily see it, and tucked her cell phone in her back pocket. It showed a missed call from Gabe, but she figured she could return that later. Walking into the Graysons' tidy backyard that looked out over the small farm, she spoke in lively tones to the little girl as she patted her tiny back. "Some day soon you'll strew this with toys. And probably make your daddy mad by leaving them out in the rain. And hand your mommy endless stains to try and get out of your pretty pink clothes."

Joy merely made sweet baby sounds and settled against her shoulder. She barely even whimpered when Avery's cell phone went off again in her pocket.

A little quick maneuvering showed her the call was from Gabe. "You'll never guess where I am," she said into the phone.

"I know you're at Heath's cooing over his baby, but you don't want to guess where I am." His voice held none of the amusement hers had. As a matter of fact, she picked up the distinct and frightening sound of Debbie's cries in the background.

Fear shot through her. "What's wrong?"

"Debbie fell off the swings. Jethro is home with Dinah

but Marlene and I are on our way to Dr. Delgado. Meet us there. It's three doors down from Lila's."

Oh, no. Dear Lord, watch over my girl, Avery prayed as she rushed back through the house to shake the Graysons awake from their peaceful nap on the porch swing.

"Is Joy okay?" Josie's startled eyes shot wide.

"Joy is fine, but I have to leave."

"We nodded off," Heath said, dragging himself awake. "Everything okay?"

"Debbie fell off the swings. Gabe and Marlene want me to meet them at Dr. Delgado's." She wished she could be calmer, but her pulse was thundering. *Debbie's hurt. Bad.* She could hear it in Gabe's voice. She deposited Joy in Josie's arms and pulled on her jacket. "Supper's in the oven. I've got to go."

"Oh, no. Of course you do. We'll say a prayer for poor Debbie. Let us know how everything turns out, okay?"

Gabe tried to keep his eyes on the road and stay within the speed limit, but both tasks were hard with Debbie's frightened cries right next to him.

"Hold that arm still now, baby girl," Marlene said in softer, calmer tones than he could hope to manage.

"It hurts," Debbie sobbed. "I want Mama."

"She's on her way, darlin'," Gabe reassured her. "She'll be right there at Doc Delgado's."

"I'm rotting!" Debbie cried with new alarm as she moved her hand from where it held her forearm.

"Rotting?" Gabe was almost afraid to ask. Visions of gruesome gashes filled his brain. He was a cool-headed manager, but little-girl emergencies were not exactly his thing.

"I'm turning black like the bananas," Debbie moaned as the tears came harder.

"Oh, sweetheart, you're bruising," Marlene said. "That's your body sending in soldiers to help take care of your arm. It's a good thing, I promise."

Gabe wasn't sure of the accuracy of Marlene's preschool description of the human immune system, but he wasn't about to argue, since the explanation seemed to calm Debbie. He turned the last corner carefully so as not to bump the tender limb. "Here we are. Doc Delgado will have you fixed up in no time."

"I'm scared," Debbie whimpered. "I want Mama."

Avery came out of Dr. Delgado's door, eyes wide with fear. "She's already here," Gabe told her.

"Baby!" Avery cried.

Gabe ducked out of the door and intercepted the panicked Avery. "She'll be okay. It's her arm. She's scared but…"

"Mama!" Debbie burst into further tears.

Avery moved to scoop up her daughter. "Mind the left arm," Marlene warned. "I don't think we want to jostle it."

"It hurts," Debbie whimpered.

"I know baby, I know," Avery said as she nearly ran toward the door. Marlene and Gabe followed fast behind. He was unprepared for how tiny Debbie's injury rattled him. He'd bought the swing set and had it installed. He felt responsible. And hang it all if he wasn't growing fond of all that tiny pinkness around the house. It felt like all of March was spiraling out of his control into places he didn't want to go.

When Dr. Delgado ushered Avery and Debbie into his office, Gabe's stomach twisted until Avery motioned him into the office with her, Marlene right behind. He'd have stayed out in the waiting room if that was her wish—

he wasn't their kin, after all—but it would have driven him crazy.

"I've seen you in church. My Martin's not much older than you. Remind me of your name, sweetheart?" Dr. Delgado's calm, quiet voice cut through the panicked chaos of the last few minutes.

"Debbie," the little girl replied as she clutched her arm. Gabe thought she looked so small and pale sitting there on the examination table.

"Well, Debbie, I'm Doc Delgado. Gabe here tells me you took a tumble off some swings."

The words sent stinging little stabs into Gabe's chest. Avery hadn't given him a "you hurt my baby" look yet, but it was only a matter of time.

"How about you let me take a look at that arm?" Dr. Delgado asked, gently peeling Debbie's other hand off the injured arm. "Look at all those colors," Dr. Delgado said, as if it was a wonder of science rather than the telltale signs of a serious injury. One Gabe had made possible. "Box of sanity," huh? What made him ever think those swings were a good idea?

"I thought I was rotting. Like a banana." Debbie sniffed with a dramatic air. Marlene offered a chuckle, but Avery gave Gabe a questioning look.

"Pretty clever association, if you ask me," Gabe replied. He felt totally out of his depth and achingly guilty at the moment, as he waited for Avery to lash into him for allowing her daughter to fall injured. She looked upset, no doubt about it, but he couldn't work out why there seemed to be so little anger in her features.

"Well, clearly something's up with that arm," Dr. Delgado said. "I'll have to take an X-ray—that's a special kind of picture that will let me see the bones in your arm. I'll even show you when we're done, if you like."

"I wanna see my bones," Debbie said.

Doc went on with a tender examination, keeping Debbie talking. With each question she answered, she seemed to calm further. Gabe was calming down himself—it still startled him how personally he'd taken Debbie's fall. When Avery and Debbie left with Dr. Delgado to go take the X-ray, Gabe felt like slumping against the wall in exhaustion.

He looked up to see Marlene's very direct gaze leveled straight at him. "Hurts to care, don't it?" He couldn't tell if she was chastising or encouraging him. The fact that it was probably both just unnerved him more.

He pointed in the direction Debbie and Avery had gone. "That's my fault. I put those swings up so they'd stay out of my hair."

Marlene leaned back against the wall cabinets and crossed her arms. "If you recall, Gabriel, I suggested the idea of some outside play equipment. And this is no one's fault—certainly not yours. Now, getting caught for breaking the speed limit twice on the way over here like you did? That would have been your fault. But not this."

He didn't have an answer to that, so Gabe simply glared at her for a moment and then began fiddling with his car keys.

"She'll be all right, Gabriel. Maybe not right away, but in time. You, on the other hand…well, I'm not so sure."

Gabe stared down the hallway. "You're right, Avery's bound to be furious."

Marlene shook her head. "I doubt that, and that's not at all what I meant. Why is it such a fearsome thing to you that you've taken a shine to those little girls? You care about them, and you act as if that was some horrible itch you can't scratch."

A horrible itch he couldn't scratch. Did Marlene have

any idea what a perfect picture she'd just painted of the way he felt? He felt it all over—and getting stronger by the minute—with an itch he absolutely should not, could not, scratch. Ever.

The honest truth was that the more he came to care about Avery and her girls, the less he could ever hope to be part of their lives. They deserved someone who wanted to be a father, who had those warm, fuzzy fatherly tendencies he couldn't hope to possess. Just because he felt a flicker of affection for the girls didn't mean his lifelong preference for privacy, peace and quiet would suddenly evaporate.

And even if he could manage to grow used to the tiny pink brand of chaos, there was a lot of baggage piled up in front of him and Avery: the long line of men who didn't stay around. His father. His grandfather. His first stepfather. His second stepfather. Her grandfather. Her father. The list tightened around his throat like a pair of hands. Those girls and Avery should be doted upon, showered with affection by a man with a strong calling to family life.

That wasn't him.

Even if it had felt as if his heart had left his chest and wrapped around that poor little girl as she wept in the truck seat beside him. The hole that would open up in his house—and his heart—after March 20 felt acres wide, and Gabe didn't know what to do about it. It made him nearly hope Avery would be furious with him for this incident—her anger would be easier to bear than those looks she had given him in the mudroom the other day.

"Ms. Marlene, Mr. Boots," Debbie called from down the hall. "I'm broken." She appeared in the door with a little blue sling and a white plastic splint secured to her arm with pink elastic bandages. Her voice had a "so there" tone about it, as if the injury had been an accomplishment instead of the pile of regret that currently turned in Gabe's stomach.

"A very small break, I'll give you that, and some serious bruising around the wrist. She should come back in two days for me to cast it once the swelling goes down."

"I can have a pink cast," Debbie said, sounding as if it was a privilege.

"I'll take those swings down first thing tomorrow morning," Gabe offered.

Debbie's mouth fell open. "No!"

"Why would you do that?" Avery asked.

Gabe nodded toward the little girl with an "isn't it obvious?" glare.

"Well, you can't go on them until you can hold on with both arms, but that doesn't mean they have to come down," Avery explained half to Gabe and half to Debbie.

Gabe took a breath to reply, but one glance at the expressions of each of the three females in front of him shut his mouth again. To his mind, the swings needed to go, but it was crystal clear he was in the minority at the moment and he was in no mood to argue.

"Let's get everyone home and settled," Marlene suggested. "I'm sure Jethro and Dinah are out of their minds with worry. I'll call them from Gabe's truck while Debbie heads home with her mama."

Chapter Twelve

It was nearly nine thirty at night by the time Avery was able to settle Debbie and Dinah in bed after all the chaos of the accident. The novelty of her current splint and upcoming pink cast had worn off along with the pain medicine, and Debbie was fussy and uncomfortable. Dinah was worried about her sister and needy herself. By the time both girls were finally asleep, Avery felt as if she was more spent and irritable than a dozen Heaths and Josies.

What happened to the lovely afternoon that was supposed to be spent cooing over beautiful new baby Joy?

Marlene and Jethro, bless them, had gone to bed also exhausted from the day. Avery was just about to follow suit when she remembered a quart of peppermint-stick ice cream in the freezer. A big bowl of that with a healthy dose of chocolate sauce sounded like just the balm for her surprisingly stressful day.

There was also one other matter to settle—and that would go better over ice cream, as well. On her way to the kitchen, Avery knocked on the door of Gabe's study, where he'd holed himself up since their return.

He looked up with a cautious startle. Was he expecting a lecture or another crazy tea-party invitation? With an inner smile Avery realized she had yet to knock on Gabe's study door with any news the man would consider "good." Tonight would be a good time to fix that.

"I was just about to eat my stress by way of a big bowl of ice cream. Care to join me?"

He looked shocked. Clearly, that wasn't the statement he was expecting.

"No special hats required, promise."

"Okay," he said with a touch of hesitation. Did he really think she'd ask him to join her for ice cream so she could chew him out? Danny couldn't even seem to embrace the concept of guilt or responsibility, but Gabe seemed to hoard it. He'd been heart stricken over Debbie's fall, and the emotion seemed as foreign as it was endearing on a man of Gabe's bearing.

Gabe kept eyeing her as he pulled a pair of bowls and spoons from the cupboard while she got out the ice cream and sauce.

"I'm not mad," she finally said, unable to stand his "go ahead, yell at me" face. "Frightened, maybe, but not mad."

"You ought to be." Avery felt as if he was going out of his way to keep his distance as he laid the scoop on the counter between them.

"I don't get mad at people for accidents. Deliberate pain? Yes, I get mad. You already know that." Avery didn't see any need to name Danny or Cyrus—Gabe knew how she felt about their manipulations. She opened the container and began scooping generous portions into the bowls. Today had clearly been a three-scoop kind of day. "But there was nothing deliberate about what happened this afternoon."

"Debbie's hurt."

"Yes, she is. But I'm thankful she wasn't hurt worse. She's a bold and brave little girl—they both are. The way

I see it, bangs and bruises—and yes, breaks—come with the territory."

When he didn't reply, Avery put down the scoop and stared straight at Gabe until he met her gaze. "I don't blame you." And then, maybe because her defenses were long past down, she added, "I'm grateful you were there to take such good care of her."

When he still looked as if he was crawling out of his skin with guilt, she pushed one bowl in front of him and walked over to the counter stool next to him. It was a little too close to him, but it felt wrong to go out of her way and scoot it farther toward the edge. She took the bottle of chocolate syrup and doused the pink mounds of ice cream. "This is the part where you just say 'okay' and stop beating yourself up about something that wasn't your fault." She set the bottle in front of him as if to say "your move."

With a rather unsteady glance in her direction, Gabe picked up the bottle, gave his ice cream a flimsy swirl of sauce and choked out, "Okay."

She eyed his bowl and hers. "Really? That's the best you can do after a day like today? You men and your sensible compartmentalization slay me."

It had been a long day. She didn't want to feel the slightest bit guilty for her indulgence. The words might have a bit more edge than they ought to have had.

With a defiant look, Gabe picked the bottle back up and squeezed a small ocean of chocolate sauce on his portion.

If he'd meant to outsauce her, he had. She laughed loudly, clamping her hand to her mouth for making too much noise and possibly waking the girls. The laugh settled into a stifled, refreshing giggle that seemed to shave all the sharp ends off the day. Avery sighed, digging her spoon in and heaving up a blissful mouthful of cold sweetness. "See now?" she mumbled in ice-cream-garbled words. "Marvelous."

"I don't see how a thousand calories of sugar solves any problems," Gabe said as he systematically assembled a spoonful of equal portions ice cream and sauce. Did the man ever stop managing circumstances?

"That's because you're a guy. Believe me, this helps. Your mentioning the calorie count, however, does not."

"I am sorry it happened. Am I allowed to say that?"

The true concern on his face touched her. Today had shown her his care for Debbie and Dinah in ways she could no longer hold at a distance. Gabe Everett wasn't staying inside the neat, controllable borders she'd drawn around him and their relationship. Ever since he'd shown her the toolboxes—and the glimpse of his heart he'd been unable to hide while doing so—Avery felt her own heart venturing into very scary territory. She could not risk any more hurt—for her or the girls.

"Yes," she replied, frightened that the tone of her single word said a lot more than was wise.

"Will she be okay, you think?" Again, the words were full of care. Affection, even. It made Avery think, *She might, but will I?*

"Yes," she said in something too close to a whisper, keeping her eyes on the ice cream. Every inch of her felt flushed and tingly. She ate another huge bite so she wouldn't have to speak more.

Gabe cleared his throat. "I know I'm gruff with them most of the time, and they are all kinds of noisy, but... I have to say they've..." He coughed again, making distracted circles with his spoon in the ice cream. "Well, the little pink things have grown on me."

Avery's chest held a fluttery, bursting sensation as if

her heart was attempting an escape. She found the notion entirely too accurate.

Once he had spoken the first words, it seemed as if Gabe needed to spit them all out before he came to his senses. "They steal my time, they invade my study, they run down my hallways and yet I went crazy thinking about Debbie being hurt, and on my watch besides. And still, I know the minute she can, Debbie will be right back out on that swing fixing to break the other arm." He looked up at Avery as though she was a puzzle to solve. "How do you do it?"

Explain parenthood to a bachelor cowboy? She could gather every word in Texas and still not have enough. "You just…do." The inadequate reply spilled a tender-hearted laugh from her. That, and a feeling of sympathy that made her heart's escape not only likely, but also impossible to stop.

Gabe was trying so hard not to care.

He was failing at it, and in a way that stole her heart no matter what she deemed best for her or the girls.

Have mercy, Lord, she wailed silently to Heaven as she looked away from his perplexed and resigned expression. *You take away the man who couldn't care enough only to give me the care of a man who's told me he doesn't want a family? You know we can't stay. You know the girls need someone who'll be over the moon for them. You know I'm raw and wounded from Danny's discarding of me. I can't trust what Gabe is stirring up in me.*

Gabe evidently misunderstood her evasion. "Please don't leave on account of what's happened. I'm trying to find Theodore—and I will, I have to—so I need you to stay."

It was the "I need you" that got to her. She could convince herself he was pleading for something other than the fulfillment of Cyrus's demands. Gabe's eyes had a way of clouding her thinking.

"Gabe..." Avery found she couldn't finish the sentence. She could feel herself falling, feel herself inventing reasons to stay close to this man when she should be planning her exit. She'd convinced herself, just now, that Gabe was as fond of her as he was of her daughters.

He shook his head, shoulders hunching over as if he'd just reprimanded himself. "I know. I know it's asking a lot."

He didn't realize that if he stood up and took her in his arms right this minute, she'd melt against him faster than the ice cream. She'd lay down the steel-willed determination that was her armor in this one-woman battle. She'd let him into her life and the girls' lives even though she knew better.

And what would happen then? Danny could withhold his permission to let her move the girls here. Cyrus's scheme could still backfire, leaving her only a broken-down cabin, leaving the boys ranch scaled back down and removing residents, and leaving Haven with the punishment of a strip mall the whole town would hate. How could she possibly stay and raise a family in the shadow of that?

Staring into his questioning gaze, Avery tried to stop herself from wondering, *What if it worked?* What if somehow they found Theodore and Gabe was the right man for her and the girls had such a warm community to grow up in and Danny cooperated? The people in Haven were behaving as if she could stay forever and be welcome. Would it be so wrong to see if they were right?

Hadn't life shown her enough to stop thinking in happy endings like that? Staying in Haven wasn't the best choice for her, and the flutter Gabe's eyes bloomed in her stomach didn't change that. *I can't trust my emotions here. The best thing would be to finish my ice cream without saying anything I can't take back.*

"I wish I had better news," Mike admitted to Gabe over coffee at Lila's Wednesday morning.

"You could have told me you'd hit dead ends over the phone." While Gabe was glad for time with his good friend, he'd assumed the request to meet meant either Mike had uncovered something about Theodore or his own team of attorneys had uncovered some loophole Harold had missed. He was wrong on both counts.

"I know this means a lot to you. I'm as frustrated as you are that your grandfather has disappeared into thin air."

I doubt that, Gabe thought bitterly. Mike was a long-time friend—one of his closest—but the failure to find Theodore wouldn't cost Mike anything but frustration. That same failure was starting to feel like it would cost Gabe everything. "I know," he conceded, not wanting the mounting tension to get to him. Gabe ran his hands down his face. "Is there anything else you can think of?"

Mike sighed. "I had my two best guys go through that will with a fine-tooth comb. I've run through the two best investigators I've got and every legal channel I can think of. Short of prayer, I don't know what else there is."

"We've got every soul in Haven praying for it now," Gabe admitted. He wouldn't admit—at least out loud—how he was getting pretty sore at the Almighty for leaving this hanging. The God he knew and loved would never let old Cyrus shaft a bunch of needy boys in order to build a silly strip mall. If he fought the urge to leave town if the whole thing went south, what must Avery be feeling? Right now he wouldn't be surprised if Avery was gone before sunup Monday morning—if not before the end of the doomed "celebration" party.

"What about the strip-mall thing?" Gabe asked in desperation. "Can we get an injunction or something to stave that off?"

"I thought of that. Even looked for a zoning loophole. I hate to say it, but Cyrus was pretty clever on this one. If there's a way to stop his 'incentive,' I haven't found it yet."

Gabe stared into his coffee, feeling as dark as the brew. This was going to hurt everyone involved, and they'd dragged Avery and her girls into the middle of it.

"But that doesn't mean I won't stop trying. We've still got four days. And the Gabe Everett I know doesn't give up." Mike sat back against the booth. "The Gabe Everett I know also would never invite a trio of females—two of them children, no less—into the sanctity of his home. How's that going?"

Well, there was a question. "I expect if you ask the six people in my house you'll get six different answers."

Mike never did fall for any of Gabe's diversions. "I'm asking *you*. Something's different about you."

"I'm stressed, I'm surrounded by pink, my house is in total chaos and I'm behind on four different schedules. Take your pick."

Mike narrowed his eyes. "Well, sure, I knew the kids would stress you out. Little ones have never been your thing. But that's not it. You're stressed, but the Gabe I know gets all hard and sharp when he's stressed. You're..." Mike grinned. "Well, to be honest, you got a bit of warm and fuzzy comin' up around the edges."

Gabe was suddenly thunderstruck by the ludicrous thought: Did it show? Could people actually see the way he felt like he was walking around with his chest cracked open? "It's nothing." He knew the minute he said it that Mike wasn't convinced. Maybe that was the real reason his friend had made the trip out here "on his way to Austin."

"Come on, Gabe. You know me better than to think I'll fall for that. What aren't you telling me?"

Gabe felt embarrassed that he actually checked the booths on either side of them to ensure they were empty. Haven had big ears and even bigger mouths some days. "It's…well, it's her." He followed the words with a pleading look, hoping Mike wouldn't laugh out loud.

"The mom? Avery Culpepper?"

Rather than confirm, Gabe offered Mike a helpless look. Gabe had, in fact, watched Mike gain the same helpless look over his current wife.

"I'm, um, she…" He couldn't even bring himself to admit it.

Mike leaned in. "Wait a minute—are you telling me you're falling for Avery Culpepper?" He leaned back with an examining eye as Gabe was powerless to deny it. The crack in his chest opened so wide it practically hurt. Every wailing country song about heartache made far too much sense to him these days.

"It's such a bad idea," he finally spit out. "We've dragged her and the girls into a calamity. She'll never stay, and I couldn't blame her a bit. I mean, come on— the timing, the circumstances, the little girls…"

Mike was stifling a chuckle under an entirely too-fake cough. "Well, what do you know? I wasn't sure it would ever happen, to tell you the truth."

"I'm miserable. You know me. I don't do kids and family. I definitely don't do little girls. This can't possibly work out—everybody will end up hurt."

The sharp tone knocked the amusement from Mike's

face. "Hey, I get it. You, me? We didn't get role models. Nobody in your family or mine would ever be up for Father of the Year. It's easy to think it's in the blood, I know. Only I never could quite understand why you looked at my happiness like some prize you could never win. We don't have to be the men our fathers were. With the right woman, we could be anything. I know I feel that way about Terri. Why not Avery?"

Gabe waited for the world to tilt. For some horrible thing to happen now that he'd admitted his attraction to Avery Culpepper to another living soul. Nothing. The world seemed to accept it far easier than he had.

"I can't make sense of it, Mike. I can't be anything close to what she needs. I can't make the pieces fit."

"You think this stuff ever goes by sense?" Mike fiddled with the gold band on his left hand. Gabe had been his best man when Mike acquired that ring. "I could give you twenty reasons why Terri and I shouldn't be together. I expect she could give you thirty. You're looking for order that won't ever come, buddy. But it's the best kind of miserable there is. Does Avery feel the same way?"

Gabe wished Mike hadn't asked that. The answer seemed to make it all so much more unsettling. "Maybe. There are moments, you know? The way she looks at me. She put her hand on my shoulder the other night and I thought I'd keel over right off the porch." He hadn't planned on sharing that, but it seemed to rush out of him through the ever-widening crack in his chest. No matter how he tried, this whole situation wouldn't stay within the neat lines he'd drawn around it, and that had to mean it was wrong.

"You do have it bad." Mike sighed. "Always figured that when you fell, you'd fall hard."

"She's leaving next week, Mike. And she should leave.

She keeps saying she's got a job and a life back in Tennessee. Why ever would she stay in Haven after the whole Cyrus mess on the twentieth—and it will be one huge mess if we don't find Theo."

"You act like there's no convincing her to stay. You said it yourself—she seems to like it here. She'd need the girls' father's permission, yes, but I've seen it happen. It's not an impossible situation."

Gabe slumped back against the booth. "Even if I could convince her—and I'm not saying I could—would it really matter without Theo? She's told me she hates the idea of living under Cyrus's shadow. Could I really ask her to stay here with the awful stuff that will happen? Would you want to raise Mikey in that kind of family baggage? I can't deny her the chance to walk away from this craziness and go back to the life the girls know."

"What about a life the girls want? What Avery wants? What you finally figured out you want? So you'll let the memory of Cyrus Culpepper and the disappearance of your slippery old grandpappy cheat you out of your happiness? Now who's choosing to live under a shadow?" Mike checked his watch. "You're better than this, Gabe. You're stronger than this, and I, of all people, know that. I've got to head to my meeting in Austin, but that doesn't mean I'm slacking up on this with you. She could be the best thing to happen to you. But you'll never know if you let her slip through your fingers, crazy bequest or no crazy bequest." He stood up, gathering his coat. "As a matter of fact—"

"Mr. Boots!" Dinah's voice clamored from behind Gabe in the restaurant. Mike smiled broadly while Gabe gulped. He turned to see Dinah, Debbie and Avery walking toward him.

"We got your note," Dinah said.

Gabe stood and made the quickest introduction possible. Mike's grin was making him so squirrelly he nearly forgot to ask what she meant. "What note?"

"The one you left telling us to meet you here after Debbie's cast was on."

Debbie held up her neon pink, casted arm, wiggling her fingers out of one end. "Doc Delgado was right—it's all kinds of pretty colors now. But just a little broke."

"Brok*en*," Avery amended. "And you left a note on our car in front of Dr. Delgado's asking us to meet you here."

Mike's grin took on epic proportions. "Wasn't me," Gabe offered.

"Well, you're here now," Mike said cheerfully. He motioned toward the side of the booth he'd just vacated. "And I was just leaving before Gabe here had any chance at dessert. Have you had the pie here yet, girls?"

"Twice," Debbie announced as she slid into the seat without hesitation. Gabe watched his planned trip to the bank and supply store dissolve right before his eyes. He was already behind on five projects—would it really matter if he was behind in six?

Mike looked down at Debbie. "Excellent! I hear pie is very good for broken arms."

"Pie is very good for anything," Dinah declared as she slid in next to Gabe.

"You didn't ask us here?" Avery questioned, holding up a note. "You didn't put this on my windshield?"

Gabe peered at the note. Whoever had been "matchmaking" all over Haven had now set their sights on him and Avery. Just when he was thinking March couldn't get any worse.

Chapter Thirteen

Gabe had feared this moment since the day he had brought the box of swing parts onto the Five Rocks. He'd done everything he could think of to avoid it. He'd dodged several requests and had become an expert at creating urgent tasks whenever it looked as if the situation would arise.

And yet here he was, pushing Dinah on the swings Thursday morning.

Well, what did you expect when you put up a swing set? he lectured himself as Dinah settled herself gleefully onto the seat.

"Really high," Dinah requested.

"Medium high," Gabe responded, thinking Avery didn't need more reasons to visit Dr. Delgado. She and Debbie were there now, getting a checkup on Debbie's cast since her fingers were still looking puffy. As both girls were barred from the swing set until Debbie healed—a tactic even he could see as necessary since having one swing and one not would result in a torrent of tears—this was perhaps Dinah's last chance to play on the swings.

He'd agreed to the idea when it was Marlene and Jethro doing the pushing. Then Marlene's sister had one of her "emergencies"—that sister seemed to have dozens of crises, and always at the worst possible times—and the task had fallen to him.

At first he tried just watching. Supervising from the porch while Dinah pumped her tiny legs to no avail. He'd finally succumbed to the endless pleas of "Push me!" and found himself in his current predicament.

"Higher!" Dinah called.

"This is fine."

"Pleeeeaaaaasssseeee?" Surely, the world had no more irritating sound than a little girl's whine.

"Noooooooo," he responded as firmly as he dared without making his voice reflect the annoyance he felt.

This went on for twenty minutes. Any adult would be dizzy by now, Gabe thought, which gave him an idea. He slowed the swing to a stop, bringing a king-size moan from Dinah.

"Have you ever spun a swing?" He tried to make it sound exciting.

"Spun?"

He appealed to Dinah's sense of adventure. "You'll have to hold on real tight."

Her eyes lit up. "I can do that."

"You're sure now? I wouldn't want you to fall off."

She rolled her eyes. "I'm not Debbie."

Gabe was glad her mother wasn't here to hear that pint-size put-down. "Well, okay, if you're sure you can hold on."

Dinah replied by gripping the swing ropes with fierce determination.

Gabe spun Dinah around slowly, winding up the swing once or twice. "Ready?"

"Yup."

He let go, allowing the swing to spin at a slow speed, unwinding the twist he'd just made. The maneuver was decidedly tame, but it made her giggle just a bit.

"Phew!" he teased. "You made it."

"You're silly," she replied. "Do it again. Do it more."

That came as no surprise. "You're sure?"

"Spin it more!"

Gabe wound the swing six or seven times. "Hang on really tight now."

The swing unwound longer and slightly faster. Nothing even remotely dangerous, but he could see Dinah's eyes register a fair amount of dizziness when the swing finally stilled. She waited a moment—presumably for the world to stop swirling around her—before she looked up at him and said, "Again!"

"Okay, but this is the last time."

"Noooooo."

"Yes." He repeated the winding, mildly enjoying her squeals and giggles as the swing twisted itself free. She was definitely wobbly by the end.

"Again!"

"Stand up first." He got down on one knee in front of her, extending his arms for the inevitable. She stood up, and then promptly toppled over right into his arms. "And that's why we're stopping."

He'd expected her to refuse and squirm out of his arms, but instead she clung to him, laughing and settling into his embrace. The simple, open nature of her action bowled him over, and he found his arms going around her before he could stop them, hugging her tight.

When was the last time he'd hugged someone? Or someone hugged him? Sure, there had been social hugs or the standard cowboy clasps on the back, but to be hugged, clung to like this? There had been one woman in his life, years back, who always draped herself on him in a way that felt suffocating. That woman had accused him—rightly so—of being cold and distant. Nothing about Dinah's arms around his neck made him feel cold or distant. In fact, he wasn't rightly sure who was hugging who more tightly.

When had he become so walled off from people that touch had left his life? It made sense now why Avery's hand on his shoulder had bolted through him like a power surge.

"You're fun," Dinah said into the crook of his neck, snuggling closer. He told himself it was the dizziness that made her clutch him, but even he could see that for the lie that it was. She looked up at him. "Can you come home with us?"

The question smacked him in the chest. He sat back on the ground, bringing Dinah onto his lap.

"The swings can go home with you if you like. It's not like I'm going to use them."

"Yeah," she said, settling herself as if sitting on Gabe's lap was a perfectly natural thing to do. "Mom says we can bring them home. But can we bring you?"

Avery had said she would leave after the celebration, and he had no right to expect anything different from her.

Except that he did.

He'd somehow persuaded himself that they could stay, that they *should* stay. He didn't like the idea of Debbie and Dinah leaving Haven, leaving his life. He certainly didn't like the idea of Avery leaving his life. When he was honest, he didn't even take to the idea of their leaving Five Rocks. For all his annoyance at shoes in the hall, crayon on his papers and five juice spills a day, the house would seem empty without them.

Lonely.

Gabe was not a man who got lonesome. His houseguests were messing with his insides, and he wasn't sure what to do about it.

"Can you?" Dinah persisted.

Clearly, she had no idea of the size or implications of her question. He had to give her an answer, but was stumped for what to say. He opted for a standard evasive tactic—ask another question. "Do you miss home?"

"I miss my bed."

Gabe could commiserate. He'd never been much for traveling, preferring the comfort of his own familiar home. "I have a mighty fine bed. I'd miss it, too."

"I know. Debbie and I jumped on it when…" Her eyes went wide. "Oops. I wasn't supposed to tell."

The thought of those two jumping on the high, wide four-poster king-size bed in his room both amused and irritated him. Those girls had gotten just about everywhere in his house. "What else do you miss?" he asked, not wanting to venture a comment on his bed's use as a trampoline.

"I miss Dad."

Another big answer. It was the first time either of the girls had mentioned their father in front of him.

"He left." She said it with a heartbreaking sigh that made Gabe want to shake the clod of a man who had walked away from this family. The man who had Avery and gave her up was nothing short of a fool.

"I'm sorry for that," he said.

"Mama says he's still our dad."

"That's true," Gabe replied. "He'll always be your dad."

"We don't ever see him." The sad tone of her voice sunk a hole in Gabe's chest right in the spot where her little head lay resting.

"I'm sorry for that, too. I didn't see my daddy growing up, either." He found his arms tightening around the girl. "Shame something like that has to happen."

She looked up at him. "Do you think he'll come push me on the swings when we set 'em up back home?"

Those sweet little eyes could tear him to bits. Based

on what Avery had told him, the answer was most likely no, which made that hole in his chest sink a mile deeper.

"I sure hope so" was all Gabe could manage to say. A fresh wave of resentment at the man fool enough to walk away from this family surged in his chest.

"Will you push me again?" Dinah asked.

Gabe said, "Absolutely," with no hesitation at all. He stood up and set Dinah on the ground in front of him. "But only until we hear Debbie and your mom coming up the drive. Then we'll have to stop."

"I know, 'cuz it's not fair." Dinah's bottom lip stuck out just the tiniest bit. "She can't swing."

"It won't be much longer," Gabe replied, consoling her as he began pushing. All the irritation had deflated right out of him thinking how Dinah had no dad who cared enough to push her on the swings. *It won't be much longer until they leave. This house will never feel the same*, Gabe thought as Dinah's giggles sailed across the spring breeze. He could never hope to be the kind of father Debbie and Dinah deserved, but today, now, he could be the kind of man who pushed a swing.

Avery and the girls were sorting flowerpots for celebration table decorations later that afternoon when Gabe walked by.

"How's the arm?" he asked Debbie.

She held up the bright pink cast. "Patching up."

"Good for you."

"The cast won't feel so tight once her swelling goes down some more. Doctor Delgado gave us the X-rays to take back to Tennessee. Six weeks in the cast," Avery added, "but she'll be fine by the time it's warm enough to swim." He resumed his walking until Avery stood up. "Gabe?"

"Yes?"

She'd thought hard about how to ask this, given the many implications. "I'd like to go look at the cabin again. Take a good look inside this time, and see what kind of shape it's in." It was a perfectly reasonable request, but given how many people seemed to think she ought to fix it up and move right in, she'd hesitated.

"You can do that anytime you like. Haverman gave you the keys, didn't he?"

"I…well, I'd like you to come with me." She started to add all the reasons why, but ended up silent.

He looked at her for a moment, rightly puzzled at her request.

She had to say something. "I know you're busy and everything, but… I just don't want to do it alone."

A warm understanding washed over his eyes. "I can take you up there." He paused for a moment, and she could see him deciding whether to say more. There was a whole delicate conversation hanging in the air, but with the way things were, and with the girls right there, it would have to remain unspoken.

"Tomorrow?" he asked, his voice unusually soft.

"That'd be just fine."

"I'll be in town most of the morning, but I can circle back and pick you up."

"No need. I've got some things to pick up in town myself, so I'll just meet you in town and we can drive out from there."

She wanted him there, but she didn't want him to take her there. She needed to do that part herself. Which made no sense. The line between standing on her own two feet and depending on Gabe was starting to blur, and that bothered her.

Because she was leaving when the weekend was over. At least she was mostly sure she was. It was getting harder to know what it was she wanted.

Chapter Fourteen

Avery walked out of the town hardware store Friday morning with a big bag of cleaning supplies. She could have borrowed all this from Gabe, but it felt better to purchase them on her own. The run-down cabin at the back of the Culpepper ranch property was hers now, so she should start to clean it up. Even if all she could do before she left was make a small dent, it would feel good to do *something*. It might help settle her mind about what to do next.

It would certainly be only a small dent, if that. The place looked to need a lot more than a good scrubbing to be either livable or sellable.

Pulling some juice boxes from her handbag, she lined the girls up on a park bench while she looked through the list of handymen that Tanner Barstow, the owner of the farm supply store, had given her.

Where to start? Avery pulled photos she'd taken of the property up on her cell phone. The pictures made her heart sink. She knew enough about houses to see that the place had good bones, but the fallen shingles, a boarded-up window and debris scattered about the foundation told her how much work was ahead of her. Or ahead of anyone she hired. *Well, maybe it will give me a reason to come back and visit*, she thought.

"That's ugly," Dinah said, swinging her feet as she sat on the bench sipping apple juice. "Who'd want to live there?"

"Nobody's lived there in a long time," Avery explained in optimistic tones. "It needs fixing up." She nervously fingered the keys to the place. "Mr. Boots is meeting us here. Then we'll drive over to the cabin to go inside and get started." She'd know for sure once she was inside, but it was a good guess the place needed major structural repairs. Could she sell it in its current shape? Would anyone even buy it? They'd be more likely to tear it down, and that felt wrong. Her grandfather had grown up there—it was the closest thing to roots she could claim.

If someone hadn't claimed it first—and by "someone," she meant a snake, or a possum, or any number of varmints she'd imagined might have taken up residence in the abandoned home.

She peered at the photo again, as if it would hold clues to anything living inside. At best, she'd encounter trash and disrepair. At worst…well, let's just say that was another reason not to have to enter alone. Maybe she should have left the girls at home for this trip.

Avery looked up to see a familiar old man crossing the street. Wasn't that Harley Jones?

"Hello, Mr. Jones!" she called, wanting to be friendly. After all, Gabe had said Mr. Jones lived in an old cabin at the back of Gabe's property. Maybe he knew a thing or two about bringing an old cabin up to snuff.

He turned, startled. As if surprised anyone would say hello to him.

"How are you today?" she asked.

"Same as any other day."

Maybe he didn't recall who she was. "I'm Avery Culpepper. We're guests of Gabe's at Five Rocks."

"I remember," he said, his sour face softening a bit. "And these are…" His face scrunched up into a collection of weathered wrinkles as she could see him trying to remember the girls' names. "Starts with *D*'s…"

"I'm Debbie."

"And I'm Dinah."

He almost grinned. Not quite, but almost. "You're sure now? You could be switching 'em on me and I'd never know."

Avery laughed. "No, they gave you the right names." She slanted a glance toward Dinah. "Not that they haven't tried that particular trick on some other folks." She sighed and held up the photo on her phone. "We're meeting Gabe here to go check out the inside of my new property."

Harley squinted at the phone display and scratched his chin. "Ain't much to look at, is she?"

"Are you a cowboy?" Debbie asked. She'd begun to ask that of anyone wearing a cowboy hat. While some of the answers she received were amusing, Avery was wondering if the charm was wearing off. Harley certainly didn't look amused, but then again she'd never seen him looking like anything but as if he'd just bitten a lemon.

"We're from Tennessee," she offered by way of explanation, which really wasn't much of a reason for a state that boasted the country music capital of the world.

Harley leaned on his cane to stare at Debbie. "Ain't they got cowboys up there in Tennessee?"

"They got cowboy *hats*," Debbie said, completely unfazed by the old man's gruff demeanor. "But anyone could wear those."

Harley chuckled. "Oh, well, you're right there. The hat does not necessarily make the man." He turned to Avery.

"Sharp girls you got there, ma'am. You're Cyrus's granddaughter. The real one, I hear tell."

Avery shrugged. "That's me." Why did everyone feel compelled to remind her someone had tried to step into her identity—and her inheritance? Considering the state of the cabin, it made the whole scheme seem that much more absurd. Who'd go to such lengths to get their hands on that mess? No one knew if there was anything more to her inheritance, least of all her.

"Whole thing's a mess, that's what it is. Only now with you here, it'll mostly shake itself out, I suppose."

Avery remembered the silhouette of Gabe hunched in defeat against the porch column. "Well, not necessarily."

"But you're here."

"Yes, but I'm only one of the stipulations." It still sounded crazy, no matter now many times she said it. "There are still the four original residents of the boys ranch to find. They've found three—and me, of course—but unless they find the last one, it won't matter. Without Gabe's grandfather, it won't matter how many of the other requirements they've met. Cyrus made sure it was an all-or-nothing proposition."

That seemed to agitate the old man. Which was understandable—even Avery couldn't understand why her grandfather had gone to such extremes. She was glad he eased himself down on the bench beside her. "Find Theodore Linley? He's long gone. They won't hold anyone to such nonsense."

"From what I hear, they have to. Seems my dear old grandfather locked the whole thing down tight—legally speaking, that is. If they don't find this man and bring him to the party, then the Triple C becomes a strip mall and the boys ranch has to go back to the Silver Star."

"They'd never do that." He shook his head. "Strip

mall? And send half the boys elsewhere? That's fool talk. It won't never come to that."

"They'll have no choice." She sat back against the bench. "A strip mall, can you imagine? My grandpa Cyrus was one wily old coot."

Harley worried at his cane handle with one gnarled hand. "You're tellin' me all that happens if that Linley fellow don't show?"

"Sad, isn't it?" Avery pulled a box of animal crackers from her bag and handed it to the girls. "It's tying Gabe into knots that he can't find any trace of the man."

"Nonsense. That isn't Gabe's fault."

"You and I can see that. And it seems pretty clear to me the guy doesn't want to be found or is long dead—but Gabe sure blames himself."

Harley turned his face to look down the street. "Takes a lot on himself, Gabe does." His tone was so sad.

"He speaks very fondly of you," she offered. The poor man probably considered himself a burden the way Danny's grandmother had in her last days. She hadn't been. She was a sweet woman who almost made Avery feel like she had a family. She hated how Danny's actions were teaching Debbie and Dinah that family was something that could be discarded when it became inconvenient. That's not how family should ever work. Not that she'd experienced much to the contrary.

Harley kept staring down the street. "Does he now?"

She remembered how often Gabe went to visit Harley with food or just to keep him company, and tenderly touched the old man's elbow. "I think you're actually quite dear to him, but you know Gabe—I doubt he'd ever come out and tell you."

That sent Harley into a chuckle that all too quickly dissolved into a rasping cough. Dinah sweetly held up her apple juice to share with the man, but he waved her off and began to struggle to his feet. "I'm sure Gabe'll be here any minute. I'd best get on."

"You're sure? You can sit with us a spell. We can give you a ride back to Five Rocks."

His face took on the sour, tight countenance she'd seen almost all the time from him. "I got my own car. I ain't so far gone that I can't get myself to town and back, young lady."

The girls looked up at his sharp tone, and he seemed to realize how harsh his words had been. "You all come tell me what you found in there one of these days," he said, backpedaling and trying to show a sliver of a smile. "I expect it'll be quite a story."

"Oh, I hope not," Avery replied. Dinah and Debbie made dual slurping sounds as they finished up their juice boxes just as Gabe's truck pulled around the corner.

"Tell Gabe I said hello," Harley called as he started down the block.

"You sure you don't want to stay and say hello yourself?" He couldn't have so much to do that an extra five minutes would be so much of a burden. Harley had to be lonely, living all the way on the back of Five Rocks all by himself.

"Nope," he called abruptly over his shoulder, picking up the pace of his labored hobbling.

What was that all about? Was Harley avoiding Gabe? Had the remark about Gabe's fondness for the old man crossed some sort of line with him?

For a small simple town, Avery thought to herself, *Haven sure is complicated.*

Avery was trying to put up a good front as she stood inside the mess of a house. She was trying to act as if inheriting this pile of lumber was a good thing. Based on what Gabe saw today, he might just tear the whole thing down if he was in her place.

She stood in the empty front room, staring at the dented, crumbing walls. "It has good bones," she declared.

Bones? he thought. No one could want to live in this skeleton. Cyrus hadn't done her any favors by leaving her this. It'd take a year's worth of work—and a wheelbarrow full of money—to make this place anything anyone would ever want. Another reason she had every right to head on back to Tennessee come Monday.

"You going to sell the place?" he asked.

"Of course," she replied quickly. "It makes no sense to keep it. We have a home in Tennessee."

Yes, she did. The fact seemed to follow him around like a shadow. He'd already come to dread the moment she would leave Five Rocks and return to Tennessee. The selfish part of him wanted her nearby, wanted her to be a part of Haven.

But in two days, she'd have no reason to stay. Everything felt like it was slipping through his fingers.

"Look, Mama!" Debbie had opened a closet door and pulled out a musty old afghan.

The large blue square was falling apart, but Gabe could still make out the faded design stitched into the center. "That's Cyrus's brand," he said, outlining the design with his finger. "I wonder if June made it."

Avery held out her hands for the relic. "June Culpepper? My grandmother?"

"She was always knitting things, I recall. Every church bazaar had a dozen hats or throws from her. Before she passed, that is."

"It smells funny," Dinah said, wrinkling her nose.

"It's very old," Avery said, touching it with a sad tenderness. "And not in good shape. I expect it's been in the bottom of that closet for decades." She pulled at one piece of the fringe and a whole corner of the afghan seemed to unravel in her hands. Avery whimpered as if wounded.

She had next to nothing from her family, and here she had to watch something crumble before her eyes. It seemed cruel. "Maybe we can save the design," he offered, having no idea if such a thing was possible. Avery had a trunkful of cleaning supplies, but they'd given up any hope of starting that within five minutes of opening the door. This house didn't need a dustpan, it needed a shovel. Maybe even a backhoe.

Gabe removed the cleaning supplies from the box Avery had brought and held it out. "Put it in here," he said as gently as he could. "You can take it to Marnie over at the ranch and see what she can do. She does all kinds of yarn stuff and if anyone knows how to save it, she will." He understood the sentiment. He had a ratty old football jersey of his father's, and that chair of his mother's—and he'd be beside himself if anything happened to either of those. Even family you resented was still family, and everybody deserved at least a piece of their roots.

The tattered afghan seemed to unhinge something in Avery. She'd kept up a nervously optimistic attitude the whole time they'd been in the house, but he could practically watch her lose the ability to keep that up. Her shoulders fell forward, she began to pace the empty room and her lips pressed together.

He felt for her, he truly did. Cyrus had put her through the ringer with all this business, and he admired that she'd held up as well as she had. It felt unfair that the one solid thing she'd gotten out of this whole mess so far was a tumble-down house that right now was more of a burden than a blessing.

"Why'd he do any of this?" She was trying not to lose it in front of the girls—even he could see that. Should he stay beside her, or invent some reason to take the girls outside and let her go to pieces alone?

Alone seemed the worse of the two, so Gabe reached out and put a hand on her shoulder. The act unleashed a short sob from her, one of Avery's delicate hands flying up to cover her mouth as if she could hold it all in.

He couldn't answer Avery's frustrated question—no one could.

It was the wrong thing to do. It would confuse the girls and cross a dozen boundaries, but Gabe could no more stand there and watch Avery unravel than he could have left her there on Roz's porch. He pulled Avery toward him, feeling her composure fall away as she dissolved against his chest and cried. Not pretty, careful tears, but great, reckless sobs that made her shoulders shake and her fists grab at his sleeves.

"Don't cry, Mama. It's not that ugly in here." Dinah's heartbreakingly tender voice came from down beside them.

Avery, of course, cried all the harder at her daughter's attempt at comfort. At another time, he might have found her misguided grasp of the situation amusing, but there was no humor in today. He wrapped his arms more tightly around Avery, startled by the sense of honor and purpose that enveloped him as he did so. Gabe felt Dinah and Debbie circle around his and Avery's legs in a tiny huddle that made his own heart twist in a surge of care and sympathy.

He'd stand here and let her cry it out because no one should have to do this alone. And because he wanted to be the one to hold her up while she fell to pieces. He wanted to lend her his strength, to shield her in this over-whelming moment.

Gabe let one hand fall softly on her hair, soothing as she cried against him. He couldn't explain why the awful moment felt right, sacred even. These three people had come to mean so much more to him than the solution to the problem Cyrus had dumped on him and all of Haven. But he also knew, with a certainty he'd been denying for weeks now, that he didn't want them to go. Not after Sunday, not ever.

Avery pulled her hands from his sleeves to wrap them tightly around his chest, clinging to him with a despera-tion that broke his heart wide open. For a moment, he al-lowed himself the indulgence of laying his chin against the top of her head, reveling in the way she tucked per-fectly inside his embrace.

It was the exquisite opposite of being alone.

He wanted to kiss that soft brown hair. He wanted to kiss away the tears and make promises he couldn't keep. Irrational promises that she wouldn't have to do any of this alone or ever be alone again.

Such promises would only make things worse for her. And so Gabe said nothing—not because he didn't want to speak his fumbling words of comfort to her, but because Avery deserved to hear eloquent words from a man who would woo her and cherish her the way a lifetime bach-elor like himself could never hope to do. He'd choke on his own silence before he added to the line of men who'd disappointed her.

But oh, how unwise promises and declarations roared in his chest, clawing against her heartbeat to set traps for the both of them. While strong and stubborn, she'd pulled a surprising admiration from him. While weak and broken, however, Avery had gone and stolen his heart.

And it was gone, he realized. He'd lost the battle to deny what he felt for her. For all three of them. He loved her.

As he held her, the thought fixed itself clear and true in his head. He loved her. But that thought came with the equally clear truth that he would love her alone. He would love her enough to give her the happiness she'd never have with him. Life had made him a creature of privacy and distance, not the rest-of-your-life family man she needed and deserved. He would bear her tears today, and be honored to do so, but he would also bear her leaving. He would never, ever risk being the source of her sadness.

It seemed to Gabe that he'd lived an hour in the span of minutes he'd held her, that time had stopped until she pulled away, embarrassed and sniffling. Even Debbie and Dinah looked up at him with tearful, confused eyes.

"It's okay," Avery said, squatting down to gather the girls in her arms.

Gabe looked down and fought the urge to pull all three of them right back into his arms. The massive hole in his chest was permanent as of this moment—they'd taken a piece of him he'd never get back.

Chapter Fifteen

All Saturday morning, Avery and Gabe had maneuvered around each other with a careful distance. No one wanted to admit the lines that had been crossed back there in the dirty cabin. No one wanted to talk about the goodbye that had to happen soon. No one had found Linley. Avery felt as if the whole house crackled with tension on multiple levels.

She fled for a bit to the boys ranch, to drop off the afghan with Marnie and pick up some mason jar lanterns that were being redecorated and repurposed from the ranch's Thanksgiving banquet. The ranch was buzzing with cautiously optimistic preparations, but somehow she didn't feel much like joining in, knowing she'd be leaving all this behind in a matter of days.

She'd just pulled the last box from her trunk when she heard it—a loud, hard series of whacks. Bangs so loud it was a wonder the whole house didn't shake. Jethro had taken the twins "fishing"—which basically meant he took the girls and a basket of cookies out to the tiny creek where no one ever caught any fish, but no one ever seemed to mind—and Marlene was sorting linens.

Whack. Tumble. Whack. Grunt. It was something out

by the barn where Gabe was, and it was far from peaceful. It was angry. Fierce. If the tension of the house had a sound, this was it.

That meant it was something she should probably avoid, but when she heard a sharp cry of pain, Avery put down her box and walked cautiously toward the barn.

She found Gabe stalking around a pile of logs, an axe sunk into one large stump. He had his back to her and was grumbling in dark and sour tones. When he turned a bit, Avery noticed he cradled his left hand in a bandana.

"Gabe?"

He looked up at her with a wild storm in his eyes. Why were they always finding each other in the midst of their wit's end? She and Gabe seemed to collide at the worst possible moments, repeated witnesses to each other's pain.

"I'm fine," he barked.

She almost had to laugh at that. "You are not."

"I just got a sliver, that's all."

Gabe Everett was a huge man. No piddly sliver would make him hold his hand like that. Were it not for the lack of blood, she'd assume his axe went through a finger from the way he grimaced.

"Should I call Marlene?"

He glowered at the idea. "Absolutely not."

She looked around at the huge pile of chopped wood. It was springtime, but he'd chopped enough for two winters. This clearly wasn't about fuel, so it wasn't hard to guess what was going on. "Taking out your frustrations on innocent tree parts?"

She'd hoped the small joke would take some of the dark edge off his features, but it didn't. At least he stopped his furious pacing. "Some."

Avery ventured a step closer. "Did it work?"

"Does it look like it worked?"

"Not a bit, actually." The last week had wound Gabe so tight she was surprised he hadn't done something more drastic than chop wood. The anniversary deadline arrived tomorrow, and watching Gabe Everett stare failure in the face was a gut-wrenching sight. "Look, Gabe, surely you know no one blames you for—"

"Don't!" he snapped before she could finish the sentence, the word so sharp and loud it made her jump. He'd grown so kind and gentle with her and the girls she'd forgotten just how imposing a man he was.

He saw her jump and cringed, then simply sank down onto a nearby log. "Just don't, okay?"

What comfort could she hope to offer? Over the last week she'd watched Gabe try every possible source, spend untold sums of money, call in favors and generally do every conceivable thing to find Theodore Linley.

And fail.

The man had virtually vanished off the face of the earth, and all those young boys would pay the price. *Unfair* didn't begin to do the situation justice.

She pointed to the hand. "Does it hurt?"

"It's nothing."

"Oh, I doubt that." He was holding it like it would drop off at any second. "You didn't cut off a finger or anything, did you?"

"I told you, it's just a sliver." He'd been pushing everyone away for hours, evidently determined to face this failure alone.

No one should have to do this alone. "Then you won't mind showing me."

"As a matter of fact, I would mind."

"Tough."

That raised an eyebrow. She'd never challenged him before—she got the impression few people ever did.

When he didn't warn her off, she walked closer, sat down next to him and held out her hand with her best "do what you're told" mother glare.

Gabe surprised her by complying. She unfolded the bandana to find a startlingly large shard of wood embedded in the base of his thumb.

"If that's a 'sliver,' the girls have gone whaling. Gabe, there's half a tree in there!"

"I've had worse."

"Well, don't you think you should get it out?"

"I was *about to* before I was interrupted. Want to watch? You know, in case I keel over or anything?" It was dark, sour teasing, but at least the near-lethal edge was fading from his eyes.

She cringed. "Not particularly." This looked like no mere "put a bandage on it and kiss it better" injury. The man looked as if he might need stitches.

"Tough," he said, throwing her own word back at her with a victorious gleam. Then, without preparation or ceremony, he simply grabbed the chunk of wood with his teeth and yanked it out of his thumb with a blood-chilling hiss. Avery felt her head swim a bit at so brutal a remedy.

It was clear the removal hurt tremendously, but he wasn't going to show it. His jaw worked and he flexed and shook the wounded hand as he spit the offending wood away with a growl. She'd probably either be crying or have fainted from such a yank, but Gabe just looked steamed. Tense and angry. Even in pain—emotional or physical—the man refused to lower his guard. *It must be exhausting to live like that*, she thought.

And yet, he'd been so kind to her when her own guard had fallen. It had come crashing down back at the cabin, surely. Gabe had been wonderful in those moments. Strong and protective and loyal—exactly what she needed, what she'd been missing for so long. The memory made heat rise up her spine. He was there for everyone else but let no one be there for him. That was as unfair as all this business with the will.

"Better?" she said softly, nodding her head into his view even as he gripped his now-bleeding thumb with his other hand.

"No," he growled, turning away from her.

It was the closest thing to an admission of pain she'd ever got from him. It wasn't better—neither the wound nor the search for Linley. There wasn't really any better to be had.

Avery knew, just by looking at him, that both would leave a scar.

She picked up the bandana off his knee and reached for his hand. He resisted. She tugged at him anyway, pulling the injured hand toward her lap and wrapping the bandana tight over the wound. "Put pressure on it. And you should go inside and wash that up before it gets infected."

He didn't move. Instead, he stayed stock-still and stared at her. Fighting, she could see, to keep the wall up between them while everything else tumbled down around him. Hadn't she been doing the same thing? She felt her heart scrambling in her chest, desperate to come open, fighting against her determination to keep it locked up tight.

"It hurts," he admitted, and she knew those two words cost him everything to speak. They were both so achingly weary, wounded in so many ways by this fiasco Cyrus had launched. It felt like a trap neither of them deserved.

She stared at the wounded thumb, then back up at the storm in his eyes. She did what any mother would do. She brought up Gabe's hand, cradled it in both of her hands and kissed it. Avery knew exactly what she was doing and why it shouldn't happen, but there was no stopping it. She wanted, even if only for this moment, to lay the battle down. To make even this tiny part of it better, if only just for now.

It crossed the line they'd carefully drawn between them, and they both knew it. She had opened her heart—partially back at the cabin, but fully at this moment. It made it hard to breathe; both exhilaration and anxiety swirled around her at the same time.

Avery looked up from the wounded hand to stare into Gabe's eyes. She made herself hold his gaze, to meet him in this moment, no matter how hard her heart pounded. She could see the precise moment his armor fell away, the change so dramatic in his eyes that it was as if they changed color. Storm clouds to blue sky. The man she'd barely glimpsed out by the toolboxes showed up now in full force; an overpowering, stunning transformation that stilled her pulse. A man far more tender than everyone else saw, but somehow far more powerful for that tenderness. A man who loved as fiercely as he fought.

Gabe felt like he was falling off some high cliff or diving into some fast-running river. Everything he'd tried so hard to keep from happening—the surge in his heart, the nonstop need to know where Avery was and if she was okay, the confounding affection for those little girls—happened anyway. He should stop it, but he couldn't. Worse yet, right now he didn't want to. Wouldn't it be wonderful to let himself really hold her? Kiss her the way he was aching to. Tell her she should never have to be alone again and lie to himself that he could be the man to make that happen.

Gabe was many things, but he never counted being weak among them. The power of his will was his greatest asset. He bent circumstances and people to his need or the greater good all the time. Served his community tirelessly, fought for causes, supervised a large and successful ranch.

And yet he'd never felt as weak, as downright powerless, as he did right now. There simply wasn't any hope for it. He couldn't make his mind or even his arms resist despite nearly yelling at himself silently in his head.

Gabe pulled Avery close to him, and when she lifted her sweet face toward his, he kissed her. The absolute delight of it nearly consumed him. After so many days of trying not to wonder how those lips tasted, the glory of tasting her nearly knocked him over. *Glory.* That was the only word he could think of—when he managed to think at all—for what it felt like.

Avery made a tiny sound and slipped her hands around his neck, and Gabe was lost. He knew it would take a hundred years to gather up the will to stop. The girls or Marlene or anyone could come around the corner of the barn at any second and Gabe couldn't bring himself to care. It felt as though kissing her was like pure oxygen and he'd spent the last weeks gasping for breath.

She was leaving, and everything around him was about to fail. The rightness of holding her—of the way his heart seemed to reach toward her, of how he felt her beside him even when they were clear across the room—was the only balm to make that pain subside. He desperately needed it, even if only for a few moments. Kissing her, having her look into his eyes the way she just had, made him feel as if he could do anything. He was unstoppable. Victorious despite the defeat that was poised to come down on his head.

He needed her, more than he felt capable of denying himself. Her sweet heart called to him stronger than his own will, and that scared him to death. He ought to push her away, end this exquisite kiss and tell her to go back to her life in Tennessee, but he couldn't. He wasn't capable of it. He didn't even want to be capable of pulling away from her.

She proved him right, pulling away first with a gasping breath he felt through every corner of his chest. "Gabe," she said, his name more of a breath than a word. Nothing could have undone him more than to hear her say his name that way with that look in her eyes.

I'm not who she needs, he pleaded with his reason. *It can't matter that I need her.* It couldn't matter that he felt like he'd been wandering through his days at everyone else's service and just now woke up to what he really wanted.

Because what he wanted—more than anything, more than was wise, far more than was good for any of them— was her. In his life, gazing at him like that every day.

He feathered his good hand against the porcelain rose of her cheeks, flushed by the rush of what had just passed between them. Sure, right now it felt as if he'd sooner die than walk away from her, but that was too marvelous to stick. The glowing in his chest couldn't be trusted, even if it was love. Parenting was hard work even when you were born to it. He'd never had those instincts, never wanted to have them. His quiet and order were how he survived— how would he live with tiny pinkness messing things up year after year? A whole life of solitude couldn't just transform in the space of a month. Sooner or later he'd have to own up to what he knew to be his true nature.

Tomorrow, he'd pay the piper for every failing.

Tonight, he'd kiss her. Again. And memorize every detail of it to make it last after he sent her away.

He'd fail at that, too. He knew, even as he settled his mouth against her impossibly soft lips, that it'd never be enough. He would wish for more of her every day of his life from here on in.

Chapter Sixteen

The anniversary celebration was by far the oddest affair Avery had ever attended. The whole thing felt like a warped blend of birthday party and funeral luncheon. Everyone wandered around the beautifully decorated barn with an air of tense happiness. There was laughter, groaning-full tables of good food, cheery hellos and handshakes, but it all glossed over the huge disappointment everyone knew was coming.

After that heart-stopping set of kisses yesterday, Gabe had pulled himself away and walked without a word into the house. She'd sat on the log for a few moments, desperately trying to sort out her feelings. Should she leave? Could she even consider staying? What she felt now, strong as it was, didn't change a single one of the obstacles facing her. It certainly couldn't be enough to risk the girls' stability.

But what about their happiness? Hers? She had wandered inside, lost in a haze of emotion and confusion. Gabe's study door was shut and she couldn't bring herself to open it. What was there to say or do? He didn't come out for supper. She could barely keep up the appearance of an appetite herself.

Sunday morning, Gabe left before everyone else rose and stayed away until timing forced his return to dress for the late-afternoon party.

She left him alone. It wasn't as if she could help what was about to happen. Last night had been a wonderful mistake, but a mistake anyway. She needed to leave. Even if she could somehow stay, if Danny consented to let her move the girls, would she really want to? Build a life as living embodiment of what Cyrus had done to this community? Back in Tennessee, she wouldn't have to watch them tear that beautiful old estate down to put in a strip mall. Watch them send boys back to places that weren't as beautiful or special as the Triple C. It hurt to leave, but not as much as standing in this party and pretending to be happy—her heart was breaking on so many levels.

Bea pulled Avery from her thoughts by clanging a spoon against a glass. The woman stood in the center of a little makeshift stage at one end of the barn, framed in dried vine arrangements Avery had helped to make.

"I'm delighted to say that the boys have prepared a little entertainment for y'all this afternoon."

Dinah tugged on her hand. "Do we get to see a show?"

"I don't know what we'll get to see," Avery replied. "You'll just have to wait and find out like the rest of us." She pointed to the stage, where the boys lined up in a bumbling sort of line, each holding a sheet of paper.

The tallest boy—Riley, she remembered from her time painting frames with the boys—stepped to the microphone. "We have a poem for you. Nothing fancy, but y'all might find it interesting. On account of most of you are in it."

"That can't be good," Jethro muttered beside Avery.

"Hush now, they might surprise you," Marlene chided.

Riley cleared his throat and smoothed his page on the podium, then began.

"Some folks think we're not much good,
"That ranch boys ain't got smarts.
"But we see more than you might think
"When it comes to lonely hearts."

"Well, this just got interesting," Marlene whispered.

Riley stepped away as Avery recognized Ben moving up to the podium.

"Mr. Tanner may sell seed,
"Or tractors, hay or twine,
"But it took more than books before
"He read between the lines!"

One of the youngest held up one of the painted frames—filled not with a boy's photograph, but with a red paper heart that read "Tanner + Macy" in big letters. He hung the frame by a colored ribbon to the decorative vines. The room burst into laughter and applause at the poem and the antics it confessed. The boys were the mystery matchmakers, it seemed.

"I suspected it was you," Macy announced.

"You did not," Ben countered, smiling all the while.

"I thought my students wrote me *not* to take up with Tanner!" Macy called as Tanner's face turned more than a few shades red.

"Well, they did, but they got a little help from us, too. Changed our mind about that, didn't we?" Ben called back.

"They do say teamwork is the first tool of management," Harold Haverman called playfully to Tanner. "Gotta respect a young man who changes his thinking and makes use of resources."

"Not in my Sunday school class I don't," Macy called back. "Y'all stop such meddling."

"No need to meddle anymore now," Ben replied. "I'd say we got the job done."

"Oh, so *you're* taking credit for this?" Tanner teased.

"Only some. Most, maybe."

That sent the room into further laughter as Ben left the podium and Diego and Stephen took their place. In tandem, they recited:

"Miss Josie may be fond of calves,
"But Rangers take her heart.
"So we sent pie and baby things
"To give those two a start."

Another frame, this one holding a "Heath + Josie" heart, rose from the smallest of boys.

"That was a pretty good pie," Heath called out. "Surely, none of *you* made it."

"Another bit of teamwork," Lila from the café added with a wide smile. "Who could resist helping out a cause like that?"

"You could have at least spelled my name right on your note." Heath pointed a finger at the boys.

"Nobody's perfect, amigo." Diego offered an exaggerated wink as he stepped away from the podium.

Avery gaped at Marlene as a trio of the younger boys took to the podium for another recitation.

"Miss Lana had to kiss some frogs
"Before she got her prince

"But little Logan's Christmas wish
"Sure looked a lot like Flint's!"

"That's a terrible rhyme," Flint moaned, his hand over his eyes as the now-expected framed heart appeared and was hung on the vines.

"Honestly, you did some terrible matchmaking, boys," Lana added. She'd told Avery about the multiple notes pointing her in the direction of some truly unsuitable "matches."

"Hey, someone had to make sure Mr. Flint looked good by comparison," one of the boys said.

"Thanks for the vote of confidence," Flint commented with a mock sour look.

"It worked, didn't it?" a second boy called back.

"So all the mystery matchmaking you told me about— it was the ranch boys the whole time?" Avery asked Marlene.

"And they're three for three, those rascals," Marlene said, giggling.

Avery thought about the note she'd received inviting her to pie at Lila's and gulped. The boys had caught on to the attraction between her and Gabe, but they wouldn't keep their "perfect score" today. How could she explain to those boys—and everyone listening—that in her and Gabe's case it wasn't enough?

It *wasn't* enough, was it?

Corey and Aiden, two other of the ranch boys, stepped up to the podium, but Avery barely listened to their poem about false invitations to a dance as part of a rodeo fundraiser. Her pulse was starting to roar over what would happen when those boys got to her and Gabe. They'd make some clever rhyme about how they belonged together, and she couldn't bear to hear it.

Because such a huge part of her had come to believe that she and Gabe did belong together. She wanted to see a frame holding their names coupled. She wanted to belong here, with these people, far more than she wanted to go back to Tennessee.

But I can't, can I?

As laughter and applause rang out for Nick and Darcy, Avery headed for the door. She couldn't hear the next verse about the veterinarian, Wyatt, and his long-lost love, Carolina. Nor could she bear to see them leave off the last verse—or worse yet, speak up—about their unsuccessful attempts at matching her up with Gabe.

She fled out the back entrance to lean against the side of the barn and gulp down air. *I can't stay. I can't bear to leave. Lord, why ever did You bring me here?*

It would be complicated and messy to stay here. She'd have to deal with Cyrus's legacy. She'd have to watch the whole town shoulder this unfair burden. She'd have to restart her business. She'd have to ask Danny for permission, and she chafed at the idea of asking him for anything, sure he'd say no just to spite her. None of those things seemed to matter in light of her heart.

For her heart had already chosen to stay here, whether she physically left or not. Her heart had fixed itself to the man about to tear out his own heart up on that stage surrounded by symbols of everyone else's happiness.

She couldn't leave him to do that alone. Not after all he'd done, after all he meant to the girls. To her. She'd go inside and stand witness to his pain. She owed him that much.

Chapter Seventeen

If a silence could roar in a man's ears, it was roaring in Gabe's. There was no doubt now who had slid the note under Avery's windshield. He and Avery had been the final target of the boys ranch matchmakers.

The final, failing target. He'd pulled the frame from the little boy's hand, silencing the final stanza of their little matchmaking skit, unable to bear whatever they planned to say.

What did it say if even teenagers picked up on the attraction between himself and Avery? Was the whole town watching them fight the pull between them? The idea made Gabe feel beyond vulnerable, made him want to disappear as totally as Theodore had done. The final empty spot on the stage vines—the spot where a frame bearing "Gabe + Avery" should have been—loomed like a black hole.

And here he thought today was already as awful a day as a man could stand.

It didn't help that he'd barely slept. The pair of kisses he'd shared with Avery burned so bright in his memory that sleep had been impossible. She'd ended their second kiss as she had their first, with a sigh of his name that cut through him. Only that second sigh was one of regret, or lost possibility, or just plain "it can never be." If God's timing was supposed to be perfect, it wasn't feeling one bit perfect at the moment. Everything felt the exact opposite of perfect.

Gabe had seen Avery leave the barn. Every bone in his body wanted to follow her, to escape this awful, gaping moment, but he couldn't. He still had one final wound to endure.

Every eye in the room was still staring at him as he set the offending frame facedown on the podium. His stomach turned somersaults over the bad news that was his job to declare. It wouldn't come as a surprise—everyone in town already knew Theodore Linley hadn't been found. That was bad enough. But to have to say it out loud? To tell the boys they'd have to pack up and move back to the old location? There wasn't a more loathsome task in the world right now.

Avery's words to him that first night on the ranch rang in his ears: *I hate him. I know I'm not supposed to, but I do.* Right now, at this moment, he hated Culpepper for toying with those boys' futures. For thinking any good whatsoever could come from the Triple C becoming a strip mall when it could be—had already become—the ranch's new home.

He hated Culpepper for forcing him to hunt for his grandfather, only to come up empty at everyone's expense.

How could Culpepper hang lives in a stupid balance like he had? His own pain was bad enough, but boys would now have to be turned away, for crying out loud.

I hate you. Gabe had always tried to steer clear of words like *hate*, but such moderation evaded him now. Hate, regret and disappointment boiled in his gut.

Gabe cleared his throat, words escaping him. He'd rehearsed this dreaded speech over and over last night, but nothing suited this tragedy. Because that's what it was—a regrettable, preventable tragedy brought about by old men who cared nothing for the generation after them.

"Well," he began, not able to look any of the boys or house parents in the eye, "y'all know the task…handed to us." His heart wanted to yell and stomp and call it an underhanded scheme, but the only gift he could give this crowd right now was to avoid stooping to Cyrus's level. "And I'm proud of how our little community pulled together to rise to the challenge. Bea found Samuel Teller, and we're glad to have you here, Sam. Heath found his grandfather Edmund, and that's a blessing. Carolina's here standing in for her great uncle Morton, who I'm sorry to say has passed. And we'd have never met—" he paused for a moment, trying to drag the words up from the place in his chest that clutched at him in despair "—Avery and Debbie and Dinah without Darcy's help. And, you know, we almost pulled it off."

He felt the boys' falling expressions as if they physically pulled him down. Each frown was a lead weight pressing on his shoulders, each set of sad eyes a stab to his gut.

"As the new sign says, boys ranch has been here for seventy years, and it will go on for another seventy if I've anything to say about it."

Half-hearted cheers of "Sure will!" and other such encouragements did nothing to make the next words any easier.

"But it won't be here. Without Theodore Linley—my grandfather—the stipulations of Cyrus's will go unmet, and we'll have to move back to the old place and go on as we always have."

There. He'd said it. He'd admitted that his grandfather's continued disappearance was the failing link in this chain; he'd confessed that he hadn't found him. So far, the ground hadn't risen up and swallowed him whole, but he found himself wishing for it. Wishing he was anywhere but here, doing anything but this.

"You mean we really don't get to stay?" Diego asked.

Just when he thought it couldn't sting any worse. "No, son, we don't."

Desperation sent his eyes out over the gathering. He was beyond thankful when he saw that Avery had come back inside. Tears wet her cheeks. He locked his gaze onto her, needing to see her face while the world toppled around him. He'd remember last night's kisses as the only good thing to come out of this whole mess, and try to be thankful for that. He'd spent the day in hiding, sure he couldn't stomach the sight of her packing her things.

"I know that's a hard pill to swallow," he went on, working to keep his voice from wavering as Avery wiped fresh tears from her eyes. "But we'll get by. This isn't the first tough challenge you boys have had to face, and I know you'll find a way through. And we'll all help every single way we can." Right now, looking at the sea of disappointed faces, Gabe would put all of Five Rocks up on the block and buy the Triple C himself if it could be done.

But, of course, it couldn't. Mean ol' Cyrus had seen to that. *I hate you, old man.* The moment the words repeated in his mind, Gabe realized he couldn't rightly say if he was speaking to Cyrus or Theodore. *God have mercy on your mean old souls, the both of you.*

"I do have a bit of good news, though. The league has made it possible for all of you to go to the rodeo championships in Waco next weekend. All of you, up-front seats, as our gift to you."

There were some smiles, and genuine attempts at "isn't that nice?" from the adults, but it couldn't hope to put a dent in the sadness that filled the room. It was a fool's hope to think it ever would. How could one day—even one amazing day like they'd have at the championships—make up for losing the Triple C to a strip mall?

The room was excruciatingly quiet. Gabe had to fix this, to find some way out of this sad mess and save the evening. There had to be some words to let these kids know they were down but not out. Only he felt so down and out himself, everything he could think of felt hollow and pointless.

Gabe cleared his throat again, sending a silent "Help me!" plea to Heaven for something—anything—to redeem the moment.

"Can I say something?"

The whole room turned to Avery.

"I came here not sure I ever wanted anything to do with this place. I never knew much of Grandpa Cyrus, and what I've learned hasn't given me a lot of affection for the guy. I'm…well, I'm just plain sorry for what he's done to all of you. And if I had the power to change it, I'd do whatever it took. I just want you to know that."

Marlene, who was standing next to Avery and the girls, wiped a tear from her own face and reached out a hand to Avery's shoulder.

"But I want you to know something else, too," Avery went on. "Something Grandpa Cyrus did do, and something he can't take away from me no matter what scheme he pulls. And that's all of you."

She walked toward the stage as she continued talking. "I came here ready for everyone to be mean. To use me for whatever it was Grandpa Cyrus set me up to be. Only it didn't turn out that way. You all have treated me as nice as you ever could be. My girls and I both. And Gabe is right—the way you all pulled together for today is something special. Something even going back to the Silver Star won't take away from you."

I love that woman. He'd known it all along—since way back showing her the toolboxes—and he'd felt it in every corner of his soul last night. But right now, it was declaring itself to him in shouts that pounded inside his chest.

"But Gabe is wrong about something. If you knew how this man is beating himself up for failing you, for not finding a way to do what no one else in this room could do, either, your heart would break. I've never seen a man so relentlessly try for something. Not because he wanted it, but because you needed it."

She'd reached the stage now, and when Avery reached for his hand, Gabe could not stop himself from taking it for all the world.

"And that's no failure," she said, smiling at him even as tears fell across her cheeks. "That's a man of honor, a man to be proud of." She hesitated just a moment, her face turning the most extraordinary shade of pink. "That's a man to love. Don't you dare let this man feel a failure for how hard he's tried on your behalf. Cyrus has taken a lot, but he doesn't get to take this from me. He brought me here, to you," she said, looking straight at Gabe, and he felt his heart gallop toward her. "And to all of you," she said to the crowd. "I've made a decision. I'd like to stay in Haven. I hope I can make my home here, if I can work it out, if you'll have me." She directed those last words at Gabe.

He wasn't a man for grand gestures. He wasn't much for speeches or public declarations. But there was only one response to a speech like that, and it didn't matter if there were one hundred or one thousand people watching. Gabe pulled Avery to him and kissed her for the true, extraordinary blessing she was. For taking the darkest moment of his life and filling it with light.

And love.

And tiny pinkness, for no sooner had he kissed her soundly than he felt the clamp of little-girl arms around his legs, squeezing him tight and yelling, "Hooray for Mr. Boots!"

She'd chosen Gabe, but then again, she hadn't. Avery stood there, watching Gabe tear his heart open in front of all those people who loved and respected him, and it was as if some irresistible force drew her to say what she did, despite all the obstacles still in her way. She had to walk toward him with her hand out. With her heart out, in defense and admiration and—yes—love for him.

Because she loved him, and she had to believe that love still conquered all.

It had begun to dawn on her late last night, while she sat in her bed trying to catalog all the reasons why it was safest to go back to Tennessee and put Haven behind her. Nothing Cyrus could leave her now would change anything—be it ten cabins, ten dollars or a fortune. Cyrus's manipulations were just an act taken by someone gone from her life. Standing outside just now, leaning against the barn, none of that mattered. Everything in the past didn't matter.

What mattered were the people in her life now, the man and the love this crazy situation had dropped in her lap. That was the true inheritance, the blessing that made everything else possible. The truth was that nothing of real value was waiting for her back in Tennessee; it all was here in Haven. In this loving community and in the love of a man who cared so much for her welfare that he was ready to deny herself that love. If God had brought her this far, couldn't she count on Him to tear down the obstacles that remained? Couldn't God give her the words to ask and receive Danny's consent to move to this place that now held the key to her happiness?

Given all that, was it really any surprise that she found herself kissing Gabe Everett in front of God and everybody in Haven, Texas? When the girls came up and wrapped her and Gabe in the wonderful circle of their arms, the last nigglings of doubt had vanished. Whatever lay in front of them because of Cyrus's crazy scheme, Haven would get through it. And she'd be there to help.

Avery didn't even hear the applause at first. She was lost in the wonder of Gabe's arms, in the exquisite perfectness of her love for him. They both realized the rather public nature of the display at the same time, pulling only a tiny bit from each other and laughing even as the girls giggled and jumped at their feet.

She could tell Gabe was grasping for what to say, but really, what was there to be said?

"I tried so hard not to fall for you," he finally whispered. "But it couldn't be helped."

Not the most romantic words ever to declare love, but to Avery, they were perfect, because they came from Gabe.

"I want to stay for you," she whispered back. "We all want to stay for you."

Evidently, the girls hadn't quite caught on to that until just now. "We can stay?" They began to chant, jumping up and down. "Mama says we're staying!"

"I sure hope so, sweetheart. I want to stay with Mr. Boots, don't you?"

Their smiles were all the answer she needed.

Suddenly, Jethro and Marlene were beside them,

boasting mile-wide smiles themselves. Marlene grabbed the frame from the podium and handed it to Dinah, who rushed to hang it in its place on the stage vines. "We've been waiting for you two kids to figure this out," Jethro said with a tender chuckle. "You sure waited until the very last moment." He grinned at Avery. "Although I give ya points for drama. That was the sweetest speech I ever heard, young lady. Clearly, you don't take after the likes of your grandfather."

"I'm sorry about all that, really I am," Avery said. "I meant what I said. If there was any way I could change it, I'd do it. It wouldn't matter what it was, I'd do it."

"That's why I will," said a voice from the crowd, and the gathering parted to see Harley hobbling up toward the stage.

"Harley," Gabe said, helping the poor man step up onto the stage. "There isn't anything any of us can do."

Harold Haverman at least had the decency to look regretful when he agreed, "Not a thing. Cyrus's terms were explicit."

Harley coughed. "That's where you're wrong." He gestured toward the microphone, and Gabe stood back, but not before casting a curious glance toward Avery. She shrugged, having no more idea than Gabe did what Harley was up to.

"Hi, everyone. I'm Harley Jones, y'all know that."

As revelations go, that wasn't much of a start. A curious silence filled the room.

"Y'all been looking for Theodore Linley. And now all kinds of sadness is happening because he couldn't be found. And I was content to leave it that way, which is a stain on my part, because I've known all along where Theo was."

"Harley?" Gabe sputtered. Avery felt him stiffen beside her—and rightly so. To have gone through all he did when the solution was known?

Harley held up his hand to silence whatever Gabe was going to say. The old man gripped the podium, and Avery noticed his hands were shaking. What on earth was going on?

"Truth was, I thought it cost too much to tell you. Only today it's pretty clear it'll cost me much more to keep my mouth shut. The fact of the matter is that y'all have found Theodore Linley, and he's in this room. On account of...well, he's me."

The room buzzed with shock and disbelief. But as Avery stood looking at the two men, the resemblance jumped out at her. The jawline, the set of the eyebrows, the shape of their hands—he was kin to Gabe. And here she thought life in Haven couldn't get any more surprising.

"I ain't been a respectable man. I done things I can't be proud of, left when I shouldn't have and, well, I expect you know most of that on account of your lookin'. Always seemed to me that Gabe was better off without me. Only I couldn't stay totally away, so I signed on as a hand to my girl's new husband so's I could keep an eye on things—on my grandson—after she died."

He turned to look at Gabe. His eyes held such pain and regret that Avery nearly gasped. She felt Gabe tighten his hand on her and gave a silent prayer of thanks that she could stand beside him at a bombshell of a moment like this.

"It was a coward's way out, but then again, that's what I am. I figured Theo Linley was no good to anybody, especially you. And then all this business happened, and it got harder to keep my mouth shut. I'd have to fess up to all kinds of things, and I didn't think I could do it."

Gabe started to say something, but Harley—or was that now Theo?—held up his hand again.

"Let me finish, son. I got a lot of silence to make up for."

Son. The word hit Avery like a wall, and she could only imagine what it did to Gabe. It was a wonder the man was still upright.

"I made up my mind to stay away from today, to just let it all lie quiet and let Cyrus win whatever battle he'd claimed for himself." Theo coughed, hard this time, and shifted his weight. Gabe was not the only man baring his soul today at great cost, Avery thought.

"Only I couldn't. The ranch had been there for Gabe when I was too much of a mess to be there for him. I came here thinking I'd fess up, then I lost my nerve."

Avery remembered that "Harley" had left the party in the middle of it—she'd just figured he was tired and went home. She hadn't seen him come back in.

Theo's eyes returned to Gabe. "And I watched you come up here, strong and steady, and own up to bad news. Like a man ought to. Like the man I couldn't be."

The old man turned his eyes to Avery, and the lump in Avery's throat grew ten sizes. There was such a pained smile in the man's eyes she felt her own eyes well up with tears. "Then you came up here, sayin' what you said, and I realized I was even prouder than you were of Gabe. Of who he is, and the people who love him. Of you saying how you'd do whatever you could do to save the boys ranch, no matter what it cost. And here I was sitting on the only thing that could save it. So maybe, just this once, I figured I could step up and be half the man my grandson is today."

"You're Theo Linley." Gabe's voice was thick with

emotion. Stunned, but with shock, not hate. "You're my grandfather."

"I am. And I'm beyond sorry for not telling you before this. I'll never be able to make that up to you, I know."

"By gum, Theo, it is you," Sam Teller shouted from his chair on the far side of the room. "I been trying to figure out why you looked familiar."

"You're my grandfather," Gabe repeated as if he couldn't get his mind around the idea. Of all the crazy things to happen since Avery came to Haven, this one topped the list.

"So now you found Theo Linley. You've saved the Triple C for the boys." Theo offered a small grin. "And got the girl, to boot. Not a bad day's work." He shrugged. "I'll go now and leave all y'all to celebratin'."

"You will not," Gabe said, walking toward the old man. After so many years of being denied their relationship, Avery wasn't sure what Gabe would say next.

Tears slid down her cheeks and Gabe grasped the old man's arm. "My grandfather isn't going to leave this party. Because I didn't save the ranch, Theo." Gabe choked on the name, and for the first time Avery heard him utter it with awe, not frustration. "You did." With that Gabe pulled Theo into a hug, sending the crowd bursting into applause.

"Hey," called Johnny, "that means we get to stay, right?"

"That it does," Harold Haverman announced.

"I can hardly believe it," Bea Brewster shouted as she hugged anyone within arm's reach. "Who'd have thought?"

Gabe was caught up in the moment with his grandfather, and Avery was glad for it, but then in a moment she found herself surrounded with well-wishers, too.

"I'm so happy for you," Josie said as she held baby Joy. "For both of you. For all five of you!"

It was true. Out of nowhere, out of strife and sorrow and scheming, God had crafted this amazing little family for her. It was a wonder. It was wonderful. Avery couldn't remember when she'd ever felt so happy.

"So this will be our new home, Mama?" Dinah asked.

"If Daddy says it's okay. Is that okay with you?" Avery brushed back her daughter's hair.

"Yup, yup, yup!" Dinah's head bobbed up and down gleefully with each word.

"You, too?" Avery asked Debbie.

"Twice as many *yup*s!" Debbie proclaimed. "Even my broke arm says *yup*."

"Now there's an endorsement if ever I heard one." Macy Swanson came up, arm in arm with Tanner Barstow. "Tanner's always said Gabe couldn't hold out his bachelor status too much longer with all this matchmaking going on."

"Oh," said Gabe as he came back to Avery's side, "they tried on us. Didn't realize it takes no arm twisting to coax me to Lila's for pie." He took Avery's hand. "Some things a man just has to figure out on his own."

Avery looked up at him and felt her heart glow. *I love him, Lord. And You knew that was coming all along. How can I doubt You'll work the rest out?*

Chapter Eighteen

Gabe smiled down at Avery. He could ponder the last thirty minutes for thirty years and still not grasp everything that had happened. Today was supposed to be one of the worst days of his life, and wasn't it just like God to turn the whole thing on its ear in ways he never imagined?

A thought struck him. "Do you think Cyrus knew what he was really doing?"

Harold Haverman gave a doubtful smirk. "Let's just say I'm of a mind that what Cyrus meant for orneriness, God meant for good."

Gabe looked at Harley... *Theo*—it'd take a while before that adjustment sunk in. His grandfather was talking in animated tones with Samuel Teller and Edmund Grayson. His *grandfather*. Right under his nose all these years. Suddenly, the powerful connection he'd always felt with Harley Jones made sense. Theo may have believed he could never be there for Gabe, but Harley had been there. In a hundred ways over the years. There was so much surprise and astonishment in his heart—especially now with Avery—that there wasn't any room for judgment or resentment. Only love, and loads of it.

Gabe pulled Avery to his side. "I love you," he whispered into her ear despite the many people surrounding them. "Have I said that yet?"

She smiled up at him with glistening, tear-filled eyes. "Not in words."

"I love you," he repeated, finding a startling delight in uttering them. "In words, this time."

"And swings, and tea parties, and doctor visits, and tumble-down cabins…and a few rather persuasive kisses." Her cheeks turned the most distracting shade of pink. "But the words are nice, too."

"Speaking of tumble-down cabins," Haverman said. Gabe tried not to begrudge the attorney for horning in on his happy moment. "Miss Avery, I believe we have some unfinished business."

"The rest of Cyrus's bequest," Gabe added. In all of the drama, he'd half forgotten that the other portion of Cyrus's will for Avery would be revealed if she stayed until today.

Harold produced an envelope from his jacket pocket. "I've no idea what's in here, miss. Don't think I've been holding out on you." He handed the envelope to Avery, who took it with an expression that seemed half curiosity, half apprehension. Gabe didn't blame her one bit. Based on Cyrus, and today, Gabe was ready to think just about anything could happen.

Avery opened the envelope and unfolded the single sheet of paper. Gabe longed to read over her shoulder, but stood silently in front of her. After a moment, however, neither man could show much more patience, and Harold said, "Well?"

"He's made me beneficiary of a three-hundred-thousand-dollar life insurance policy in addition to the cabin. 'Enough to make a home and a life in Haven if you choose,' he says." She also shook the envelope to let a key slide out. "And this is to a safe-deposit box that's filled with family photos and my grandmother's jewelry."

She looked up at Gabe, blinking away tears. "I didn't know any of that existed. I thought it all was lost. Daddy never talked about any of it." She turned the key over in her palm. "When Rhetta gave me that one photo, it made me so lonesome for more—for any bits of my family. And now I have a whole bunch of them."

"And a nice little sum to set you up comfortably," Harold added. "I know he could be a stubborn old goat, but I like to think Cyrus wanted to do good by you in the end." Harold stared out at the party, still in full swing. "Look at them. Theodore, Samuel, Edmund, the boys in their new home, you two—could you ever think Cyrus could do so much good while putting us through so much trouble?"

Gabe put his arm around Avery. "He always did have a talent for stirring things up."

"I suppose he's having a good laugh right about now," Avery said. Gabe reveled in the way her arm slipped about his waist. She felt so perfect settled under his arm—it made him wonder how he hadn't noticed how empty his arms were before they held this marvelous woman.

"I can't believe I'm saying this, but thank God for Cyrus Culpepper." True enough, Gabe did feel an honest sense of gratitude to God for what Cyrus's crazy scheme had brought him. One look into Avery's eyes told him she felt the same way.

Suddenly, a burst of cheers went up in the far corner of the room. Harold, Avery and Gabe all looked at each other. "What now?" Harold asked, echoing what Gabe was thinking.

Seconds later Marlene came up with a huge smile.

"Well, that molasses of a man finally did what he oughta," she declared.

"Meaning?" Gabe asked.

"Pastor Andrew finally found his nerve and popped the question to Katie Ellis. Just now in front of God and everybody."

Avery nodded her head toward the hugs and laughter bursting out of that corner of the room. "And she said yes?"

Marlene chuckled. "Honey, I don't even think she let him finish the question."

Gabe watched as several men clasped the pastor on the back. "Some days I think that reverend was the last person in town to realize how sweet Katie was on him."

Marlene gave Gabe a look. "Some men just take their time wising up to things, don't they?"

A week later, Avery sat nestled against Gabe on the porch staring up at the brilliant collection of Texas spring stars. This had become their favorite time of day, when the house was quiet and the girls were tucked away in bed. "Well, that's the last call. I've thanked them all for praying while I talked to Danny."

Gabe exhaled in relief. "With that many prayer warriors lined up, he didn't stand any hope of saying no to your request."

"It didn't take much convincing, actually. When I told him how happy I'd become here, how the girls loved it, he said yes. Almost right away. I treated him like Cyrus, Gabe. I turned him into some kind of monster based on how abandoned I felt. But he isn't. He's far from perfect, but he wants what's best for the girls." She looked at Gabe. "And that's you."

His eyes glowed. "I love those girls. I love their mama

even more." He kissed her again, long and slow and full of wonder. The last of the obstacles had been removed, and the world was settling down into a perfect future for her and the girls.

"I've been thinking about what to do with the money Grandpa Cyrus left me."

Gabe's arm tightened around her. "Have you, now?"

"Of course, I'll need some of it to restart my decorating business down here. But I've been thinking about how different my life would have been if I'd have had a place like the ranch. So many boys' lives have been changed. Why not girls' lives? The cabin isn't big enough, but the land around it is. Maybe there's just enough to start renovating and expanding that old place."

Gabe's gaze fell out over the land in the direction of the boys ranch. "I think it's a great idea. I expect the league would donate toward the cause in a heartbeat." He planted a tender kiss on her forehead. "The president is rather fond of you, you know."

"Well, yes, there's that. And I rather like the idea of Cyrus doing even more good than he planned."

He carefully took both her hands in his as he slowly asked, "But if you give away the property for a girls ranch, where will you live?"

She turned to look at him. She'd been trying to find a way to say this for a week now, but couldn't work out how or when. "There's only one place in Haven I want to call home." She took a deep breath. "So you'd better hurry up, cowboy."

Gabe's eyes took on a playful gleam. He had clearly caught her meaning, but pasted a puzzled look on his face and asked, "Hurry up and what?"

She sat up and yanked on the hands he was holding. "You molasses of a man. Am I gonna have to call over a crowd of mystery matchmakers from the ranch to explain it for you?"

"Well, I don't know. What do I need with a bunch of meddling boys when I've got this?" With that, Avery watched Gabe slip one of his hands from hers and reach down under the wicker couch. His hand came back up with a small black box.

Avery's heart bubbled up like a fountain at the sight of the glistening ring inside. It sparkled like the starlight she loved so much in the sky above Five Rocks.

Gabe's eyes grew intense. "I know it's quick, but I'm done waiting. I'd have done it even sooner but I knew you needed word from Danny. And now we've got that, and I don't ever want you to leave Five Rocks. Not for a day. So I figured I better make an honest woman out of you fast as I can."

"Gabe." It felt so splendid to sigh his name. Yes, it was quick, but even the girls had sensed how things had settled down in perfect places. Gabe was an honorable man. If they waited, he would insist they move off Five Rocks, and she knew what he knew: no one wanted that. If putting plans in place to become a family—the family they had in many ways already become—meant moving quickly, then Avery felt they couldn't move quickly enough. The girls deserved to stay where they were for the same reason she did: they loved it here.

All of this was rushing through her heart so fast that Avery didn't realize Gabe was staring at her. "Speaking of slow as molasses…" he said, raising one playful eyebrow.

She'd already said yes so many times in her heart it had escaped her she hadn't voiced the words. "It's yes! It was yes before you ever asked." She kissed him soundly, just to underscore her point.

When they pulled apart, breathless with happiness, Avery thought of something. "How shall we tell the girls?"

Gabe actually blushed a bit—something so endearing Avery thought her heart might actually burst. "Well," he said, reaching into his shirt pocket, "I've been thinking on that." He produced a little silk bag. "I figure I ought to ask them, too. And when I saw these in town, I knew just how."

He opened Avery's hand and spilled the contents of the little bag into her palm. Two silver rings tumbled out with a jingle—tiny but real silver and inlaid with sparkly mother-of-pearl.

In the shape of cowboy boots. "How else would Mr. Boots ask for their hand…hands?"

"Oh, Gabe, they'll just die of happiness." She slid her arms around his neck. "I think I already have. If I didn't want you all to myself, I might just go and wake them up right now."

Gabe's eyes burned with the same glow that filled her heart. "It can wait. Right now, I just want to kiss my wife. My future wife." And he did.

"How does tomorrow sound?" he asked, his voice so breathless she tingled all the way to the tips of her toes.

"Too soon," she laughed into his chest.

"Can't blame a man for trying."

Avery held up her hand, watching the diamond sparkle in the moonlight. "Now that I think about it, I could be persuaded to consider next week."

He grinned. "I've been told I'm very persuasive."

"I've been thanking God twelve times a day you persuaded me to bring the girls out to Five Rocks. For all of it. I know all this craziness seemed chaotic and unfair along the way, but I can see it all leading to this now. To us, together. And I'm glad. I never thought I'd say it, but I'm glad."

Gabe pulled her back against his chest and they settled in together to stare up at the brilliant sky of stars. "I believe I am the happiest man in Haven, Texas. Maybe the whole world." She felt his chin settle against the top of her head. "It is an amazing thing, my loving you. I hope it never stops startling me every time I think it."

"Why Gabriel Everett, what a downright romantic thing to say."

She could hear the smile in his tone. "A tidal wave of tiny pinkness will do that to a man."

* * * * *

CLAIMING HER COWBOY

Tina Radcliffe

This first book in the Big Heart Ranch series is dedicated to John Croyle and the staff and children of Big Oak Ranch. Big Oak Ranch is a Christian home located in Alabama for children needing a chance.

"That they might be called trees of righteousness, the planting of the Lord, that he might be glorified."
—*Isaiah* 61:3

A great deal of thanks goes to my wonderful agent, Jessica Alvarez, for partnering with me on this exciting new series. Thank you, as well, to my editor, Giselle Regus, for her ideas, which ultimately led me to Big Heart Ranch.

What time I am afraid, I will trust in thee.
—*Psalm* 56:3

Chapter One

If Lucy Maxwell had learned one thing, it was that when life appeared to be going smoothly, it was time to listen closely for the other boot to drop.

Because it always did.

The attorney who stood at the head of the conference table, in his finely tailored suit, with his impossibly thick black hair and deep charcoal eyes, was definitely sigh-worthy. He even had a slight dimple when he smiled. Which he didn't do very often. Except for his off-center nose, with the scar at the bridge, he was perfect. It was a good thing she was not taken to sighing over near-perfect men with dimples.

The man was unfamiliar to her. After working closely with the Brisbane Foundation for several years, she thought she knew everyone. But not him. She would have definitely remembered Jackson Harris.

He began to speak. The icy disdain that laced his voice as he reviewed the last twelve months of charitable funding to Big Heart Ranch obliterated any fanciful thoughts in Lucy's head. Instead, she blinked to attention and sat up straight, adjusting her sundress and blowing her thick fringe of bangs from her eyes.

"After a lengthy consultation with the foundation accountants, I recommend a significant reduction in funding to Big Heart Ranch for the upcoming fiscal year," he concluded.

Lucy gasped at the attorney's words. The sound was loud enough to cause the board members seated at the enormous conference table to turn and stare. She fanned her damp skin with the meeting agenda. It seemed that the cool air had been sucked from the room, leaving it as sweltering as the Oklahoma summer outside the conference room windows.

Reaching for her water glass, Lucy took a long drink. If ever there was a need for divine intervention, it would be now. Big Heart Ranch's own budget for the next year could not be finalized until the foundation's donation had been secured.

She should have suspected something was up when her presence was requested at this meeting. Usually, the ranch accountant met with the Brisbane Foundation accountant. And it was generally a simple transaction. Not this time. This time the director of the ranch was invited to the meeting. Lucy took her director responsibilities seriously and had arrived early and eager.

The start of the meeting seemed a lifetime ago. Now her hands trembled as she set the glass back down. Lucy clasped her fingers together tightly in her lap and turned to the other end of the table, where the chief executive officer of the Brisbane Foundation sat.

"Mrs. Brisbane?" Lucy prompted.

Meredith Brisbane had paled beneath her silver coif. She cleared her throat and touched the pearls at her neck, as if to reassure herself she was still breathing.

"Lucy dear, I can assure you this is as much a surprise to me as it is to you. Though my nephew is newly appointed to the foundation, I am certain he has our best interests at heart."

Nephew? How had she missed that significant bit of information?

"However, through no fault of his own," Meredith added, "Jackson has a limited understanding of why we partner with your organization. I take full responsibility for this omission. Lucy, perhaps you could enlighten him on how funding to the ranch is utilized."

"Yes. Yes." Lucy nodded, while her mind raced. "I'm happy to."

After all, Big Heart Ranch *was* Lucy, and her brother, Travis, and her sister, Emma. They'd single-handedly built the Timber, Oklahoma, local charity for orphaned, abandoned and neglected children.

Lucy paused, her confidence waning. She could provide the smug attorney with numbers until the ranch cows came home. Like the fact that the average cost of raising a child was well over two hundred thousand dollars, and that the ranch was raising sixty children. However, something told her that Jackson Harris would not be impressed with numbers. What *would* get through to this man?

She blinked. Like the kick of a stubborn mare, out of nowhere, inspiration struck. Lucy smiled and turned to face him.

"Spreadsheets and PowerPoint presentations can't possibly show you the true heart of our ranch, Mr. Harris. The best way to understand the big picture is to come to the ranch. Spend time with us. I'd love to show you our ministry in action." She paused. "Of course, I'm happy to provide you complete access to our financials, as well. You have an open door to anything you need from us."

It was Jackson Harris's turn to show surprise. He

opened his mouth, but before he could respond, his aunt chimed in.

"Why, Lucy, that's a splendid idea. I couldn't agree more. He needs to see the scope of the ranch's reach."

Jackson's gaze moved from his aunt and then back to Lucy. He narrowed his eyes. "What exactly did you have in mind?" The words were measured and precise.

Lucy scrambled for a plan. "Summer," she burst out.

"Summer?" The attorney tugged at the collar of his dress shirt.

"Yes. We're about to start our summer program at the ranch. It's our busiest and most ambitious undertaking of the year. Not only do we work with our own sixty children, but we invite the children from the State of Oklahoma orphanage in Pawhuska to the ranch for vacation Bible study at rotating intervals."

He adjusted his silk tie and said nothing.

Lucy continued. "We're about to start our annual series of old-fashioned trail rides and campouts." She flashed him what she hoped was a confident smile. "The summer events are capped off in August, with a black-tie fundraising gala hosted by your aunt."

Had she imagined his jaw tightening as he reached for his water? The board members seated at the table glanced away and carefully examined the paperwork in front of them. An awkward silence stretched for moments until a melodic ring filled the large room. All hands shuffled and reached for cell phones. Meredith shot Lucy an apologetic smile as she retrieved her own phone.

"I'm so sorry. I must take this." Phone in one hand, cane in the other, Meredith stood and wobbled precariously. As she reached out for the table ledge, her cane fell to the thickly carpeted floor with a soft thud.

Lucy jumped up in time to grasp Meredith's forearm and gently steady the benefactress.

Jackson was around the table and at his aunt's side in seconds. "Are you okay, Aunt Meri?" he asked. Genuine concern laced his voice—the first sign of humanity Lucy had seen in the man.

"Oh, my. Sorry to give you two a fright." Meredith glanced from Lucy to her nephew and frowned. "An inner ear issue, the doctor tells me. Sometimes I'm a bit off balance. This getting-old stuff is not for sissies."

"How are you feeling now?" Lucy asked.

"I'm fine. Thank you, dear. I simply need to remember not to stand quite so fast."

Lucy nodded as she picked up the ebony cane and handed it to Meredith.

Head held high, Meredith's measured steps were nothing short of regal as she moved across the carpet. The room remained silent until the door closed behind her.

Harris again turned to Lucy. The man's unflinching gaze was anything but warm and fuzzy. The dark brows were drawn into a serious frown.

Lucy glanced around the room. Had she missed something here? Why was he so irritated?

"Visiting the ranch is out of the question, Ms...." He faltered for a moment. Clearly, he'd forgotten her name.

"Maxwell. Lucy Maxwell."

"Ms. Maxwell, I can't—won't—leave my aunt." Harris gathered up his papers and stood without sparing another glance in her direction.

Lucy folded her hands and willed herself not to panic. The other boot had officially dropped.

"Jackson? Is Lucy gone?" Meredith asked from the doorway of the great room.

Jack turned from the tall window that overlooked the front lawn and circular drive. "If she drives a beat-up mustard-colored Honda, then yes, Aunt Meri, she's gone."

Lucy Maxwell. He shook his head. He'd never met anyone like her before. A sunflower. That was exactly what she reminded him of, with that cap of dark hair and round chocolate-brown eyes, along with a smattering of freckles on her golden face. A petite woman, she wore a pale yellow dress along with red hand-tooled cowboy boots. When she walked, the dress fluttered around her calves, capturing his attention, whether he liked it or not. And he did not. Con artists came in pretty packages too, he reminded himself. He'd been taken in once before, and even put a ring on her finger. Never again.

"When will you start at the ranch?" Meredith asked.

"Hmm?" He blinked and met her gaze.

"What are you thinking about?" His aunt smiled. "Lucy, perhaps?"

"What? No." He gave his aunt his full attention. "I'm sorry. What did you say?"

"I asked when you will be heading to Big Heart Ranch."

He paused for a moment at the question, planning his strategy. "I'm not leaving you to spend time observing a ranch."

"Oh?" She smiled. "Then you're approving the original donation amount?"

Jack crossed the room and put an arm around his aunt's thin shoulders. "Aunt Meri, you know you're my favorite aunt."

She chuckled. "I'm your only aunt."

He grinned. "True. And while you are as generous as you are kind, you can't give away the foundation money to every shyster that comes along."

Meredith gasped. Her sharp blue eyes blazed, taking

him back to his childhood days of misbehaving and facing his aunt's wrath. She had never hesitated to serve up well-deserved punishment for his crimes. Jack took a step back when she straightened to her full five-foot-nothing height.

"Lucy Maxwell is not a shyster!"

"What do you really know about the woman, Aunt Meri?"

"What I know is that the bulk of the foundation's income is from mineral and oil rights. My husband inherited those rights from his great-great-grandfather, who was one-half Osage Indian. The foundation was set up to ensure that the funds were invested locally." She pinned her gaze on her nephew. "Big Heart Ranch is as local as it gets, and they are an investment in this community's future."

He wasn't going to point out that she hadn't answered his question. Instead, he tried another tactic.

"You've proposed nearly doubling the donation to this ranch. Why?"

His aunt narrowed her eyes and exhaled sharply. "Have you been talking to your father?"

"What makes you say that?"

"He's made it quite clear that he believes I'm not fit to manage the foundation. Oh, he thinks he's being subtle, sending you out here as in-house counsel, but I know what he's up to."

"Aunt Meri, Dad's concerned about your health, that's all."

She offered a harrumph at his words. "I'll tell you what I told him, Jackson. Vertigo does not equal diminished mental capacity."

"What about the chemo?"

"My treatments are completed and I've been given a

clean bill of health by my physicians. The cancer is in remission. Shall we have my oncologist contact your father?"

"Aunt Meri, please don't get upset. The bottom line is I'm here as the foundation's attorney. Not to inspect a ranch in Timber."

"I don't see why you can't do both. They have internet and telephones at the ranch, so you'll be able to stay in touch. My assistant has all the numbers. Besides, while the ranch is on the outskirts of Timber, you're still only twenty minutes away."

"Twenty minutes is forever if you need me."

She paused and gave him a hard, assessing glance. "What are you really doing in Oklahoma, Jackson? You've been in New York since forever. I have a hard time believing your father didn't pressure you to come out here."

"Not at all. Dad would never do that."

"Oh, please. Your father could talk a peacock out of his feathers."

He laughed. She was right, he'd give her that. Except the truth was more complicated. His father did want him to check on his aunt. It was a coincidence that Jack desperately needed a change of scenery.

"He told me the position was open, and you were vetting candidates. Perhaps it was… What's that saying of yours? A God thing."

Her expression said she didn't believe him for a second. "You made it clear once you left for college that you prefer the big-city skyscrapers over the red clay of Oklahoma. You've been gone a long time. What happened to make you quit your job and take on the foundation position?"

"Let's just say that I'm reevaluating my options."

"In my day, a man like you would have been considered a catch. Why haven't you settled down, Jackson?"

"Aunt Meri, I'm not much of a family man."

"What does your fiancée say about that? Isn't she still one of your options?"

"That's over."

She slowly shook her head and glanced past him, out the window. "I'm so sorry to hear that. What happened?"

"Let's just say she was more interested in my wallet than me."

"Ahh, so that's why you're being so hard on Lucy."

"My personal life has nothing to do with Big Heart Ranch."

"No?" She cocked her head.

Silence settled between them. "What's going on?" his aunt finally said. "You've been unhappy for some time. I could tell from your phone calls."

He met his aunt's perceptive gaze. Was he unhappy? Or simply disenchanted and searching for something real in his life?

She frowned. "You always wanted to make a difference, Jackson. What changed?"

"Make a difference? Did I say that?" He scoffed. "If I did, then you're correct. That was a long time ago. What's changed is that I'm not an idealistic attorney anymore."

"I think maybe deep inside you are." She placed her hand on his arm. "Don't get me wrong, I'm glad to have you here, but as far as Lucy Maxwell and Big Heart Ranch are concerned, you couldn't be more off base. I still contend that you can't make a decision to cut off their funding without investigating the situation."

"Off base? I did my research. That ranch is a money pit."

She offered a sound of disgust. "That doesn't mean they're mismanaging the funds. I don't believe for a minute that anything shady is going on at that ranch, and I challenge you to find one bit of evidence to support your claim."

Meredith gripped her cane and walked to the wall of family portraits. Her hand trailed the ornate, gilded edges of the frames. A huge portrait of Jack's grandfather hung next to a smaller one of her husband, followed by another of Jack's father. She stopped at a painting of Jack with his twin brother, Daniel. They were nine years old, mirror images, with matching grins and dark curls. There, however, the similarities ended. Daniel was charming, outgoing and impulsive, while Jack was shy, hesitant and introverted.

A wave of sadness and guilt slammed into him as he stared at the painting. Twenty-five years had passed, yet nothing would ever be the same. Daniel was gone and it was his fault. He'd been minutes behind his brother that day and hadn't been able to save him.

"I miss Daniel," Meredith murmured with a soft sigh. He was surprised when she turned and wrapped her arms around him in a loving hug.

The scent of his aunt's lavender perfume carried him back years. "I miss him, too, Aunt Meri," he whispered.

His father's words from when Jack left New York raced through his thoughts. *When we lost your brother and your mother left, your aunt was there for both of us. This is an opportunity for you to be there for her. She won't ask, but Meri needs help.*

He swallowed hard as he stared at his brother's smiling face. "I'll go to the ranch, Aunt Meredith."

Jack grimaced when he realized that the words had actually slipped from his lips. When his aunt's face lit up, he knew that it was much too late to take them back.

"Oh, Jackson, I knew I could count on you to do the right thing. I'll call Lucy immediately."

The right thing.

For a moment, he'd let his guard down and sentiment had strong-armed him. Jack took a deep breath. He suspected his orderly life was about to be blown wide-open, and he placed the blame squarely at the feet of Little Lucy Sunshine, the director of Big Heart Ranch.

Chapter Two

"I need a favor." Lucy stood in the doorway of the children's therapist and child care director of the Big Heart Ranch office. It belonged to her sister, Emma.

"Good morning to you," Emma said. She tidied the bookshelf in her already immaculate office and turned to Lucy. "What sort of favor?"

"Can you handle my calls for a couple of hours? I have to start a new volunteer."

"Sure. Only because then I can remind you that you need to hire an assistant."

"Not going to happen."

Lucy glanced at a platter of chocolate muffins artfully arranged on a table. "You made muffins? Like you don't have enough to do?" She nodded toward the portable cribs set up in the back of the huge room. Inside, her twelve-month-old twin nieces slumbered, thumbs in mouth and bottoms in the air.

Emma shrugged. "So tell me what happened at the Brisbane Foundation yesterday."

Lucy grabbed a muffin and peeled back the paper. "Meredith said to tell you hello."

"Was that before or after she handed you a sizable donation check?"

"Things didn't exactly work out that way."

"What do you mean?"

"Meredith has a new attorney who hasn't approved the funding. I'm sure everything will be taken care of soon."

Emma sank into a chair and nervously fingered her braid. "Lucy, we need to finalize our budget. I don't understand what the holdup is. She sent us preliminary numbers weeks ago."

Lucy met her sister's worried gaze. "The attorney is doing things differently."

"Is Travis aware?" Emma asked quietly.

"Yes. But you know Travis. All he cares about is the cows."

Emma glanced at the calendar and cringed. "This puts everything on hold."

"I know. Which brings me to the other news." Lucy dusted off her hands. "Leo quit."

"What? Why? He's our best ranch hand."

"He was offered more money at a ranch in Driscoll. I simply can't match the offer."

"So we'll hire someone else."

"I'm not going to hire anyone until the budget situation is resolved. In fact, I may have to lay off staff if we don't get the Brisbane Foundation backing by the end of summer." She met Emma's gaze. "All expenditures outside of the day-to-day ranch maintenance are on hold."

"What about the gala? I've already placed deposits for caterers, waitstaff and flowers. Not to mention the entertainment. Meredith always funds the gala."

"The gala is low on my worry list. Let's try to focus on what's really important. The kids."

Emma nodded.

"The Lord has been the financial backing for Big Heart Ranch since day one," she said. "This is His ranch. These are His children. He will continue to provide more than we can ask or imagine. Right?"

"Right," Emma said. "I couldn't agree more."

Lucy took a bite of the muffin and glanced toward the parking lot.

"Was there something else?"

"Yes."

Travis stuck his head in the door. "That new volunteer is here, asking for you, Lucy." He offered her a conspiratorial wink.

"Thanks, Travis. I'll be right out."

"What was that all about?" Emma asked. "And who's this new volunteer?"

"Jackson Harris."

"Who is Jackson Harris?"

"Meredith's nephew and her new attorney."

"What?"

"Perfect timing, isn't it? He'll replace Leo."

"No one can replace Leo. He did the work of three ranch hands." Emma stood and walked to the window.

"All the same, we should be grateful to have the help for the summer."

"I'm confused. Why would Meredith's nephew agree to volunteer on the ranch when it sounds like he's opposed to giving us the funding?"

"His aunt is very persuasive." She turned to Emma. "No one is to know that he's from the Brisbane Foundation."

"Why does Travis know?"

"He was here last night when the call came through from Meredith."

"Why the secrecy?"

"Mr. Harris is vetting us. I want his experience here to

be positive. He needs to know we have nothing to hide. It's the only chance we have that he'll change his mind."

"Is that him?" Emma asked.

Lucy peeked over her sister's shoulder at the tall attorney whose back was to them as he talked to Travis.

"Yes. That's Jackson Harris."

Emma chuckled. "Look at him, all shiny and new in his designer jeans, Italian leather shoes and that dry-cleaner-starched shirt. Lucy, why would you take on a city slicker?"

"I'm not in a position to be choosy."

"Can he even ride a horse?"

"Meredith says he can."

Lucy edged closer to the window. When Jackson Harris turned around, she caught her breath.

"Oh, my," Emma said, her face lighting up. "Well, I suppose you could do worse."

Lucy turned to her sister. "What do you mean, I could do worse?"

"The man is mighty fine-looking, that's for sure. And you'll be working closely with him all summer, dear sister."

"Don't get any ideas. *If* I was looking for a man in my life, it certainly would not be another temporary cowboy." She shook her head. "I have most definitely already been there and done that. And I have an empty house in the woods to prove it."

"Just remember that sometimes the Lord brings us what we need, not what we want."

Lucy tossed the muffin liner in the trash and dusted off her hands. "This discussion is over."

"Six weeks!" Jack Harris stood outside a log-cabin-style bunkhouse next to Lucy Maxwell, trying to digest her words. "Where did you get the idea I was here for six weeks?"

"Your aunt," Lucy said. "She called me last night and said you want the Big Heart Ranch experience, and that you'd be filling our ranch hand position for the summer."

Stunned, Jack rubbed a hand over his chin and closed his mouth when he realized it was hanging open.

"Do you want me to call her?" she asked.

"No." He shook his head. "Look, between you and me, my aunt isn't as strong as she used to be. She thinks she is, but those cancer treatments have taken a toll on her overall health."

"Apparently, she's well enough to pull one over on you," Lucy murmured. Her lips twitched as she concentrated on the ground, creating a line in the dirt with the toe of her boot.

Jack's gaze followed. She wore the red boots, this time with jeans and a bright red T-shirt with the Big Heart Ranch logo on the front and the word Staff on the back. Once again, she reminded him of a bright flower. This time a poppy. He averted his gaze and considered her words.

Lucy had assessed the situation correctly. He'd been bamboozled by his seventy-year-old aunt. Aunt Meri was right about one thing: Jack had been away from Oklahoma for a very long time. Long enough to forget how stubborn his aunt could be once she got a bone between her teeth.

"For some reason, she's convinced I'll change my mind if I see the ranch up close and personal," he muttered.

"Why is it you constantly think the worst of Big Heart Ranch?"

"This isn't personal. I have a job to do as the foundation's counsel. And I happen to love my aunt. I'm simply trying to protect both interests."

Lucy stared at him, obviously biting her lip. The dark eyes glittered with unsaid words. It was clear he'd pushed her buttons and she was working hard to control her temper.

"You seem to think we've committed an offense," she said. "If so, what happened to innocent until proven guilty?"

"Shouldn't I be the one on the defense here?" he asked. "First, you fingerprint me like a criminal. Then you make me sign a release for a complete background check. Now you're telling me I'm stuck here for six weeks." He shook his head. "The kicker is that I get to do it while living with two other guys. I mean, come on. You must be kidding."

"You'll be living like all the other volunteers. Think of this as summer camp for grown-ups." Lucy looked him up and down. "As for the other, we're entrusting you to care for our children. Children who have already suffered more in their short lives than you can even comprehend. These are children who have been abandoned, neglected and even abused. This isn't kiddie rehab, Mr. Harris. They don't come here to be fixed. They come here to live a normal life. We are their life. We are their family. Forever." She paused. "Makes your trivial complaints seem insignificant, wouldn't you say?"

"Believe it or not, I did my homework, Ms. Maxwell. I understand the ranch mission statement."

She raised her brows.

"First Corinthians thirteen. Faith, hope and love. Faith in God, hope for tomorrow, and unconditional love."

When her lips tilted into a huge smile, the effect nearly knocked him over. A guy could get addicted to a smile like that if he wasn't careful.

"You memorized our mission statement." The words were a hushed whisper. "I'm impressed."

"Somehow I doubt that," he muttered.

"A lot of prayer and thought went into that mission statement, so yes. I am impressed."

He offered a short nod.

She handed him papers from the clipboard in her hands. "A list of recommended gear you'll need for the summer. Oh, and the schedule and a map of the boys' ranch, girls' ranch and important facilities. Phone numbers are listed, as well."

Jack glanced down at the form on top of the papers. "What's this? Yet another form?"

"Waiver of liability. If you choose to ride our horses without the recommended safety helmet, we need this signed."

"Do you wear a helmet?"

"It depends on the situation." She met his gaze. "Oh, and by the way, other than me, only Travis and Lucy are aware you're from the Brisbane Foundation. You are simply a summer volunteer, as far as everyone else is concerned."

"So I'm undercover? Why the big secret?"

"I don't want anyone to panic, and actually, Mr. Harris, it's to your advantage."

"How's that?"

"If everyone believes you're part of the team, they'll be open and transparent while you're here."

"If you say so," he replied.

"I do." Lucy pulled out a key and opened the bunkhouse door before dropping it into his hand. "Welcome to your new home. This is bunkhouse number one. It has all the amenities you should need—coffeemaker, microwave. If you need something more, let us know. We'll vote on it at the next budget meeting. Of course, that won't be until after the foundation makes their funding decisions."

A smiling Travis greeted them at the door. "Hey, Jack. You're bunking with us? Great." He held open the screen. "Come on in."

Jack folded the papers from Lucy and put them in his

back pocket as he moved into the living quarters. "You live here?"

"Only during the summer," Travis said. "It's easier than driving home after a twelve-hour day, so I moved my stuff over today." Travis tossed his black Stetson on a bunk and winked at Lucy. "Besides, it keeps the boss happy, because if the boss isn't happy, nobody is happy."

"Keep it up, little brother," Lucy muttered.

"Who..." Jack waved a hand at the other bunk.

"Tripp Walker," Travis said. "The horse whisperer. Doesn't talk much. If it involves horses, though, Tripp is your point of contact."

Jack nodded.

Travis looked from Lucy to Jack. "Madame Director giving you a hard time?"

"One might conclude that."

"Her bark is worse than her bite," Travis returned, as though she wasn't in the room.

Lucy offered her brother a slow nod, obviously letting him know he could expect payback for his comments. Jack couldn't help but smile at the affectionate sibling interaction. A part of him was envious at their bond. Would he and Daniel have been like Lucy and Travis? He brushed the thought away.

Travis turned to Lucy. "I just got a call. Beau is loose. We're on lockdown."

Lucy released a breath. "Of course he is. Any sightings?"

"Not yet."

"Did you drive the Ute over, Trav?" Lucy asked.

"Yeah. It's parked behind out back, on the street."

"Mind if I borrow it to take Mr. Harris on a little tour?"

"No problem." He tossed her the keys.

"Ute?" Jack asked as he followed Lucy out the back door and down a gravel walk.

"Utility vehicle. Like if a Jeep and a golf cart had a child."

Jack smiled when he saw the black vehicle with the ranch logo emblazoned on the hood. "That's a fitting description," he said as he slid into the doorless passenger side.

"What was Travis talking about? Beau?"

"The boys' ranch mascot. Beau is literally an old goat. He's nearly blind, mostly hard of hearing, yet somehow, he manages to get out of his corral now and then."

"A goat?"

She nodded. "You better fasten your seat belt, Mr. Harris. Around here you never can tell what might be waiting down the road."

He stretched the seat belt across himself and connected it with a click. "Couldn't you call me Jack or Jackson? Mr. Harris seems a little formal."

Lucy shrugged. "That's fine. However, our children will be calling you Mr. Jack. Those are the rules."

"What about you?" he asked.

"What about me?" Lucy put a hand on the gearshift knob.

"What do they call you?"

"Miss Lucy works." She paused. "I mean for the kids. You may call me Lucy."

"Thanks, Lucy."

She shot him a sidelong glance.

"Can you tell me about the ranch?" he asked.

Lucy turned in her seat. "I'm sure you had us investigated. Exactly what is it that was left out of your report?"

"Your family's qualifications for running this operation."

"I'm an orphan." The words were a flat admission. "Obviously, my brother and sister, as well. We cycled through the foster care system until we were adopted out." She shrugged and started the Ute. "More than you probably care to know."

Jack paused. He understood and cared far more than

Lucy Maxwell would ever know. When his brother died, he too had been orphaned. His mother had taken off and his father had checked out.

Aunt Meri had saved him. He needed to remember that. His aunt was the only reason he was giving Big Heart Ranch a second chance.

She steered the Ute toward the main ranch road. "I have a master's degree in business management from Spears College of Business Management. Travis majored in animal sciences and graduated from the Oklahoma State University College of Agriculture and Natural Sciences. Emma also attended OSU and is a licensed social worker with a master's degree."

"How did three orphans manage that?"

Lucy's head jerked back at his question and she inhaled sharply. Slowing the Ute to a stop, she shifted into Neutral to look at him. "Excuse me?"

He raised a palm. "Don't read something into my words I didn't intend. My questions are simply part of my due diligence."

Silence reigned for moments, as she stared straight out the windshield of the Ute. When she turned to him once again, her eyes were shuttered.

"In addition to scholarships, we sold snake oil on Saturdays to fund our education."

Jack met her gaze. She didn't give him time to respond.

"As I stated, we were in the foster care system for several years. A cousin of our mother tracked us down and adopted all of us. I was ten, Travis was eight, Emma five. At the time, we were living in separate homes with monthly visitation."

"Separated from your siblings? That had to be tough."

"I'm not looking for pity."

"I wasn't offering pity."

She nodded and said nothing for several moments.

"You inherited the ranch?" Jack asked.

"Yes. Our property is bordered by that hewn wood fence," Lucy said as she pointed to a fence in the distance.

Fingers tight on the wheel, she turned the Ute left and drove down a shady, tree-lined street. The redbuds and maples were thick with green foliage. The aroma of freshly mown grass rode on the slight breeze.

"These are the boys' homes." Lucy pointed to the red-brick, two-story, Colonial-style houses, each spaced two lots apart, occupying the right side of the street. The left side was fenced, and horses grazed in the pasture.

A group of helmeted cyclists rode by, all young girls with arms extended to offer enthusiastic waves. "Hi, Miss Lucy!" they called in unison.

Lucy raised a hand out the vehicle in greeting.

"Why aren't they in school?"

"It's summer, Mr.— Uh, Jack."

He turned to look at the pasture on the right. "Cattle? That seems ambitious."

"That's us, and why not? Travis has graduated from the OSU Master Cattleman Program. He's worked several area ranches over the years."

"He's an impressive guy."

"There's not a person on the ranch who isn't impressive. We function with a staff of qualified professionals and volunteers. We need and value everyone. I hope you'll note that when you review our funding."

Jack stared out the window as they passed horses nibbling on grass and clover, their tails swishing at flies in the summer heat. The ranch was beautiful, he'd give her that. A part of him longed to walk through the fields spread before him, like he had as a child, when he hadn't had any cares. He and Daniel would lie on their backs in his aunt's pasture, finding shapes in the fluffy clouds that slowly moved across the endless blue Oklahoma summer sky.

A drop of sweat rolled down the back of his shirt, bringing him back to reality. Jack shifted uncomfortably. "I'd forgotten about how hot it is here in July."

Lucy shrugged. "You'll get used to the weather. The nice thing about the Oklahoma humidity is that it makes everything grow. You should see our vegetable garden."

He turned to her and raised a brow. "Vegetable garden, as well?"

"Yes. I hope you're sensing a pattern." Lucy offered a proud smile. "We want to be as self-sustaining as possible. Growing things also gives our children an appreciation for everything the Lord provides. We don't ever want to take that for granted. The more we do for ourselves, the better stewards we can be of the financial blessings we receive."

Jack said nothing to the obvious jibe.

"Look over there. Through the trees," Lucy said. "Girls' ranch. You'll actually get a close-up of everything after you receive your chore assignment."

"Chore assignment?"

"Everyone at the ranch has chores."

Jack wrapped his mind around that bit of information and stared out the window. A moment later, Lucy hit the brakes hard. He lurched forward, thrusting a hand to the dashboard in protection as the vehicle suddenly came to a complete halt.

"Sorry," Lucy said. "Are you okay?"

"Yeah. Is this how you usually drive?"

"No. Look to your right."

Jack glanced out in the field. "More cows."

"Our missing goat is out there, too."

"What's that?" Jack pointed to a black hen that strutted along the right side of the road, her black tail feathers raised regally.

"Mrs. Carmody got out, too!"

"You lose animals often here at the ranch?"

"They must have heard you were coming. However, to be fair, Beau and Mrs. Carmody escape every chance they can."

"You name all your chickens?"

"We do. Come on, let's go get her."

Jack blinked. "What?"

"You walk toward her and I'll circle around behind."

"What about the goat?"

"He'll be easy. I told you he's got vision and hearing issues. As for Mrs. C., she's an old hen and doesn't move very fast. She'll be easy, too."

"How'd she get out anyhow?"

"I don't know. Let's catch her and then I'll be sure to ask."

Jack frowned at the response and stepped from the Ute.

"You walk toward her and I'll circle behind."

"Are you sure this is going to work?"

"No. I'm not sure of anything," she said with a grin. "If you have a better idea, I'm open to suggestions."

Jack moved toward the chicken.

"Flap your arms," Lucy said.

"Flap my arms?"

"Why?"

"Let her know you're friendly." She cocked her head. "You don't have any medical conditions that preclude you from flapping, do you?"

"No. But I try not to look like a fool on principle."

Lucy began to laugh.

He paused for a moment at the sound of her laughter

bubbling over. Then, despite his better judgment, Jack tucked his hands under and moved his arms up and down.

The chicken wasn't impressed. She slowly scratched at the ground and then began to run toward him on wobbly claws. "Why is she charging me?" Jack yelled.

"This is Mrs. Carmody and she doesn't follow the fowl rules."

Jack's eyes rounded when the bird attempted liftoff, her black wings flapping furiously. *Could chickens fly?*

This one managed a small liftoff before landing on her backside. Regrouping, the beady-eyed bird targeted him, one step at a time. Suddenly she picked up speed.

"Old and not very fast, huh? That bird is going to attack!"

Jack turned and ran, straight into a pile of something soft and wet. "Oomph!" His feet slid out from under him, and he landed on his back in the sweet grass.

"Good thing that grass hasn't been mowed yet," Lucy observed.

He opened his eyes. Mrs. Carmody was tucked neatly against Lucy, who stroked her feathers with her other hand. The chicken squawked and fussed for a moment, but Lucy held firm.

He had to give the ranch director credit; she'd grabbed the bird and was now doing an admirable job of trying not to laugh.

"Yeah, good thing," he returned as a black feather danced through the air and landed on him.

"Why did she run at me?" Jack asked.

"She was running to you. Big difference. I think she mistook you for Travis. You're both about the same size and coloring. Travis always brings Mrs. Carmody treats."

"So you're saying that I ran for nothing."

She glanced away, lips twitching. "Um, yes."

"And the flapping?"

"To get you into the moment."

Lucy held out a hand, and he grasped her palm, heaving himself to a standing position. Their eyes met and he froze for a moment, lost in her gaze. Then he glanced down at his once spotless shoes, lifting one and then the other to inspect the soles. A pungent odor drifted to his nose and he cringed. "Manure? Is that what I slipped on?"

She nodded and sniffed the air. "Horse, I'd say. Fresh."

"Do you know how much these shoes cost?" Jack rubbed his feet back and forth on the long blades of grass.

"My guess is enough to feed one of our kids for a year."

Jack only grumbled in response, and then he stopped what he was doing and stared at Lucy.

"What?" she asked.

"Could you have caught Mrs. Carmody on your own?"

"Probably." She said the word slowly.

"That's what I thought. So you were having fun with the city guy."

"I'd like to think of it as breaking the ice. You and I have a whole summer to work together. We need to get along. Besides, if it's any consolation, you passed chicken flapping with an A plus."

Jack couldn't help himself. He started laughing, and when he stopped, his gaze met Lucy's.

Her lips parted sweetly, and he realized they had at least reached détente. In that moment he became aware that his obligation to remain objective while he investigated the ranch for the Brisbane Foundation would be compromised every time Lucy smiled at him.

"What about your goat?" he asked.

"You hold Mrs. Carmody and I'll go grab Beau."

He stepped back and held up his hands. "Ah, no thank you. Why don't I get the goat?"

"You're okay with that?"

"I'm okay with pretty much anything if it means not holding a chicken."

This time Lucy laughed as well, and her eyes were bright with amusement. "You know that chickens are on your chore list, right?"

"Not seriously?"

She nodded.

"So, how do I get Beau?"

"He's docile. Gently grasp the rope around his neck and lead him to the Ute."

"What about the cows?"

"Nary a bull in sight. You'll be fine."

Jack started across the field. He grimaced and shook his head as he skirted around a cow patty. Day one on Big Heart Ranch, and already he'd gotten up close and personal with a chicken and was about to bring home a lost goat.

Yeah, it was going to be an interesting summer.

Chapter Three

Jack checked his watch as he tugged his shirttail free from his jeans. He'd made it through day one and would be off duty soon. All he had to do was get his final chore assignment of the day completed. Then he'd be on his way to T-town, a little shopping and a nice steak. Free until the alarm sounded tomorrow at 5:00 a.m.

He pulled the paper Lucy had given him from his pocket and checked the dates. No chicken assignment until after the trail ride and camping trip were complete. If things went in his favor, Mrs. Carmody would release all the birds before then. He'd even pay the bird to stage a coop-break.

For a moment, he simply smiled, thinking about the whole chicken incident. Lately, women had been getting one over on him left and right. Feathered females included.

At least the goat had cooperated.

He shook his head and turned the paper in his hand over. Stables, straight ahead. Or equestrian center, as Lucy Maxwell called the building. He'd been assigned his own horse. That thought alone made him smile.

It had been a long time since he'd been responsible for

a horse. Twenty-five years ago, Aunt Meredith's horses had been his saving grace. His aunt worked him so hard the summer Daniel died that he didn't have time to blame himself for his little brother's death. He'd mucked stalls, fed and exercised a stable full of horses from sunrise until bedtime. Then he fell into a hard sleep, too exhausted for the nightmares.

There was no denying the thrum of excitement that accompanied Jack as he entered the equestrian building. Except for the soft whinny of horses, it was quiet.

Jack smiled. He'd forgotten how good quiet was. The lights were on as he took his time walking down the center of the stables, his left hand reaching out to touch the gates of each stall he passed, like he was a kid again. He let the smells of horse sweat and hay nudge his memories while he searched for the sorrel mare he was about to groom.

Spotless. The boys' ranch stables were spotless, no strong urine odors to indicate the stalls were anything but clean. A chalkboard on the outside of the very last stall on the left had "Grace" printed in white chalk in a childish scrawl. He looked around and found the tack room, situated next to an office, whose door was shut, lights off. The sign on the door read Tripp Walker, Manager.

The familiar scent of new leather drifted to Jack's nostrils as he entered the tack room and grabbed supplies. He juggled a currycomb and soft brush in the air and caught them easily. His steps were light as he opened the latch to Grace's stall.

Jack Harris, in a barn. No one would believe it if they could see him now. He didn't believe it himself.

The mare shifted and raised her tail. Jack sidestepped, though not fast enough to avoid stepping in steaming and aromatic horse patties. He grimaced and held his breath. Twice in one day.

His life as an attorney was filled with horse patties, but today was a record.

Nope, no one would ever believe this, either.

"Grace," he told the mare. "I thought we were going to be friends. This is no way to treat a guy on our first date."

The horse merely nickered in response.

Jack grabbed a pitchfork and buried the foul evidence in fresh wood chips that he moved to the corner of the stall, before pulling the currycomb and a brush from his back pocket. He ran his open palm slowly along the coarse coat of reddish-gold of the animal's flank to prepare her for the session, and then gently began to comb the horse.

"There you go, Grace. Feels good, doesn't it?" he soothed. "When we're done, I have a nice carrot for you." With two fingers, he massaged the animal's wide forehead until she relaxed.

Jack stuck his nose right into her neck and rubbed the mare's ears as he inhaled. Yeah, this was the real perfume of summer. The sweet, subtle sweat of horse hair. Pleasant memories of days with Aunt Meri tumbled through his mind.

Jack continued to brush the mare, one hand on the brush, the other on the animal's silky-soft back. The tension he didn't realize he held evaporated into the small space.

"You're doing it wrong," a small voice whispered.

Jack paused, and Grace's ears perked at the voice. A quick glance around the stall revealed nothing and no one. Jack continued brushing.

"Circles. You gotta do it in circles."

He opened the metal gate and took a quick peek down the main walkway and then into the stalls on either side of Grace's. Both stalls had horses, but they appeared to be the nontalking variety. "Where are you?" Jack asked.

"Up here."

Jack frowned before glancing straight up. To the right was a hay storage shelf where a little boy, no more than five or six, smiled down at him with a toothy grin. His upper front teeth were absent.

"Are you supposed to be up there?" Jack asked.

The urchin with a dirty face and hair the color of straw shrugged. "No one cares."

"I bet Miss Lucy cares," Jack said.

The kid wore jeans and battered red sneakers, the laces untied. Scooting to the edge, he dangled his legs. The movement knocked bits of straw into the air. Hay and dust danced on their way to the ground. Some landed on Jack and Grace.

"Kid, you're messing up my work here."

"Sorry." Which came out as *thorry* due to the missing teeth.

"What's your name?"

"Dub Lewis."

"Your name is Dub?"

"Uh-huh. What's your name?"

"Jackson Harris."

Dub screwed up his face and giggled. "What kind of name is that?"

Jack smiled. No filter. His brother had been the same way. Said whatever came to mind, whenever it came to mind.

He chuckled. "Touché, kid."

"You want me to show you how to do that?" Dub asked.

"Do what?" Jack looked up again, and then down at his hand paused on the horse's flank. "*This?* I've been grooming horses since I was your age."

That might be a slight exaggeration, but it silenced the kid, who was obviously five going on thirty.

Jack pulled out the soft brush and began to clean the area the currycomb had covered.

Silence reigned until Jack began to pick Grace's hooves.

"Are you supposed to be here?" Dub asked.

"Yes." Jack cocked his head. "I think the real question is, are you supposed to be here?"

"I gots permission."

"So you said."

"Grace is my horse. Leo said. And he's going to teach me to ride Grace."

"Who's Leo?"

"Leo. You know. Leo."

"Actually, I don't know. But I can ask Miss Lucy about it if you want me to."

Again with the shrug of the bony shoulders. Jack stared at the kid for a moment. He couldn't remember the last time he'd been around a child. Normally, he avoided them. Too much responsibility and too many memories.

Jack moved on to the next hoof, battling an urge to check and see if the kid was giving him an approving scrutiny. *Hoof picking, Harris.* He reminded himself. *You've got this covered.*

"Aren't you going to the meeting?" Dub asked.

"Meeting?"

"Uh-huh. Right before dinner."

"Maybe *you* have a meeting, but I don't think I do."

"The meeting's for everyone," the kid insisted.

Jack vaguely recalled a meeting listed on his schedule for today that he planned to miss.

"I don't think I need to attend."

"Everyone does. Miss Lucy said it's for the trail ride."

"You're kind of young for a trail ride. How old are you, anyhow?"

"I'm five and I'm going." He gave an adamant shake of his blond head. "Yeth, I am."

"Okay. Fine."

He grabbed the tools and closed the stall behind him before offering her the carrot. "Good girl, Grace."

The mare snorted and accepted her treat.

"She likes carrots best."

Jack nodded. "She sure does. So, Dub Lewis, I don't suppose you know where this meeting is?" Jack asked.

"Uh-huh. The chow hall. Want me to show you?"

"I'll find it." Jack put the tools away and looked up at the little boy. "How are you going to get down?"

"Ladder."

"Be careful, kid, would you?" he said as he finished with Grace and closed the stall gate behind him.

A moment later Dub Lewis appeared at his side. The kid seemed small for his age. But what did Jack know about kids? Nothing. And he planned to keep it that way.

"Why aren't you wearing boots?" Jack asked. "It's dangerous to be in the stables without boots on."

"I wasn't in the stall," he lisped.

"Sure you were."

Dub shook his head. "I was in the loft. You don't need boots in the loft."

Jack opened his mouth and closed it again. What was he doing? He was arguing with a five-year-old, that was what. Once again, the kid reminded him of Daniel. Same forthright attitude and stubborn streak.

"I'm watching Grace," Dub said. "We're friends."

"Oh, yeah?"

Dub nodded, and his short legs did double time in an

effort to keep up with Jack, who continued to put the supplies away in the tack room.

"Yeth," he said. "Sometimes I get to ride Grace, but I gotta wear a helmet."

"They let you run around the ranch all by yourself, too?" Jack asked.

"I'm not running around. 'Sides, I told you. I gots permission."

"Gots, huh?" Jack resisted the urge to smile. This was serious stuff. A five-year-old had no business running around without supervision. He knew only too well what could happen. Jack swallowed hard, finding himself getting tense and annoyed all over again.

Dub tugged on Jack's shirttail. "Come on, Mr. Jackson, or we'll be late."

He regarded the pint-size kid at his side. "I'm Jack. Mr. Jack."

And what was with this "we" stuff?

"Hurry, Mr. Jack!"

"How do you know we'll be late?" he asked Dub. "You don't have a watch on."

"I could see from the window up there. Everybody's walking to the chow hall."

"Okay, fine. Show me the way."

Dub was right. There were a lot of kids walking toward the training building. Now that he thought of it, he recalled a cafeteria in that building.

A few adults were up ahead, but it was mostly kids. Lots of kids. Boys of different ages laughed and talked as they headed to the meeting.

Somehow the whole kids at the ranch thing had slipped Jack's mind. He hadn't connected the dots. Or he had, and then blocked it out. Jack swiped a hand over his face and swallowed, willing his heart rate to slow down.

It didn't matter—he wasn't here for kids. He was here as a ranch hand. He'd do chickens and goats, and anything else the director lady threw at him. But kids were definitely not part of his repertoire. Not now and not in the future.

He stole a glance at the boy beside him. A prickle of apprehension raced over him, and he realized that he needed to make his no-kids policy completely clear to Lucy Maxwell.

And to Dub Lewis.

Lucy blinked.

What was Jack Harris doing with Dub Lewis? At well over six feet, he had to lean over every now and again to catch what the small child was saying. Dub seemed to be talking nonstop, skipping at intervals to keep up with Jack's long strides. Jack's dark head was next to Dub's blond one. Lucy's heart gave a little swoon at the picture they made. But Jack wasn't smiling. The attorney limped as he walked—a sure sign those fancy shoes were causing him considerable discomfort.

"Did you get all moved in?" she murmured as he approached.

"I did," he said with a curt nod.

"You spoke with your aunt?"

"My aunt." He chuckled. "Aunt Meri cleverly left town to spend a few days with a friend."

Lucy smiled and glanced from Jack to the little boy at his side. "I see you met Dub."

"Met? He seems to have permanently attached himself to my shadow. I have a few questions for you," Jack said, his words for her ears only.

Lucy knelt down next to Dub. "Hey, Dub, why don't you go ahead and find a seat inside?"

Dub glanced at the box of camping supplies at her side. "Don't I need those, too?"

"Miss Lorna picked yours up for you."

"Okay. Are we still going for ice cream?" He searched her face hopefully. "With my sissies?"

"What did I tell you?" she returned.

"You said that you'd pick us up tonight after dinner."

"That's correct, and I always keep my promises."

Relief now shone in Dub's eyes.

"Now go ahead and find a seat inside, please."

"Okay." He turned to Jack. "I'll save you a seat, Mr. Jack."

"Uh, thanks, kid."

Lucy's gaze followed Dub as he raced into the open door of the building.

"What's his story?" Jack asked.

She turned to face him. "What do you mean?"

"Seems like he should be in an orphanage so he can be adopted. Your facility isn't licensed for adoption."

"You really did your research," Lucy said with a grudging smile. "Once again, I'm impressed."

"Don't be. I'm sure I'll annoy you again very soon."

"Dub is here as a favor to the court."

"Why?"

"He's one of three."

"Three?"

"Yes. Triplets."

Jack's eyes rounded. "There are three of him? Where are his brothers?"

"Sisters. Ann and Eva. They're at the girls' ranch."

"How's that work?"

"Normally different-sex siblings have visitation weekly. We provide extra family time together for the triplets."

"So why are they here?"

"You understand this falls under the medical confidentiality agreement you signed. We expect that of all staff members."

"I'm an attorney. I'm accustomed to keeping my mouth shut."

Though she sorely itched to spout the hearty comeback on the tip of her tongue, Lucy recognized that she was supposed to be making nice with the man, so she bit her tongue instead.

"Finding foster parents willing to take triplets isn't easy. Dub was in a separate foster home from his sisters and he became very depressed. In fact, Dub has been in three different foster homes already this year. He ran away from all of them."

"Why? Why does he run away? Do they treat him poorly?"

"Not at all. Dub simply feels obligated to take care of his sisters. That's his burden. So he leaves to find them."

"That's a heavy load for a five-year-old."

"I know." And she did, far more than anyone would ever understand. It had been her job, like Dub's, to keep track of Emma and Travis when the three of them were in foster care.

"How far does the little man get?" Jack asked.

"Oh, you'd be surprised." She released a sigh. "Our Dub is very resourceful."

"Now he's here."

"Yes. Dub and his sisters are here for the summer at least, to keep them together."

"How long have they been in the system?"

"A year. They were removed from their home due to neglect and abandonment. Poor kids were left alone quite a bit, and expected to fend for themselves by the only custodial parent."

Jack grimaced. "Mother?"

"Yes."

"And the father?"

"Unknown."

He shook his head and glanced at the building Dub had gone into. Lucy blinked at the emotion Harris wore on his face. It was the first emotion she'd seen him express for anyone besides his aunt.

"That's a tough break for a kid," he muttered.

She nodded. "Another reason they're here is to see if Dub flourishes when his only responsibility is being a kid. At the ranch, he knows his sisters are being taken care of. A few times he's randomly asked to see them in the middle of the day. It was as if he needed to be sure they were safe. We complied, and he was able to stop worrying. Dub trusts us to keep our word."

"How is his being here going to help with the adoption process?"

"We're actively trying to find Dub a home, and we've agreed to facilitate any potential foster or adoptive parents who are interested in all three children."

Jack offered a short nod, annoyance still evident on his face. "The kid was in the stables." He shot her an accusatory look. "Alone. No supervision."

"Dub always asks permission, and he knows that he's not allowed in the stalls."

"That's not the same as supervision."

"Dub understands the rules."

"So he kept telling me. Yet seeing him in the loft, a good fifteen feet above the ground, I was not reassured."

She stepped closer and lowered her voice. "We have security cameras and microphones in the stables. Off-site security is monitoring most of this ranch, except for the pastures. Soon we'll have cameras out there, as well."

It was her turn to look him in the eye. "If our budget is approved."

"Cameras don't take the place of adults supervising kids. He was in the loft. Is that allowed?"

"That would be a loophole in our agreement. Kids tend to find those. You're an attorney—surely you understand loopholes."

"A loophole?"

"Yes. He wasn't technically in the stall. But I appreciate the heads-up. I will discuss that with Dub." She paused. "I do want you to know that we've been operating for five years, and no child has ever been seriously injured."

"Trust me. It only takes one second for things to spiral out of control. And in that moment, the rest of your life is changed. *Forever.*"

She stared at him, assessing the rigid posture, the hands shoved into his pockets. More emotion. Where was it all coming from? Jack Harris was hiding a painful secret, of that she was certain. Her words were slow and measured when she responded. "Are you asking for Dub as your buddy for the summer? Is that what this is all about?"

"What?" His head jerked back and his hands came up, palms out. "No. I don't even know anything about buddies."

"You have to pick someone. Why not Dub? He certainly seems to have attached himself to you."

Jack lifted his palms again and stepped back. "Whoa. I have zero experience with kids."

"Weren't you a kid?"

"That was a very limited engagement. It ended when I was nine."

"What?"

He grimaced. "Trust me. I am not the man to be in charge of a kid."

Lucy opened her mouth to answer and then closed it again. Somehow she knew that he was telling the truth, and his words troubled her. What had happened to Jack Harris to make him so nervous at the thought of being with a child?

She pushed back her bangs. "All you have to do is accompany him on the various summer activities. Be his designated adult. Give him your undivided attention and unconditional love."

Was she imagining things, or did Jack pale as she spoke?

He wiped his palms on his jeans. "How long does this buddy thing last?" he asked.

"Until the end of summer."

"You expect me to babysit Dub for six weeks?"

"Please lower your voice." Again, Lucy glanced around. "We don't call our ministry at the ranch babysitting. We're sharing and caring."

"Sharing and caring." Jack ran a hand over his face and rubbed the small scar on the bridge of his nose with his index finger.

Lucy stepped closer to Jack as a few volunteers and children walked past her and into the chow hall. "Are you all right?" she asked quietly.

He skirted the question with one of his own. "What if he doesn't trust me? You said he already has issues."

"Jack, it's obvious Dub's already bonded with you."

"What makes you think that?" The lawyer's eyes narrowed.

"Dub Lewis doesn't follow everyone around. Besides, part of the connection is that horse. Grace. You're assigned to Grace and he loves that mare."

Jack knit his brows together. "Dub says Grace is Leo's horse."

"No, Leo was just in charge of cleaning the stalls. Leo is actually gone."

"What happened?"

"He needed a raise that we were unable to provide, given our current, uh…economic situation. It's unfortunate because Leo did the work of several employees."

This time Jack's eyes popped wide. "Does that make me the new Leo?"

"In a manner of speaking, yes, I guess so. However, whether you buddy with Dub or not is your decision." She shrugged. "You will be assigned a buddy."

"What part of 'I don't want a buddy' don't you get?"

Lucy grit her teeth and tamped back a surge of irritation. "What did you think you were going to do at the ranch? Ride a horse and play cowboy?"

"I didn't *think* at all. You insisted I see what the ranch was all about."

"Yes. That's because you were about to pull the rug out from under us. We're privately funded. Meredith believes in what we do here. I'm hoping you will, too. We need that funding."

"I'm not here to take care of kids." His words were flat.

Jack Harris had returned to his hard-hearted self. That was too bad, because she was starting to sort of almost like him.

"Look, Jack, this ranch is the real thing. You are expected to fully participate."

"What does that mean?"

"Not only will you have a buddy assignment, but starting tomorrow you'll start your full chore list and participate in all required activities, including the trail ride and campout."

"But…"

"Is there a problem? You certainly were quick to dismiss us to your aunt. Now that you actually have to get your hands dirty, you're having second thoughts? I'm happy to call Meredith."

"No. There's no need to bother my aunt."

Lucy glanced at her watch. "I have to start this meeting soon."

She reached down and grabbed a pup tent and sleeping bag from the boxes next to her and shoved them at Jack.

He staggered backward in surprise.

"If you lose them, you buy them." When she moved toward the doors Lucy was surprised to discover Jack matching his steps to her own.

"Tell me about the trail ride."

Lucy kept walking, stopping only to open the glass doors for him since his arms were full. "It's exactly that. The junior high and high school kids participate each year for three days and two nights. This first session is the boys' ranch."

Jack repositioned the tent pack and the sleeping bag in his arms. "Three days in the saddle?" he asked.

"No, we only ride horses there and back. It's a camping experience. We take the chuck wagon and live outside with no electronics."

"No cell phones?"

"None. Not that it really matters. Cell reception is nil where we're headed."

"You're telling me that they actually like doing this?"

"The staff and the children look forward to this particular event every year."

"Really?" His eyes narrowed as he considered her words.

"You know people pay a small fortune for this kind of outdoor experience. We offer it to our kids free of charge."

Lucy looked at him. The man was privileged. Could he possibly understand? "You have no idea what an opportunity this is for kids who have been forgotten in foster care or suffered the emotional abyss of abusive situations." She couldn't help herself as the words began to tumble from her mouth unfiltered. "Please don't discount this event until you've experienced the trail ride for yourself."

For once Jack Harris was silent.

"Are you up for the challenge?" she asked.

"Do I have a choice?"

"Everyone has a choice. You and I need to put our differences aside for the summer because the children of Big Heart Ranch come first."

When he didn't answer, she took a deep breath. "Can we work together for six weeks or not, Jack?"

"I guess we'll have to try, won't we?"

"It's all up to you, Jack." Lucy nodded toward the back of the chow hall, where Dub Lewis waved his stubby arms. "Your buddy has your seat saved."

Jack released a resigned sigh as his gaze followed hers. When he started across the room, a limp was still evident.

"Oh, and Jack?"

He turned, brows raised. "Yeah?"

"Moleskin."

"Excuse me?"

"Try moleskin and a little triple antibiotic ointment for those blisters."

His gaze shot to his shoes, and he immediately stopped

limping. "I don't have blisters. The only thing rubbing me the wrong way is this ranch."

Lucy clutched her clipboard to her chest as she inhaled slowly, counting to ten while willing herself not to respond. Keeping her mouth shut every time Jack Harris pushed her buttons might very well prove to be the most difficult challenge of the next six weeks.

Chapter Four

They'd been on the trail almost three hours. Jack pushed his ball cap to the back of his head and pulled off his sunglasses to peer at the clear azure sky. The July sun's merciless rays mocked him.

He shifted in the saddle, to no avail. His backside still ached and his T-shirt clung to his damp skin. Who went on a trail ride in one-hundred-degree weather? The humidity made the air so thick that he could taste it each time he opened his mouth.

From the bits of conversation that drifted back from the front of the line of horses and riders, everyone else seemed to be in good spirits.

Yeah, this was definitely an acquired taste. Jack took a swig of water and positioned Grace so the horse trotted behind the chuck wagon.

Covered with waterproof canvas and led by two horses, the wagon looked like an old-fashioned movie prop. More important was that it was large enough to hide Jack from inquisitive eyes as he peered at his banned electronic device.

Grace offered a snuffle and snort, shaking her head

back and forth as though in warning when he slid his phone from his pocket and checked for reception.

No signal.

Again.

He had to admit that it irked him that so far Lucy Maxwell had been right about everything. From his blisters to the cell reception.

At the back of the wagon, the right canvas flap flew open and Dub Lewis stuck his head out, a huge toothless grin on his freckled face.

"Hi, Mr. Jack!" he called.

"Hey, isn't that dangerous?" Jack returned. "You might fall out of there."

"I have a seat belt on."

"Yeah, well, be careful."

"I will."

"You better," Jack grumbled.

The smile on Dub's face widened as he continued to chatter. "You've got Grace. Can I ride her?"

"Maybe." Jack offered a begrudging smile at the kid's enthusiasm.

"Did you know that we're having carrot cake later?"

"Oh, yeah?"

Dub nodded, eyes rounding.

"It's Auggie's birthday," a familiar female voice said from behind Jack. The soft thud of horse hooves and the jingle of tack told him she was approaching on his right.

Lucy. Jack slid his phone back into the pocket of his jeans.

"Who is Auggie?" he asked, turning slightly in the saddle.

Seated confidently on a black mare, in Levi's and her red ranch logo T-shirt, Lucy was all smiles today. She held the reins with soft chamois gloves and nodded up ahead, where a dozen or so boys wearing riding helmets bounced gently in the saddle, along with the rhythmic motion of their horses.

"See the tall boy with the black helmet? The one on the chestnut mare? Near the end?"

Jack nodded.

"This is the first time in his life he's ever celebrated his birthday."

"What do you mean?" Jack said, hoping her words weren't literal.

"Exactly that."

"How is that possible?"

"Neglect and abuse situations. We see it more often than you want to know." She shrugged. "But today he's already had a birthday breakfast and opened presents before we started the trail ride. Plus, our cook for the trip has brought along a cake and a few surprises."

"That doesn't sound like roughing it to me."

"Aw, come on, Jack. Lighten up, would you? It's a birthday. We consider them part of creating family traditions for our kids."

"Traditions?" he muttered.

"Sure. Things you probably take for granted, like holidays and special celebrations, and yes, birthdays."

"What about you?" he asked.

"What about me?"

"Did you have traditions growing up?"

"Things became a little blurry once we lost my parents." Lucy pulled a foot from the stirrup, showing off one of the hand-tooled red leather boots. "See these boots?"

"Yeah, they're hard to miss."

"I asked for red boots for my birthday one year when I was a foster. I wanted them so badly. Of course, I didn't get them. But the biological daughter of my foster parents did. For no reason. It wasn't her birthday, and she hadn't asked for them."

Lucy smiled and glanced down at the boot with pride, carefully placing her foot back in the stirrup. "I bought myself these boots. Every single time I put them on I am reminded of why I do this job. It's because every kid deserves red boots for their birthday."

Jack did his best to keep what he was feeling from showing on his face. Lucy Maxwell wouldn't want to be pitied. He flashed back to his last birthday with his brother. Blowing out candles and opening presents.

Bicycles. They'd both wanted bicycles, as badly as Lucy had wanted her boots.

He swallowed hard. They'd gotten them, too. Daniel's bicycle was still somewhere at his aunt's house. Before he could dwell on the thought, the flap of the wagon popped open once more.

Dub stuck his head outside to flash them a smile and disappeared again.

"Is that safe?" Jack gestured toward the wagon. "Seems to me he could go bouncing around."

"The wagon was specially made for the ranch, and not only does it have an authentic flour cupboard and a cooking shelf on the outside, but it was also fitted with four seats that have full seat belts. It's very safe."

"Once again, I'm impressed. Where did it come from?"

"Donated by a local carpenter."

"Is Dub the only one riding inside of there?"

"Yes. He's the only child under ten on this trip."

"Was that in my honor? Because he's my buddy?"

"You flatter yourself." She tipped the brim of her straw Stetson lower against the sun. "Dub's entire ranch family is on the trail ride. House parents included. We thought it would be good for him to join us."

"There are lots of things for a little kid to get into on a camping trip. Accidents happen when you least expect them."

"Sounds like you have firsthand knowledge. Care to share?"

Jack stiffened. No, he wasn't ready to bare his soul to a woman he hardly knew. A woman he was supposed to be investigating. He shook his head and glanced away.

"He knows the rules, Jack. And he's going to stick to you like…well, you know."

"Terrific. He's not going to be in my tent, is he?"

"No, he's sleeping with two of his ranch brothers."

"What exactly is the point of this trip?"

"The point?" She released a breath and stared at him, hands on the saddle horn. "Does everything have to have a point?"

"Yes. You're utilizing plenty of ranch resources. Donated resources. I'm trying to understand the value."

"Jack, it's about planting seeds. Sometimes you can't see the harvest. You have to trust that by doing what you are called to do, what this ranch is called to do, the harvest will be there."

"How does the trail ride fit into your harvest?"

"First and foremost, this is all about fun. Think like a kid for a minute, instead of an attorney. These are children who are accustomed to going to bed on broken glass, emotionally. In their former life, they went to sleep uncertain what tomorrow would bring. We promise them that they don't have to think about tomorrow. They can simply be kids." Her chocolate eyes continued to pin him.

Against his better judgment, he paused to consider her words. *Just be a kid?* He hadn't been "just a kid" since that summer so long ago. Jack raised his head and met her gaze. Words refused to come.

Lucy sighed when he didn't respond. "Ah, Jack, you don't understand." The words were laced with deep regret.

Jack swallowed hard. He did understand. Far more than Lucy would ever realize.

Up ahead, a horse whinnied and laughter broke out, soon turning into raised voices. The raised voices changed into shouts of anger. The unexpected stop of the chuck wagon caused the rear of the entourage to stop. Like dominos falling over, horses were forced to sidestep with the sudden halt. Their protesting whinnies filled the morning air.

"Excuse me," Lucy said. She picked up her reins and nosed her horse off the well-worn path, through the wild grass and around the wagon.

"Hit him again, Matt," a voice rang out.

Jack pulled Grace's reins to the left in an attempt to figure out what was going on. And then he saw what everyone was looking at. Two teenage boys were entangled on the ground, rolling from the dusty trail to the grass with fists flying. Jack ushered Grace ahead and into a trot.

"Stop this, right now!" Lucy yelled. She slid from her horse as two men pulled the boys apart. Good-size teenagers, they struggled to get free and reach the object of their wrath: each other.

The riders up ahead had stopped and turned in their saddles to see what was going on behind them.

The boys stumbled around, kicking up dust with their boots, stretching from the hands that held them, fists flailing in the air as they continued to struggle.

Lucy stepped into the space between the boys.

"Not a good idea," Jack muttered. "Never get between two opposing forces."

One of the boys broke loose. When he shot forward to grab his opponent, his shoulder knocked into Lucy.

"Lucy!" Jack shouted, realizing the warning was coming much too late.

Down went the ranch director.

"You hit Miss Lucy," a voice accused.

Gasps, followed by a hushed silence, filled the air as Jack leaped from Grace to the ground beside Lucy's limp body.

A stunned Lucy blinked when Jack wrapped his arm around her shoulders and helped her to a seated position. Then the dark lashes fluttered closed, resting against her too pale cheeks.

Jack's hands trembled as he held her, and emotion slammed into him as hard as the protective urge that rose when he tucked her slim frame against his chest. From deep inside, his brain furiously balked at the unexpected tenderness so suddenly roused. But for the first time in a long time, he ignored that analytical voice. Right now, all that mattered was that Lucy was okay.

Around him, denim-clad legs crowded closer as riders hovered.

"Move back!" Jack thundered. His words were laced with an unspoken threat, and he didn't care who heard it.

"Go get Rue," someone urged.

Jack assessed the too still woman, fear and adrenaline kicking his heart rate into overdrive.

"Everyone, please stand back. We need a little air," a female commanded a few minutes later. A tank of a middle-aged woman with gray curls, wearing a faded and wrinkled version of the red ranch T-shirt and a straw Stetson with a hole in the brim, slid to the ground next to

Jack. With a brief glance in his direction, she opened a battered leather medical bag. "What happened?"

"She got in the way of an argument," Jack said. He looked up at the crowd surrounding them. The guilty teenager swallowed hard, his face pale and filled with shame.

"Matt and Abel." The woman glanced up at the boys. "Seriously? Again?"

"I take it they don't like each other," Jack said.

"No, they love each other. They're biological brothers. That's the problem."

"Are you a doctor?" he asked when she tossed him a pair of surgical gloves and slipped on another pair herself.

"Correct. Dr. Rue Butterfield." She nodded. "Consider yourself deputized as my assistant."

"Code of the West?" he asked, as he picked up the bright blue gloves.

"Yep." She gently checked Lucy's pulse. "Lucy? Honey, can you hear me?"

Lucy moaned, her eyes opening and then closing again. "What happened?" She reached a hand to touch the back of her head. "Ouch."

"Sit still and lean forward," Rue said when she tried to stand. "Let me check your head."

Rue pointed to a gauze pad. "Can you tear that open for me?"

"She's bleeding?"

"A small cut at the back of her head, along with a small lump."

Jack tore open the package and handed Rue the gauze pad.

"So you're Leo's replacement."

"Am I?" He met her no-nonsense dark eyes.

"Jack Harris, right?"

"Yeah. How'd you know?"

"Word travels faster than a sneeze through a screen door around here. We heard Meredith Brisbane's stuck-up lawyer nephew stopped the funding to the ranch."

"Rue," Lucy whispered, her voice shaky.

The woman continued despite Lucy's protest. "I heard that there was a volunteer here for the summer taking his place." Her gaze was intent as she assessed him. "You have your work cut out for you, Jack. Leo did the job of two men."

"I heard it was three," he returned.

Rue laughed. "Probably true. Point being, he wouldn't have left if Lucy could match the pay he was offered elsewhere. It's too bad our director here is the one picking up the slack. I'd like to give that attorney holding up the money a piece of my mind."

"Rue. Please," Lucy said with a warning tone in her voice.

"A real jerk, huh?" Jack said.

"Yep. I'd like to see him walk a day in Lucy's shoes. Then he might understand."

"That sounds like a really good idea," Jack said with a smile. "Maybe we can arrange it."

Rue smiled back. "I like you, Jack." She pulled a penlight from her pocket and checked Lucy's pupils. "And I appreciate you stepping up to save the day. We need more men like you around Big Heart Ranch."

"Thanks, but perhaps you should hold your kind words until summer is over."

"I'm a good judge of character. I doubt you can do anything that will change my opinion." She winked and turned to Lucy.

"Anything in particular hurt, Lucy?" Rue asked. "Besides the head."

"My dignity."

Rue pulled a stethoscope from her bag. "I'll take a quick listen and do a little palpation, honey. Just want to make sure you didn't break a rib or anything."

When she finished her evaluation, Rue pulled the stethoscope from her ears and nodded. "So far everything seems fine."

Lucy attempted to stand.

"No. Not just yet." She looked to Jack. "I'm going to go get ice. Keep an eye on her. She may have a concussion."

"Will do," he said.

"You're going to expel those boys who were fighting, right?" Jack asked once Rue was out of earshot.

"It was my fault. I got between them," Lucy said.

"Lucy, you were knocked down."

"It was an accident."

"I'm not so sure. You could easily file charges. Aggravated assault."

"Against who? Jack, the ranch is responsible for those boys. I'd be filing charges against my own ranch."

He paused, stymied by her logic. The woman was right again.

"Besides, they're brothers. Siblings fight. That's normal. Didn't you ever fight with a brother or sister?"

The question knocked him in the gut. Sure, he and Daniel had fought. And he'd give anything for another day to fight with him.

"Jack?" Lucy whispered. "Are you okay?"

"I don't have a sister," he said. "And my brother is dead."

She released a soft gasp. "I'm so sorry."

"Yeah. Me, too."

Once again, Lucy tried to stand.

"The doc said to sit still."

Rue returned with a plastic bag of ice in her hand. She looked between them. "Everything okay?"

"Your director is being stubborn."

Rue offered a hearty chuckle. "What else is new?"

"Hey, I'm right here," Lucy protested.

"So you are," Rue said. "Wrap a bandanna around the bag of ice and apply it to the lump on your head for as long as you can tolerate. Twenty minutes or so at a time. I'll be checking on you to be sure you don't have a concussion. Let me know if you're nauseated or dizzy."

"Shouldn't she go back to the ranch?" Jack asked.

"No!" Lucy interjected, sitting up straighter. "I'm fine. I'm also in charge this week."

Rue held up a hand. "Whoa, now, Lucy. Take it easy."

"I know the symptoms of a concussion. I'll be careful," Lucy said.

"I trust you will, and that you'll ride in the wagon with Dub," Rue said.

"My horse..."

"I'll handle your horse," Jack said. "How much farther is it anyhow?"

"About half a mile," Rue said. She turned to Lucy. "Do you want me to ride in the wagon with you?"

Lucy waved a hand. "Completely unnecessary."

"All right," the other woman said. "I'll check on you after we make camp."

"Thank you, Rue," Lucy said.

Jack echoed her words.

"No problem. It's my job. And thank you for your help, Jack." Rue offered him a broad smile.

"You certainly impressed General Butterfield," Lucy muttered as the doctor left. "That doesn't happen often."

"Did I?" He chuckled. "Why did you call her General?"

"Retired US Army. She volunteers full-time at the ranch."

"No kidding." He shook his head. "Could have fooled me when she said she was a doctor. A general, too?"

"Not just a general. A two-star general. Judge nothing by its cover at Big Heart Ranch." Lucy put a palm on the ground and began to stand.

"Wait, let me help." He held out a hand.

Lucy grabbed her straw Stetson from the ground, dusted it off and jammed the crown on her head over her chin-length dark hair. With a sigh of resignation, she accepted Jack's outstretched palm. Her small hand fit neatly in his as he carefully assisted her to a standing position. "Feeling okay?"

She blinked and took a deep breath, but didn't meet his gaze. "I'm good," she murmured, slowly extricating her hand from his.

Lucy turned away from him in a quick movement and stumbled in the process. He reached for her arm.

"I've got it." Lucy nodded her thanks, before stepping away from his hand on her elbow. She dusted off her jeans and grimaced at the red dirt and grass stains marring her once pristine T-shirt.

Her eyes widened when he stepped toward her. "You've got stuff in your hair," Jack said. He reached forward, plucked a piece of leaf and twig from the dark tresses and placed them in her palm. "There's still…"

Nodding, she removed her hat and ran her hands through the short cap of hair, ruffling the strands and releasing bits of grass and dirt.

"You got it," he said.

They stood facing each other, silent for a moment. "Thank you," Lucy murmured.

"No problem." When he pulled down the steps to the

wagon and yanked back a flap of canvas, Dub instantly appeared.

The little man's jaw dropped for a moment, and then he screwed up his face. "Miss Lucy, are you okay?"

"She fell down," Jack said.

"We gots to pray for her, Mr. Jack."

"What?" Jack's head jerked back at the words.

"We gots to pray for her, right now."

"Dub, we can pray later," Lucy suggested.

"No. Miss Lucy, we learned in Bible study that you should pray now. Not later. Later doesn't always come."

"I, ah… I haven't prayed for anyone in a long time," Jack said.

"Don't worry. I'll show you how," Dub said. He took Lucy's and then Jack's hand in his small ones. "Now, close your eyes. I'll talk to God. Don't worry."

Jack swallowed hard and looked to Lucy, hoping for an escape route.

"Planting seeds," Lucy murmured.

Jack shook his head and then closed his eyes, swallowing hard as he recalled that he hadn't prayed in over twenty-five years. Not since that fateful day his brother died.

So today he would pray, because a five-year-old orphan had told him to, and because he realized that Dub was right. Despite his misgivings about Big Heart Ranch, Lucy Maxwell still deserved his prayers.

Jack opened his eyes and rested his gaze on Lucy, and his thoughts whispered softly, reminding him how right the woman felt in his arms. In that moment, he reluctantly admitted that maybe he needed prayer, too.

"So you're sort of a white-collar rebel. Aren't you?" Lucy asked as she approached Jack Harris.

"Is that a trick question?"

The light from the campfire silhouetted his strong profile as he stood in front of what was supposed to be his tent. It also illuminated the cell phone in his hand, and Lucy clucked her tongue in dismay.

"Everyone else set up their tents hours ago." She switched on the flashlight in her hand and shone the beam over the tarp and poles at his feet. "What are you doing?"

Jack casually eased his phone into the back pocket of his blue jeans, picked up a pole and fit it into another. "Is that a rhetorical question?"

She slowly shook her head. "You know, I would have never taken you for a rule breaker."

"Rule breaker?"

"You're using electronics."

"I'm trying to put a tent together, ideally before midnight."

He looked at his watch, an expensive electronic gadget that no doubt cost more than her car.

"Nice watch. Does it talk to your phone and your laptop, and monitor your heart rate and the size of your ego and all that good stuff?"

"Yeah. It does. Except for the ego part." He met her gaze and raised a hand. "I know what you're thinking, but in my defense, this tent did not come with instructions."

"That's because everyone knows how to put a pup tent together."

"We don't have pup tents in the Financial District."

"And yet the bottom line remains the same. Electronics are not allowed."

"I wasn't—"

"A simple rule. The children understand this rule."

"But—"

Lucy cleared her throat. "We're communing with nature, Jack. Enjoying everything God gave us. Didn't you enjoy the trail ride here? The scenery is pretty stupendous. What about that campfire stew and those sweet potato biscuits? Our cook used to be a chef at a Michelin three-star restaurant. He's a volunteer, too."

"The meal was delicious." He nodded. "To tell you the truth, I might have enjoyed the ride, if it were two hours shorter."

"Nonetheless, you were warned. No electronics."

"Technically, I wasn't using my phone. It was a tutorial on putting up tents that I downloaded earlier." He glanced at the pile of tarp and poles in front of him once more and grimaced.

"I know an electronics infraction when I see one, Mr. Harris."

"Are we back to, Mr. Harris?" He turned and met her gaze. "How's the head?"

Lucy gingerly touched her fingers to the back of her head. "I'm perfectly fine. It doesn't even hurt."

"Then why are your eyes crossed?"

She stiffened. "They are not." Refusing to be distracted, she held out her palm. "If you're trying to earn brownie points with the electronics police, it's not working."

"Apparently you're feeling better." He stared at her outstretched hand and held up two fingers. "How many fingers?"

"Two." Lucy stretched her hand even closer to him.

He stepped back. "What if my aunt tries to reach me?"

"The sympathy card won't work, either. Meredith has all the ranch numbers. They'll contact us immediately. We even have a two-way radio for emergencies." She put her hands on her hips. "We've been doing this for a long time, Mr. Harris. We have a contingency plan for everything."

"No electronics," he repeated. "Do you mind telling me how you're going to wake everyone up in the morning? And what about breakfast?"

"Actually, I will have the pleasure of rousing our camp. I wake daily at dawn automatically. It's a little-known talent of mine."

"Why am I not surprised?" he muttered.

"Pardon me?"

Jack knelt down to smooth the ground cloth. "And meals?"

"We have a fire permit for the evening campfires, and our cook will be using a camp stove with a propane tank. Authentic meals, I'm afraid. Right down to the coffee."

Jack took a deep breath.

"Now, may I have your phone?" She paused. "And your watch."

He stood and hesitantly placed the cell in her hand. When their hands touched, Lucy stepped back and looked away. How could a simple touch be so potent? This was new territory for her and she was admittedly confused.

"What happens at night?" Jack finally asked.

"At night?"

"While we're sleeping. If there's an emergency. Coyotes, wolves, bears." He frowned and glanced around at the looming dark shadows of the woods that surrounded them, as though evaluating the merit of her words. "Or illness."

"We have security. I hired two wranglers to watch the camp during the night to ensure our site is secure, and because I am aware that kids will be kids. I don't want any problems while I sleep. They'll ride to the ranch in the morning and be back again at night."

"That was a three-hour ride to get here."

"They took the shortcut on the other side of the woods. It connects with the main road."

"Any special reason we had to commune with nature this far out, as opposed to, say, one hour on the trail?" Jack glanced at her. "I would have been okay with the one-hour back route. I've got aches where I didn't even know I could have aches."

"I thought your aunt said you were experienced in the saddle."

"I was. A long time ago."

"Where did you ride?"

"Aunt Meredith's stable used to be filled with horses. My brother and I spent every summer in the saddle."

"Good memories?"

"Yeah, the best. I would have savored them more if I'd only known."

"Known what?" Lucy asked.

He shook his head, dismissing the subject.

"Well, if it's any consolation, there are actually other reasons for being this far out. I'll explain when it starts raining."

She followed his gaze when he glanced up at the night sky. A stretch of deep blue-black edged with the fading orange of the setting sun filled the skies. Around them, the only sounds were the katydids singing and the muffled chatter of tent conversations.

"Doesn't look like rain to me," he finally said.

"All meteorological indicators point to rain tomorrow afternoon, and it's going to be a gully washer."

"A what?"

"I'll explain that tomorrow, as well," she said. "In the meantime, relax. Enjoy yourself, and I'll have Rue drop off some ibuprofen."

He stared at the pile of poles and fabric at his feet. "Enjoy. Yeah, I'll get right on that."

"Would you like some help with your tent?" Lucy asked.

"It's a simple pup tent. I ought to be able to put it together myself." He turned his head to look at the other tents, all efficiently raised and ready for the night.

"I'll send Dub out to help you. Please escort him back to the camp wagon when he's done."

"You're telling me that a first-grader knows how to put up a tent?"

"Kindergartener." She nodded. "And yes, Dub is extremely intuitive."

"Great. First undermined by a chicken, now I'll be schooled by a five-year-old."

"We're all about sharing our special skills here."

"Are you?"

"Yes. Oh, and do hurry, or you're going to miss dessert. Dub is so excited about ice cream and cake that he's sitting in that wagon talking to the cook nonstop."

"Ice cream?"

"Anything is possible at Big Heart Ranch."

"It's got to cost a fortune to bring ice cream out here in the middle of nowhere in July. That's how you allocate donations?"

"Put away your calculator heart, Mr. Harris." She pointed a finger at him. "This did not come out of our budget. The mayor of Timber donated the ice cream. They're bringing it out on dry ice with the Ute, from the main road."

"The mayor?"

"Yes. He supports our ranch one hundred percent. It helps that he owns an ice cream parlor, as well."

"We better get the Dubster over here to save me, so he can have his cake and ice cream."

"Will do." She turned to leave, but then stopped and faced him. "I didn't thank you for coming to my assistance this afternoon. Thank you."

Jack nodded without meeting her gaze. Head down, he shifted position as though unaccustomed to thanks, and tucked his hands into his front pockets. This was a vulnerable side of the man she hadn't seen. It was oddly attractive.

"And thank you for praying with Dub earlier. I have no idea if you're a praying man, but Dub needed that. A male role model and all."

"Me? A role model?" He scoffed. "I don't think so."

"You underestimate yourself, and you were great with Dub."

"Hmm. Was I? Aunt Meri had me in church all the time when I was Dub's age."

"And now?"

"I seem to have misplaced a good excuse for why I haven't given God the time of day."

She nodded slowly. "You're very close to your aunt, aren't you?"

"I owe her a lot. My aunt gave me hope when I needed it most."

"She gave us hope, too. Once she got on board, the entire community followed. Now that's exactly what we offer in return at the ranch. Hope. No one understands that more than Meredith Brisbane."

"My aunt is getting older. I'm not sure about her decision-making ability anymore."

"It isn't necessary for you to keep reminding me that this isn't personal. I get that, Jack. All I'm saying is that you shouldn't rule out the possibility that God has a hand in all our lives—yours, mine, your aunt's and Dub's. Have you considered that you might be here for a reason, and perhaps it has nothing to do with Big Heart Ranch's donation?"

"You really believe that?"

"You've been with us only twenty-four hours, and already I'm sensing a change in you."

His gaze met hers, and for once the gray eyes were without shutters. He stared for a long moment as if searching for something. Maybe the same thing she was—trying to figure out what was happening between them.

"I believe anything is possible, Jack," she whispered. "And trust me, that thought scares me as much as it does you."

Chapter Five

"Rise and shine."

Jack groaned and opened his eyes. This was probably the strangest dream he'd ever had—bordering on a nightmare when he realized that it was Lucy Maxwell's voice. He smelled bacon, too. *Odd.* Patting the ground beside him, he searched for his phone, but his fingers only came up with the cool, damp fabric of the ground cloth.

He blinked and realized where he was. In a tent. On the Big Heart Ranch epic trail ride and campout. In the middle of nowhere, Oklahoma. Without his cell phone or his watch.

"Mr. Jack?" A soft pummeling on his tent wall ensued. "Time to rise and shine. Miss Lucy said so a long time ago. Didn't you hear her?"

Dub Lewis.

"I'm up."

"Hurry. You missed breakfast and we gotta start the scavenger hunt."

"I missed breakfast?" Jack rubbed his eyes. But he was sure it was only minutes ago that he'd heard Lucy's voice.

"Are you coming?"

"I am. Be right there, Dub. Don't move."

"Yes, sir. But I have to make a trip down to the outhouse. And I gots to go bad."

"Go. I'll be right there."

"I'm not allowed to go by myself. I have to go with my buddy." There was a long pause. "That's you."

"Okay. Hang on a minute." Jack unzipped his sleeping bag, tried to stand and fell over in a tangle. "Oomph."

"You okay, Mr. Jack?"

"I'm fine," he muttered. Once again he automatically reached for his phone to check both the time and the temperature. No phone. *Right.* Drill Sergeant Maxwell had confiscated it.

He grabbed his paddock boots, unzipped the tent and crawled out, managing to hit his head on a tent pole. "Ouch."

"Mr. Jack, your tent is lopsided."

"Yeah. I got up in the night and forgot I was in a tent and bent the pole. Maybe we can fix that today."

"Okay."

"How did you sleep, Dub?"

"Good, until the big boys came in."

"Big boys?"

"Yeah. Stewie and Henry. They're twelve. They're my brothers here at the ranch. We live in the same house. Miss Lucy made them sleep in the wagon 'cause they were naughty."

"Oh, yeah?"

Dub nodded. "They tried to scare me with creepy stories, but I plugged my ears."

"Good for you."

Jack glanced down at the little man outside his tent. Today he wore jeans, a striped T-shirt and the red sneakers he favored. A small backpack was slung over his shoulder. The boy wriggled in an antsy dance, moving back and forth from one foot to another.

"I guess you're ready to go."

"Uh-huh." Dub shot ahead down the path to the creek.

"Wait for me. Those woods can be dangerous," Jack called. "Stop moving. Stand right there."

"You missed the meeting," Dub announced when Jack caught up. "Miss Lucy said she tried to wake you up, but you yelled at her."

"I did?"

"Yeth. She said sometimes it's better to let people sleep."

"I had a hard time falling asleep," he muttered. If he'd had his phone, his alarm would have ensured an early rising and that he didn't miss anything. Plus, he'd know the forecast. The weather app on his phone would have provided the humidity, UV index, wind factor and temperature. Without an information overload, the world seemed off.

His gaze scanned the sky, which held low layered clouds. Okay, fine. No weather app needed today. Nothing said rain louder than cumulonimbus or nimbostratus clouds. Yesterday he would have said that it was impossible for the humidity to get any higher. Yet today it was so thick, he could easily swim down to the creek. Muggy Oklahoma air had drowned out the scent of pine and campfire cooking.

Yes. It was going to rain. All part of Lucy's nefarious plot to annoy him.

"Ouch." Dub slapped a hand to his forearm.

"You okay?"

"Yeth. Just a skeeter."

"Skeeter?" Jack frowned. "Oh, a mosquito. Don't scratch the bite."

Dub nodded. "Miss Lucy passed out the scavenger hunt papers. I gots one for us. She said that if it rains, we're going through the woods to the other side."

"What's on the other side?"

Dub shrugged.

"Anything else?" Jack asked.

"Watch out for poison ivy. Some of the boys already have the itches. Miss Lucy says she's real allergic to poison ivy. So we should go see the general if we get allergic, not her."

Jack picked up a long stick near the edge of the woods and tapped it on the ground, testing its sturdiness. Then he began to strip the bark.

"What's that for?" Dub asked.

"To keep us out of the poison ivy."

"What's poison ivy look like?"

"It looks like a plant."

"But Mr. Jack, the woods have lots of plants."

"You're right, Dub. Which is why we have to be extra careful. It's a tricky plant."

"How will we know?"

"Poison ivy has three leaves." Jack stopped and glanced around as they walked deeper into the dense brush. "Wow, there's a lot of poison ivy in these woods." He crouched down to inspect the brush. "See?" Jack nodded toward the foliage and used the stick to point out the three-leaf configuration. "This is what I'm talking about."

When Dub reached out a hand toward the plant, Jack's arm shot out to hold him back. "You can't touch. At all. It has oil that gets on your clothes and your skin and causes all sorts of itchy problems." Jack stood. "We'll stay on the trail. But don't touch anything that looks like this."

"Three. Three. Three," Dub repeated as he headed

down the trail. Then he stopped and glanced around. "You hear that noise?"

"July in Oklahoma means singing bugs." Jack reluctantly grinned. One more thing he'd nearly forgotten. "Those are the cicadas. They sing in the daytime, and the katydids sing at night."

Dub's amused laughter rang out. "Singing bugs."

At the end of the trail, the underbrush thinned and finally separated to reveal two outhouses on the right and a bubbly tree-lined creek straight ahead.

Jack entered one outhouse door and Dub the other. When they emerged, Jack pointed to the water. "Let's wash in the creek."

Dub dipped his hands in the water and swished them around. Then he stood and stepped back, eyes wide. "I saw something move in there." Excitement laced his voice, and he splashed his hands in the water again. "Maybe it was a fish."

Jack stepped closer and knelt on the muddy shale stones of the creek bank. "Pollywogs."

"What's a pollywog?"

"Those are baby frogs. Little swimmers."

Again, Dub laughed at this new word. Fascinated, he knelt at the creek's edge, scooting close to Jack, eyes on the water for long minutes. When he started to slip forward, Jack grabbed a handful of T-shirt and pulled him back.

Dub turned, eyes wide. "I almost fell in."

"I know. You have to be careful." Jack stood. "Ready to go?"

"Uh-huh. But don't you want your breakfast?"

"What?"

Dub pulled off his backpack and brought out a plastic bag with toast and bacon and offered it to Jack.

"Where'd this come from?"

"I asked the cook to save some for you, and he did."

"Dub, thank you." Jack stared at the little guy in wonder, touched by the gesture. "Come on. Let's find a chair."

"A chair?"

"Yeah. See those tree stumps. We can sit there."

"Poison ivy?"

"It's safe." Jack sat and pulled the bacon from the bag. "Want some?"

"Yeth, please."

Jack handed the bag to Dub.

"It sure is pretty out here, isn't it Mr. Jack?" Dub chewed slowly, savoring the bacon. His little feet tapped on the long grass that grew around the stump as he glanced around.

"Yeah, Dub, it is." Jack's gaze followed Dub's. Mature trees lined the creek, shading the frothy water from the sun's rays. The creek wound through the fingers of a willow whose roots were embedded in the bank and covered in moss before the stream moved over fallen logs at a leisurely pace. As the water passed over rock and shale, a tinkling song reached out to those who listened.

The song of the creek settled between Jack and Dub as they ate.

"Do you like kids, Mr. Jack?"

"Huh?" Jack turned to Dub. "Where did that come from?"

"I was just wondering. Stewie said you look sorta like you don't like kids."

"What?"

"'Cause you don't smile."

"I don't smile?" Jack pondered the words. "I guess I think a lot."

"What do you think about?"

"Everything. Too much of everything."

"Do you have a mom and dad?"

Jack nodded.

"Sisters and brothers?"

"I used to have a brother. He was a lot like you. Smart and happy and he talked all the time. I liked to listen to him talk." Jack swallowed back emotion that threatened. Emotion he thought he'd buried long ago.

"What happened to him?" Dub asked.

"He died."

Dub was silent for minutes, then he slid off the stump and walked over and placed a hand on Jack's arm. "Don't be sad," he said solemnly. "I'm your buddy. You have me."

"I, ah… Thanks, Dub."

"Maybe you can meet my sisters."

"Maybe."

"I'll ask Miss Lucy. Maybe you can take us for ice cream, too."

"Maybe." Jack smiled.

"When can I ride Grace?"

"Kid, you segue faster than a trader on Wall Street."

"Huh?"

"Never mind. Do you have boots?"

"Boots? No. I have sneakers. Miss Lucy calls them tennis shoes, but I don't know how to play tennis."

"We need to get you a pair of boots like mine before you can ride Grace." Jack glanced at Dub's sneakers. "Can I see one?"

Dub frowned. "You want to see my shoe?"

"Yeah."

Dub slipped off a sneaker and offered it to Jack.

"Size twelve." He handed the shoe back. "Now, where's that scavenger hunt list?"

Dub fished a damp and crumpled paper from his pocket and handed it over. Jack chuckled and smoothed the sheet on his leg.

"Okay, here's what we have to find. A heart-shaped stone. A snakeskin. A feather. Tree bark. A pine cone. A green leaf and a dry brown leaf. Seeds. A stick shaped like a letter. Oh, and something red."

The sound of campers marching through the woods interrupted their conversation. Jack recognized one of the voices. *Lucy.* He feigned deep concentration with the list.

"Mr. Harris, how lovely of you to get up at the crack of noon," she called out.

"I don't have a watch, so I don't know what time it is," he returned without looking up.

"I did try to wake you, but you threw a shoe in my general direction."

"Yeah, sorry about that. Nothing personal. I'm not responsible for my actions when I'm asleep."

"I'll make note of that sad story. In the meantime, Dub can probably teach you how to tell time by looking at the sun. Right, Dub?"

"Yeth, Miss Lucy."

Jack grudgingly met her gaze as she breezed past with two boys at her heels.

"You'll have to get moving if you want to win." She smiled indulgently at him. "Early bird catches the worm," she taunted.

"Nope. There isn't a single worm on the list," he muttered.

"That's Stewie and Henry," Dub said.

"Those boys with her? Miss Lucy has two buddies?"

"Uh-huh."

"Figures. Overachiever."

"What's that mean?"

"It means that we better get going." Jack shoved the rest of the toast in his mouth and held up the empty plastic bag. "Here. You hold this for our scavenger hunt stuff."

"Okay."

"We're going to find everything on that list, Dub."

"We have to do it faster than Miss Lucy."

"Yeah. We will. Don't worry. I have a long history of winning."

"I dunno. She's good."

"Miss Lucy might be good, but Mr. Jack is better." He offered Dub a fist bump, and the little guy grinned as he touched his small fist to Jack's big one.

Jack pointed to an area to the right. "Look. A red leaf."

"I see it. I see it." Dub grabbed the leaf and put it in the bag, grinning.

"Now what?"

"We're going to unexplored territory. Where Miss Lucy hasn't been."

"Huh?"

"We're crossing that creek, Dub."

Dub blinked. "It's cold and deep, and very, very scary."

"You're going to ride on my back."

"But you'll get cold."

"It's already at least eighty-five degrees. I don't mind a little cold water."

"What if we fall?" Dub looked at him, his lower lip trembling. "I don't how to swim."

Jack crouched down and met the boy's wide blue eyes. "Do you trust me?"

Dub sucked in his lips and nodded.

"Okay, then climb on my back." Jack grunted as Dub hopped on and clung tightly. "Hold on tight, buddy."

When Jack splashed through the shallow creek to the other side, Dub started to giggle. Jack splashed harder, stomping through the water, inciting more laughter. His heart swelled with something he hadn't felt in years. Pure joy.

"There you go." He eased the boy down to the ground. "Now you find a piece of tree bark and I'll find that heart-shaped stone."

"Yes, sir, Mr. Jack."

Jack chuckled, then suddenly paused as reality set in. His little buddy was beginning to grow on him.

That couldn't be a good thing. Could it?

Lucy stood very still watching Jack Harris.

He was stretched on the ground beneath the shade of a redbud tree with a ball cap over his eyes. His head rested on a rolled-up sleeping bag, and his arms were crossed over his broad chest.

Ugh. Why did the man look so good? They'd been out here for two days now, and lack of hygiene was already evident on everyone except him. There was no doubt that she looked appalling, and smelled like eau de insect repellent and Oklahoma dirt, as well.

Lucy pushed her Stetson from her head until it hung by the leather cord down her back. She finger combed her hair, tucking it behind her ears, pretending that the preening would make a difference.

"Jack?"

He slowly raised the visor of the cap from his face and eyed her with suspicion. "Yes, Drill Sergeant?"

"Why aren't you napping in your tent?"

"My tent doesn't like me." He dropped the cap over his face.

"I see." She crossed her arms and bit her lip, hoping for a natural opening to the next topic on her mind.

"Was there something else?" he mumbled.

"Um, yes, actually. I want to talk to you about Dub."

"Am I in trouble again?"

"You tell me."

Jack offered a dramatic sigh and sat up.

"Dub says you agreed to go for ice cream with him and his sisters, and that you're going to let him ride Grace."

"I believe the operative word I used was *maybe*."

"There's something you need to understand. While children pretend to understand maybe, the reality is that there is no 'maybe' in a child's vocabulary," Lucy said. "There is only 'you promised' and 'you lied.'"

Jack blinked and frowned. "Oh."

"Yes. Oh. So I trust you will follow through and keep your promises."

"I can do that." He nodded. "By the way, don't forget to pencil me in."

Panic tap-danced in her stomach at his words. "Pencil you in for what?" She stared blankly at him.

"Remember what Rue said? Walk a mile in your shoes. I'd like to spend the day with you in your office."

"I can provide you with any number of ranch financials or paperwork you want to review. Transparent is my middle name."

"No. I want to spend the day understanding what the director does."

Lucy took a calming breath, imagining Jack in her itty-bitty messy office. She wouldn't be able to breathe with him that close. "Is that necessary?"

"I think so."

"Fine," Lucy muttered. Which meant that she'd find a way to prevent that from ever happening in her lifetime. She turned on her heel. "But for now, you might want to head over to the field. We're dividing up into teams for softball."

"Seriously? We've been going nonstop since what I

believe was 6:00 a.m. I don't have a watch, so I'm not sure." He paused. "First there was the scavenger hunt, followed immediately by the hike from—"

Lucy cleared her throat loudly and swung back to face him. "Language, Mr. Harris."

"What? The hike from my nightmares."

"You're a big-shot attorney. I bet you usually work from dawn to dusk. So what's with the whining about long hours?"

"Yeah, I do—at a desk, with an ergonomic chair, and climate-controlled air."

"What kind of attorney are you anyhow?"

"An extremely boring one. Contract law."

"Quite lucrative, I imagine."

"Imagine away," he said as he adjusted his ball cap. "Just remember that I'm not Mr. Lucrative anymore."

Her eyes rounded, and she gestured wildly with her hands. "You didn't think I was assessing your financial worth, did you?"

"It wouldn't be the first time."

Lucy choked. "Oh, my, my, my. That ego of yours is so enormous, it's a wonder you can stand upright."

"Okay, sorry. I might have jumped to conclusions based on past experiences."

"You think?" She shook her head. "All I was getting at was that you invested years and money in your career and climbed the corporate ladder only to give it away?"

"I still own a walkup in the city and have a gym membership that doesn't expire for twenty-four months."

She laughed. "That's a long way to go for aerobics."

"True. When clearly I can get the same thing here for free, right?"

"Right. So what's the plan?"

"I don't follow."

"Eventually you're going realize that Big Heart Ranch is not a shady fly-by-night outfit. So what's the plan after that?"

"There is no plan. I'm here to help my aunt," he said.

"No plan?"

"It doesn't take a genius to figure out that you're big into plans, Madame Director, but I'm trying to leave my options open. Go with the flow."

"When will you go with the flow back to New York?"

"In a rush to get rid of me?"

"You city folk all get tired of playing cowboy and eventually head back to wherever you came from. I've seen it enough times."

"No bitterness there," Jack muttered.

Lucy stared at him. "What did you say?"

"Sounds like you've had some history with temporary cowboys."

"We're talking about you. Not me."

Jack stood and dusted off his pants. "My ticket is open-ended."

Lucy ignored the comment. "So, you and Dub have really bonded, haven't you?"

He turned around and stared at her. "Have we?"

"It certainly seems that way."

"You gave me an assignment, and I take my assignments very seriously."

"An assignment."

"Was that the wrong answer? Lucy, Dub is my buddy. What else do you want?"

"I want you to be very careful." Lucy said the words softly as Dub approached them with a grin on his face and a blue ribbon pinned to his chest.

She addressed the little boy. "Congratulations again, Dub. You did a great job with the scavenger hunt."

"Not just me. Mr. Jack, too. We hunted on the other side of the creek. It's a secret." He began to giggle, hands over his mouth.

Lucy glanced from Dub to Jack. Though Jack's face remained impassive, his eyes sparkled with amusement at Dub's words. The man could run, but he couldn't hide from what was happening to him.

"Can I have the treasures we collected, Miss Lucy?"

"Absolutely, but keep that snakeskin in the plastic bag, okay?" Again she looked between them. "You two were the only ones who found the snakeskin."

"We're real good. Right, Dub?" Jack said.

Dub nodded and approached Jack. "Here, Mr. Jack, this is for you." Dub opened his hand, where the heart-shaped stone rested in his small palm.

With a broad smile, Jack took the stone from Dub's little hand. "Thanks, buddy."

Lucy's heart melted. Oh, this wasn't good. Not at all. What was she thinking? Dub was falling for Jack Harris. Soon he'd be tired of Oklahoma and back to his life in New York. And little Dub would be left with a broken heart.

Jack stared at the stone, a tender expression on his face. He slowly lifted his eyes, and his gaze met hers. When Lucy's stomach did a little flip-flop, she knew she was in trouble. Dub wasn't the only one who might be falling for the temporary cowboy.

Chapter Six

"Come on, Maxwell. Bases are loaded. This is your chance," Jack said from behind home plate. "Look sharp."

"Jack, don't coach her. She's on the opposite team!" Rue Butterfield called out from the pitcher's mound.

"Coach! In his dreams. The man is trying to rattle me," Lucy said as she warmed up, swinging the bat in an arc with a fierce deliberation. She turned and glared at him before lowering the brim of her red-team ball cap and getting back into position.

Jack grinned and flipped his own blue-team cap around until the bill was to the back, before he squatted down and punched the center of his catcher's mitt for good measure. For a micromanaging director, Lucy sure was cute. Distractingly so, in her jeans and red boots. Who played softball in cowboy boots? He chuckled and forced himself to focus on the pitcher. All Rue had to do was strike Lucy out, and the red team would be shut out.

On the mound, General Rue Butterfield began to wind up. Clearly, the general knew her way around a pitching mound. She stood with her left leg slightly elevated, followed by the synchronous movement of her hip as she released the ball.

It flew through the air toward Lucy, faster than a homing missile.

Crack!

Whoa! The woman could bat!

Jack jumped up to keep his eye on the ball as it sailed impossibly high and far. He blinked. It seemed apparent he'd underestimated this particular batter.

"Long fly ball," someone called out. Lucy dropped the bat and headed to first, red boots moving faster than he imagined the cowgirl could run.

"Way to make something happen," one of the teenagers on the red team yelled. The chants of support became louder as each runner rounded bases and headed home.

"Take 'er home, Lucy! Take 'er home!" another player called.

"Go! Go! Go!" Dub screamed from his spot on the sidelines. His normally pale complexion was ruddy with the exertion.

Rue backed up and positioned herself to catch the ball the outfielder tossed to her, just as Lucy passed third, her eye intent on home.

Jack cupped his hands around his mouth. "Slide! Slide! You can do it, Lucy!"

Lucy dove at the same time Jack caught the ball Rue threw to him. Red dust filled the air in a cloud, making it impossible to determine the outcome.

"Safe!" the umpire called, arms crossing and then spreading wide.

Lucy stood, a goofy grin on her face, along with a film of dusty red clay. She smiled at him and rubbed her chin with a hand, revealing a bright red abrasion where her face had kissed the ground.

"Nice job, Jeter," Jack said. "Uh, you cut your lip and your chin is bleeding, as well."

"All part of the job," she said. "All part of the job."

"No, really. It's bleeding," he said.

"I'm fine." She lifted her fingers to her face, carefully touching the area, and grimaced.

"Right. I've heard that song somewhere before," he muttered.

"Jack, you seem to be under the impression you are on Lucy's team," Rue observed as she approached from the field, her mitt tucked beneath her arm. She pulled a well-worn copy of the rule book from her back pocket. "Do you need to read this?"

Jack laughed. "Not necessary, General. I have a firm policy of always rooting for the underdog. Another facet of my diverse moral compass."

"Moral compass? You should have been a politician," Lucy panted as she worked hard to catch her breath. She stood staring at him with indignation flushing her face. "And I am not an underdog. You started rooting for me so you'd be on the winning side in your mind."

Jack chuckled, unwilling to admit that rooting for Lucy sort of came out of nowhere. He couldn't help himself.

Rue glanced at Lucy. "Nicely done, dear, but you need medical attention."

Overhead light streaked across the darkening summer sky, followed by the ferocious roar of thunder.

"It will have to wait," Lucy said, her gaze fixed on the fast-moving black clouds above as thunder ripped the air again moments later.

Dub rocketed into the air from his position on the batter's bench and screamed, "Thunder!" His voice quivered.

"Easy, Dub. Easy," Lucy soothed. She shook her head. "Those clouds are moving quickly, but the flash-to-bang count says the heart of that storm is still two miles away. We should have enough time to get to safety. Barely."

Jack met Lucy's gaze. "Did you minor in meteorology in college?" he asked.

"You've got to stay keenly tuned in to the weather when camping. Especially in Oklahoma. This storm was only supposed to be precipitation. Once again I was trumped by Mother Nature." She put her hands around her mouth. "Game called due to weather! Pack up your gear and grab your horses. We are out of here in five."

Groans went up as players left the field and jogged toward the tents.

"What do you mean the game is called? We were about to win," Jack said.

"When pigs fly. My team was about to win," she smoothly replied before turning to Dub. "Get in the wagon quickly, and put on your rain slicker and seat belt."

"Yeth, Miss Lucy."

Then she pointed to Jack. "You'll need to roll up your tent and pack. You have five or six minutes."

"Five minutes? You've got to be kidding. It took me four hours to put the thing up."

A glance at the sky confirmed her words. Large drops began to sail through the air and splatter on them. "Jack, I'm serious here. We leave as a group in five. Any longer and we'll increase the risk of being struck by lightning. Get Grace packed up, but don't ride her."

"Why not?"

"Visibility is going to be an issue, and we don't want any injuries. To horses or humans. Simply keep her calm."

"Where exactly is safety?" he asked.

"There's another route that will take us around the creek. We can make it in ten minutes."

"Make it where?" He turned around. "Lucy?"

The director had disappeared. Five minutes later, when she blew on the giant silver whistle that hung around her neck, he was still struggling with his tent poles.

"Line up!" she called.

"Jack, do you need help?" Rue asked as she straightened her clear plastic rain slicker and pulled the hood up over her silver curls.

He held up the plastic tent poles. "Why is it these things never go back in the package the way you found them?"

Rue only laughed. In under a minute she had the tent and poles neatly tucked into the pouch. "Practice, dear. Practice."

"Uh, thanks. Why aren't we waiting out the storm?" he asked the physician.

She shook her head. "We won't last the storm, not to mention that we're a target for a lightning strike out here in the open. Put on your slicker and prepare for the worst. This is a real Oklahoma gully washer."

"Gully washer again," he muttered.

"Indeed. The water moves fast and creates a dangerous torrent as it travels across the hard clay. Through the woods is the backup plan."

"To grandmother's house we go?"

"Something like that," Rue said as she flicked on her flashlight. "Follow me."

Lucy blew the whistle yet again, and all heads turned toward the director. "We will be walking our horses very carefully. Stay calm and they will, too." She pulled the hood on her cherry-red rain slicker over her hair as rainfall steadily increased, along with the wind.

"Once we get through the woods and arrive at the barn, stable your horse and wipe them down!" Now Lucy was yelling to be heard over the storm. "After you lock the stall, meet General Butterfield at the front of the barn for head count."

The clopping of horses' hooves and the steady drumming of falling rain provided the backdrop for the campers walking through the dark woodland trail. Grace shook her head, tossing moisture from her mane as the rain sluiced down her broad face each time there was a gap in the tree coverage overhead.

Jack shivered and pulled up his shirt collar against the water that ran down his back. The sweatshirt he'd shrugged over his head back at camp was already heavy with moisture. "How far is this place?" he asked Rue.

"A straight shot. Ten minutes at most." She looked him up and down, a frown on her face. "Where's your rain slicker?"

"I might have forgotten to bring one."

Rue chuckled. "And your flashlight?"

"Confiscated. It was on my phone."

"Ah, right, city boy." She thrust an old-fashioned battery-operated flashlight into his hands. "Here. I have a spare. Not as cool as yours, I'm sure, but it works."

"Thanks, Rue." He shined the light toward the back of the procession. "Where's Dub and the chuck wagon?"

"The chuck wagon detoured straight to the main road and around. They'll meet us there." She smiled and patted his arm. "Don't worry about your buddy. He's safe."

Jack paused at Rue's words. Yeah, he was worried. Only a week, and already he was attached to the little guy. Attached and also responsible for him, even though he'd promised himself never again. There went his good intentions.

"I'm going to the rear to round up the stragglers,"

Rue said. She clucked her tongue and led her horse away from him.

A sudden gust of wind and rain nearly pulled Jack's ball cap off, before he repositioned it snugly on his head and wiped moisture from his face with the back of his hand.

"How do you like the weather?"

Jack jumped at the words and turned to see Lucy. "You're kind of like a ninja, aren't you? You appear silently out of the darkness." He glanced at her dark chestnut horse. "Even your horse is stealthy."

"Right. Cowgirl ninja and her faithful horse, Blaze."

Yet again, a streak of lightning lit up the sky overhead, followed by thunder. Grace whinnied nervously, and her hooves clopped on the wet ground in a fretful two-step next to him. Jack grabbed the reins tighter and ran a hand over the horse's forehead. "Easy, girl," he crooned.

"Grace doing okay?" Lucy asked.

"Actually, Grace seems to really like the rain. It's that noise she's not crazy about."

When Grace nodded and nickered in agreement, both Lucy and Jack laughed.

"How safe are we from lightning in the woods?" he asked Lucy.

"Safer than we were in that open field. Safer than if there were only one or two trees. I've been praying since that first lightning strike, Jack. That's all I know to do when the going gets tough. That and move quickly."

The trail narrowed and Jack pushed back the wet, low-hanging leaves of a maple and held them for Lucy and several campers to pass through. Then he blinked at the sight before him.

Not far ahead was a huge two-story log home lit up like a candle in the storm to welcome them. A rust-colored barn was angled to the left of the house. The chuck wagon had been parked in the drive, right in front of the house.

"What is this? You've been holding out on me," Jack said when he caught up to Lucy. "This was here all along?"

She stopped and they stood side by side, staring at the shelter from the storm straight ahead. "Don't get too excited. It's an empty house."

"An empty house in the middle of nowhere?"

"That's right."

"Running water?" he asked.

"Yes. Well water."

"Electricity?"

"Yes."

"What do you use this for?"

"I don't use the place, although it's kept stocked with emergency supplies. Canned food, candles, powdered milk, blankets and first-aid supplies. The usual doomsday stuff."

"Just in case of a zombie apocalypse?"

"Exactly," Lucy said. She turned to him with a slight smile.

He stared, fascinated, as the rain landed on her long eyelashes. When moisture ran down her nose, Jack was unable to resist reaching out a finger to catch the errant drops.

Lucy's dark eyes rounded at his touch, yet she didn't move away.

"Sorry. You were dripping."

For the longest moment, they stared at each other as they stood beneath the branches of the tree, the rain falling around them like a curtain. Jack leaned forward slightly.

"We don't want to go there, Jack," Lucy murmured, her voice a shaky whisper.

He stepped back.

She was right. Again.

Jack gripped the reins in his hand and turned toward the house, thankful for the shadows and questioning his impulsive gesture. Questioning his sanity when Lucy Maxwell was around.

They walked in silence across the clearing, getting closer and closer to the two-story structure.

"Where did it come from?" he finally asked.

"Wh-what?"

"The house."

"It's mine."

"You built a house that you never use?"

"I already said that."

Did he detect annoyance in her voice?

"I don't get it. What am I missing here?" Jack asked as they edged nearer to the property.

"What's to get?" She shrugged. "Sometimes the boot drops, plans change and you move on."

Something like nostalgia—or was it regret?—crossed Lucy's face as she stared at the house.

Jack nodded, his gaze assessing the ranch director. This was all very odd. He'd get to the bottom of this house-in-the-woods mystery eventually.

"We'll divide up into groups, and you'll be sleeping on the floor in your sleeping bag," Lucy continued.

"My own room?"

"Nice try."

"And yet, there are no tent poles to deal with. No mosquitos biting or katydids to sing all night." He stopped at a sudden thought. "I don't suppose there's cable and internet."

"The ban on electronics is still in place. Our roughing it simply got a little less rough." She looked at him, her eyes sparkling. "Wait until you see the fireplace in the great room. We can take turns roasting marshmallows tonight."

"S'mores?"

"I never got to be a Girl Scout, but I do understand the importance of s'mores. The cook will have plenty of supplies." She squirmed and scratched her arm.

"Poison ivy?"

"A touch."

"I can go get the general. She's not far behind."

"No. I'm fine. No big deal." She nodded toward the barn. "Come on. First things first. Head count, and then I need to get the horses settled for the night."

"Is there feed in that barn?"

"Of course. Everything is ready for the animals. All part of Plan B."

"How did you know we'd need one?" Jack asked.

"My life is an extended series of Plan B's. I've learned to stay one step ahead of them."

He frowned. "That's too bad."

"Is it?"

"You just said you live with a permanent worst-case-scenario agenda."

She frowned for a moment and pursed her lips. "I like to think of myself as extremely well-prepared."

"No. You're a pessimist who plans for failure."

"That's neither true nor fair. You hardly know me. At least not well enough to judge me." Lucy released a sigh. "I happen to be a very positive and optimistic person, unlike you, interviewing campers in your spare time, hoping to uncover some evil plot at Big Heart Ranch."

"I'm being friendly."

"Perhaps we can agree to disagree on this matter."

"Sure. But I'm still right," Jack murmured.

For long moments the only sound was Blaze's soft snort and Grace's whinny as rain continued to fall in silent sheets.

They crossed the gravel yard in front of the house and stopped outside the barn, where several riders and horses were already waiting. Lucy pulled back the metal slide bar and yanked open the big wooden double doors.

"Is there a light?" Jack asked.

"To your right. On the wall," Lucy said.

He hit the switch, illuminating the huge barn. The place was as nice as the stables at Big Heart Ranch. Hooves clopped on the plank floors as young riders and volunteers led their horses into the dry building. The campers' chatter echoed their relief. Jack also looked forward to getting out of wet clothes.

Lucy led her own horse into a stall at the far end of the barn, grabbed a towel from the stack on a shelf and began to briskly rub down Blaze. He followed suit and opened the stall next to hers. A towel and brush were ready on a shelf. He removed Grace's tack, and carefully dried it and hung the saddle up to dry out. Grace whinnied and shook her head, sprinkling water everywhere.

"Grace," Jack murmured. "You're giving me a shower." He inspected the horse and brushed down her silky flank.

Minutes later, Rue appeared outside Lucy's stall. "I've done a head count. Everyone is accounted for and in one piece. We have three with poison ivy. I'm glad we're at the lodge tonight."

"The lodge?" Jack asked.

Rue smiled. "A nickname for the house." She turned

back to Lucy. "I'll have the affected children shower first, and I'll bag up their clothing."

"Calamine and cortisone cream?" Lucy asked.

"Yes. We have plenty. And good thing—the poison ivy really is out of control this year."

Lucy shook her head, a troubled expression on her face. "I should have had someone up here to spray the grounds before we came."

"Lucy dear, you cannot possibly think of everything. When three children who were previously warned play in the poison ivy, you cannot blame yourself. Mother Nature will win every time."

"Still. I'll have the grounds sprayed before Travis brings his group out next Wednesday."

"Of course you will." Rue smiled and offered an indulgent nod. "We're heading into the lodge then."

"I'll be along shortly," Lucy said.

"Let someone else do the stall check," Rue said as she pulled her hood up over her head again.

"I'll sleep better if I do the job myself."

Rue stared at her and silently shook her head. "Don't take too long. You don't want to miss the treats, or the hot water before it runs out." The general led the line of boys and staff to the front door of the lodge, and they all disappeared inside.

Outside, the rain began to pound on the metal roof of the barn, *rat-a-tat-tat*, like a stranger demanding to be let in.

"Thunder and lightning have stopped," Jack observed. "But the rain is really picking up."

"I suggest you take cover, as well. Head for the house," Lucy said.

"What about you?"

"I'm going to do a visual check of all the horses first, and then I'll be in."

"I'll help you."

"That's not necessary."

"Lucy, how am I going to fill Leo's shoes if you keep turning down my help?"

"Okay, fine." She ran her fingers through the wet tangles of her hair.

Weariness seemed to have settled on her like a heavy blanket, and he found himself longing to ease her burden. Despite their differences, he had to admire the woman. She was always first on the job and last to leave. Her work ethic rivaled any he'd ever seen.

Lucy released a breath and tucked her shoulders back, as if rallying for a second round. "I'm going to inspect the horses. You check the stalls to be sure every horse has sufficient feed and enough water for the night."

"I thought someone did that already."

"We do it again at night check. Those are the rules."

"Seems repetitive, if you ask me."

A smile twitched at her lips. "Ah, yes, but I didn't ask you."

"Touché, Madame Director."

Chapter Seven

"**O**uch," Lucy murmured as Rue dabbed antibiotic ointment on her chin.

"Sorry, dear." Rue stepped back and assessed Lucy's face. "You've had quite a week. A near concussion, cut lip and chin, and now the poison ivy!"

"Yes, but that home run was worth every last scrape and bruise. Did you see Jack's eyes bug out of his head when I knocked that ball to the moon? I'll be savoring that for a long time."

Rue chuckled as she placed the tube of medication on the kitchen counter. She sniffed the air and stepped back. "What is that on your shirt, Lucy?"

Lucy looked down. "Blaze spit up on me."

"I trust you're going to shower tonight?"

"As soon as the hot water tank recovers."

"That may be a while." Rue shook her head. "You look exhausted, dear."

"I'll be fine." As she said the words, her body begged for rest from this very long day. Soon. Very soon.

"Yes. Fine as always," Rue returned with an arched brow. "Now, let's see those rashes."

Lucy slipped off her lightweight, zip-front sweatshirt

and stretched out her arms. "So far everything is mild. Thank you for the cortisone cream."

"You're welcome. We're headed back in the morning, right?"

"Late morning. Cook is making Belgian waffles outside with the portable stove before we go."

"Despite the fact that this trip has been a comedy of errors, we certainly have eaten well."

"True that," Lucy said.

The older woman smiled. "You know, if we hadn't had a rainout, I do believe your team might have come close to winning the game."

"Rue. We did win."

"Oh, no, dear, you called the game, and we weren't even close to the fourth inning. We call that a scratch. We'll have to have a rematch."

Lucy groaned. "Scratch? That's not a regulation softball term, Rue."

"Nonetheless—"

Jack popped his head into the kitchen. "Sorry to interrupt this sports discussion, ladies."

"Ah, our catcher. Just in time. You agree with me, right, Jack? That game was a scratch."

"I'll get back to you on that, General." He turned to Lucy. "They've cleaned us out of every last s'more, and it was suggested that I find you to signal the official bedtime roundup."

Lucy pulled her silver whistle from around her neck and held it out to him, her arm limp.

His eyes widened and he stepped back. "The whistle? You want me to take the official whistle?"

"You've certainly earned the privilege, after today," Lucy said.

"I don't know. I'm only a stand-in for Leo," he returned with a wink to Rue, who chuckled.

On impulse, Lucy stepped close and placed the whistle in his hand, then closed his fingers around the shiny metal. "You can do this. I have faith in you, Jack."

Jack's mouth tilted upward. "Thank you, Lucy," he murmured, his other hand closing over hers, his gaze intense, as though they were alone in the room.

Lucy nodded and swallowed, her heart thumping in her chest. She slipped her hand from his and turned to the sink.

"My, my, my," Rue said quietly.

"What?" Lucy overturned a stack of paper cups, righted them and fumbled with the faucet until the water cooperated.

"I had no idea."

"No idea what?" She filled the cup and chugged back the water, nearly choking in the process.

"Nothing, dear. Nothing." Rue gathered the supplies spread over the counter into her medical bag, snapped the brass closure in place and smiled. "Sleep tight."

Even after a shower, sleep remained oddly elusive. Lucy paced back and forth across the wide first-floor porch while the rain continued to patter against the eaves and drip from the gutters, splashing inches away from her feet.

Turning back to one of the two large rockers on the porch, she picked up her blanket and cocooned herself before sinking into the chair's deep seat.

Maybe it was the incident with Jack earlier. But which one? That moment in the woods or the one in the kitchen? What had she been thinking, taking his hand? Lucy Maxwell didn't do impulsive things like that. Hadn't she learned long ago to avoid situations where failure was not an option?

The screen door creaked, and Jack Harris stepped outside while pulling a dark sweatshirt over jeans and a white T-shirt. "May I join you?"

"Jack," she murmured. Just what she didn't need right now.

"Was that a yes?" he asked.

"Sure," she murmured. With the blanket draped around her, Lucy stood and moved to the far end of the porch. "Insomnia?" she asked as she peered into the darkness, working hard to remain nonchalant.

"I suppose so. It's always difficult to sleep when it's raining. Seems like I should be awake and enjoying the sounds."

"That's an interesting way to look at the weather. Where does that come from?"

When he leaned against the rail and rolled up the sleeves of his sweatshirt, her gaze was irresistibly drawn to him.

"My aunt, I guess. Wow, long time ago." He paused and ran a hand through his disheveled hair, as though struggling to recall distant memories. "I had nightmares often as a kid, and one night they were especially bad. A thunderstorm contributed to the issue, I suppose. Aunt Meri opened the French doors and we sat beneath the eaves, just like this, for hours. Aunt Meri said the storm was a private show from God, just for us." A small smile touched his lips.

"Your aunt is an amazing woman."

Jack nodded and offered a weary smile.

"Why the nightmares?" Lucy asked.

He shrugged and crossed his arms, dismissing the subject. "This is a great house, you know."

Lucy studied his strong profile as he stared out into the night. There were plenty of secrets hidden inside Jack Harris. That was the only thing she knew for certain after a week with the man.

"You're missing a great opportunity here," he mused.

"What opportunity is that?"

Jack turned to face her. "Your lodge is an untapped gold mine that could single-handedly keep your ranch afloat."

"What are you talking about?" Lucy asked, knowing that she probably shouldn't ask questions she didn't want the answer to. An uneasy shiver ran over her when he assessed the house before once again pinning her with his gaze.

"You were going on about cattle and vegetables and a self-sustaining vision for the ranch and all, correct?"

"Your point?"

"A little tweaking and you can rent this place out. Vacation rentals are big right now. Then there's weddings and retreats and small group programs. You know, if you add a few horses you have—"

"A dude ranch!" Lucy said, horror lacing her voice.

"They don't call them dude ranches anymore. Guest ranch is the term. Tourists really love that stuff."

She stiffened with indignation. "I don't think so."

"Why not?"

"Do you know how many guest ranches there are in the state of Oklahoma?"

"Come on, you were the one who said that people pay a small fortune for this kind of outdoor experience."

Lucy sank down into the nearest chair and gripped the wooden arms of the rocker. "I need to keep my big mouth shut."

"Visualize the chuck wagon in front of the house. Add

picnic tables, and you've got more authentic Oklahoma experiences for very little overhead." He gestured with a hand, excitement simmering in his voice. "You were right, Lucy. Camping. Trail rides. Outdoor meals. Rustic adventure. They eat it up, and you've got the perfect place sitting empty, waiting for you to tap into."

"They can eat it up somewhere else," she grumbled.

"Are you against making money?"

"No."

"All the profits would go directly back into the organization. Even your accountant would approve."

"Is everything about money with you, Harris?"

"Some people think that's a good thing. And who knows? If this takes off, you don't have to be as dependent on my aunt's donation. On anyone's donation."

"We are not dependent on your aunt's money. We are dependent on God."

He cocked his head. "Then why am I the new Leo?"

"We…we can't finalize our budget until we know what our estimated donations will be."

"With this idea, you never have to worry."

Lucy bit back the response on the end of her tongue and silently counted to five. "We don't worry. Big Heart Ranch belongs to God."

"Great, because I can't see God disapproving of using your resources for the kids. You said you want to be good stewards of the finances."

"But…but…" She struggled with the words, her mouth suddenly dry. "I thought you were here to approve the ranch for the donation."

"I'm here to get an understanding of what you do at the ranch. How the funds are allocated."

"How's that going for you?"

"Lucy, I'm not saying I will or will not approve of

the funds. This is apples and oranges. But you should at least think about what I'm saying. My aunt isn't going to be around forever. I'm offering you a way to ensure the ranch will be, and you're telling me that you aren't interested."

"You're twisting my words around. What I said is that I have no interest in any commercial venture that would include this house, Jack."

"What if your sister and Travis are interested?"

Lucy opened her mouth and closed it again. Her stomach dipped, and a queasy, unrestful feeling settled in the pit. It was her house. She longed to stamp her feet. If she had her way, she'd simply knock the place down. Raze it until it was gone, along with any evidence of how naive she'd been. And how her heart and her dreams had been broken into a zillion little pieces. The log house represented a happily-ever-after she'd never have.

"Tell you what," he said. "I'll make this easy. Let me do the legwork. This is the sort of thing I'm good at. I'll present you with my findings and we can go from there."

She frowned, growing more and more annoyed.

"Do we have a deal?"

"Fine. But I do not want a dude ranch here. I can't risk an unsavory presence on the property."

"We can find a way to make this work and keep the two entities separate."

"Can we?" She rubbed absently at the rash on her arms. The skin burned beneath her shirt.

"Sure. Where's your spirit of adventure?" He paused and pinned her with his gaze. "Why weren't you a Girl Scout anyhow?"

Lucy shook her head and looked at him. "You might consider refraining from prying into people's personal lives, Harris."

He offered a distracted nod at her words. "You know, it just occurred to me that maybe your childhood snuffed out any opportunity for being adventurous."

She stiffened. "I'm as adventurous as the next gal."

"So why no Girl Scouts? You sounded sort of bitter when you mentioned it earlier."

"No one shells out money to fosters for frivolous things like Girl Scouts."

"Fosters, huh?" He shook his head. "What happened to your parents, Lucy?" Jack asked quietly.

Around them, the rain had slowed to an almost intimate rhythmic patter. Lucy shivered as a cool breeze slid past. She pulled the blanket closer and stared out into the night.

"They died together in a motor vehicle accident. We were driving through the mountains in Colorado. A boulder broke loose. They said it was the result of a heavy spring runoff. It crashed the front of the car. Travis and Emma and I were trapped in the back."

Jack inhaled sharply. "I'm so sorry, Lucy."

"Stuff happens." She swallowed hard, focusing on a tiny chip of paint on the arm of the chair.

"Yeah, it does."

"Their deaths were just as painful as being separated from Travis and Emma. That's why this ranch is so important. I got a second chance. Giving kids a second chance is what we're called to do. It's a huge responsibility that I can't afford to mess up."

"Lucy, believe it or not, I do get that. I'm not immune to what you're trying to do, and believe it or not, I understand second chances."

She nodded slowly, wanting to believe him.

Jack tucked his hands in his pockets. "So, the house. You never did explain where it came from.

"The house is not part of Big Heart Ranch."

"Is there something you're hiding?"

"Not at all." She released a breath. "I was engaged. We built this house. The engagement didn't work out, and I bought my portion of the house from him." There. Now he had it. Her pitiful story.

"I'm sorry it didn't work out."

"It was a long time ago."

He frowned and looked at her. "You're still emotionally attached to the property, aren't you? Maybe you have hopes for reconciliation."

"Hardly," she scoffed. "He's moved on. Married a woman who doesn't come with baggage and sixty children." Lucy paused, realizing that her words were true. She had moved on. The pain that usually clawed at her chest when she thought of her former fiancé was gone.

When had that happened? How had she not noticed?

"The ranch? That was the problem?"

"Come on, Jack. Not many men want to marry a woman with a houseful of kids. Or in my case, a ranch-full."

"You do bring new meaning to the terms baggage and married to the job." He chuckled.

"I'm glad you find my pain so amusing."

"Aw, come on. If you don't laugh, what else can you do? Trust me, you aren't the only one who's been dumped."

"Not you? Big New York attorney?" She paused. "Let me guess. Supermodel?"

He straightened, looking almost offended. "How'd you know that?"

She laughed. "Because you're Captain Obvious."

"I like to think of myself as an open book."

Lucy choked on a laugh. "So why did you split up? Her ego was bigger than yours?"

"No. My bank account wasn't big enough."

"Ouch. That had to hurt."

"Surprisingly, not as much as I would have thought. We'd been lingering in the nowhere zone for so long, I didn't realize the relationship was dead until she'd been gone for two weeks and I hadn't even noticed."

Lucy looked up at Jack. She would have never guessed that his heart had suffered the same pain as hers. That didn't make them kindred spirits, though, she reminded herself.

Jack had buried his heartache, looking for all the world unscathed as he put on his lawyer face each day.

If only she could be so emotionless.

She shifted and tucked her feet beneath her. "Okay, this is getting far too maudlin for me. Can we change the subject?"

"Sure. How about food? I'm hungry."

"Didn't you eat s'mores?"

"Are you kidding? Those kids scarfed them down so fast, I would have lost fingers if I got between them and their appetites."

"The cook locks everything up at night."

"There isn't a single snack in this place?"

Lucy hesitated. "Well…" She met his gaze. "I do have my own personal locked closet downstairs in the pantry. I'm sure there's something in there. Whether it's edible or not is the real question."

He smiled. "Got the key with you?"

"I do." She folded up her blanket and stood, moving to the door. "Come on. But be quiet."

Jack held the door and followed Lucy through the entry and down the hall to the kitchen. He nearly knocked her over when she stopped in the middle of the room.

"Jack!" she hissed as he stumbled. "You're supposed to be quiet."

"I'm sorry. Why did you stop?"

"Because this is the closet." Lucy nodded to a tall door and pulled keys from her pocket. After fitting one into the lock, she turned to him. "I can't turn on the light until the door is closed. No one must see the inside of this closet."

He narrowed his eyes. "What sort of contraband do you have in there?"

The hardware creaked when she eased the door open.

"Come on," Lucy whispered.

When he didn't move, she grabbed his shirt and yanked him into the darkness before closing the door behind them.

The space was tight and she could sense when Jack turned slightly, as if trying to orient himself in the shadowed space. When the light came on, he blinked, shielding his eyes with a hand. He stepped back and knocked into her shoulder with his arm. "Sorry."

Lucy froze, caught in his gaze. His dark eyes widened, as he stared at her. Could he hear her heart beating out of control? She inched away, her back against the shelves.

This was a very bad idea. What was she thinking? How long had it been since she'd been this aware of a man? Too long. Why did it have to be this man?

Jack stared at her, and then his gaze slowly moved to the shelves behind her. The moment between them disappeared as his lips parted in amazement.

Lucy waited for the inevitable.

"Whoa. What is all this?" he said.

"Shh." She cringed and faced the shelves for the first time in three years. It was exactly as she'd feared. Nothing had changed. Every single space from top to bottom had been claimed. Even the floor was knee-deep in boxes.

Suddenly she saw everything through Jack's eyes, and humiliation slammed into her. Heart hammering, Lucy leaned over to catch her breath. "I didn't know what to do with everything when we called it off."

"Are you all right?" Jack asked. "You're hyperventilating."

She took a deep breath, closed her eyes and nodded.

"Are these wedding gifts?" he murmured.

"No. I returned all the gifts, along with apology notes."

"Then what is this stuff?"

"I'd been collecting things for months in preparation for…for our life. Our future together."

He eyed the appliances, towels, and blankets. "Why didn't you donate everything, or use it at the ranch?"

"Opening this closet was a reminder of my impaired judgment. It was easier to lock everything up and turn the key than deal with my issues."

"You haven't opened this door since then?"

"Correct."

Awkward silence fell between them.

Finally Jack brightened and opened his mouth. "You could always repurpose everything if you turn the lodge into…"

"Thank you, but no."

Jack stared at her. "Have you moved on or not?"

"I have." Lucy straightened.

"Great." He picked up a large package of chocolate bars, which had been tucked into a sealed Ziploc bag. "What's the expiration date on chocolate?"

"I don't know. Everything you see has been in here for three years."

"Three years!" His eyes widened. "What was this chocolate for?"

"Favors. They're engraved with our initials."

Jack inspected the fancy monograms on the silver and white wrappers. "Are you opposed to eating them?"

She stared at the bag in his hand and hesitated only a moment before responding. "White, milk or dark?"

"I'm a dark chocolate guy."

"That's my favorite, too."

He handed her the plastic sack. "I think you should be the one to open the bag."

Lucy stared at the chocolate for several moments before unzipping the top and offering him a bar.

Jack tore open the wrapper and took a tentative bite. "Pretty good." He frowned. "I take that back. This is amazing chocolate."

Lucy bit into hers, releasing a flood gate of tamped-down memories and emotions. She chewed and swallowed, savoring the rich flavor. "Of course it is," she said to Jack. "Did you read that label? Imported from Belgium. His mother insisted."

"Highbrow?"

"One hundred percent."

"What did he do for a living?"

"Attorney."

When uncontrolled laughter spilled from his mouth, Lucy slapped a hand over his lips. "Quiet."

Jack gently removed her hand. His eyes locked on hers, and his fingers gently stroked her palm.

Lucy shivered. He was saying something, but she lost her concentration as she stared at his lips.

"Lucy?"

"Hmm?"

"We're not all jerks, you know."

"No?" She tugged her hand from his.

"No."

She bowed her head and reached for a bag of candy-coated, button-shaped chocolate pieces.

"Those are engraved, too," he noted. "Nice font."

Lucy tore open a bag and shoved a handful into her mouth.

"Good?"

"Amazingly satisfying," she said around a mouthful. "I should have done this years ago."

"Thank you for the chocolate," Jack said.

"You're welcome." She met his gaze. "Thanks for listening, Jack."

"I'm honored you shared with me."

"I didn't really have an option. It was either spill my secret or let you think I'm a crazed hoarder. I knew that wouldn't bode well for you approving the donation to the ranch."

"Lucy, look, we may have started out on the wrong foot…" He paused.

"But…"

Jack opened his mouth as if searching for the words.

Lucy cupped a hand to her ear. "I do believe I hear the sound of a Plan B thudding to the ground."

"No. Lucy, come on. It's not like that at all. I'm recognizing that I may be of use here at the ranch."

"You mean besides investigating us for corruption?"

"That's not why I'm here. I'm the fiduciary duty guy. Every organization can use a little assistance with management and reevaluation of fund distribution. The ranch has been around for five years, right?"

She clutched the bag of chocolates in a death grip. "What are you saying, Jack?"

"I'm saying that I'd like you to consider restructuring Big Heart Ranch."

Her stomach began to revolt. "Please, tell me you aren't serious."

"I'm very serious."

Quickly swallowing, she handed him the keys and the bag of chocolate. "Lock up when you're done."

"Lucy…"

She held up a hand. "Jack, I thought I'd prepared for every possible disaster, but you've managed to pull the rug out from under me. For the first time in a very long time, I don't know what to say."

"You're making too much out of this. I'm talking about working together."

"You and me? Managing Big Heart Ranch?" she sputtered.

"For a time. Yeah. See, I knew you'd get it."

"No. I didn't say I get anything. In fact, I can't imagine why you'd want to take over my ranch."

"Take over? What would I do with a ranch full of kids? I can barely handle one kid without breaking out in a cold sweat and hives."

Lucy stifled a sound of aggravation as she tried to move around him. She didn't remember his shoulders being so wide.

"Lucy, wait, please. We're only talking. Discussion is healthy."

"I feel less than healthy at the moment. In fact, all this chocolate is making me somewhat nauseous. Please move."

"So that's it? One minute we're sharing chocolate and the next I'm gum on the bottom of your red boots?"

"Jack, I'm tired and my blood sugar level is now off the charts, so while I'm willing to concede that I may be blowing this out of proportion, the idea of you restructuring my ranch is not something I want to discuss in this particular closet."

"You're right. I apologize. We can discuss this next week. I'm sure everything will look much better on Monday."

"Somehow, I suspect everything will look exactly the same on Monday," Lucy muttered as she walked out the door. She'd opened her heart and talked about her past for the first time in three years, and in return, Jack Harris had used her moment of weakness to betray her.

Maybe he was right; she did always prepare for the worst-case scenario—and this was exactly why.

Chapter Eight

Jack knocked on the open office door and peeked in. Lucy's sister had her head buried in paperwork, but it was obvious even with her head down that Emma Maxwell was a slightly taller version of Lucy, with long dark hair.

He knocked again. "Excuse me? I'm looking for Lucy."

The petite brunette's head popped up. She smiled and quickly stood. "You must be Mr. Harris. Our new volunteer." She offered a conspiratorial wink.

Jack approached the desk and held out a hand. "Jack. And you're Emma?"

"Yes. Delighted to meet you. How's your aunt?"

"Doing well, I think. She's been mysteriously difficult to locate since she sent me out to the ranch."

Emma laughed.

"Is your sister around?" he asked.

"Lucy should be in anytime now. She did leave me a message to pass along to you." Emma reached for a notepad. "Ice cream around six tonight." She looked up. "Will that work for you?"

"It might. If I had my phone to check my schedule."

"She confiscated your phone?" Emma nearly choked on a laugh.

"Yeah, I tried to reach her all weekend on the bunkhouse phone without any response."

"Off the grid, no doubt, after I insisted she go home. That must have been some trail ride. Lucy looked like she was run over by a Mack Truck that backed up after to finish the job."

He smiled at the colorful yet oddly accurate description. "I'm a little surprised she went home without an argument. I haven't known your sister long, but it's pretty clear that she prefers to be the one giving orders."

"That's our Lucy." Emma glanced at the wall clock. "Do you want me to try to reach her? She's probably caught in traffic, but she'll have her Bluetooth on."

"Traffic? Where could there possibly be traffic around here?"

"Downtown Timber gets downright busy on senior discount day at the Piggly Wiggly."

"I hadn't considered that. I'll try back later today." He frowned. "Or maybe not. I have a chore list a mile long."

"Not that long, surely."

"Are you kidding? I'm Leo's replacement, and everyone tells me that Leo did the work of six men." He offered a wink.

Emma chuckled in return. "That might be a slight exaggeration."

"I'm beginning to think not." He glanced at his wrist where his watch used to be. "Do you suppose Lucy would mind if I used her desk to make a few quick calls? I'm researching a project for her."

"Jack, as far as I'm concerned, you can do whatever you like. If you'd be more comfortable, there's a small conference room down the hall, as well."

"Does that mean you aren't upset about the holdup of funds from the foundation?"

"I've heard all sorts of good things about you from General Butterfield. So, no, I'm no longer concerned."

"You're much more laid-back than your sister."

"Youngest child syndrome. And mostly everyone is more laid-back than my sister."

"Tell me, what do you think about the lodge?" Jack asked in an effort to gauge her reaction.

"It's a sad story isn't it?"

"Yeah. Too bad we can't turn things around and make it a functional part of the ranch."

"Lucy's broken engagement?"

"No. I'm talking about Big Heart Ranch Retreat Center." He smiled. "That's my working name for the project."

"Okay, now you have my curiosity."

"Picture a hewn wood entrance arch with the name branded across the top in dark letters." Jack gestured with his hands. "Can you see that?"

Emma's eyes lit up. "Yes. Yes, I can. Tell me more."

"I'm still working on the details, but I'm thinking combination vacation rental, event venue and guest ranch. The bottom line is a solid income stream for the ranch."

"That's a fantastic idea. What did Lucy think?"

Jack grimaced. "Your sister wasn't as enthusiastic as you are, which is why I'm working on a full presentation."

"Shot you down, huh?"

Jack nodded. "Faster than I could say 'think about it.' For some reason she's taking my idea as a personal attack. I'm in awe of what Lucy does around here. My ideas for that house would make her life easier."

"Lucy doesn't handle change well."

"I noticed."

"You have to remember that she's a lot like Dub. She's had responsibility on her shoulders all her life. Lucy never really got to be a kid. The only thing that ensures she can sleep at night is being in control."

He tilted his head, considering Emma's words. "Any thoughts on how I can get Lucy on board?"

"Try to understand that you've terrified her, Jack. However, there is hope. I have learned over the years that it's always best to present ideas in layers. Give Lucy time to wrap her head around the idea first."

"You certainly know your sister."

"Yes. I do."

"So what do you suggest?"

"It depends on you. Travis and I have different approaches. I move slowly, like I'm trying to gentle an anxious mare. Travis gallops ahead, does what he wants and apologizes later. He'd rather ask for pardon than permission. Both are surprisingly effective techniques. It simply depends on how much time you have."

He pondered Emma's words for a moment, understanding dawning as he recalled the terror in her eyes when he'd suggested restructuring the ranch. How could he get Lucy to understand he wasn't threatening her control, but trying to ease her burden?

Jack turned at the sound of labored breathing behind him. A portly gentleman in a white short-sleeved dress shirt and mud-brown trousers, and with a faux-leather briefcase, filled the doorway, pausing to catch his breath.

"Mr. Fillister," Emma said. "I didn't realize you have an appointment with Lucy?"

"Woo-ee. Hot out there. I'm sweating like a politician on election day." He wiped his brow with a rumpled handkerchief. "Lucy's not around?"

"Not at the moment."

"We didn't officially have an appointment. I wanted

her to review the new contracts for the office supplies and equipment."

"I can do that," Jack said without thinking.

Emma stared at him, eyes wide.

"Would that be okay?" Jack continued. "I mean, it *is* what I do for a living. Contract law."

"Go ahead, Jack. Lucy should be along any moment, anyhow."

The salesman frowned as he assessed Jack. "I don't think we've met, sir."

"Jackson Harris. I'm helping out at the ranch this summer."

"I can tell you ain't from around here," the man drawled.

"How can you tell?"

"That accent is a dead giveaway."

"*I* have an accent?"

"Shore do."

"Huh. I had no idea." Jack offered a hand, which was accepted.

"Fred Fillister. Fillister World-Renowned Office Supply, Timber, Oklahoma."

"World-renowned?"

Fred laughed. "In this part of the world, we like to say."

Jack couldn't help but laugh, too. "I like that, Fred."

"Why don't I show you gentlemen to the conference room?" Emma offered.

It was less than thirty minutes before a door slammed in the building, followed by muttering and the rapid shuffling of feet outside the conference room. Lucy Maxwell had no doubt arrived. A moment later, the conference room door opened.

She stood with one hand on the knob. With the other she pushed her bangs off her face. "Mr. Fillister, I'm so sorry I was away from my desk." Her gaze took in the papers strewn across the table, the empty coffee cups and the box of doughnuts, and her eyes widened a fraction. Her jaw tightened. "Did we have an appointment? How may I assist you?"

"Actually, your attorney has taken care of everything."

"My attorney?" Lucy's gaze chilled as it slid from the salesman to him.

Fred Fillister tilted his head as he assessed her. "Are you all right, Lucy? You look like you haven't slept in a few days."

She moved into the room and smiled brightly. Too brightly. "I'm fine. Wonderful." She glanced at the papers on the table again. "What's all this?"

"I brought those contracts for the office supplies and copiers."

Jack cleared his throat. "I've been reviewing the contracts with Fred here."

"Oh?" Her left eye twitched.

"We agreed that Fillister World-Renowned Office Supplies can do better."

"A better deal. From Fred?" Lucy swallowed.

"Yes. He's going to increase the discount and throw in an extended warranty."

Her eyes rounded. "That sounds excellent."

Jack smiled. "Fred and I thought so. He understands that while you want to support local businesses, this is a competitive market."

"Yes. Definitely," Lucy agreed.

"I'll get those contracts updated and stop by next week," Fred added as he stood and brushed doughnut crumbs from his shirt. He pointed his index finger at Jack. "Front and center on the webpage?"

"Right there with our other valuable donors."

Fred grinned. "'Preciate it, Jack."

"Thanks, Mr. Fillister," Lucy chirped as the salesman waddled down the hall. She turned to Jack once their guest was out of earshot. "Front and center on the webpage?"

"Is that an issue for your web guy?"

"It will be, if you promise front and center to all our vendors. And by the way, meet the web guy."

"Why am I not surprised?"

Lucy crossed her arms, and he waited for what was coming. The dark eyes sparked with thunder and lightning. A storm was about to hit.

"Look, Jack, while I'm very grateful, and actually stunned that you got Fred to budge, I have to ask, what do you think you're doing?"

"There is no nefarious plan brewing, Lucy."

She eyed him with doubt.

"You weren't here and I was. I'm good at negotiation. I can be very persuasive."

"I'll remember that." She began to clean up the table.

Jack reached out to stop her. When their hands collided, she drew back. "You shouldn't be cleaning up," he said. "Don't you have an assistant?"

"Assistant what?"

"You know, a secretary, clerk, personal admin. Someone who can prepare a conference room for meetings, and then go out for doughnuts."

Lucy stepped around him and closed the doughnut box.

"Who got the doughnuts?" she asked.

"Emma."

Jack picked up the trash can and brought it to the table. "Lucy, you're running an organization. It's efficient to have an assistant. Perhaps one with basic web skills."

"We're family here, Jack. Travis or my sister are happy to help me when I need assistance."

"Would that be your sister with the sign on her door that says Children's Therapist and Child Care Director? The one with the two babies in her office, who also runs some company called RangePro?"

"Assistants cost money." She stopped and stared at him. "You're the one causing the cash flow issues."

"That's not exactly correct. My job is to be sure Big Heart Ranch is utilizing the funds from the Brisbane Foundation in a fiduciary manner."

She offered a dramatic sigh. "Life was much simpler when your only agenda item was to prove I'm a lowlife crook, preying on the elderly."

"That might have been somewhat true last Monday, but six hours in a saddle and seventy-two hours on the trail have persuaded me that the bigger problem here is the allocation of resources."

"Speak for yourself, Jack. You may have a problem, but we do not. This is my business and I have been running the ranch for five years without your fiduciary duty."

"All the same. Brisbane Foundation sent me here. You and my aunt decided it would be six weeks. So I plan to share my thoughts with you until my time here is complete."

"Great," Lucy muttered. "Just terrific!"

He stepped back and looked at Lucy. Really looked at her. Besides the bruised chin from the ball game, she had dark circles under her eyes and the sparkle was missing from her gaze.

"Are you feeling okay?" he asked.

"Why does everyone keep asking me that?"

"Maybe because you look a little rough, and as I heard often enough on the trail, you act like you have a burr under your saddle. Have you considered taking the day off?"

"Thanks. I appreciate the ego boost, but I can't stay home and leave everything to Emma again."

"If you had an admin, you could."

"Way to hammer home your point, counselor," she said. "If you'll excuse me, I have a job to do." Lucy swept from the room and started down the hall.

He followed. "You said I could shadow you."

"Today might not be the best day."

"Fair enough. How about later in the week?"

"Sure. I'll let you know this evening. Okay?"

"That works, but may I have my phone and watch back in the meantime?"

She stopped and turned, her face becoming red. "Didn't I return them?"

"No."

"You went the entire weekend without your phone and watch?" Lucy sighed. "I'm really sorry." A frown crossed her face. "Let me check my saddle bag. It's in my office."

"It was actually sort of liberating to go off the grid. I hear you do it often."

"Not often, but on occasion. I have a lot of things crowding my mind here at the ranch. Sometimes God and I need to be alone."

Jack stepped closer. Close enough to see the weariness that rode on her shoulders. "You do too much."

"Excuse me?" Attitude and annoyance began a slow stampede across her face.

"You've got to start delegating, or you're going to burn out. Trust me. I know."

"At the risk of sounding harsh, Jack, I might be able to delegate if the Brisbane Foundation funding comes through. Right now I'm on a tightrope, trying to pull a Plan B out of my hat while balancing the funds we do have."

"Lucy, with or without budget approval, you aren't going to change your management style unless you're pushed. Consider this me pushing."

"What exactly is my management style?"

He hesitated, rubbing his chin. "You do lean toward micromanagement."

Her eyes rounded, and Jack checked for smoke coming out of her ears. He waited for the backlash.

Instead of responding, she started walking again.

"Lucy?"

"Let me get you your electronics, Mr. Harris."

Uh-oh. They were back to Mr. Harris.

Jack followed her down the hall to an office that would have terrified a lesser man. His gaze took in the haphazard stacks of paperwork and books. He was fairly certain that there was a desk somewhere under the various piles. An ivy plant in a colorful porcelain Western boot sat on the window ledge begging for water.

"Did you file a police report?" he asked.

"What?" Lucy sputtered.

"Someone ransacked your office."

"Funny, Harris."

"This is a pretty small office for the ranch director," he observed.

"I don't need much room to micromanage," she returned.

They faced off across her desk. All five feet two inches of Lucy Maxwell stared him down. What was it about this particular woman that made him want to protect her and kiss her at the same time? She was as stubborn as he was, and therein was the irony. He'd rather argue with Lucy than spend time with anyone else.

"So I'll see you tonight?" he murmured.

Lucy blinked. "What?"

"Tonight. Ice cream. It's a date?"

Pink tinged her cheeks. "Ice cream, yes. Date? Hardly."

"Maybe you and I should go to dinner sometime," he suggested.

Her mouth opened but nothing came out. Flustered again.

Jack turned with a smile, realizing he should leave while he was ahead. For once. "See you at six, Lucy."

"For the record, Lucy, I think Jack is adorbs," Emma said as she sorted the stack of mail in her hands.

Lucy nearly choked on her coffee. Clearing a place among the paperwork, she cautiously set the mug down on her desk before pinning her sister with a pointed gaze. "Adorbs? What are you? Sixteen?"

"No, but I hang out with adolescents all day." Emma sighed. "I need to get out more. You and Travis and Tripp are the only grown-ups I ever see, and Tripp doesn't talk."

"You've been a single mom too long. It wouldn't hurt for you to get a sitter on occasion and have a mental health day. Have lunch with friends. Go to a movie."

"You're giving me social life advice? You haven't gone to lunch with a friend in years and a date, well, not since…you know," Emma said as she placed the stack of mail on Lucy's desk.

"I'm going out…" She glanced at her watch. "In fifteen minutes, as it so happens."

"With three five-year-old escorts. Not exactly my idea of a hot date."

"Who would I go on a hot date with?"

Emma raised a hand. "Hello. Are you paying attention? Jack, of course. Minus the triplets." She looked Lucy up and down. "Is that what you're wearing?"

Lucy glanced down at her sundress and boots. "What's wrong with this?"

"There's a new dress shop in Timber. You could get some serious clothes. After all, this is Jack Harris we're talking about. The man is the whole package. Tall, dark and handsome. If you made an effort, he might ask you out. Alone, I mean."

Lucy's thoughts tumbled to the man who only hours before had stood at her desk, leaving her speechless when he'd made the very same suggestion. "Jack?" she repeated.

"Yes. Jack." She started checking off on her fingers. "He's smart. Doesn't live with his parents. Is gainfully employed and doesn't play video games all day."

"While that is all true, Jack and I have nothing in common."

"You're wrong, Lucy. You and Jack are so much alike it's almost scary."

Lucy paused. She quickly shook her head, discarding the possible truth of her sister's words.

"Everything he said tells me that the man genuinely respects you and cares about you."

"You and Jack discussed me?" Her voice raised an octave.

"It wasn't like that. We were discussing the ranch."

Lucy blew a raspberry. "The ranch. Yes. The truth is Jack Harris only cares about taking control of the ranch."

"That's not true. He's an attorney. The man has more options than Italian loafers. Why would he want our ranch?"

"I haven't figured that part out yet, but I will." She fingered the stacks of paper on her desk. "Did you give me my messages?"

Emma reached in her back pocket and handed over a neat wad of pink memo notes.

"That's a lot of memos. I was only gone three days."

"The budget hasn't been approved. Checks are delayed. Contracts haven't been signed. Everyone wants to know what's going on."

"You know what's going on. Jack Harris."

"Yes. I know, and I get it, but you haven't told anyone else but me and Travis. Maybe you should."

Lucy flipped through the papers one by one. "We ran out of supplies for VBS? Order them. Overnight, if necessary. You don't need my approval for that."

"With the state of the budget, I've been afraid to do anything. And Travis is no help. I mention finances and he suddenly has chores to do. In a pasture, without cell service."

Micromanager. Jack's words slapped her in the face.

Emma and Travis did whatever she told them to. They waited for her to lead them. Maybe it was time to delegate more than ordering doughnuts and answering her phone.

Jack might be right. Her stomach churned at the thought.

"I'm sorry, Em," she murmured. "Thank you for handling things while I was gone."

"Not a problem." Emma picked dead leaves from the pathetic ivy in Lucy's window. "What did you do to this plant?"

"Nothing. I bought it because the lady said you can't kill ivy."

"And yet, you seem to have proven that theory wrong."

Lucy grabbed a bottle of water from her tote and moved to the window. "Did he mention the lodge?" she asked.

"Jack?"

"Who else?"

"He might have."

"I rest my case."

"At least give his idea a chance," Emma said. "You're dismissing him on principle."

"That's not true." Lucy frowned as she carefully released a stream of water into the plant pot.

"Stop," Emma said, grabbing her wrist. "That plant needs a drink of water. Don't drown the sucker."

Lucy plunked the bottle on the windowsill and turned to Emma, hands on hips. "Admit it. I'm a terrible director, aren't I?"

"Whoa, where did that come from? You're a business school graduate. You're a Godly woman, inside and out. And you love these kids."

"Too much. Maybe this ranch needs someone with a calculator heart like Jack's instead of…" She swept her hand around the room. "An unorganized mess."

"Where is this coming from?"

"Jack, that's where."

"Give yourself a break, would you? You've been under a lot of stress lately. Maybe you need a vacation."

Lucy stared out the window at the ranch she loved, her gaze taking in the little chapel across the way, surrounded by redbuds and a huge magnolia. "Or maybe it's time I stopped fooling myself."

The administration building's front glass doors closed with a bang, and both sisters swung around in time to see Jack in the doorway.

Lucy glanced at the clock, almost expecting to hear the tolling of the executioner's bell as the clock struck six.

"Oh, look, here's Mr. Adorbs now," Emma whispered.

Lucy elbowed her. "Stop that."

He glanced at both sisters. "Everything okay? Did I dress appropriately?"

"You're fine," Lucy said, taking in his tan chinos and open-neck blue cotton shirt. The man's annoyance factor failed to distract from his good looks.

"Better than fine, Jack," Emma gushed, taking the words Lucy would never dare utter right out of her mouth.

"Thank you. How about you, Lucy? How are you feeling?"

"Okay. That's it." Her glance slowly swept over Jack and Emma. "No one is to ask another question about my health, mental or otherwise. Got it?"

Emma nodded.

"I guess that means you're feeling fine," Jack said.

"You guessed right. Now you and I have an appointment with triplets. We promised, and you know my thoughts on that. The girls and Dub will be waiting for us at the meeting hall." She turned on her boot heel and headed outside, with Jack a step behind.

"Have fun, you two," Emma called out. "Stay out as late as you like."

"Remind me to fire her when we get back," Lucy said.

"Can you fire your own sister?"

"I can try."

Jack laughed. "You're fortunate to have Emma."

Lucy grumbled in response as they walked along the sidewalk.

"I've got my car parked behind your admin building," he said.

"Are you still renting a car?" she asked. "Isn't that sort of expensive?"

"Cost of doing business."

"Nice for you. We'll take my car. I know where the place is. I'll drive." She glanced over at him, taking in the expression on his face. "You have a problem with me driving?"

"Not at all, I'm just a little concerned about your vehicle. Old Yeller."

"Old Yeller?"

"Yeah, that mustard-colored car of yours. It's like a Labrador retriever who's overdue for doggie retirement."

"Jack, don't spare my feelings. Tell me how you really feel."

"You're the ranch director. You deserve a respectable vehicle."

"I don't spend ranch funds on my personal needs."

"Lucy, a decent car is part of doing business. It's not a luxury, it's a necessity. You shouldn't drive potential donors around the ranch in that old jalopy. You're the director. That requires you play the part."

"My car isn't that old."

"Not old? It appears quite, uh, vintage to me."

"Vintage. Not even close. If you want to talk vintage, let me tell you about my father's truck. He had a wonderful red hump-backed Chevy pickup. He'd take us for ice cream once a week in that truck. Thinking about that Chevy reminds me how much I miss him, and miss those times as a family."

"I'm sorry, Lucy."

"It's all right. Good memories last forever, you know."

"Do they?" He raised a brow. "So what happened to the pickup?"

"Who knows? A lot of things disappeared after my parents died. Until my cousin finally showed up, it was assumed we didn't have any living relatives."

"That's too bad."

Lucy nodded.

"How old is it? Your car?" he asked.

"The Honda? Eighteen years."

"Eighteen! Good grief. That car is over one hundred and twenty in dog years."

Lucy stopped and stared at him. She burst out laughing at the absurdity of his comment. Moisture blurred her vision as she kept laughing. Finally, she cleared her throat and held out a hand. "Okay. You win. You can drive."

"My car?"

"Yes. Only because I'm afraid I'll spontaneously start laughing if we take mine, and that might be hazardous on the road."

"Thank you." He smiled.

"You won't be smiling when there are kids' fingerprints and other unidentifiable residue all over your pristine vehicle."

"Residue?"

"Uh-huh. Kids pick up anything and everything. Then they shove it in their pockets or in their noses. It always winds up on your windows, or smashed on the floor mats."

He stared at her for a moment, mouth slightly ajar with horror.

When they reached the chow hall, Jack held open the glass door. A pleasant-looking middle-aged woman waited for them just inside.

"Lorna, you remember Jack Harris from the trail ride?" Lucy asked.

"Oh, yes. The catcher who couldn't decide which team he was on."

Jack grimaced.

"Where are the kids?" Lucy asked.

"The girls are using the restroom one last time."

"How've they been?" Lucy asked.

"Good. The girls are so envious of Dub's snakeskin and blue ribbon. They can't wait to meet his buddy."

Lucy looked past Lorna to a table where Dub sat, swinging his legs back and forth and fiddling with the buttons of his shirt.

Lorna followed her gaze. "That boy is so excited."

"Anxious, too," Lucy added.

"Excuse me, ladies," Jack murmured. He walked to where Dub sat clenching and unclenching his hand.

Dub's face lit up with obvious relief when he saw Jack. Her breath caught as the little boy gazed up at Jack with his heart in his eyes.

"You came," he breathed, eyes wide.

"I said I would," Jack said quietly.

Lucy blinked, swallowing past the lump of emotion in her throat. She knew what it was like to be disappointed over and over again. Little Dub would never go through that again if she had her way.

"Yeth, you did." Dub nodded. "My sisters are here."

"Good. I want to meet them."

Two replicas of Dub came out of the restroom. They looked like girly girls, with flyaway, fine blond hair held back with headbands. One wore a white headband, the other pink. It was obviously the only way to identify the girls, as they were mirror images, down to their pink tops and patterned pink shorts. They smiled, revealing that they too were missing their front teeth like their brother.

Jack offered an exaggerated bow. "Ladies, I'm Dub's buddy, Mr. Jack. Pleased to meet you."

Both girls giggled.

"Can you guess which one is Ann and which one is Eva?" Lucy asked from behind him.

"I can't. They look like identical princesses to me," he said.

Pleased smiles lifted the girls' lips.

"Ann always wears the white headband," Dub said.

"Ann," Jack said. He turned to the other little girl. "Eva," he said with a grin.

Lucy's heart melted as the little girls soaked in the special attention. Every little girl should have a daddy who made them feel like a princess.

"You okay?" Jack murmured as he turned toward her. His warm breath tickled her neck.

"Yes. Yes. Of course."

"Ready to go?" he asked.

"Yes. We're ready. Right?" Lucy asked, her glance taking in the triplets.

All three nodded.

"Mr. Jack is driving today."

A worried frown crossed Dub's face. "Do you know how to get to the ice cream store?"

"My car can find anything." He took Dub's hand. "Come on. I'll show you. It talks."

"Cars can't talk." Dub laughed.

"Not every car. But mine sure can."

Dub's eyes rounded and he looked at his sisters, wiggling his eyebrows up and down.

"Stooping to cheap party tricks to win them over?" Lucy whispered.

"Absolutely. Whatever it takes," Jack returned. "I have no shame."

"Finally. Something we can agree on."

Chapter Nine

"This was a lot more fun than I anticipated," Jack said. His gaze followed the triplets, whose laughter was unleashed like a kite tail as they raced around the gravel playground.

"I'm guessing your expectations were quite low."

"Gloating is not an attractive trait, Lucy."

She chuckled as she bit into her cone, releasing melted vanilla ice cream onto her chin.

He grinned as she struggled to catch the drips that ran leisurely over her fingers.

"You can stop laughing and hand over the napkins."

He offered a stack of napkins.

"You and the kids shoveled in a lot of ice cream and toppings in a very short amount of time. In fact, I'm pretty sure your sundae was mostly chocolate sauce."

He leaned back against the bench. "Shoveling in ice cream like a kid. I haven't done that in a long time."

"No? You caught right on, like an old pro."

"Which is why I am recovering on a bench, while they run around," Jack said. He turned to Lucy. "The park was an excellent idea."

"If you feed kids sugary treats, you have to let them run it off. That's rule eighty-six."

"Right after 'don't break promises'?"

"No. 'Don't break promises' is near the top."

"Exactly how many rules are there?"

She shook her head as she seemed to consider his question. "Too many to count."

Jack stretched his arm along the back of the bench, accidently touching Lucy's warm shoulder. For once she didn't move away, and he allowed himself to pretend that she welcomed his touch.

"Excuse me?" a voice said from behind the bench.

Jack and Lucy both turned to see an elderly couple standing behind them, with a beagle on a leash. Jack stood, as did Lucy. "Yes, ma'am?" he asked.

"Your children are simply adorable. And so well behaved."

"They—" Lucy began.

Jack interrupted. He put an arm around her shoulder and pulled her close. "Thank you so much."

"You certainly are blessed," the woman added.

"That we are," Jack said.

"Would it be all right if our little pup said hello to them? He so loves children, and he never bites."

"Of course." He took Lucy's hand and they followed the couple to the triplets. Once again, Lucy didn't resist.

"What are you doing?" she whispered.

"Let's not disappoint them."

Dub, Ann and Eva petted the little dog for several minutes. As the couple walked away, Dub raced to Jack.

"Jack! Jack! That man thinks you're my dad."

"He does?"

A small wistful smile settled on Dub's lips. He looked up at Jack. "I wish you were my dad, Jack. I do."

"Thank you, Dub. That's the nicest thing anyone's ever said to me."

Dub raced back to his sister, and Jack's gaze followed. Worrisome thoughts nipped at him. He turned to Lucy and reluctantly released her hand.

"What will happen to Dub and his sisters at the end of summer?" he asked.

"They'll go back into foster care." She glanced away, her expression solemn.

"Separate homes?" A knot twisted his gut.

"Once they leave the ranch, it's out of my hands. Of course, the ideal scenario is one home, but the likelihood of that is slim."

"Have you ever thought about taking them in permanently?"

"Me?" Stunned surprise crossed Lucy's face as her eyes connected with his. "You mean fostering them?" Her eyes widened with alarm.

"Or adopting. You've obviously got what it takes."

"I do?"

"Hold that thought," he said, while pulling a ringing cell from his pocket. His aunt.

"Sure, Aunt Meri. Not a problem."

"Everything okay?" Lucy asked when he ended the call.

"She asked me to swing by," Jack said.

"I can call Travis to pick us up."

"No. This won't take long. She'd love to see Dub. I've told her about him."

"You told your aunt about Dub Lewis?"

"Sure. Why not? He's my buddy."

"I thought you were allergic to kids, Jack."

He shrugged, unable to explain what he didn't understand himself, that Dub had wormed his way into his heart and even cured him of kid-itis.

The time spent with Dub had begun to ease the crushing pain of Daniel's death, as well.

Lucy slowly shook her head. "Jack, you never cease to amaze me. Whenever I think I have you pigeonholed, I'm either pleasantly surprised or totally annoyed."

"I like to keep you on your toes." He winked. "You might want to wipe that ice cream off your nose before we leave."

She groaned. "Why didn't you tell me?"

"I just did."

She ineffectively swiped at her nose and looked to him for approval.

"Missed it by a mile." Jack leaned forward, the pad of his finger touching the tip of her nose. His gaze rested on her lips, and for a moment he silently debated eliminating the space between them. He took a deep breath and moved away.

"Am I okay?" she asked.

"Lucy, you are more than okay," he said softly. "In fact, once I convince you to repurpose the lodge, you'll be perfect."

"Things are going so nicely today. Don't start." Lucy stood. "I'll get the kids into the car."

When they pulled up to the large, circular drive outside the Brisbane estate, Jack parked beneath the shade of a big magnolia near a small fountain.

Dub and his sisters unbuckled their seat belts and scrambled out of the car to stare at the water bubbling over a mermaid sculpture perched on the edge of the fountain.

"Are you sure your aunt is okay with this?" Lucy asked

quietly as they approached the front door. She nodded toward the children.

Jack shot her a curious glance. "Why wouldn't she be?"

"There's five of us. We're like a..."

"A family?"

Her eyes rounded. "I was going to say a troupe."

"She'll love our troupe," he said.

"Look. Bunnies," Dub said.

Near the front door, the children crouched down to examine a concrete lawn ornament nestled in the grass. The figurines depicted a family of bunnies.

Jack pressed the bell, and a shadow appeared behind the stained glass panels. A young woman opened the door.

"Come in. Mrs. Brisbane is on her way. Hello again, Mr. Harris. Good afternoon, ma'am." She held out a hand for Lucy. "I'm Estelle, her personal assistant."

"Nice to meet you," Lucy said.

With gentle hands on the children's backs, Lucy led them into the house. The little faces turned upward to stare at the ornate crystal chandelier.

The soft tap of Meredith's cane on the marble floor preceded Jack's aunt into the large entry hall.

A smile lit up his aunt's face as she eyed the children standing behind Lucy. "Who do we have here?"

"Dub, Eva and Ann," Jack said.

"Triplets. They're adorable. Please, do come in."

"Kids, this is my aunt, Mrs. Brisbane."

"Oh, please, they may call me Aunt Meri." Her face warmed with pleasure at the trio.

"Aunt Meri, what was it you wanted to see me about?" Jack asked. "Is everything okay?"

"Let's move to the solarium. The children might enjoy my fish."

Dub's ears perked. "Fish?"

"Yes. I have a giant aquarium. Follow Miss Estelle. She'll take you right to them. I'm a little slow, but I'll be along."

Once the children were busy observing the large tank, Meredith ushered Jack and Lucy to a seat on the wicker divan. Large windows with crisp off-white Roman shades provided a view of the grounds, and though it was summer, air conditioning kept the room comfortable.

"I'm having a small soiree next weekend, Jackson, and I was hoping to persuade you to attend."

"You could have asked on the phone."

"True. However, I find my powers of persuasion function best in person."

"A soiree?" he asked.

"Yes. Lucy, you are of course invited, as well. Actually, this is quite providential." She smiled. "I had no idea that you and Jack…"

"Oh, no. Your nephew and I are not… I'm only here because…" She paused. "Jack is Dub's buddy for the summer. This was a promised outing." Lucy flashed him an appeal for assistance.

"Lucy didn't know if I could handle three kids, much less one, all by myself. She took pity on me."

"Nonetheless, Lucy dear, you would do well to get to know more members of the Timber community. Your ranch could only benefit. I've been singing your praises for years. Jackson will escort you."

Lucy's gaze skittered nervously to him and then away. "Um, thank you, Meredith. I'd love to attend."

"Was that all, Aunt Meri?"

"A few more things." She turned to her assistant, who stood near the tank talking to the children. "Estelle, dear, do you mind asking the chef to bring in lemonade?"

"Of course not, Mrs. Brisbane."

Meredith turned back to Jack. "That friend of mine in New York would like to talk to you about subletting your place."

Jack raised a brow and scratched his head. "Really?"

"Yes, and she mentioned a very nice price."

"I'm going to have to think about that."

"What is there to think about, Jackson? There's nothing in New York for you anymore."

"What about Dad?"

"Your father lives in hotels and is rarely in the same city long enough to call any place home. In fact, if you're here full-time, he might be encouraged to visit."

"I'm still going to have to think this over."

"Don't think too long." She pulled a card from her pocket. "Here's the phone number."

"Thanks, Aunt Meri." He fingered the card and put it in his back pocket.

"Now, about the stables." She glanced outside in the direction of the building that used to house the horses. "It's been empty for years. I've decided to lease the building and the yards."

"Good idea."

"Yes. Could you do a quick walk-through of the building? Most everything has been boxed up. Take anything in there you want before I have a local charity haul the rest away."

"I can do that."

"Perhaps you could take Dub with you. I'd like to spend some quality time with the ladies, so we'll enjoy some lemonade and talk about you while you are gone."

Jack laughed. "Fair enough. Dub, would you like to go to the stables?"

"Yeth." The little boy rushed to follow them.

Meredith stood. "Let me locate those keys for you."

As they approached the front hall, his aunt pulled the keys from her pocket.

"I thought you had to find the keys."

"I wanted a chance to talk to you." She smiled. "I see you and Lucy are working together?"

He frowned. "Yes. But don't get any ideas. We're working. That's all."

"Does that mean you're going to release the donation documentation? It's already two weeks overdue. Lucy must be extremely stressed."

"I'm actually doing my best to take some pressure off Lucy."

"Oh? Why not approve the proposal and be done with it?"

"If I approve the funds, I won't have a reason to stay at the ranch."

"You want to stay? I'm a bit confused."

"Aunt Meri, it turns out you were right about the ranch."

"Aha! I told you so."

"Yes, you did. I have a few ideas to help Big Heart Ranch, and ultimately help Lucy, in a very big way. The problem is that she's a little set in her ways. The only leverage I have is that unsigned donation proposal."

"Jackson, you're playing with fire here. This cannot end well."

"I disagree. I'm giving my all to this project. To tell you the truth, Aunt Meri, for the first time in a very long time, I'm really enjoying myself and I'm excited about what I'm doing. I believe I'm contributing to something that will benefit Big Heart Ranch and the children and staff."

"I don't understand why you're taking the long route around instead of the direct route."

"Trust me, Aunt Meri, I know what I'm doing."

She placed a hand on his arm. "I hope so."

Jack kissed her cheek. "Come on, Dub, let's go exploring."

They walked outside across the drive and around the back of the house to the large stables complex.

"You gots horses, Mr. Jack?"

"Not anymore. We did when I was younger."

"Are you fixin' to get horses?"

"Sort of. My aunt is going to let someone else keep their horses here." Jack unlocked the massive wooden door and pulled it open. Warm air rushed past them, struggling to get out.

"Wow, sure is a big stable," Dub said. "Bigger than the one at the ranch."

Their voices and footsteps echoed through the empty building.

"Hot, too." Jack strode through to the back and opened the double doors on the far end, to get the summer air circulating. Then he hit the switch to start the blades of the large overhead fans.

Beside him, Dub bent down and picked up something shiny on the ground. "Look. I found a quarter. Can I keep it?"

"It's yours."

Dub pointed overhead. "Is that your loft?"

Jack glanced up. "Yeah. It's dusty up there. You might want to wait down here."

"I wanna go with you."

"Okay, but hold that rail and be careful." The wood creaked as they mounted the dozen steps to the loft.

Dub sneezed. "This doesn't look like a loft. How come you don't have hay?"

"Because we don't need hay without horses."

"Oh, yeah." Dub nodded.

They both stared at the stacked and sheet-covered furniture that took up one entire wall, along with dusty boxes.

"Furniture?" Jack murmured.

"Lots of it," Dub said.

"Maybe enough to fill an empty house." He'd have to make sure his aunt didn't get rid of anything until he had more time to inventory what was here.

"Look, Mr. Jack. A bicycle. It has training wheels, too."

Jack turned and smiled at the sight. Propped against a spindle-legged chair was a red bicycle, complete with a bell and a basket. "That's my bicycle. See the baseball card in the spokes? I put that there."

"Cool. Can we take it downstairs?"

"Sure. But let's look around some more before we do that."

"I know how to ride," Dub announced.

"I bet you can."

"How old were you when you rode that bike?"

"I think I was your age. I got another bigger bike later, and this one was tucked away."

"Did your brother have a bike, too?"

"He did. I don't know where his bike is." Jack glanced around. Beneath a window, a large box with his name and one with Daniel's sat side by side. "Dub, can you sit on the floor for a few minutes while I check out these boxes? I might find something in there for you."

"Treasures?" Dub asked as he settled cross-legged on the floor.

"You never know. I can't remember what's inside."

Jack pushed open the small attic window before he,

too, settled on the floor and tugged the box with his name toward him. He slid his hand under the flap.

"What is it?"

Jack pulled out hardbound childhood classics. "Books."

"My sissies read lots. Can we bring them books?"

"Sure." Jack pulled out a plastic bag filled with metal toy cars. "Look at this, Dub."

Dub clapped his hands. "Whoa. Cars. What are you going to do with them?"

"They're yours, if Miss Lucy says it's okay."

"She will. I know she will. Can we ask her?"

"Absolutely." He held the bag out to Dub. "Why don't you hold them for me?"

"Yes, sir, Mr. Jack." Delight spread like jam across Dub's freckled face.

"I want to look for…" Jack grinned as he pulled boots and a helmet from the box. "This is what I hoped we'd find. Boots. My old riding boots. You know what that means?"

"What?"

"You can ride Grace."

Dub's eyes lit up. "This has been a real good treasure hunt."

"It has." Jack reached for his brother's box, hating that he was going to look inside, but unable to stop himself. The box held bits of his brother's life and right now, at this moment, he needed to see those pieces.

He inched back one flap at a time. Toys. The letters DH had been written on the tag of a chocolate-brown chenille-stuffed bear. Lifting the toy to his face, he inhaled. How could that be? The soft fabric still smelled like Daniel.

Twenty-five years. How was it possible that in one

breath he was nine years old again, having his heart torn from his chest once more?

Jack's jaw tightened as he gripped the toy. He swallowed hard, his eyes filling with emotion.

"Jack?"

He turned at Lucy's soft voice.

"Everything okay up here?" she asked from the top step to the attic.

"Yeth," Dub answered. "Look, Miss Lucy. I have cars. Mr. Jack says I can keep them if you say I can. Can I?"

"Sure, Dub. Let's take them downstairs."

"What about the bike?" Dub asked.

"I'll bring the bike downstairs and we can put it in the trunk of the car," Jack said. "Go with Miss Lucy, Dub. I'll be right there."

"Mr. Jack, I like it here. Your aunt is nice and I like the fish, and the lemonade, too. Can we come back?" Dub asked quietly.

"Maybe." Lucy met his gaze and he sighed. "We will come back, Dub. I promise."

Jack sat where he was, staring out the small attic window at the tops of the peach trees in the orchard. Minutes later he heard footfalls on the steps again. "Jack, I can take the children to the ranch and come back for you later," Lucy said softly.

"No. I'm coming. I…" He faltered. "The heaviness in my heart I'm used to. This… I didn't expect this."

"Your brother?"

"Yeah. Funny. You think you have a tight lid on your emotions. Everything is under control, and then when you least expect it, you're blindsided."

She sat down on the floor next to him and took his hand. "I'm so very sorry, Jack."

He shrugged. "Why are you sorry?"

"I'm sorry because you're hurting."

She spoke with care, as though he were a child. And in a way, when it came to Daniel, he still was.

Lucy continued. "I understand grief. Maybe it's the one thing you and I have in common. It isn't just about loss. It's about the past, the future and the now. Grief touches everything in our lives."

Her petite hand clutched his with a strength he hadn't realized she was capable of. "Despite the fact that you and I don't see eye to eye on everything, I actually like you. I never want to see people I care about hurting."

When he turned to her, tears were freely slipping down her face.

Jack released the tight, hard breath he was holding, allowing the sadness inside him to be released into that one breath. Dust scattered in the air.

"Lucy, there's something you should know." Jack closed his eyes as shame filled him. "It's my fault my brother is dead."

When he opened his eyes, her caring gaze met his.

She wiped her eyes and placed a hand on his arm but said nothing. The warmth of her touch encouraged him to continue.

"We were playing outside. My family lived in Tulsa then. Typical for me, I was so engrossed in reading that I didn't notice when Daniel ran out from in-between two parked cars to chase his ball. Right into the street. He was hit by a car."

A long silence swirled around them.

"How is that your fault?" she whispered.

"I'm the older brother, by minutes. Daniel was…impulsive. It was my job to look after him. That was always understood."

"Oh, Jack, surely you must see what an impossible burden that was for you at that age. Like our friend Dub downstairs. You were a child, Jack. A child. And it was an accident. A tragic accident."

Jack sucked in a breath of air. He wanted to believe that. Desperately. But he couldn't.

"You will never be free until you give this burden to God and let it go."

"I'm sure even God is disappointed in me for that day."

"It's been, what? Over twenty-five years?

"You don't understand."

"Oh, but I do. I do. There were a thousand what-ifs about that day in the car with my parents."

Jack reached out, and this time it was he who took her hand, enveloping her softness in his large hand as though it was something he did every day. She didn't pull away. "I've never told anyone about this," he murmured.

Lucy nodded.

"My mother left us when Daniel died."

"It's a horrible thing to lose a child. We can never say how we might react." She sighed. "This is why my job at the ranch is so important to me. I want to save all the children." Her voice cracked. "Sometimes you can't, can you?"

"No. I suppose not."

Moments later, he turned his head and met her gaze. "Thank you, Lucy."

"Jack, we're sort of friends now. Friends are there for each other."

"Sort of friends?" The words made him smile.

"Yes," she breathed softly in response.

He still held her hand, and he could feel her pulse jump when she looked at him.

He leaned forward and touched his forehead to hers.

"Sort of friends. Right," he said with a soft chuckle. Then he stood and pulled her to her feet. "Come on, let's go down."

"Yes, we better. Your aunt is feeding the children lemonade and cookies. They should be bouncing off the walls by now."

"You left my seventy-eight-year-old aunt with three kids?"

"She was having a great time. Maybe you should consider making promises to Dub more often. She'd love that."

"More promises. That's a little scary."

She patted his arm. "It gets easier every time."

He looked into her eyes and realized that things were only getting easier because of Lucy. That thought alone shook him.

Lucy waved a hand in front Jack's face as he leaned against the pen fence. "Are you awake?"

"I'm sleeping with my eyes open. A trick I learned as a law student riding the subway to class."

"Impressive."

"Not really." He grimaced and shot an accusatory look at the sky. "The sun has risen, so I guess it's too late to go back to bed."

She inhaled and assessed the deep blue panorama overhead. "Don't be silly. This is going to be a lovely day. Not nearly as hot as usual, either."

Jack yawned and stretched. He glanced around. His expressive face clearly said he was unimpressed with the sight of the ranch at 6:00 a.m. "Remind me why you're here?"

"Pardon me?" she squeaked.

"That's not what I meant. I promised Dub. You

shouldn't have to be inconvenienced." He pulled out his phone and groaned. "Aren't the horses still sleeping?"

"I'm here because you aren't a certified instructor, thus you are not qualified to take Dub horseback riding alone."

"Did you just insult my equestrian skills?"

"You were on a saddle for the first time since you were a kid two weeks ago. I'm a certified instructor. I'll help you with Dub. My insurance carrier will be much happier that way."

"Fine, boss. So which horses?"

"Dub wants Grace."

"Isn't Grace a bit more horse than a five-year-old can handle?" he asked.

"Grace is a beginner horse. All the kids start on Grace."

He was suddenly wide-awake, his gray eyes round with a pointed accusation. "You put me on a kiddie horse for the trail ride?"

"You did fine."

"That's because I didn't realize I had training wheels."

Lucy laughed. "You hadn't ridden a horse in two decades. What did you expect me to set you loose on?"

"Was everyone laughing behind my back?"

"Not at all. You did great."

"I can't believe Grace never let on. She kept eating those carrots I gave her and never said a word." Jack shook his head with obvious disgust. "So which horse will I be riding today?"

"Chloe. She's spirited, yet very well trained."

"That still doesn't explain why we're doing this so early."

"Apparently your coffee is not doing its job." She slowed her words. "You promised Dub. The stables are very busy during the summer months. There's a sign-up sheet for recreational riding and training. We were completely booked. I had to pull strings to get us this Friday-morning slot."

"Maybe you missed the sign on your parking space, but you're the director," he said.

"That doesn't matter. I play fair."

She assessed his fancy stainless-steel container of coffee. "You know you can't take that on the ride. Right?"

"Why not? I take it in the car."

"When you ride, you focus on the horse, not coffee."

"Yes, Madame Director."

Lucy nodded toward the curb. "Lorna just dropped off Dub."

They both turned in time to see Dub race to the stable entrance in his new riding boots. He wore a red polo shirt tucked neatly into his jeans.

"Wow, Dub, you look like a real equestrian," Lucy said.

"What's that mean?"

"It means you are ready to ride." ·

He puffed out his chest and looked at Jack. "Ready to go, buddy?"

"I can see you are," Jack said. "Nice boots."

Dub grinned and stared at his feet. "Thanks, Mr. Jack."

Lucy slid open the stable door.

"What's my horse's name again?" Jack asked.

"Chloe."

"Chloe." He started walking down the center aisle of the stable.

"Dub, do you know how to tack a horse?" Lucy asked the little guy.

"Yeth. Leo showed me. 'Cept I'm too little."

"We don't have much time today, so Mr. Jack will tack for you, okay?"

"Okay."

"Tack his horse, Jack?" she called.

Jack nodded as he inspected each stall. When he stopped outside Chloe's stall, his eyes rounded. "Lucy, this horse is as old as your Honda."

"That is not true, and do not let Chloe hear you say that."

He peeked over the stall door. "How about this one instead?"

Lucy carefully chose her words. "Zeus? That gelding is a bit strong-willed."

"I can handle strong-willed." He looked pointedly at her.

"Jack, I really don't think…"

"Lucy, I can handle Zeus."

"Fine. If you insist, but you will wear a helmet."

"I didn't wear one on the trail ride."

"That was with Grace. No helmet, no Zeus. If you keep pushing me, I'll have to insist on a riding vest, as well."

"Helmet it is." He rolled his eyes.

"Role model, Mr. Jack. Role model," she murmured.

Lucy led Grace outside the barn once Jack had the horse saddled up. She gave Dub a boost onto the mare's back. "Collect your reins," she instructed.

"Like this?"

"Very good. Blaze and I are going to walk next to you this session. Grace and Blaze are good friends. Did you know that?"

"They are?"

She nodded.

"Where will we go?" Dub asked.

"Just down the trail to the big corral."

"Keep your hands low and together on her neck," Lucy instructed. She stroked Grace's mane. "You're a good horse, Grace."

Lucy slid her foot in a stirrup and hopped onto Blaze at the same time that Jack trotted past them. Zeus offered an unhappy snort.

"Jack, you're a little tight on the reins. Ease up. Zeus gets cranky if you pull on his mouth."

"I got this."

Zeus began to move faster.

"Don't kick him," Lucy said. "He doesn't like to be kicked. A gentle squeeze will be sufficient."

"Now you tell me!" Jack called back.

The discordant and loud vibrating trill of an old-fashioned alarm clock ripped through the quiet morning.

A cell phone alarm? It must be Jack's.

Clearly distressed, Zeus began to buck.

"Hold on to the horn!" Lucy yelled as Jack flailed back and forth in the saddle.

She turned to Dub. "Keep Grace very still. Okay?"

The little boy nodded.

Lucy clicked her tongue and nudged Blaze toward Jack. "Toss me the phone, Jack."

Without looking, he threw the device in her direction. It bounced on the ground, but the alarm kept going.

Lucy slid off Blaze and scooped up the phone, fiddling with the screen until the noise stopped.

"Whoa. Zeus. Whoa," Jack said. Though he pulled up on the reins, he began to slide sideways off the saddle.

When Zeus finally obeyed and stopped, Jack was dumped unceremoniously to the ground on his backside.

Lucy ran and grabbed the horse's reins.

"Mr. Jack, are you okay?" Dub hollered.

Jack stood, dusted himself off and yanked off his helmet. "Oh, yeah, I'm fine. Cowboys slide off like that to protect the horse. Happens all the time."

Dub stared at him, confusion and concern on his face.

When Dub looked away, Lucy leaned over. "He can't hear you. You can whimper now."

"No, really," Jack said. "I appreciate your concern, Madame Director, but I'm fine. Even though that crazed horse just threw me off, and I could have broken every bone in my body."

She handed him his phone. "You slid to the ground."

"Whatever." Jack stared at the cracked screen and slowly shook his head. Grabbing Zeus's reins from her, he started walking toward the stables.

"Come on, Jack, you have to get back in the saddle. Literally."

"Seriously? This horse hates me."

"I didn't mean Zeus. Chloe would love a morning ride. We'll meet you at the corral."

"Chloe, huh?"

"Yes. You can untack Zeus when we're done. We only have the corral for the next twenty minutes. In the meantime, we're burning daylight."

"You aren't going to say I told you so?"

Lucy put her foot in the stirrup and mounted Blaze. "No. We all make mistakes. The important thing is that we don't waste our time with Dub."

Jack stared at her for moments. Then he nodded. "You're right." A slow smile spread across his face before he turned toward the stable. "Thanks for reminding

me of what's important. It's not every day I get to go riding with two of my favorite people."

Lucy's eyes rounded at his words. If he was messing
with her, someone needed to notify her heart right away,
because it had melted and she was dangerously close to
falling for Jack Harris.

Chapter Ten

"Big Heart Ranch. Lucy Maxwell speaking."

"Maxwell? This is Alberta Hammerton, returning Mr. Harris's call. Is he available?"

"Mr. Harris?" Lucy blinked, confused.

"Yes. Your retreat facility coordinator. I have those quotes he requested."

"May I take your number and have him call you back? He stepped out for a moment."

"Who did you say you are?"

"Lucy Maxwell. Ranch director."

"Thank you, Ms. Maxwell. Oh, and he has my number."

"Perfect."

She dropped the phone into its charger. "Retreat co-ordinator? Yes. Absolutely perfect."

She turned to her computer, fingers flying across the keyboard until she pulled up the staff and volunteer schedule. A quick search on the spreadsheet directed her to Jack Harris's schedule.

Stall mucking. Knee-deep in horse manure, and the man was still causing problems. A multitasking trou-blemaker.

The phone rang again, and Lucy grabbed the receiver a second time. "Big Heart Ranch, Lucy Maxwell speaking."

"Oh, I'm terribly sorry to disturb you on a Monday morning, Ms. Maxwell. I know you must be extremely busy. This is Erin with Timber Staffing Agency. May I speak to Mr. Harris?"

"Could I take a message? Mr. Harris is involved in another project at the moment."

"Would you tell him I have two candidates to schedule for interviews?"

"Interviews?"

"Yes. For the admin position. I can assure you that they are both highly qualified. He told me how particular you are."

Lucy took a deep breath. "I'm sure they are. I have your number on caller ID. I'll have him check back with you as soon as he's free."

When the phone rang a third time, she stared at the receiver for a moment, and then began to count backward. "Really, Jack?" she fumed.

"Lucy?" Emma called out. "Is that your phone?"

"Yes. I've got it."

"Maxwell speaking."

"USA Rentals. I've got a sixteen-foot truck available. Do you want to schedule?"

"Truck? What truck?"

"Just a minute." Papers rustled before the man spoke again. "Jack Harris requested a sixteen-foot truck. We've got one ready to go. Does he need furniture pads and a hand cart?"

"I'm not sure. May I have your name and have him call you right back?"

"Roscoe. This is Roscoe. He has my number. I talked

to him yesterday. Tell him to hurry before I have to release the truck."

Lucy grabbed the keys to the Ute. "I'll be back," she said when she passed Emma's door.

Parking the Ute outside the stables, Lucy slowly walked through the building, checking stalls on either side of the large space. No Jack Harris in sight, but the stalls were clean—evidence that he'd been by recently.

Tripp was in his office, hunched over a laptop. Lucy gently knocked on the door.

"Come in," he grunted without looking up.

"Ah, Tripp, have you seen our new volunteer, Mr. Harris?"

"Chickens."

"Thanks." She paused. "Everything okay?"

Tripp leaned back in his chair, and his ice-blue eyes pinned her. He absently rubbed the scar that ran down the left side of this face. "Truthfully, Lucy, I could use some help with this paperwork. We talked about hiring someone last spring. It's only getting worse. I'm stuck in here crunching numbers and ordering supplies when I should be out there with the horses and getting ready for the ranch rodeo."

Mouth open in surprise, Lucy simply stared. She'd never heard the taciturn cowboy string together that many sentences at once. "I, um, I'll see what I can do. Right now we're on hold until the budget is approved."

"Don't hang me out to dry."

"I won't forget your request, Tripp."

She carefully closed the door and returned to the Ute, where she sat for several minutes in stunned surprise. Tripp's words and Jack's comments echoed in her ear. Was it possible she was being narrow-minded and inflexible with the ranch budget? Once again, she found herself rethinking her role as director and praying for guidance. "What do You want me to do, Lord?" she whispered.

Lucy buckled her seat belt and headed down the road to the coops. Rue Butterfield met her in the middle of the chicken yard. She held a basket of eggs in one hand and a mangled straw Stetson in the other.

"Rue, what are you up to?" Lucy asked.

"I came by to visit Mrs. Carmody."

"Is there something wrong with our favorite hen?"

"Not at all. We're friends. I like to visit on occasion. We old birds have to stick together."

"Old is not a word I would ever use in connotation with General Rue Butterfield."

"Well, thank you, Lucy."

Lucy glanced around. "Have you seen Jack?"

"Yes. He was here." Rue gestured toward the basket of eggs. "I offered to wash these and run them over to the chow hall for him."

"Did he mention where he was headed?"

"I believe he said he had to get cleaned up for an appointment in town."

"An appointment." Lucy nodded absently.

"You know, dear, I think there must be something wrong with his schedule."

"What makes you say that?"

"He has stall mucking and chicken coops. Both chores are scheduled every day for the entire summer. We never assign both of those chores together. It's always one or the other."

"It's no mistake. And why not? The man's on a mission to fill Leo's shoes, so I'm helping the process along."

Rue started laughing. "Oh, my," she said, catching her breath as she carefully balanced the eggs. "So he's been doing both all summer? Is that what you're saying?"

She nodded.

"Oh, Lucy, I believe you may have finally met your match."

"My match? What do you mean?"

"Anyone else would have complained about the assignment. Not Jack. He's determined to prove he's not simply a pretty city slicker. The man wants to pull his weight. Or Leo's weight, in this case. You two were cut from the same cloth, if you'll excuse the cliché. Neither of you will back down from a challenge."

"Jack and me? Alike?"

"Yes. You're both single-minded and stubborn."

"Those are my best features, but I'm not so sure that makes me like Jack."

"You might want to give it some thought," Rue said.

"Not likely. I don't sleep at night as it is."

"Lucy, do you mind if I ask what the deal is with Jack?"

"What do you mean?"

"Oh, come on. He's polished, well-educated and reeks of old money. This is a man who probably speaks three languages and went to an Ivy League college. Yet he's running around trying his best to replace Leo and not getting paid for his efforts. I imagine Jack Harris has better things to do with his time than hang out on Big Heart Ranch in the middle of summer, shoveling horse manure."

Lucy was speechless for a moment. Rue had certainly nailed the man. "He's a volunteer," she finally said.

"Yes. I'm aware. And when he's not volunteering?"

"Rue, I'm not sure you really want to know. I don't know if it's a good idea to tell you, either."

"How long have I been working at the ranch, Lucy?"

"Four years."

"Have you ever known me to be indiscreet?"

"No," Lucy murmured.

"The United States government handed me a top secret security clearance. If Uncle Sam trusted me not to sell them out, maybe you could, as well."

"Jack is Meredith Brisbane's nephew. He's the attorney holding up the funding." Lucy released a breath as the words came out in a rush.

Rue's eyes widened with surprise, her mouth sagging open with a gasp. "I never saw that coming." The general began to laugh. "You're telling me that Jack is the jerk who hasn't signed the donation proposal." She laughed again and wiped her eyes. "Oh, the irony."

"Yes, I nearly lost it when he agreed with you on the trail ride."

"You've been protecting him?"

"I suppose I have. I wanted him to evaluate the ranch without bias."

Rue paused and narrowed her eyes. "Are you threatened by Jack Harris, Lucy?"

"I'm intimidated by the fact that he's been here three weeks and has come up with some great ideas for the ranch. Ideas that I, as the director, should have come up with."

"So that's why you're questioning your role at Big Heart Ranch."

"Rue, I've been running everything for five years. Maybe it's time for me to take a back seat. To tell you the truth, as much as I hate to admit it, he's good at what he does. Right now he's screening personal assistant candidates for me."

"Marvelous. You need one."

"Yes. So everyone feels free to tell me."

"Is he going to approve the funding?"

"Most days I'm certain the answer is yes. The rest of the time, he skirts the issue while he explores new ideas for the ranch. We continue to butt heads because he refuses to keep me in the loop."

"Oh, so this is all about control."

"It's my ranch!"

"If he felt like you'd listen to him objectively, he might not be working behind your back."

"Whose side are you on?"

"Are there sides?"

Lucy opened her mouth and closed it.

"Dear, you have to be willing to open that closed fist of yours in order to allow people to help you."

"I'm going to have to think about this," Lucy said. She turned to go and then stopped. "Rue, what's a soiree?"

The general smiled and cocked her head. "I haven't heard that term in a long while. A soiree is like a cocktail party held later in the evening, and usually with some sort of musical entertainment. They're generally quite romantic affairs. I've been to many a soiree in my day," she mused. "Why do you ask?"

"Meredith Brisbane has invited me to a soiree at her estate this weekend."

"Oh, my, isn't that great timing?"

"Why do you say that?"

"Well, she's head of the Brisbane Foundation. She must really like you if she invited you to her soiree. That bodes well for our budget approval."

"I pray you're right." Lucy frowned. "Um, Rue?"

"Yes, dear?"

"What should I wear?"

Rue glanced at Lucy's staff T-shirt, jeans and boots. "Not your red boots."

Lucy sighed. "I was afraid of that."

"A lovely young woman such as yourself certainly has at least one sophisticated dress tucked into the back of her closet."

"Rue, I have flannel shirts tucked into the back of my closet."

"Didn't you have some fancy events while you were in college?"

"I worked at the ranch when I wasn't in class. There was no time for fancy anything."

"You need to get yourself to Tulsa and find a dress and shoes." She assessed Lucy. "A stop at a salon for a trim and manicure are not out of the question, either."

"I don't know the first thing about where to shop in T-town."

"When is this soiree?"

"Saturday."

"Nothing like waiting until the last minute." Rue arched a brow.

"In my defense, it was a last-minute invitation." Lucy glanced down at her daily ranch outfit and sighed. "Who am I kidding? I don't have a clue what I'm doing. My life is spent in jeans and the occasional sundress from the Western store. I have no idea what to wear or the proper etiquette for an event at the foundation."

"Clear your schedule and take Emma with you to the big city."

"Is that really necessary? They have shops in Timber."

"When was the last time you had your hair trimmed?"

"At the start of summer, at the Timber barbershop."

Rue groaned. "Oh, Lucy. The barbershop? Didn't anyone ever tell you that good hair covers a multitude of things?"

"I don't see you with fancy hairdos, General."

"That's by choice. Not omission. There's a difference.

I've put in my time in dresses and heels." Rue stopped and looked at Lucy again. "But you. No excuse. You represent the ranch, so you should be prepared to dress for this occasion and others."

"Rue," Lucy groaned.

"You know, Lucy, it's bad enough your childhood was stolen. I will not allow you to go any longer without some girly fun."

"Girly fun?"

"A salon and spa day."

Lucy gulped and stepped back. "I don't do salon and spa days."

"You do now. I'll make all the arrangements for you and your sister. Why, I'll even babysit the twins." She nodded. "I'll inform Emma, so you don't weasel out."

"I don't do salon and spa days," Lucy whined under her breath. She stomped her way to the bunkhouse and pounded on the door. Her hand was raised to knock again when the door swung open and she nearly fell over.

"Whoa," Jack said, catching her fist. "Stand down there, Madame Director."

Freshly showered, his dark hair was combed back and his face cleanly shaven. He looked almost the way he did when she'd first met him. Powerful. In control. The man smelled good, too. For a moment, she simply stared.

"Lucy?"

"I, um…"

"Lucy? Did you need something? I've finished my chores early and I'm not scheduled for the rest of the day." He glanced at his watch.

"Don't let me bother you. Your personal time is your own. I wanted to give you your messages." She held out the pink slips of paper.

Jack winced and pulled out his phone, which was held

together by duct tape. "I apologize. This must be really annoying. My phone keeps cutting out. The new one arrives today or tomorrow. I left your number with my contacts."

"Retreat facility coordinator?" she asked. "Really? Was King of the Mountain taken?"

He grimaced. "It's not as bad as it sounds. I have to talk the talk and walk the walk if I want people to take me seriously." He took the papers from her and neatly folded them.

"Take *you* seriously. You. Not me."

"Are you offended that I'm doing this? You did say—"

"I know what I told you, Jack. Yes, in a moment of weakness and complete exhaustion on the trail ride, I agreed that you do can the legwork and present your findings. I simply had no idea you would be moving at the speed of light."

"It only seems like I'm moving fast because you move so slow."

She released a soft gasp. "I can't believe you said that. What's that supposed to mean anyhow?"

"Lucy, it isn't normal to leave a house abandoned for three years. To have a closet full of appliances and household gadgets you never even look at."

"When did I say I was normal?" She gave a sad shake of her head and turned away. "Wow, I never imagined you'd use the confidence I shared with you against me. I trusted you, Jack. I shared my chocolate with you and I trusted you."

"Lucy, wait. I'm sorry. That's not what I meant."

She met his gaze. "What did you mean, Jack?"

"I don't know… I'm just sorry. That was uncalled for."

She paused. "How sorry are you? Sorry enough to sign the proposal?"

He rolled his eyes. "The mission of the foundation is to serve the local community. If I can help the ranch become more self-sufficient, then less money will be needed at Big Heart Ranch, and other organizations will benefit from the Brisbane Foundation funding. So the answer is no. I'm not going to sign anything until my work here is done."

She crossed her arms. "What is this obsession you have with the lodge?"

"It's not an obsession. I'm exploring options."

"Couldn't you explore your options from your office at the estate? You'd even have a phone and an admin."

"I promised my aunt and Dub I'd be at the ranch for the entire summer. I'm sort of locked into Leo's chores, too. You might not miss me, but those chickens would."

Miss him. She hadn't even thought that far ahead. Nor did she want to. It would be far better to simply imagine him gone and pretend he was never here rather than miss him.

"I guess this whole retreat thing is sort of fun for you, isn't it?" she asked.

"Sure. I'll admit I like a challenge."

Lucy nodded, as an odd tightness squeezed her chest. What would happen when he wanted more of a challenge than Lucy and Dub, and Big Heart Ranch in Timber, Oklahoma, could offer? When he left in search of his next adventure?

"You okay, Lucy?"

"I'm fine." She met his gaze. "What's the rental truck for?"

"I'm helping my aunt empty out the stable loft." He glanced at his watch again and straightened his tie. "I really have to go. I'll be back in a couple of hours. We could talk then."

He started down the walk and then stopped. "I finished my chores, if that's what's behind this. In Leo fashion, I might add. Dub and I did arts and crafts this morning."

"I never doubted you for a minute."

He frowned.

"What about the interviews, Jack?"

"I'll handle them until we get down to the final candidates. No use wasting your time until the field is narrowed. I put an ad in the Timber paper, so we still have a few more candidates to review."

"You paid for an ad? To hire an admin I said I can't afford?"

"Utilizing the lodge would eliminate that problem."

"Again with the lodge." She got in the Ute, wishing there was a door she could slam.

"You might be overreacting here, Lucy," he called.

"Who, me? The invisible director of Big Heart Ranch?"

Jack cleared his throat. "This might not be a good time to ask when you want me to shadow you."

"Whenever works with your schedule, Jack. I don't want to inconvenience you."

He nodded, her sarcasm clearly sailing right over his head. "What time?"

"Whenever. Stop by my office. If I'm not there, Emma will know where you can find me."

"Okay."

She nodded. "Jack?"

"Yes?"

"Your tie is crooked."

"Thanks." He glanced down, adjusted the silk material, walked over to the Lexus and got in.

Three weeks at the ranch, and the man remained exactly the same. Aggravatingly perfect and unaffected by his time with them. While she, on the other hand, had been turned upside down. She gave the man an inch and he took far, far more. It was then that Lucy realized with stark clarity that she better start guarding her heart, before he took that, too, because she certainly couldn't handle that sort of disappointment once again.

Jack pulled the Lexus to the curb outside the traditional two-story redbrick house with black shutters. A bicycle lay on the front path. He got out of the car, ready to spend time shadowing Lucy.

He'd give anything to be able to share the news that he'd gotten a great response from the local chamber of commerce regarding the Big Heart Ranch Retreat Center with Lucy. But the ranch director wasn't ready to consider that good news. He'd wait until he had all his cows in a row before he shared everything with her. Maybe then she'd be able to see the big picture.

Down the street, Lucy stood at the back of the Honda pulling grocery sacks from the trunk. He picked up speed and met her on the sidewalk outside the house. She glanced through him.

"Let me help you," Jack said.

"I don't need help," she returned, rushing toward the house steps ahead of him.

"Are you mad at me?"

"Mad? No. I'm aggravated, irritated and annoyed."

"Fair enough. Where are you going in such a hurry?"

"I have sick house parents. They have the flu, as do two of the kids in the house."

"What can you do about that?"

"I'm going to take over for them. Cook, clean and handle the kids until they feel better."

"I'll help."

"You signed up to shadow me at the office." She stopped and turned around, assessing his khaki slacks and polo shirt. "I don't think you're up for this particular assignment."

"I can handle anything you can, Madame Director."

"Have you had your flu shot, Jack?"

"All up-to-date."

"Okay, but don't say I didn't warn you." Lucy offered an ominous chuckle and kept walking up to the front door, where Dub stood at the screen.

"Dub," Jack said. "What are you doing here?"

The little boy laughed. "I live here, Mr. Jack." He looked to Lucy. "Mr. Bill and Miss Lorna are resting. They have a fever and sick stomachs."

Lucy pulled open the screen. "Where's your big brother?"

"He's upstairs getting ready for work."

"Work?" Jack asked. He followed her into the neat two-story home.

"Yes. Many of our high school students have jobs in the community during the summer."

"Dub, whose bicycle is that on the sidewalk?" Jack asked as he stepped into the home.

"Stewie's. Mine is in the garage. I take real good care of the bicycle you gave me, Mr. Jack."

Jack grinned, foolishly pleased that Dub was riding his old bike.

"Where are Stewie and Henry?" Lucy asked.

"In bed. They're sicker. They puked even."

Jack grimaced, and his stomach clenched. "So that's the ripe odor around here."

Rue Butterfield came down the carpeted stairway with

her medical bag in her hand. "Lucy. Jack. I see the cavalry has arrived."

"I'm not so sure about that. How is everyone?" Lucy asked.

"Quite the flu epidemic we have going on at the boys' ranch."

"Don't tell me that. You offered the flu vaccine last spring. Didn't anyone take you up on that?"

Rue raised a hand in gesture. "The joys of modern medicine. Apparently, another strain has hit the ranch. The good news is that this seems to be a hard-hitting and short-lasting virus."

"Good news, huh?" Lucy returned. "I'm out of replacement house parents."

"We've isolated our patients. Hopefully, things will slow down. Remind everyone of the importance of good hand washing. Are you aware that the flu virus lasts up to twenty-four hours on hard surfaces?"

"Ugh, I had no idea." Lucy walked over to the counter and pulled two containers of antiseptic wipes from a grocery sack. "However, I did bring these."

"Excellent. Wipe down anything that isn't moving."

Dub's eyes rounded and he hid behind Jack. "Not me!"

"No." Rue laughed. "Not you."

"Thanks, Rue." Lucy sighed. "This has been some summer, hasn't it?"

"I like staying busy," Rue replied. "Retirement is for old people. This is much more fun."

"Still, this has been ridiculous and over-the-top busy."

"True." Rue washed her hands and addressed Jack. "And look at you. You're quite the volunteer. Trail rides, stall mucking, chicken coops and now house parent duty?"

"Jack-of-all-trades. Pun intended," he said.

Behind him, Lucy scoffed.

Rue eyed Jack as she rolled down her sleeves. "What is it you do when you're back in your world?" She winked at Lucy.

"I'm sort of between worlds right now."

"Between worlds. I like that, and how fortunate for us."

"Not everyone agrees." He met Lucy's gaze.

"Oh, I don't know," Rue said. "I can provide you with a list of folks around here who are very thankful you've been with us this summer. We couldn't have done it without you, Jack. Especially with those budget issues hanging over our heads, stressing everyone out."

Again, Lucy met his gaze and the arrow of guilt pierced his conscience. Time to step up the work on the lodge.

A small hand tugged at his shirt tail. "Mr. Jack. Can we have lunch now?"

"Sure." He smiled. "Will you excuse us, General?"

"Absolutely. I need to head home to clean up and have lunch myself." She saluted them on her way out the door. "I'm sure I'll see you two soon."

"Thanks for stopping in," Lucy called.

"We gots pizza in the freezer," Dub said.

"How does soup and sandwiches sound instead?" Lucy dug into the grocery sacks she'd brought with her.

"Pizza sounds really good," Dub repeated.

"I agree," Jack said. "Frozen pizza is in my limited repertoire, too."

"Does that mean we can have pizza?" Dub asked.

"It sure does." Jack opened the freezer and assessed the box. "How many should I take out?"

"One should do the trick. There's just the three of us,"

Lucy said. She leaned over to read the instructions on the back and then turned on the oven.

"Don't forget the baby," Dub said.

"Baby?" Jack looked down at Dub. "There's a baby here who eats pizza?"

Dub giggled. "She doesn't eat pizza."

"The baby is sleeping," Lucy said.

"Wanna see the baby?" Dub asked him.

"Not particularly," Jack admitted.

"The pizza will take twenty minutes," Lucy said. "Maybe you can look in on the kids while you're waiting. I'll start loading the dishwasher."

"You mean the *sick* kids?" he asked.

"Yes. Stewie and Henry. The baby isn't sick."

"But you want me to check the baby, as well?"

"Yes," Lucy said.

"What am I checking the baby for?"

"If she's awake, check her diaper."

"Check it for what? Its existence?"

"Very funny." She frowned at him. "Check and see if it needs to be changed."

He raised a palm. "Nope. Stop right there. I don't change diapers."

"Jack, in a perfect world, no one would change diapers."

"Lucy, I'm willing to do a lot of things outside my comfort zone, and I think I've proven that over the last month, but changing diapers is not one of them."

"Someone has to do it, and you asked to shadow me today. In fact, you insisted."

He groaned and ran a hand through his hair. "Have you really thought this through? Sending me in there is not in the baby's best interest."

"Seriously, Jack? Are you making this up?" She stared at him, exasperation raw on her face.

"I wouldn't know how to make this up," he said with a grimace.

She dried her hands and faced him again. "Are you able to take out trash? Or is that outside your comfort zone?"

"Trash?" He perked up. "Yes. Trash happens to be my specialty. I'll handle all the trash."

"Terrific. When you're done I'll give you some chores from the children's chart."

Jack assessed the chore chart with its little gold stars for a job well-done. "This day isn't turning out quite the way I'd anticipated," he muttered.

"Tell me about it."

He grabbed the trash and headed outside. When he returned, Dub was waiting at the door.

"Mr. Jack? I don't feel so good." Dub rubbed a hand over his stomach.

What? Wait. No. This could not be happening. Jack whipped around. Where was Lucy? He picked up the baby monitor and yelled into the device. "Lucy!"

She raced downstairs, her feet thundering on the steps, eyes frantic with concern. "What is it? Why did you do that? You woke up the baby."

"Dub doesn't feel good."

She sighed and laid a hand on Dub's forehead. "Get him into bed. I'll be up to take his temperature."

"What are you going to do?" Jack asked.

"I'm calling Emma to come and take the baby." Lucy handed Jack a plastic bucket.

He met her gaze and shook his head. "Is this for what I think it's for?"

"Yes. Take it, Jack, you may need it."

"I don't want to need it."

Lucy jammed her hands on her hips. "Jack, get him up those stairs right now."

"Yes, ma'am." He grabbed the bucket, scooped up Dub and took the stairs two at a time. "Which room is yours?"

Dub pointed to the first door. Jack peeked in. Stewie and Henry were asleep in bunk beds.

"Are you going to be sick?" he whispered.

"No, but my head hurts. Can you pray for me?"

"I, ah…"

"Please Mr. Jack?"

"Sure, Dub. Get under the covers." Jack pulled back the sheet and the blanket on the twin bed and handed Dub a stuffed turtle from under the pillow. When Dub was settled, Jack held his small hand. "Lord, please help my buddy Dub feel better, and everyone in this house. Amen."

"Amen. Thanks, Mr. Jack." Dub's lower lip quivered. "I don't like being sick."

"It's going to be okay. Close your eyes."

"Will you sit with me until I fall asleep?"

"Absolutely, buddy."

Dub's eyes fluttered closed, and Jack gently pushed the flyaway blond hair from his forehead. His little face was flushed, particularly high on his cheeks, with the emerging illness. Within minutes the regular rise and fall of the five-year-old's chest said he was asleep.

Jack was hesitant to leave. Finally, he tucked the covers carefully around Dub and eased off the edge of the bed.

"Oh, Dub," he whispered. "How did you manage to crawl right inside my heart when I wasn't looking?"

Jack's steps were slow as he left the room.

Lucy met him at the bottom of the stairs. "How's he doing?"

"Asleep." He headed to the sink to wash his hands.

"Good job, Jack. Gold stars for you."

"Yeah. Even though I'm diaper-phobic?"

"We all have our proficiencies. And deficiencies. Did he...you know?"

"Nope. I'm beyond grateful."

The oven pinged, and Lucy turned off the alarm and slid the pizza out. "Lunch."

"I'm not hungry anymore." He leaned against the counter. "So what do we do now? What's Plan B?"

"Jack, this *is* Plan B."

"Yeah? How do parents do this? I've only been here a short time, yet I can tell you this was harder than Mrs. Carmody and mucking out stalls combined."

Lucy smiled. "I know, but when you love someone you do anything for them. There's a lot of love around these homes."

"Even though they aren't their biological kids?"

"That's not even a consideration, Jack. Falling in love with a child has nothing to do with biology. It's a choice." She wiped the counter down with an antiseptic wipe. "There's something to love about every child."

"I'm not sure I could do what they do."

"You did it today."

He paused at her words. "I did what I had to. For Dub."

"That's the start of parenting. Common sense, love and putting their needs before your own." She shrugged. "Nobody looks forward to cleaning up after a sick child. It's part of the job description, offset by the moments when they look up at you like you're Superman."

"Superman?"

"That's the way Dub looks at you."

"He does?"

"You've never noticed?"

"Maybe I've tried not to notice. Summer is more than half over. Not a day goes by that I don't think about what will happen to Dub at the end of summer." He looked at her. "Have you thought any more about fostering?"

"Yes, but I'm not sure I'm suitable. My job is pretty demanding. I don't know that I'm a good candidate."

"You raised your siblings, right? If you don't want to raise another family, that's understandable."

"No, that's not what I'm saying. I suppose that after my engagement debacle, I stopped thinking about my own family. I blocked out the idea. It was safer that way. Now I'm really doubting myself."

"Lucy, I can't think of anyone who would be a better candidate than you. Look how you handled tonight."

"You helped, Jack."

He laughed. "I took out the trash."

She shrugged, obviously dismissing the topic. "What are you going to do when the summer is over?"

"Who knows? I did sublet my place in the city."

"Not going back to New York?" Her eyes widened.

He met her gaze, his own skimming over her brown eyes, her pert nose. "Oklahoma is growing on me."

Lucy shook her head. "Your lips were moving, but the words were all wrong. It sounded like you said Oklahoma is growing on you."

Jack laughed. "Funny."

"Look, Jack, um, I need to apologize. I overreacted yesterday. I promised you could gather information for your project and present it to me, and I intend to keep that promise."

"I appreciate that, and you'll be glad to know I'm almost done."

"Are you?"

"Yeah." He nodded toward the laptop she had set up on the kitchen table. "Looks like you're working on a project, as well. What's all this?"

"We've got another big milestone event at the ranch coming up a week from Saturday. The annual alumni barbecue and rodeo."

"Tripp's been grumbling about it at the bunkhouse. Big deal, according to him."

"It is a big deal," she said. "It's the end of summer for the kids visiting from the Pawhuska orphanage, and at the same time, all the children who graduated and left the ranch return. It signifies the official end of summer is upon us. Another year is about to begin."

"Sounds like fun."

"Really? I was sure you'd balk."

"I like hot dogs and hamburgers as much as the next guy, Lucy."

"You and Dub will need to sign up for a few events, as well."

"Events?"

"The usual. Three-legged race, tug-of war, that sort of thing."

"What about you?"

"Stewie and Henry are my buddies. We'll be out there."

"Can't wait for more of that healthy competition."

Lucy glanced at the wall clock. "Things have settled down here. You can go ahead and go. The worst is over. I've got work to do, so I'll spend the night on the couch monitoring the situation. No doubt Lorna and her husband will be able to take over in the morning."

"Are you sure?"

"I am. And Jack?"

"Yeah?"

"About Saturday."

"You aren't begging off, are you? My aunt is looking forward to your presence at her soiree."

"No. I'll be there. In fact, I'll meet you there."

"Lucy, I'm happy to drive you."

"There's no need. We're both attending, but it's not like it's a date or anything."

"Right. We wouldn't want to take a chance on this looking like a date." He glanced around. "Have you seen my keys?"

Lucy lifted up a stack of papers on the counter.

"Ah, there they are." Jack reached around her and scooped up the keys at the same moment she turned right into him.

Jack froze, waiting, watching. His heart kicked up its rhythm a notch as Lucy Maxwell stood very still in the circle of his arms.

Her gaze dropped to his lips, mere inches away, and then moved to his eyes. "I…" She opened her mouth and closed it very slowly. "Thank you again for your help."

Her soft breath touched his face like a caress.

Jack longed to lower his lips to hers. Instead, he nodded and stepped away with more regret than he would have imagined when he landed at Big Heart Ranch.

"In and out and no one gets hurt," Lucy murmured. "Ask open-ended questions. Gather information, but share little." She stood in the Brisbane estate foyer, handing the silver threaded silk pashmina that Rue had gifted her to a maid before pausing to review Rue's soiree mingle advice one last time.

"Lucy? Is that you?"

She frowned and turned at Jack's voice.

"You know, I thought you ate, slept and lived horses

and kids. Who knew there was a different Lucy outside Big Heart Ranch?"

"What are you talking about? I don't look any different." A glance at herself in the hall mirror confirmed her words.

Jack did a slow and appreciative assessment, from her satin heels to her demure black dress. He swallowed. "Oh, yeah, you do. Lucy, you're more lovely than you can possibly imagine."

"That's silly. It's only a dress." Lucy stole another peek at herself, noting the pink that warmed her face. She wasn't accustomed to such flattery, but she could easily get used to Jack's sweet words.

"It's not just the dress. That little frown line across your forehead is gone, and you're relaxed."

She laughed. "Hot stone massage. Every muscle in my body is happy."

"Really?"

"Yes. Followed by a mud bath. Emma and I had a salon and spa day, courtesy of the general."

"That's great. You deserve that and more. You work far too much." Jack cocked his head and looked at her again. "Your hair…" He gestured with a wave of his hand. "Something's different there, too."

"Oh, that. I brushed it."

He laughed. "You're in good spirits, as well."

Her own gaze swept over his charcoal blazer, striped dress shirt—open at the neck—and white slacks. "What about you? You look all cricket and polo and lawn parties, Mr. Harris."

Jack offered a half smile that nudged a dimple to life. The effect was potent, forcing her to glance away as she recalled the almost kiss earlier in the week that had left her weak-kneed and confused.

"Is that a good thing?" he asked.

"It is. You know, Jack, something about you has changed since I met you at that budget meeting at the start of summer."

"Changed?"

"Yes. You smile more."

"I have more to smile about than I did then."

He left her to ponder his words as he took her arm and led her away.

"Let me show you around my aunt's house. Have you ever seen the great room?"

"No. I've never seen anything except the boardroom and the solarium."

"My apologies. We have been remiss."

Jack opened the double doors of the great room and flipped on a switch. The reflective lights of an unusual crystal chandelier lit up the room.

The walls were buttercream, the carpet Aubusson in ribbon patterns of pale blue. Robin's-egg-blue satin couches faced each other around a circular glass coffee table with a crystal bowl of potpourri in the center. The faint scent of lemongrass and verbena welcomed them.

"That chandelier is amazing," Lucy said.

"A wedding present from my uncle. All imported Belgian crystal. If you look closely, you can see that many of the crystal pendalogues are heart-shaped."

"That's so romantic."

"Would that be the way to your heart, Lucy?"

She laughed. "Not exactly. Where would I put a crystal chandelier? And who would clean the crystals?"

"Ever practical."

"How did they meet?" Lucy asked.

"My uncle's family is Native American, and they've owned this land since before statehood. He was a bachelor for a long time. Apparently he'd given up on the idea of marrying."

Lucy nodded thoughtfully as her gaze went to the portraits that filled an entire wall.

"When they found oil on the land, Aunt Meri was with the team of assessors from the oil company."

"Your aunt worked for the oil company? In what capacity?"

"She's a geologist."

"I never knew that."

"As my aunt tells the story, it was love at first sight, for both of them. If you can believe that."

"I'm not sure I do."

"Right. That wouldn't fit into your Plan B theory, would it?"

When he said it like that, she realized that she did sound like a pessimist. But love at first sight? Could that possibly be real?

Jack met her gaze and offered a rueful smile before he continued. "She quit her job when they got married. Uncle Jeb was much older than her and they didn't want to waste any time."

"No children?"

"None."

"So your father is her brother?"

"That's correct."

"Who is this?" Lucy asked, pointing to the picture of twins on the wall.

His voice softened. "That's me and my brother, Daniel."

"You're a twin." She looked at Jack's profile and then back to the picture several times. "An identical twin. You never told me. You only said that you were older."

He shrugged. "I was. By minutes."

"Do you have other siblings?"

"No. Daniel was my one shot, and I blew it."

Lucy inhaled sharply at his words. "You're so hard on yourself. Doesn't everyone deserve a second chance? That's what Big Heart Ranch is all about," she said softly.

"Yeah, I get that, but don't we need to pay for the mistakes of yesterday?"

"Yesterday is long gone, Jack. Stop bringing it back. His blessings are new every morning. I think it's time for you to start looking ahead and not behind."

He paused as though considering her words, and glanced at the picture one last time. "I'm spoiling the party. Come on, let's go find some of those expensive hors d'oeuvres my aunt is serving."

Lucy was only too aware of his hand on her back as Jack led her through the open doors of a large room. Her gaze spanned the high walls of the room that reached up to a domed vaulted ceiling and back down to the marble floors.

"This is even bigger than the great room."

"Aptly called a ballroom."

"I thought soirees were a bit more intimate of an affair."

"This is intimate to Meredith Brisbane." He glanced toward the buffet table. "Uh-oh, she's headed this way. Once Aunt Meri corners you, you'll be stuck chatting with a dozen people you don't know."

"Rue prepped me."

He laughed. "I've been doing this all my life. No one can prep you for my aunt's people."

At the far end of the room, the music began. A small trio provided slow jazz sounds. Though the room was large, the music and dim lighting created intimacy.

"Providence is in your court," Jack murmured. "My

aunt's been sidetracked and has accepted an invitation to dance from a silver-haired gentleman."

"Good for her," Lucy said.

"What about you, Lucy?" Jack asked. "Would you care to dance?"

She hesitated as he held out a hand.

"One dance." He repeated the request, his dark eyes intent.

"Yes." The word slipped from her mouth while her heart whispered that this was a very bad idea.

Jack caught her by the waist and hummed as he led her across the dance floor.

"I've never glided before," Lucy murmured. "In fact, I'm not much of a dancer."

"Sure you are. It's a partnership, and you've got the right partner. Stick with me. We might even do a little foxtrot later."

"You're very good," she said. They turned and swayed, and he led her past Meredith and her dance partner.

"My aunt is pretty much responsible for every good thing there is about me."

"Dance lessons?"

He nodded and dipped her slightly, his face close enough to smell the faint sandalwood tones of his aftershave.

As the music came to a close, he directed her to the open French doors that led to a veranda. "Wait right here and I'll go in search of sustenance."

Lucy stepped outside, rested her arms on the marble rail and looked out into the garden below. Strings of twinkling white lights had been wrapped around the trees and glittered festively in the night. Overhead a full moon had made an appearance for the event. It rode high in the sky, a hazy blue disc against a carpet of black velvet spilling a generous amount of light onto the world below. The sweet scent of freesias filled the air, and she inhaled deeply.

Lucy sighed at the perfection of the evening. Had she ever imagined an evening with Jack Harris's arms around her on the dance floor? An evening pretending she wasn't a foster child who ran a ranch for kids? Maybe for a few moments she could imagine she was simply a woman enjoying the company of an attentive man.

She glanced at her fingers splayed on the marble rail. She'd gotten a manicure at the spa. This was the first time in a long time that her nails weren't torn and ragged, and her hands weren't reddened and chapped from the daily ranch chores.

Tonight she was Cinderella at the ball.

And yet it couldn't last. This was Jack's world. Not hers.

Jack returned a moment later, balancing a plate full of food in one hand and two glasses of sparkling water in the other.

"Why do I think you've done this before?" she said.

He winked. "I'm an expert. Check my jacket pocket for silverware and napkins."

Lucy laughed as she pulled the utensils from his blazer.

"Won't your aunt be looking for us?"

"No worries, the night is young. There's still plenty of time for boring conversation with my aunt's acquaintances."

"Acquaintances? Not friends?"

"Money only buys acquaintances and ex-fiancées."

"I see your mantra is intact, as well."

His lips curved into a small smile of acknowledgment.

Lucy speared a bit of food onto her fork and inspected it for a moment. "What is this?"

"That looks like foie gras."

"Which is…?"

"Ah, some things are best to enjoy. I'll explain later." He took a long drink of water. "By the way, I've been sharing business cards for the Big Heart Ranch Retreat Center with a few very select guests."

She stiffened. "What business cards?"

Jack swallowed and held up a hand. "That was a misstep. We aren't talking business tonight." He reached out and touched her forehead with his finger. "Relax that frown."

"Jack, you're pitching a venue that hasn't even been approved. And even if it is, there are still licenses and business plans to complete. I thought we had a deal here."

"We do. Calm down."

"Calm down?"

Her eyes widened with uncertain surprise as Jack leaned forward until his lips touched hers. Her head began to spin and her heartbeat raced, but she kissed him back, without hesitation. When he raised his lips from hers, Lucy kept her eyes closed for a moment. A moment to block out the real world where men like Jack Harris didn't kiss women like her. For tonight she could pretend.

"What was that?" Lucy murmured when they broke apart, a hand to her mouth.

"I was trying to change the subject before everything went south. Did it work?"

She blinked. "I…um…"

"Are you all right?" Jack murmured.

"I'm not sure," she whispered, meeting his concerned gaze.

"Should I apologize?"

"Can I get back to you on that?"

"Sure." He ran a hand over his face. "Am I forgiven for bringing up business?"

"Jack?"

"Yeah?"

"My head is spinning. I'm going to need you to talk a little less." She took a deep breath and quickly stepped away from the veranda railing. "We should return to the party. Right away, before I forget I'm only visiting your world."

Chapter Eleven

"Ready to ride, little buddy?"

Dub leaned against the door of the stables with his helmet in his hand and looked around. "Are we going without Miss Lucy?"

"She'll be along." At least he hoped she would be. This was Monday, and she'd had all of Sunday to think about that kiss. As far as first kisses went, it was a good kiss. A simple kiss, yet a good start. Surely Lucy had come to that same conclusion.

Jack glanced around the stable. No Lucy.

Maybe not.

What was he thinking, kissing the director of Big Heart Ranch? He was a professional here with a job to do. It didn't include kissing.

"Why don't we tack up our horses while we wait for Miss Lucy?" he asked Dub.

"I'm too little. I can't reach Grace."

"You can help me with Grace. You tell me what to do and I'll do it. Deal?"

Dub's laughter trilled into the morning air.

Jack smiled. He was going to miss that laugh.

"So what's first?"

"Brush Grace so there's nothing under the saddle that could scratch her." Dub handed Jack the brush. "Then you gots to rub her behind the ears and tell her she's a very good horse. She likes that." His face was solemn as he observed Jack's actions.

Grace snorted and snuffled with pleasure at the rub down. "How did I do?"

"Pretty good, Mr. Jack. You're lots better than when you first got here. You're as good as Leo now."

"Whoa, Dub. I appreciate that, buddy."

"Put on the pad. Miss Lucy says to put it a little bit over the withers.

Jack grabbed the flannel pad and positioned it on Grace. It landed slightly crooked, and Dub jumped up to straighten the edges.

"Dub, have you grown?"

"Yeth, Miss Lorna says I'm growing out of my clothes." He grinned with pride.

Jack stared into space for a minute. Dub was growing. Summer was almost over. Soon the little guy would outgrow his riding boots. Who would get him new ones? Who would take Dub riding? Would his new foster home even care that Dub loved Grace?

"Mr. Jack, are we going to the rodeo on Saturday?"

"Sure are."

"Stewie and Henry say they're going to win the greasy pig."

"Greased pig?"

Dub nodded.

Jack sighed. "You really want to try to wrestle a pig, huh?"

"Yeth, please."

Jack grabbed the saddle and hoisted it carefully onto Grace. "So chasing a greasy pig is supposed to be fun?"

"Uh-huh."

He narrowed his eyes and tried to imagine the pig scenario. "Nope. I don't see it, but I respect your right to try. I'll sign you up."

"You'll come watch, too?"

"Of course. We're buddies. Amigos. Pals. We support each other."

"And the sheep?"

"The sheep what?"

"Mutton busting, Jack," Lucy said from behind him. "My team won last year."

"A nice girl like you busts mutton?" He secured the saddle into position and lowered the cinches and stirrups before turning to Lucy.

She laughed. "No. The little kids…"

When his gaze landed on her lips, Lucy paused, suddenly flustered, her face pink. She quickly turned to Dub. "You ride the sheep, right, Dub? Tell him about it."

"We ride without a saddle," Dub explained.

"Isn't that cruel?" Jack asked.

"Bareback. I know some rodeos use a saddle, but we do not. In fact, we're quite humanitarian about it. Even the greased pig competition is one-on-one. We don't let our pigs or sheep get trampled by kids."

"A humanitarian rodeo. Good to know. I'm down with the pig, but the whole bareback mutton thing seems a little harsh."

"Maybe you could observe first, before you make any snap sheep judgments."

"I'll try to be objective, but no promises." He tightened the cinches, checking the tightness before he looked up at Lucy. "What's today's plan for our riding lesson?"

"I checked the stable records. You've gotten in over

ten hours with a certified instructor—me. I'm going to authorize you to ride the corral with Dub on your own."

"Whoa. I graduated?"

"Yes. You did."

He lifted his hand for a high-five with Dub.

"Way to go, Mr. Jack."

"Couldn't have done it without you, pal."

"Continue to ride Chloe and keep Dub on Grace. Everyone wears a helmet, and you stay in the corral. No new maneuvers, please."

"No worries. I can't afford another cell phone."

Lucy chuckled.

"So you're leaving?" he asked.

"I am. I have a ton of work and two buddies of my own to fit into my day." She paused. "By the way, I found out what foie gras is."

"Delicious, right?" He grinned.

"Not the word I was looking for. Let's just say that it was wise of you not to tell me at the party."

Jack leaned closer. "Are we okay, Lucy?"

"Okay?"

He shrugged. "You know."

"Oh, that. We're fine," she said, quickly dismissing the subject.

"Hey, did I mention your admin starts next Monday?"

"Oh, which one did you hire?"

"Iris. You said her résumé put her up front."

"Yes. But that doesn't mean you're going to take my input. You've been here over four weeks and have pretty much ignored every single one of my recommendations, unless push comes to shove or a cell phone is destroyed."

"That's not true."

"It's absolutely true. Case in point—the lodge. Guest

ranch, rec center, vacation rental." She waved a hand in the air. "Whatever you're calling the place these days."

"Big Heart Ranch Retreat Center."

Lucy crossed her arms. "I'm getting impatient. When will you have your presentation ready?"

"Soon, really soon."

"I hope so. It's been a month."

"Wednesday is a month. It takes time for due diligence."

"It took you five minutes to decide I was a crook."

"I was wrong. Which is why I want to be more thorough."

"You're running out of time for thoroughness. If I don't have a signed proposal or a check in hand soon, we can close the gates and send everyone home."

"Summer is over in two weeks, Lucy. I get that."

"What about the gala?" she continued.

"That's Aunt Meri's thing. My aunt loves a party. If anything stands in the way of that gala, she'll pretty much shoot me. The Brisbane Foundation will cover the expenses for the gala in full."

Lucy released a breath. "Thank you."

Jack looked over his shoulder at Dub, who was happy to walk Grace around the yard outside the stables in circles. "What will happen to Dub?"

"You keep asking me, but you know these things take time." She sighed and clasped her hands together. "I'm working on that, Jack. In fact, I need to get back to my office to work on a stack of paperwork."

"Paperwork? Why not wait until Iris starts and let her help you with your paperwork?"

"This is time-sensitive. I'm applying to the State of Oklahoma Department of Human Services for their Bridge Foster Program."

"You're really doing it?" A joy he hadn't felt in a long time welled up inside at her words. Jack grabbed Lucy around the waist and swung her around.

"Jack, stop. Put me down."

"Lucy, this is fantastic."

"Please. Keep this confidential. If it doesn't work out, I don't want to disappoint them. The end-of-summer transition from Big Heart Ranch is going to be difficult enough. If they get excited about this and it falls through, they'll be devastated." Lucy sighed. "I'll be devastated. Besides, you know how I feel about promises."

He stared at her, speechless for a few moments at her admission. "You've really applied to foster Dub, Ann and Eva?"

She nodded.

"Lucy, you are amazing."

"Don't give me too much credit. And please don't tell anyone. I may not be approved."

"Don't be ridiculous, Lucy. Everyone approves of you."

"Jack, I'm serious. I don't want anyone to find out. You know, just in case."

"Right. In case the other boot falls. In case the zombies take over. Especially in case Plan B doesn't work, either."

Her expression faltered for a brief moment at his words.

"Oh, Lucy." Unable to resist, Jack snaked his arm around her waist and gave her a swift kiss.

Lucy put a hand to her mouth and stared at him, her face flushed with color. "Jack!" She backed up and looked around. "What are you thinking?"

"That you are a generous and giving woman."

"Thank you, but you can't kiss me in public."

As quickly as the kiss of a moment ago was over, a

thought raced through his mind and he froze, stunned. Dub wasn't the only one he was going to miss. He'd miss Lucy Maxwell as much as the little guy.

How had that happened?

Jack turned to Travis. "What's this?"

"What?" The cowboy stopped cleaning his boots to glance over at Jack.

"There's a box on my bed."

"Yeah. It was there when I got here. Looks like a hat-box to me."

Jack opened the round box and unfolded the tissue inside. "What is this?"

"Jack, I know you're a city boy, but I'm thinking even you greenhorns know a straw Resistol when you see one."

"Resistol?"

"Yeah, see that Resistol insignia pin on the band?" Travis shook his head. "That's not a cheap hat, either. The ranch will be full of lovely ladies today. Wear it with pride, bro."

Jack put the hat on his head, examined himself in the mirror and laughed.

"Good fit," Travis said. "Someone knows your hat size."

"Yeah, and they got it big enough to fit my ego. Only one person could have done that."

"My sister, huh?"

"Exactly." He looked at himself again. "You don't think I look a little ridiculous?"

"Jack, a man never looks ridiculous in a hat if he earns the right to wear it. You've put in the time this summer. You earned the right."

"Thanks," Jack murmured.

Travis looked him up and down. "Going to the rodeo, right?"

"Yeah, me and Dub."

"You need a proper shirt. Thankfully, you've come to the right place. I've got shirts." Travis opened his closet and fingered through over two dozen crisply starched and ironed Western shirts. "This one." He handed Jack a black-and-blue plaid Western shirt with snap buttons and black pipe trim on the pockets.

Jack grinned. "Thanks, Travis."

"I'll expect it returned in the same condition."

"Absolutely."

Tripp stepped into the bunkhouse and stood for a minute, staring at Jack without saying anything. Then he went to his drawer and pulled out a belt and brass buckle and handed them to him.

"Here."

Jack's eyes widened at the oversized trophy buckle with a cowboy and bronc engraved on the front, along with the words Guthrie Frontier Days. "Thanks, Tripp."

Tripp nodded and left the bunkhouse without another word.

Jack put the shirt on over his T-shirt and then pulled the belt through the loops on his jeans. He adjusted the hat on his head. "You're sure I should wear this hat?"

"I'm not telling you again," Travis said. "Cowboys wear hats. It keeps your head cool, keeps the sun off your face and keeps the dirt out of your eyes. A cowboy without a hat just ain't right."

"Is that a song?"

"Could very well be."

Jack nodded and pushed his hat to the back of his head and scooped up his keys. "Thanks again, Travis."

"No problem."

Jack strode back across the rodeo grounds for twenty minutes, past cowboys and cowgirls of all ages and sizes before finally admitting to himself he was lost. The ranch was packed with people, but so far the only thing that called his name was barbecued chicken and beef. If he didn't find someone familiar soon, he was going to give up and go eat.

The tent in front of him displayed a colorful banner announcing musical performances on the hour. He stuck his head inside and looked up and down the bleachers.

"Jack?"

He turned to see Rue in a white fringed Western shirt and denim skirt with boots. When he realized her straw hat was exactly like his own, he stood a little straighter.

"Look at you," she said with a sly grin. "Our temporary cowboy looks like one of the locals today."

"You don't think it's too much?"

"Too much what?" She smiled. "Take a peek around you, cowboy. You blend right in with this crowd."

"That's a relief."

"Are you here for the yodeling competition?"

"What?" He stepped back out of the tent. "No. I'm looking for Dub. Do you know where the children's competition is being held?"

"Right over there."

She pointed left, and he took off. A moment later, a small hand slipped into his. "Jack, I like your hat. It matches mine."

He glanced down at the little boy. "So it does."

"Miss Lucy got it for me. She got one for Ann and Eva, too. They have pink hats." He laughed. "I didn't know cowboys could have pink hats."

Jack pulled out his phone and checked the time.

"We've got to hurry and find the greased pig competition."

Dub grabbed his arm. "We're right there. It's in that corral."

"Did you tell Miss Lorna you'd be with me?"

"Yeth."

"Are you sure you want to do this?"

"I've been practicing."

"How do you practice?"

"I chase Stewie and Henry."

Jack laughed. "But listen, Dub, I've been studying up on this, as well."

"You've been studying greased pig?"

Jack looked up. Lucy smiled at him, nearly knocking him off his feet. She wore the yellow sundress with her red boots. The one that made her look like a sunflower. The one she'd been wearing when they met.

"Wow, you're the whole package today, aren't you?" she said, assessing his clothes. "Even have a Western shirt and buckle."

"Courtesy of my roommates." He nodded toward her hat. "I see we all match."

"I thought it might be easier to find you and Dub, but everyone pulled out their straw hats today."

"Thank you for the Resistol," Jack said.

"Yeth! Thank you, Miss Lucy."

"You're both welcome. Now tell me about this greased pig strategy."

"No way. You're the competition," he said.

Lucy sighed, feigning disappointment. "Are you going to be that way?"

"I am, and Dub is going to win today."

Dub grinned when Jack led him to a private area.

"Show me your left hand," Jack said.

Dub shot up his left hand.

"The pig is going to go left, so you have to be ready. Always be prepared to go left. Grab him around the neck, land on his back and hook him with your feet so he can't go anywhere."

Dub offered a solemn nod as he took in the instructions. "How do you know the pig will go left, Mr. Jack?"

"Google." Jack patted his back. "Do your best. That's all you can do."

The announcer called out Dub's name and Jack stood at the fence, hands gripping the rail.

That was his kid in there.

The crowd roared when the gate opened, releasing a sow covered in grease. Dub's little legs moved down the field after the squealing animal.

"Go, Dub go! Go left! Go left!"

Dub focused on his target, pulled the pig to the ground by the neck and hooked his back legs around the animal's torso.

"With a time of forty-five seconds, and the time to beat, Big Heart Ranch's own Dub Lewis!"

Dub raced out of the arena and into Jack's arms. "Jack, I'm the time to beat!"

Jack offered a high-five. "Whoa, that's some grease on you, pal."

"Stewie and Henry are going now."

They stood side by side at the fence, hands gripping the rail as each competitor had their moment of glory in the ring with the pig. Lucy, too, cheered her buddies from the sidelines.

"And the winner of the junior greased pig competition, with a time of forty-five seconds, is Dub Lewis."

Dub's eyes rounded, and he started to jump up and down. "Jack. Jack. I won!"

"Yahoo!" Jack shouted. He scooped Dub up and raced him through the applauding crowd to the winner's circle to get his ribbon.

"That was great, guys," Lucy said. She mussed Dub's hair. "I am so proud of you."

Dub held his ribbon up for her to examine. "Look, Miss Lucy. Mr. Jack told me how to grab the pig, and it worked."

"Oh, Dub. Wait until your sisters see this."

"Do you know where my sissies are, Miss Lucy?"

"They're with Miss Lorna at the line dance competition. We'll find them later. Don't worry."

"Dub, let's pin this on your shirt," Jack said as he wiped his hands on his jeans. He knelt down next to Dub and grabbed a wad of fabric, but the ribbon kept dangling crooked.

Lucy knelt next to him. "Let me help."

Their hands touched as she took the ribbon and expertly attached it to Dub's shirt. Lucy's gaze met his and she smiled, a soft, smile that reached her eyes and warmed him inside and out.

"Thank you, Lucy," Jack murmured.

"You're very welcome."

He stood. "Which way is the food? Us cowboys need to eat after a hard day tackling greased pigs."

"Follow your nose," Lucy said.

"Left."

"Correct." Lucy grabbed his arm. "Look, Jack."

He turned in time to see a vintage red humpback Chevy pickup truck pull into the parking lot.

"It's exactly the same as my dad's."

"Wow, she's a beauty. Do you recognize the driver? An alumni?"

"Let me go check." A moment later she returned with

a smile on her face. "He's the husband of an alumni and he restores cars." She waved a business card. "I've got his number. I'm going to stop by and take the Chevy for a test drive."

"Way to go, Lucy. I'm proud of you."

"What for?" she asked.

"For doing something for Lucy, for a change." He smiled, sharing her enthusiasm. "So you're getting rid of the Honda?"

"Old Yeller? Yes, I'm warming to the idea." She grinned and looked back at the truck. "A test drive, Jack. That's all."

"Can we get our food now?" Dub asked.

"Single-minded, aren't you, Dub? I guess that's what makes a greased pig champion." Jack pointed to a picnic table in view of the Chevy. "I'll grab the food. Why don't you and Miss Lucy wait here?"

"Burger for me, please," Lucy said.

"Me, too," Dub chimed in.

When Jack returned to the bench, Dub was asleep with his head on Lucy's lap.

"He's beat. No mutton busting for this little guy." Lucy smoothed back the hair from Dub's forehead. "Lorna said he's been having trouble sleeping again."

"Again?" Jack sat down on the other side of Dub and placed the food on the picnic table.

"Yes. He couldn't sleep when he first came to Big Heart Ranch."

"What's going on now?"

"Dub knows the end of summer is almost here. He's worried. For himself and his sisters."

Moisture welled in Lucy's eyes. She bit her lip and stared ahead. "No child should have to worry like that. Dub Lewis has grown-up problems, and it's not fair. A little boy shouldn't have to sacrifice his childhood to protect his sisters."

A sucker punch hit Jack straight in the gut as a lone tear rolled down Lucy's cheek.

"What can I do to make sure the fostering goes through for you, Lucy? Whatever you need. I'm your guy."

"Pray, Jack. Pray."

He could do that. The Lord had given him plenty of practice this summer at Big Heart Ranch. He'd developed a proficiency for stall mucking, coop cleaning and prayer. Time to put that last one to work.

Chapter Twelve

"Here you go, Iris. Two Big Heart Ranch staff T-shirts. Jeans or slacks are the uniform. No sneakers, and absolutely no open-toed shoes. This is a working ranch and you could be called out into the field at a moment's notice, so keep a pair of boots at the office."

"Yes, Ms. Maxwell," the young woman replied with a nod.

"Call me Lucy."

"Yes, ma'am. Um, Jack said I'd have my own office."

"Of course he did." Lucy laughed. This was yet another one of those "oh, that Jack" moments she was learning to take in stride.

Lucy opened the door to the supply closet. "Unfortunately, until Jack builds you an office from pixie dust, we're going to have to be creative." She shoved the copier against the wall with her hip and propped open the door.

"Do I have a phone?"

"Yes. I would have ordered you one sooner, however, *someone* failed to let me know you'd be starting today. He told me Monday. The phone company technicians promised that an installer is on his way. Make sure they give you a jack in here, along with your cable connection. Oh, and the guy who does our computers is coming this afternoon."

Iris glanced at the boxed computer on the floor. "Oh, I can take care of the computer. All your tech will need to do is download the software."

"Really?"

"Consider it done."

"Terrific."

"Would it be okay to reorganize this room?"

"Of course. Make it your own. There's a closet down the hall and a conference room. Anything you can discreetly move into either of those locations is fine with me."

"Thank you, Lucy."

"No. Thank you, Iris. Despite my lack of preparation for your first day, and the fact that this is Friday and my brain already checked out, I'm excited you're here. One glance into my office will verify that. I have a ton of work to dump on you." She smiled. "Of course, I mean that in the nicest possible way."

Iris chuckled, and Lucy was certain that despite her misgivings, things were going to work out. If Iris relieved Lucy of the day-to-day stressors of the office, then Jack would be proven right. She did need an admin.

"Thank you, Jack," she whispered.

Rue had a point—she did need to learn to allow people to help her, without being afraid.

Was partnering with Jack to review the ranch funding such a bad idea? She hadn't reevaluated the expenditures in five years. Sure, they'd hired an independent auditor each year, but those results simply kept the books in order. Suddenly the idea of her and Jack working together held an exciting appeal.

Lucy's desk phone rang the moment she sat down.

Soon someone else would be handling these calls. She glanced at the ivy on the windowsill. Perhaps Iris could resuscitate the plant, as well.

She pushed the stack of fostering paperwork ready for the Department of Human Services aside and picked up the phone.

"Lucy Maxwell, Big Heart Ranch."

"Ms. Maxwell, this is Asa Morgan with Morgan and Masters in Manhattan. I'm trying to reach Jackson Harris. The numbers we have on file for him aren't functional and his aunt referred me to you. I understand Mr. Harris is doing pro bono work with your ranch this summer."

Emma peeked her head in, and Lucy put her hand over the receiver.

"Lucy, I'm leaving for court," she whispered. "The judge requested my presence. There's a juvenile that they'd like to place at the ranch. I gave Iris my phone number in case something comes up."

Lucy nodded and returned her attention to the phone call. "Yes. Mr. Harris is with us. I'm pulling up his schedule right now. Please bear with me. Ah, yes, he's with Mrs. Carmody right now."

"Oh, I don't want to take him away from a client. Could you have him return my call as soon as possible? We're hoping to get him out to New York immediately."

"I will give him the message."

"Off the record, Ms. Maxwell, we've heard some very good things about his activities in the nonprofit sector. Could you comment, as his employer this summer?"

"Mr. Morgan, you know that employment law forbids me from confirming or denying anything, except to say that Mr. Harris is indeed here at Big Heart Ranch for the summer."

He chuckled. "Right. Forget I even asked."

"Forgotten. I'll have Mr. Harris call you back immediately."

"Thank you."

Lucy put the phone down and stared at the calendar in stunned silence as the conversation she'd just had sank in.

"Oklahoma has grown on him, huh?" she said aloud. She should have known he'd last about as long as his worthless promise to volunteer through the end of summer.

What did she expect? The silly thing was that she should have seen this one coming in a Brooks Brothers suit, and a mile away, too, despite his kisses.

Or maybe she meant in spite of them.

Lucy swallowed and bowed her head. Every single red flag was there. Yet she'd let herself believe that Jack Harris really did care about her. That his kisses meant something.

What about Dub and the ranch? Did he care about them?

"This isn't personal, Lucy," she whispered. "Jack Harris is a temporary cowboy here on an assignment for the Brisbane Foundation. That's what he said, and that's exactly what he's doing."

If she'd been fooled, it was her own fault.

"Lucy? Am I interrupting?"

When she looked up, Iris stood hesitantly on the threshold of Lucy's office.

"I was talking to myself. I should have warned you about that."

Iris hesitated.

"Come on in. I know it looks terrifying in here, but really, it's harmless."

"Um, your sister called to ask if you authorized a moving truck."

"A truck?"

"Roscoe from USA Rentals. He was apparently lost and she directed him to the lodge."

"The lodge?" Lucy blinked, a knot forming in her stomach. "You're sure he went to the lodge?"

"Yes, ma'am."

Lucy stood. "I'm going to check on this. I'll need you to listen for the front door and take messages if anyone stops by. Don't worry about the phones." She paused and offered a grimace. "Can you handle all that? This is your first day, and I don't want to overwhelm you."

"Ma'am, I've got everything under control."

"Control," Lucy murmured. "Control is a good thing." She headed out the door of her office and backtracked. "The forms! Could you please get this paperwork mailed to the Department of Human Services? It needs to be taken directly to the post office and overnighted."

"Yes, ma'am."

"Thank you, Iris. When I get back, we'll work on that ma'am stuff. It makes me feel like your grandmother."

"Yes…okay, Lucy."

Lucy got into the Honda and turned the key. The car sputtered and coughed but refused to turn over. She put a gentle hand on the dashboard. "You're upset because I looked at that pickup truck, aren't you? I'm sorry."

She tried the ignition again. Not even a click this time. With a groan, she got out of the car and headed to the stables.

Riding to the lodge was the only solution. Lucy picked up speed, finally breaking into a run until she reached the open doors of the stables. Catching her breath, she checked the schedule.

Blaze was free. After a hurried tack up, she offered the gelding feed before they took off. "Blaze, we're going to take a shortcut through the woods. I'm going to need you to cooperate."

The moving truck pulled up to the turnoff to the lodge just as Lucy cleared the woods. Her eyes widened with surprise at the professional sign at the entrance to the lodge. Though she sat on Blaze, positioned at an angle, she could still see the lettering on the sign.

Big Heart Ranch Retreat Center had been burned into its wooden archway. The truck barely cleared the sign as it chugged slowly up to the log cabin house.

Lucy clicked her tongue and nudged Blaze forward, as well. She slid off the gelding's back and tied the reins in a clove hitch around the horse post outside the stables.

All the while, her gaze was focused on the lodge. She walked toward the log cabin house with measured steps. The change took her breath away. It was as she had imagined a lifetime ago when she'd bought the place.

The windows held boxes that overflowed with red and white geraniums. Huge clay pots stood guard at either side of the front door and were filled with more flowers and elephant ear plants. The porch held hanging pots of massive Boston ferns.

Red Adirondack chairs and footstools had been placed casually on the porch and under the willow tree and welcomed a seat in the shade.

Almost ready for his presentation? That's what he'd said. She hitched a breath and swallowed hard.

"I need your signature."

Lucy whirled around. "Excuse me?"

"I need your signature on this load." A stout man pulled a pen from his uniform pocket and tapped on his clipboard.

"No, I'm afraid I don't know anything about a load."

"Jack Harris around? He was supposed to meet me here."

"Then I'm sure he'll be along."

She strode toward the house.

"Lady, time is money."

"I'm sure it is, Roscoe, and you can bill Mr. Harris. This is his problem. Not mine."

Keys. She'd given Jack her keys. Then she remembered the emergency key in a fake rock under the massive redbud in the front yard. Three years ago she had put that key in the rock and buried it.

On her knees, she searched the base of the tree until she located the spot. After three years, the rock had sunk into the red clay and was now practically embedded into the ground. She used her car key to dig it up. At least Old Yeller was still good for something. Sitting on her haunches, Lucy pulled the rock from the ground and opened the shell case.

She grinned and held up the key.

The mat outside the front door had been engraved with the words Welcome to Big Heart Ranch Retreat Center.

"All the personal touches, right, Jack? No wonder this took you so long. You weren't planning a presentation— you planned a done deal. So much for working together. For partnerships." She released a groan of frustration.

Lucy stood at the threshold, a hand on the knob and the key in the lock, though her feet seemed unable to move. Overwhelmed, she closed her eyes and slowly inhaled.

Last night she'd tossed and turned thinking about Jack Harris and his kisses. She realized with stunning wonder that she was falling in love. Not with the attorney, but with the volunteer who had replaced Leo and stolen her heart. And she actually liked the idea. A lot.

But that was last night. This was now.

Fear paralyzed her for a few moments. Finally, she turned the knob and pushed the door open.

A small and elegant reception desk faced the door, surrounded by baskets of overflowing ferns and ivy. On the desk, another basket held menus to local eateries that delivered. Yet another held mints with the ranch name and number on black-and-gold wrappers.

The once-empty main living room behind the desk had been converted into a stylish cross between a hotel lobby and a real lodge. Cozy seating arrangements were placed around the room, along with an internet charging table. Jack had brought high-speed internet to the lodge. Of course—if it could be done, Jack was the man to do it. No amenities had been spared.

The fireplace had stacks of wood on either side. Over the mantel, a reproduction of a Bob Timberlake painting that depicted a ranch in winter hung. Mesmerized, she stared at the painting.

Lucy wandered into the kitchen next. Shiny pots and pans hung over the center island. Unable to resist, she opened cupboards and drawers. Dishes, silver and even thick kitchen towels filled the drawers.

Her suspicions were verified. Jack Harris had never planned to propose a facility at the lodge. He'd forged ahead and created something beyond her imagination. The place was amazing. He was not a man of half measures. The evolution of this house from empty to visionary revealed the real Jackson Harris. A man who went after what he wanted, no matter the cost.

How had she not seen this coming?

Her closet.

Lucy willed her heart to stop pounding so hard. She stared at the pantry closet for moments, grappling with her emotions. Her hands trembled as she remembered sharing the painful secrets with Jack in there. The memory burned, and she held her hands to her flushed face.

Twisting the knob, she realized the pantry was unlocked. Lucy slowly opened the door and turned on the light. Nothing had been touched. It remained as it was the last time she was there. With Jack.

Lucy put a hand on her heart and realized it was beating overtime, and her breath was coming in shallow pants. Hyperventilating again. She leaned over, hands on her knees, and willed herself to relax.

From the other room, the sound of the front door opening and footsteps echoing on the pine floor filled the silence. She turned her head in time to see Jack step into the kitchen with a smile on his face.

Their gazes connected, and the smile faded.

"Lucy, what are you doing here? I didn't see Old Yeller."

"I rode Blaze."

"This was supposed to be a surprise."

She sucked in a shaky breath. "Surprise!"

He stepped closer. "I can explain."

The time for explanations was long past. About four weeks too long. Lucy struggled to keep her voice calm.

"What's in the moving truck, Jack?"

"More furniture."

"More?" She nodded, thoughtfully considering that one word.

"For the upstairs rooms."

"You bought furniture, too?"

"No. My aunt had furniture in the stables. I figured upcycling was a good thing."

"That's green of you."

The awkward silence was broken when Roscoe came in carrying a rocking chair.

"Where do you want this stuff?"

"Put everything in the bedrooms upstairs," Jack directed.

"There was a call for you," Lucy said when Roscoe left the room. "Asa Morgan with Morgan and Masters in Manhattan. He's very impressed with what he's heard about your nonprofit work."

She stared at him, trying to figure out who Jack Harris really was. How had she been so easily duped?

"Is that all we are at Big Heart Ranch, Jack? An opportunity for you to build your résumé, sharpen your skill set?"

"What do you want me to say, Lucy?"

"I want you to say that you really do care about Dub. That you believe our ranch is the real thing, and that the last few weeks haven't been simply a chance for you to explore your entrepreneurial side at our expense before you head back to New York."

"They're courting me. I didn't reach out to them. Summer is almost over. The fact is, I have to make some hard decisions soon."

She bowed her head.

"Whatever you think I've done, you're wrong." He shrugged. "But you've already convicted me. Right, Lucy?"

"Why did you lead me to believe you were busy drawing up plans and proposals all this time?"

"I had to work around the fact that you keep your expectations low. That you weren't ready to move on."

Lucy met his gaze. "What does that mean?"

"It means that you can't let go of the past long enough to see the future. Telling you about the future wasn't going to work. I knew I had to show it to you. Show you possibilities, or you'd continue to define this house as your epic failure."

"It is my failure."

He shook his head. "Lucy, you've taught me so much about second chances. About leaving the past behind. Why is it you give everyone a second chance but yourself? This house is not a failure. It's a possibility, just like your kids. Maybe even like us."

"Us? There is no us. You lied to me."

"I didn't lie. I dodged the truth. If I'm guilty of anything, it's caring too much. I suggested working together, but you wouldn't even hear that option. I made a decision to work around you, in an effort to get through to you." He ran a hand through his hair. "My aunt tried to warn me that this wasn't the right approach. I didn't listen to her."

"How did you fund…" She waved an arm around the room. "All of this?"

"Consider it a donation from a private donor. Me. Not my aunt."

"Thank you for not touching my closet," she murmured.

"You're the only one who can empty that closet."

A phone began to ring, and Lucy reached into her back pocket and pulled it out. "Sure, Iris. I'll be right there." Lucy headed for the door.

"Where does this leave us, Lucy?" Jack asked.

"The same place we were five weeks ago. I represent the children of Big Heart Ranch and implore you to approve the donation funds."

"What about us?" he pressed.

"Seriously, Jack? Relationships are messy and complicated, and they take time and dedication. You can't plan them out on one of your spreadsheets. Your money can't buy love." She turned away. "I'm sorry you don't get that."

* * *

Jack blinked, his eyes gritty from lack of sleep. He led Zeus from his stall out to the pen. The horse offered an agitated whinny on principle.

"Don't you start on me, too." Jack grabbed the shovel. The cowboy's cure for insomnia. He started mucking with a vengeance. Stall by stall, and in under a few hours the stables were cleaner than even the amazing Leo could have produced.

Leo. Maybe he should give the guy a call and see if he'd consider a raise to return to Big Heart Ranch. He felt guilty leaving the ranch in the lurch. Jack pulled off a glove and made a note on his phone.

"Jack, just the man I want to see."

He raised his head and narrowed his eyes at General Rue Butterfield, who stood in the middle of the stables.

"Normally those are exactly the words I want to hear. Today, not so much."

"What happened between you and Lucy?"

"Nothing. A big fat nothing."

Rue sighed and put her arms on top of the stall gate. "Jack, I never figured you for a coward."

"I'm not."

"Let's pretend for a moment that those words are true." Jack raised a brow.

"What about the ranch funding?" she asked.

"Signed on Friday, General. The certified check should be on the director's desk…" He glanced at his watch. "What day is it? Time flies when you spend your time banging your head against a wall."

"Wednesday."

"I met with the accountant yesterday. It will be on Miss Maxwell's desk tomorrow afternoon."

"That's a relief."

He couldn't think of a single satisfying response, so he pulled on his glove and stabbed at the straw with the pitchfork.

"Less than two weeks left. You're staying until the end of summer?" Rue asked.

"I always keep my word."

"Good to know. What about the gala?"

"That's my aunt's department. I'd rather get tossed off Zeus than attend another party."

"What will you do once the summer is over?"

"I couldn't tell you."

"You're going to walk away?"

"I've examined this situation carefully. I don't see that I have any choice."

"Let me get this straight. You'd rather walk away from the possibility of everything and jump straight into a future that holds nothing than fight for what you want."

He looked at her. "Admittedly, when you say it like that, it doesn't sound too smart."

Rue laughed. "At least your sense of humor is still intact."

"Always."

"Mr. Jack?" Dub stuck his head around the corner. "Are we having lessons this week?"

"Yeah. Right on schedule, tomorrow afternoon at three."

Dub pulled a shiny quarter from his pocket and held it out to the general.

"What's that you have, Dub?" she asked.

"A quarter. Mr. Jack said I can keep it." Dub cocked his head and watched Jack. "You okay, Mr. Jack? You're not getting sick, are you?"

"I'm good, Dub."

Dub turned and walked out of the barn, tossing the quarter in the air and catching it again as he went.

Jack winced. He was getting sick all right. The thought of leaving Dub behind turned his stomach.

"He's in tune to you, Jack."

"What does that mean?"

"It means he knows something is up." Rue shook her head. "Sadly, Dub is the one who's going to suffer when you walk away."

"There's nothing I can do to fix things. Lucy's happy to see me leave. She thinks I'm heavy-handed and dishonest."

"Are you?"

"My intentions were honorable. But yeah, I messed up. Big time. What can I do, General?"

"I don't know, but I'm sure you'll think of something, because come ten days from now you won't be the only one in a world of hurt."

Jack swallowed hard as Rue left the barn. He'd come to Big Heart Ranch an empty man. If he left things as they were, he'd be walking away exactly the same. Somehow he had to find a way to get Lucy to forgive him, because he wasn't willing to turn his back on everything he loved.

Chapter Thirteen

"This arrived by courier, Lucy."

Lucy looked up from her desk at the official-looking envelope Iris held out to her.

"By courier? We're twenty minutes from Timber, Oklahoma. Who sends things by courier?"

A frown crossed the admin's face. "Is that rhetorical?"

"Yes." Lucy cleared a place on her desk, which she noted was significantly less messy since Iris had started last Friday. Another thing to thank Jack for.

"Don't you want it?"

Lucy pointed to the spot she'd cleared, and Iris dropped the envelope on the desk.

"Oh, and General Butterfield called and asked for a few minutes of your time. However, she didn't wait for an answer. She's on her way over."

"I always have an open door for the general."

Iris nodded. "Do you mind if I run some errands for Emma tomorrow morning? She's swamped with preparations for the gala."

"Of course. Thank you for being so flexible, Iris."

"I like it here, Lucy. I don't have any family. Big Heart Ranch sort of feels like home."

"I'm glad to hear that."

Lucy stared at the envelope. The embossed return address was from the Brisbane Foundation Legal Department. That would be attorney Jackson Harris's department.

He was everywhere.

A shiver raced over her. She clenched and unclenched her hands, knowing that the future of Big Heart Ranch was inside an unremarkable white envelope delivered by courier on a Thursday in August.

She'd been asking around, and though she hadn't run into him since last Friday, as far as she could tell, Jack was still living at the bunkhouse. According to a little surreptitious checking, she'd learned that he continued to fulfill his promise to stay at the ranch through the end of summer and fill Leo's shoes.

Lucy rubbed her forehead. How had things gotten so out of control so quickly? She glanced at the red-team ball cap sitting on her bookcase and smiled, remembering Jack yelling at her to slide into home at the ball game. Jack and Dub laughing as they created monster ice cream sundaes together. That wonderful kiss at the soiree when she was naive enough to think she might be falling in love with Jack.

Soon it would all be a memory, tucked away like a pressed flower.

Eight more days until the gala. The gala was supposed to be a jubilant time when they celebrated the year's blessings. Another year of mending broken hearts and providing second chances.

What about Dub? His little heart would be broken when he and his sisters went back to the Pawhuska Children's Orphanage.

Though it was ridiculously too soon to expect a response, Lucy pulled up her email to verify no one had contacted her from DHS about the foster program.

She released a dramatic sigh and held the envelope to her desk lamp.

"Aren't you going to open it?"

She looked up at Rue, then put the envelope on the desk and folded her hands over the top. "I haven't decided."

"Come on, Lucy, open the letter."

"I'm not sure I'm ready for what's inside."

"Everywhere I go on this ranch, folks are dancing to the same tune."

"Okay, I'll bite. What tune would that be?"

"The chicken dance."

Lucy chuckled. "Does this mean you've stopped by to share some sage wisdom with me?"

"Whenever I can. You don't get to be my age without learning a thing or two. Usually the hard way." Rue shook her head. "If I can save some folks the heartache I suffered needlessly due to my own pigheadedness, then by golly, I'm going to try."

"I'm sure there's a lesson in there somewhere."

"Open the envelope. That's the lesson for the day."

Lucy took the letter opener from her drawer, slid the point beneath the letter's gummed flap and sliced the envelope. The check fluttered to the desk.

Lucy slowly reached out and turned it over. She trembled as she read the amount.

"This is the largest donation to the ranch that we have ever received from the Brisbane Foundation," she whispered. "It's more than we requested."

"Isn't God good?"

"Wait until Travis and Emma find out." Lucy put a

hand to her heart in a futile effort to slow its wild beating. "Oh, my goodness. I'm speechless."

"You deserve this, Lucy. You've worked hard for that check."

"Yet I'm humbled. I had moments when I doubted the Lord and even whined a bit. I definitely have time on my knees in my immediate future."

"Do you think you can handle more good news?" Rue's eyes twinkled.

"I'm not sure." Lucy blinked and cocked her head. "What are you up to?"

"I made a few phone calls, and your fostering paperwork has been expedited."

"What does that mean?"

"It means you've been selected to foster Dub, Ann and Eva, pending inspection of your domicile and, of course, approval of the children."

"Rue, I live in a one-bedroom apartment."

"It's okay. DHS understands. The children will stay in their homes on the ranch until you locate a place suitable for all of you."

"How did you do this?" Moisture blurred her vision as she spoke.

"There's really not much point in being a general if you can't pull in favors every now and again." She shrugged. "It's always good to have friends in high places."

Lucy stood up and came around the desk to hug her friend. "Oh, Rue. That little boy and his sisters are going to get the second chance they deserve."

Rue wiped her own eyes. "I promised myself I wouldn't blubber."

Lucy sniffed and handed the older woman a tissue.

"The hard part is going to be up to you," Rue said.

"You mean talking to the children?" Lucy paused before she sat down. "You're right. What if they don't want me to be their foster parent?"

"Get real, Lucy. Those kids love you."

"What hard part are you referring to?"

"You have to talk to Jack."

"Jack?"

"Don't leave him out of this. He recommended the increased funding, and he's your biggest cheerleader. I know for a fact that he and his aunt also spoke to the DHS regarding you fostering."

"They did?"

"Yes."

"How do you know all this?"

Rue shrugged and glanced at the calendar. "Don't make the mistake of thinking you have all the time in the world to make this right, Lucy. You don't."

"There's a lot of hurt between Jack and me. I don't know if I can bridge that. Besides, he has job offers in New York City."

"He's still here. It doesn't seem to me that he's in any rush to leave. Jack will stay in Oklahoma if you ask him. Deep down inside, he wants you to ask him. He longs to be part of something that's forever, just like you do."

Lucy was silent, overwhelmed by Rue's observations.

"Second chances are great, Lucy, until you miss the window of opportunity."

"Are you suggesting I beg him to stay?"

"No, I'm suggesting that you tell him how you feel."

"I don't think I can," Lucy murmured.

"I think you better. You can't afford to leave things unsaid." She smiled sadly at Lucy. "You of all people should have learned this long ago."

"What if he doesn't… What if he says no?"

"You can't lose until you saddle up and try."

"Okay, Rue. When the time is right, I'll talk to Jack."

"I know I can count on you," Rue said.

Iris appeared in the doorway. "I'm so sorry to interrupt, but Lorna has been trying to reach you on your cell, Lucy. She says it's urgent. Dub Lewis is missing."

Adrenaline shot through Lucy. She grabbed her purse. "Rue, can you head over to the security office and ask them to check the cameras? I'll phone you when I have details."

"Of course."

"Jack. I have to find Jack." Lucy jumped into the Ute and put her phone on speaker, hitting the auto dial button over and over.

Jack Harris wasn't picking up.

"What?" Jack sat straight up in bed.

The banging at the bunkhouse door had him scrambling for his phone.

Six p.m. He'd fallen asleep for four hours?

The banging didn't let up.

He pulled open the door, nearly knocking the ranch director off her feet. "Lucy? What's wrong?"

"Dub is missing."

"Missing?" Jack struggled to breathe. Realization hit him like a solid punch in the gut. "I missed his riding lesson. I fell asleep."

"What time was the lesson scheduled?"

"Three," he groaned.

"Lorna went to check on him when he didn't come down for dinner. He wasn't in his room."

"What about his house brothers?"

"Stewie and Henry don't know anything. But his bicycle is still in the garage."

"Is he with his sisters?"

"No, she already called over there."

"We can take my car," Jack offered.

"Jack, it'll be better if we split up. You check the boys' ranch. I'll go to the girls' ranch and look around. Rue is working with security."

He grabbed his boots and shoved his feet into them. "This should have never happened, Lucy. That kid has way too much freedom."

She grimaced and turned away. "Please, don't play the blame game, Jack. Not now. I love that little boy as much as you do. I'm planning my future around him."

"Then why did he leave?"

"Why do you think? Dub is smart. He knows summer is over in a week. And he knows you're leaving. You missing that lesson today must have had him in a panic that you were already gone."

"It's my fault."

"Stop. Focus on Dub. We'll find him."

"All it takes is one moment, and your life changes forever."

Lucy's face paled at his words.

"We have to find Dub," Jack said, fighting emotions that threatened to paralyze him.

"You're right, Jack. We both understand that only too well. But this isn't about you or me. This is about a hurting child who is afraid he's going to lose everything once again. This is the time for prayers, not accusations or self-recrimination."

She walked out the front door without looking back.

Jack grabbed his keys and got in the Lexus. His thoughts flashed back to his brother, and for the first time in twenty-five years he once again felt the sinking despair of helplessness pressing down. He couldn't lose someone he loved again. Not like this.

"Dub, where are you?" Jack rested his head on the steering wheel and began to pray. "Lord, that boy means more to me than I realized. Help me find him. Help me make things right."

For several minutes, Jack stared out the windshield at the ranch where activities were winding down around him.

The loft.

Dub would be in the loft if he was anywhere.

Jack started the car and headed to the stables.

The front door stood open as children and staff finished grooming their horses for the day. Jack walked to the end of the building. Tripp's office was dark. Outside Grace's stall, something shiny winked at him. He crouched down and scattered the straw, uncovering a quarter.

Grace whinnied and nodded. She shook her head toward the loft overhead. "Thanks, Grace," Jack whispered, rubbing the mare's ears.

He took the back stairs and nearly stumbled over the sleeping child at the top.

"Dub," Jack whispered, his relief raw.

Dub had neatly placed Grace's pad on the ground and lay on the flannel, curled on his side, his hands tucked beneath his head, quietly sleeping. Tear tracks had dried on his dusty face.

The five-year-old had been crying.

Jack closed his eyes and ran a hand over his own face. "I'm sorry, Dub."

He eased down to the loft floor next to Dub. For minutes he simply watched the child sleep. Swiping at his eyes with the back of his hands, Jack released a silent prayer of thanks.

"What am I going to do, Lord?" he whispered. "I can't leave this boy."

Dub's eyes fluttered open. "Mr. Jack?" A small smile crossed his face.

"Yes, Dub."

"I thought you were gone. Stewie and Henry said you were going away. You didn't come for my lesson."

"That was an accident, Dub. I'm so sorry. I fell asleep."

"You're here now."

"Yes, but you're right—I'm leaving when the summer is over. I have a few more days."

"I'm going back to the orphanage," Dub said as he sat up. "My sissies, too."

Jack nodded.

Dub twisted his hands in his lap. "I thought if I prayed hard, God would hear, and me and my sissies could stay at the ranch."

"Oh, Dub. I know God is listening. Sometimes things don't happen when we think they should, but He always hears our prayers."

"I wish He'd hurry up."

"Me, too."

"What about Grace?" Dub frowned as if in pain. "Who will take care of Grace? She needs her carrots, and her ears rubbed. She'll be sad if you and me both go away, Mr. Jack."

"Mr. Tripp takes good care of all the horses. Don't worry about Grace."

Dub gave a resigned nod.

"Miss Lorna and Miss Lucy are worried about you, Dub. You missed dinner."

"I'm thorry." Dub grabbed the flannel pad and stood up. He shook the straw from the fabric.

"I'll take care of that later. Are you hungry?"

"No." Dub stared at the stables stretched out before him, then finally looked up at Jack, his lower lip quivering. "I don't want to leave the ranch. It's like a real home."

"I know, Dub. I don't want to leave, either."

"Maybe Miss Lucy will let us stay. We can ask her, can't we?"

Lucy's words came back to him. *Don't make promises you can't keep.* Jack's lips were a thin line as he looked at his buddy without offering him the promises he desperately needed to hear.

Dub nodded. "It's okay. Don't be sad, Mr. Jack. I know sometimes we gots to follow the rules."

Jack choked on the emotions overwhelming him. Without thinking, he scooped the little boy up in his arms. "I love you, buddy."

Dub Lewis tucked his head into Jack's chest. "I love you, too, Mr. Jack."

Chapter Fourteen

Lucy saddled Blaze and led her out into the sunshine. She'd checked Jack's schedule before she snuck into the stables. He'd be in the chicken coops for at least another hour. This would be as good a time as any to take the shortcut to the lodge and empty that closet. She might figure out what to do about Jack Harris while she was cleaning up her life.

As she approached the house, she was once again struck by the transformation. The place welcomed visitors. Encouraged them to sit on the porch or rest beneath the willow tree.

Jack was right. It made sense to use the lodge to support the ranch. She'd been stubborn on principle, and he'd been high-handed. The two of them were quite a pair. Controlling to the bitter end, and where had it gotten either of them?

Control had served her well when she was a foster child looking after Travis and Emma. She was a long way from those days. With a glance at her hands, Lucy opened the palms. "I'm finally giving it all to You, Lord."

Lucy had barely unlocked the front door and walked in when the doorbell rang. She turned to discover Meredith

Brisbane on the porch, carrying an enormous bouquet of long-stemmed sunflowers, wrapped in green floral paper.

"Meredith?" Lucy looked past the elegant matriarch to the limousine parked outside the lodge.

"Hello, Lucy. Your assistant told me you'd be here."

Lucy opened the screen, and Meredith handed her the bouquet. "My nephew once said that sunflowers reminded him of you."

She did a double take at the words. *Jack said that?*

"They're lovely." Lucy fingered the bright yellow petals. "What are they for?"

"Your foster request was approved."

"Yes, it was. Thank you so much for putting in a good word for me."

"I adore those children. So does Jackson. We both know you'll be a wonderful mother."

"A mother." The words rolled off her tongue, and she paused to consider them, sinking down into a chair. "Things have been so incredibly busy that I hadn't even stopped to think about that. I'll be someone's mom. Wow."

"I'd say a few wows are in order."

"Come on in, Meredith. Let me put these in water." She stood and headed to the kitchen. Suddenly Lucy stopped and turned. "Where's your cane?"

Jack's aunt held up her empty hands. "I'm feeling so much better. No cane needed."

"That's wonderful."

Lucy led Meredith into the kitchen and searched the cupboards for a large vase, but came up empty. "Excuse me a moment."

Second shelf on the right. Tucked near the back. Exactly where she'd put it three years ago. Lucy opened the pantry door and carefully removed the vase from the original gift box. She placed the crystal cylinder in the sink under running water.

"This is your house?" Meredith asked, her gaze sweeping the open spaces and high ceilings.

"Yes. I bought the place a long time ago. It's been empty ever since."

"Why has this house come between you and Jackson?"

Lucy took a deep breath, turned off the faucet and faced Meredith. "I could tell you that he and I have had differing views on the future of the ranch, and this house. But the truth would be because we're both bossy and pigheaded."

"That's a shame." Meredith stepped into the open living room. "So this is where he brought all that furniture." She walked across the room and stood in front of the fireplace to admire the painting. "Bob Timberlake. It looks like a first edition print."

"Is it? I don't even know where it came from," Lucy admitted.

"Oh, Jackson, I imagine."

Lucy's gaze followed Meredith's. As she glanced around, she realized how nicely the furniture and accessories fit in the lodge. It was almost as though they were supposed to be there.

"Lucy, did you see the chandelier in the great room at the estate?"

"Yes. It's incredible. The heart-shaped crystals."

"My husband bought it for me because he had it in his head that the chandelier was something I longed for." She smiled serenely. "I didn't really. However, every time I look at that chandelier and see the prisms of light reflected from those hearts I remember how much he loved me. That chandelier was his expression of love."

Lucy was silent as Meredith continued.

"Have you ever considered that what my nephew did with this house is his expression of love?"

Lucy's eyes widened.

"Jackson knew right away that you weren't a crook, and that Big Heart Ranch was legitimate. He respected and admired your steadfast devotion to the ministry God gave you." Meredith laughed. "He's been more than a little perturbed that you care more about his stall-mucking ability than his bank account or his family ties."

"I don't understand. Then why didn't he sign the paperwork?"

"I asked him the same thing that day when you were at the house with the children. He said that if he signed it on week two, he wouldn't have a reason to stay at the ranch for the summer. Jackson cared for you right from the beginning." She smiled again. "He was determined to make sure you'd never lose Big Heart Ranch. I believe he said something about a Plan B."

Lucy's jaw sagged at the words.

"My nephew loves you."

"He certainly has a funny way of showing it."

"Oh, don't get me wrong. He was completely in the wrong. I told him that from the start. He made a mistake."

Meredith stepped closer and took Lucy's hands. "I've grown to love you as well, Lucy. You're an amazing woman. It would be my dearest wish if you could find it in your heart to forgive Jackson. To give him a second chance. Do you think you can do that?"

Emotion stinging her eyes, Lucy nodded.

"What are you doing?" Jack asked. He assessed the boxes spread over the kitchen floor. Lucy Maxwell was on the closet floor, with her boots sticking out into the kitchen of the lodge.

She jerked when he spoke, and the sound of her head connecting with a shelf echoed in the kitchen. "Ouch."

Jack groaned. "Sorry. I didn't mean to surprise you."

Lucy crawled out of the closet and looked up at him. "What does it look like I'm doing?"

He opened his mouth and then closed it, determined not to make a mess of things today. *Focus, Jack.* The reason he was here was to fix what he'd already messed up.

When she dusted off her jeans and began to stand, Jack quickly offered her a hand.

"Thanks. I was getting a little stiff." Their gazes connected, and she paused, glancing down at her hand in his before stepping back.

"Dust bunny at twelve o'clock," he said.

"Huh?"

Jack plucked a ball of dust from her hair and offered it to her. Lucy laughed when he placed it in her palm.

He smiled. Lucy laughing was a very good sign.

"So you were saying?"

"Saying?" Lucy frowned, confused.

"The closet."

"Oh, that." Lucy gestured with a hand. "I'm moving on with my life." She picked up a stack of small boxes and put them on the kitchen island. "Six trivets, Jack. How many trivets does one woman need?"

He frowned. "I don't know the answer to that question."

When she laughed again, the tightness in his chest eased. Maybe this wasn't going to be as painful as he thought.

"Thank you for the check. And the flowers and the recommendation you provided to DHS." Her cheeks went pink, and she offered an embarrassed smile. "Actually, I have quite a bit to thank you for."

"You're welcome." He shoved his hands in his pockets. "Look, Lucy, I'm here to apologize. Let me do that before I put my foot in my mouth again."

"Okay," Lucy murmured.

"I steamrolled you with this whole Big Heart Ranch Retreat Center plan of mine."

"Yes. You did."

"I was an idiot. I thought I could force you to face your fears when I had no intention of facing mine until you made me." He released a breath. "I'm sorry."

"You are quite forgiven."

"Yeah?" He cocked his head. "I expected a lot more, you know…"

"Groveling?"

Jack nodded.

"Normally, I would require that."

"Oh?"

"Except I have so much to be thankful for, I'm feeling benevolent today." She paused. "And it's possible that despite your arrogant and high-handed ways, you actually did me a favor by forcing me to face my fears and let go of control."

"Um, thanks. I think." He met her gaze. "But it goes both ways. By twisting my arm, and pushing me to be a buddy to Dub, you helped me move past the guilt of my brother's death."

An awkward silence stretched between them. Jack met her gaze. "What are we going to do now?" he whispered.

Her expression was solemn as she lifted her chin and really looked at him. "I don't know."

"You're still afraid, aren't you?"

She sighed. "Well, duh. Of course I am. I'm terrified. I don't have any more closets, Jack."

"I'm not that other guy, you know. I won't ever leave

you. I'm not perfect. When life gets messy and complicated, like you said it would, I won't ever disappear."

"What are you saying?"

"I'm saying that I love you, Lucy Maxwell."

Tenderness filled her eyes, followed immediately by wide-eyed panic.

"It's only been six weeks, Jack."

"Yeah. How about that? Six weeks is all it took for me to fall in love with you."

Lucy's mouth formed an O of astonishment. "You're really in love with me?"

"How could I not be? You've been turning my life upside down since day one."

"Your life? What about mine? I now have an admin and a guest ranch. With the new budget, we'll be able to add a few more houses to the boys' and girls' ranches. That means we can help a few more kids. Thanks to you."

"Don't give me the credit." Jack aimed his thumb heavenward. "I've been asleep for twenty-five years. He and my aunt woke me up by sending me to Big Heart Ranch. They're quite a team. They get all the credit."

Lucy gave a hesitant nod. "Yes. With a little help from the general."

"You know that this means you have to trust me. No more Plan B. No more waiting for the other boot to drop. I get that this ranch is your ministry, and that doesn't scare me."

"Maybe it should."

"Not at all. These are God's kids. This is your job. God willing, I'll partner with you in that job and at night we can go home to our children, Dub, Ann and Eva, each night."

Lucy gasped and reached for the counter as her knees wobbled. "You want to adopt them?"

Jack slipped an arm around her waist and helped her to a chair. "Of course I want to adopt them. I'd be lost without them. Without you."

"Adopt?" Lucy repeated the word. "Five hearts will get a second chance, Jack."

"A family. A forever family."

"Except I haven't even told Dub and his sisters about the foster plan yet. I haven't asked them if they want me to be their mom."

"Of course they do. But why haven't you told them?"

"I'm waiting for the official paperwork to be delivered. I can't tell them until then. What if..."

He put a finger to her mouth. "No more what-ifs, Lucy. No more zombie apocalypse backup plans."

She nodded. "You're right. You're completely right."

For a few moments, Lucy simply stared at him. Then she stood and wrapped her arms around his neck. She closed her eyes tight and opened them. "Oh, Jack," she murmured. "Who ever thought I'd fall in love with the ornery lawyer with the cute dimple?"

"I have a cute dimple?"

When she nodded, Jack lowered his head to meet her lips.

"Ah, Lucy," he breathed when they separated. "We have to get busy."

"How so?"

"We've got paperwork to file if we want to finalize the adoption in time for the wedding."

"What wedding?"

"Lucy Transparent Maxwell, will you marry me?"

"Oh, Jack," she murmured again, reaching up to kiss him. She leaned back in the circle of his arms.

"A wedding," she breathed.

"Yeah."

"With Dub and Ann and Eva."

"Is that a yes, Lucy?"

"Yes. It's a yes." She reached for a notepad on the counter. "We have so much to do. We're way behind schedule, Jack. We have to catch up and start making those forever memories for those kids. For us."

He laughed and took the paper from her. "We have a lifetime, Lucy. A lifetime for our little family."

"I love you, Jack."

"I love you too, Lucy."

* * * * *

SPECIAL EXCERPT FROM

Love Inspired®

Could this bad-boy newcomer spell trouble for an Amish spinster...or be the answer to her prayers?

Read on for a sneak preview of
An Unlikely Amish Match,
the next book in Vannetta Chapman's miniseries
Indiana Amish Brides.

The sun was low in the western sky by the time Micah Fisher hitched a ride to the edge of town. The driver let him out at a dirt road that led to several Amish farms. He'd never been to visit his grandparents in Indiana before. They always came to Maine. But he had no trouble finding their place.

As he drew close to the lane that led to the farmhouse, he noticed a young woman standing by the mailbox. A little girl was holding her hand and another was hopping up and down. They were all staring at him.

"Howdy," he said.

The woman only nodded, but the two girls whispered, "Hello."

"Can we help you?" the woman asked. "Are you...lost?"

"*Nein.* At least I don't think I am."

"You must be if you're here. This is the end of the road."

Micah pointed to the farm next door. "Abigail and John Fisher live there?"

"They do."

"Then I'm not lost." He snatched off his baseball cap, rubbed the top of his head and then yanked the cap back on.

Micah stepped forward and held out his hand. "I'm Micah—Micah Fisher. Pleased to meet you."

"You're not *Englisch*?"

"Of course I'm not."

"So you're Amish?" She stared pointedly at his clothing—tennis shoes, blue jeans, T-shirt and baseball cap. Pretty much what he wore every day.

"I'm as Plain and simple as they come."

"I somehow doubt that."

"Since we're going to be neighbors, I suppose I should know your name."

"Neighbors?"

"*Ja.* I've come to live with my *daddi* and *mammi*—at least for a few months. My parents think it will straighten me out." He peered down the lane. "I thought the bishop lived next door."

"He does."

"Oh. You're the bishop's *doschder*?"

"We all are," the little girl with freckles cried. "I'm Sharon and that's Shiloh and that is Susannah."

"Nice to meet you, Sharon and Shiloh and Susannah."

Sharon lost interest and squatted to pick up some of the rocks. Shiloh hid behind her *schweschder*'s skirt, and Susannah scowled at him.

"I knew the bishop lived next door, but no one told me he had such pretty *doschdern*."

Susannah's eyes widened even more, but it was Shiloh who said, "He just called you pretty."

"Actually I called you all pretty."

Shiloh ducked back behind Susannah.

Susannah narrowed her eyes as if she was squinting into the sun, only she wasn't. "Do you talk to every girl you meet that way?"

"Not all of them—no."

Don't miss
An Unlikely Amish Match *by Vannetta Chapman,*
available February 2020 wherever
Love Inspired® *books and ebooks are sold.*

LoveInspired.com